Dragon Slayers

Dragon Slayers

J. Bernier

Chapter 1: How It All Began

I think this crazy story all began on that one peaceful early-spring day. My three friends and I were all chilling at our usual hangout spot, which was a hidden, overrun sword-training ground at the edge of town. It was concealed by big bushes and trees that enclosed the place. We sparred with each other with our swords throughout the day until we eventually stopped for lunch.

While we were eating, my friend Charles randomly said, "Hey, so I've been thinking—" then got immediately interrupted before he even finished his sentence by my friend Jack:

"Oh geez, you've been thinking! When was the last time you ever thought of something?"

Charles then loomed over him with his arms crossed, then simply shoved him out of his seat, and a mini brawl broke out like usual with the two, with Charles pinning Jack to the ground.

Charles was the tank of our team. He was tall, at six foot four, with jacked muscles that could swing heavy swords like nothing. His full name was Charles Collins. He was a huge, jolly goof who used only one brain cell to think, but we always listened to his dumb ideas and then did them.

He had tan skin, dark-brown eyes, and short reddish-brown scruffy hair with a classic goatee on his chin. He almost always wore a thick red tank top, ragged washed-out blue jeans, and light-brown work boots with tan soles and laces, no matter what weather we had outside. Charles was nineteen at the time.

On the other hand from Charles, Jack was the brains of our team. He was kind of weak with almost no muscles, but he was almost as tall as Charles at six foot one. His full name was Jack Williams. Jack was an absolute genius strategist who could come up with all kinds of crazy ideas and solutions. But he was also kind of a jerk and liked to make fun of all of us. Jack had olive skin, hazel-green eyes, and short straight jet-black hair that stuck up in the back along with his bangs, which almost did the same. He wore an old ragged brown jacket with an emerald green short-sleeved shirt underneath, loose black cargo pants that had one pocket on each leg to the side above the knees, and cleaned-up dark-brown leather dress boots with black soles and laces. Jack was about one year younger than Charles.

As they fought each other, me and my other friend Bolt just watched them, dumbfounded by how fast this had escalated into a mini brawl.

"Hey, should we… well… do something to stop them?" Bolt asked.

I said back to him, "Nah, it's funny watching them mock each other over some stupid comment."

"Well yeah, it happens all the time anyways. I was mostly just curious on what Charles was going to say. What did you think he was going to say?" he asked.

"Eh, probably something stupid like usual," I answered back.

This was Bolt: he was my dearest friend. Bolt was the archer of our team. He was super good at using range weapons, throwing, and general aiming. Then he had some really good hidden charisma. His full name was Bolton Lee. Bolt was the kindest, purest person in the world. No matter who you were, if he saw you hurting, he'd lend a helping hand. He was also a bit quiet and didn't like to draw attention to himself. He was also not as tall as the others, only five foot eight. Bolt had pale mixed-olive skin, light-blue eyes, freckles on his cheeks, a scar across the top of his nose, and midlength yellowish-blond hair with bangs that parted in the middle and swooped over to both sides of his head above his eyes. He always wore a light-yellow hoodie with a white short-sleeved shirt underneath, all tucked into his pants, which were light-blue jeans with a brown belt, and beige ankle boots with tan soles and black laces. He also had a beige messenger bag with him most of the time that had the basic necessities inside. Bolt had just turned seventeen about a month before.

Bolt and I were pretty close. He was my first good friend, and we were the same age. I was just a few months older than him. Bolt and I were roommates, and we lived with Bolt's uncle. We first met back when we were fourteen years old. I saw Bolt having trouble with some bullies, so I decided to help out. After I helped him, we talked for a bit, and he found out I had no place to sleep. So he offered to help me out, and I ended up staying with him. Sometime later he introduced me to Charles and Jack. Then before I knew it, this was my life now: hanging out with these idiots every day.

Charles and Jack had stopped their little fight and sat back down.

"So anyways…" Charles said. "What I was trying to say before Jack started that fight was, I've been thinking about signing up to join the Dragon Slayers. Do any of you guys want to join me so we'll all be in a squad together?" he asked.

We all turned silent, thinking to ourselves about what we wanted to do.

"Like to become Dragon Slayer soldiers for Infinitas?" Bolt asked.

"Hell yeah, we'll become Slayers for Infinitas!" Charles said, excited.

Infinitas was the name of the kingdom we lived in. This kingdom was quite large and was known for its powerful Dragon Slayers army. Infinitas had quite a small army but had one of the strongest out of any neighboring kingdoms around in our land. The kingdom's motto was "Your possibilities are infinite," but nobody really brought up this motto. The only people who used this were traders or employers, to draw people in.

"Why become one now?" I asked.

"Because now Bolton is seventeen, and that's how old you need to be to sign up for training. And it would suck if none of you were there with me. Or if you guys did want to join and if I already had, I would be a year or two ahead of you guys just joining. And, well, it would be hella fun if we were all together training, you know. So what do you all say?" he explained.

"I'm in!" Jack shouted. "If I'm in the Slayers, they can't say shit to me if they ever find the documents I stole about Dragonborns!" he said, laughing to himself a little as he pulled out a document with a picture of a scaled humanoid creature with claws and horns, then slammed it down on the stump.

"Uh… okay, I guess. So what about you two?" Charles asked. Then on the side of me, I heard Bolt muttering to himself,

"The training takes about five years to complete, to be a certified pro at least. That means by the time we graduate, we'll be living well for a while if no major injuries ever happen to us."

"What do you say, Bolt? I hear you muttering stuff about the benefits of this job. What do you think?" Charles asked. Bolt was quiet for a good minute, thinking to himself, until he finally said,

"You know what, maybe I will join you guys. Maybe it won't be so bad, right?"

"Hell yeah, I knew you'd all say yes to joining!" Charles shouted.

"Hey idiot, Aika hasn't agreed to it yet," Jack said, ruining Charles's little celebration.

"Oh, dear! Sorry about that. So what do you say, Aika? Will you join us?" Charles asked me.

"Oh… uh, let me think about it for a bit. I'll let you know by the end of the day, okay," I told him.

"Eh, that's fair," he said. Then Charles and the others started a different conversation, but I sorta just spaced out during it.

In our world, about five hundred years ago these monsters known as Dragonborns suddenly showed up. Some people thought they were gods and made religions to honor them; others thought they were devils and should all be killed. Dragonborns were a race of humans with supernatural abilities such as enhanced vision and extra-flexible joints. Their most notable feature was their aura powers, which swirled around their bodies as they moved. Their aura allowed them to create fire from their body to attack with or shield themselves. They also use their aura to materialize dragon-like wings for flight. When activated, it makes their irises glow the same as their aura.

But what made people think they were godlike was their elemental power: it could be wind, electric, ice, fire, or worst of all, toxic. Each element had its own different abilities and sets of possible aura colors and accent aura colors. What made people call them devils was their armor form. This form was what got them their name, Dragonborn. They looked like any other regular human, but when they swapped to this form, they looked like the monsters people called them. They had dark-colored scales that matched their aura, which covered their entire body and extended over their face like a mask. Then hard metal-like plates on their scales protect them. These plates often resembled armor like soldiers and were located on their forearms, shoulders, chest, shins, knees, hands, and feet, and those plates resembled the claws of a dragon. On their hands their scales on their fingers curled down at the end, creating claws like a beast. Then on their heads they had horns like dragons, demons, or goats that could be ridged or smooth. These horns were made up of plates like their armor, which were both the same color—usually silver tinted with the color of the Dragonborns' aura. Finally, their eyes in their armor form turned the color of their aura, and their irises were their accent aura, which was usually a slightly darker color than their aura, and their eyes glowed brightly in the dark alongside their aura. The only other place that the accent aura could be seen was in the center of their fire and the rims of their wings.

Dragonborns seemed impossible to kill until people created Dragon Slayers not too long after they appeared. They were an army of people willing to risk their lives to protect their homes from attacks by Dragonborns. Dragon Slayers defeated them by overwhelming them with attacks from swords and sending traps and arrows to throw them off guard. Slayers did this until it became too much for Dragonborns to handle and they flew off. Their attacks were somewhat rare, but every time Slayers did battle them, they learned more about them. Such as how Dragonborns used their powers and where they might had originated from. When Slayers weren't battling, though, they helped the kingdom or village's people with their problems and crimes. They took down criminals and threw them into grimy dungeons until proven guilty and sent to jail or set free.

Throughout the rest of the day, I could not focus on anything at all. I was stuck only thinking about what Charles had asked me. "Should I join the Dragon Slayers?" I thought. I then began to think of a plan so crazy that it seemed stupid yet genius. At the end of the day, I said to everyone,

"Hey, know what, I'll join you guys too. I'll become a Dragon Slayer as well."

Charles then shouted, "All right! Tomorrow I'll grab the form to sign up. How about we all meet up here tomorrow afternoon to fill it out, does that sound okay to everyone?"

We all agreed with each other to meet up the next day.

Finally, I'll talk about myself. My name was Aika. I wasn't really like any other person like my friends, and that was because I was actually a Dragonborn, a person with powers unlike any other. At the time and for a while after, no one knew I was a Dragonborn. I had kept my powers a secret from everyone for years. There were many things I did to keep them hidden, such as the people I talked to and the specific clothing I wore. Every day I wore my jacket, a dark-blue oversize open jacket with a folded-down collar and slightly droopy long sleeves. It was long, extending halfway down my thighs. Under my jacket I wore a plain white V-neck short-sleeved shirt with black belts. The first one ran across my chest and back from my right shoulder to my left side. Then the second connected with the first and wrapped around my stomach. Those belts helped me carry around something secret under my jacket. Then my shirt was tucked in my pants, which were slim-fit dark-turquoise trousers, held up by their own belt, which was also black.

My pants were also tucked in like my shirt into my combat boots. They had thick black soles and laces, and were made of a gray leather that was almost mid-calf length. Then finally I had simple black fingerless tactical gloves with thin armor on the top for protection and a leather pad on the palms for extra grip with white wrappings underneath. I had long, slightly wavy dark-brown hair that ended below my shoulder blades with bangs that swooped over to the right above my eyes. I had bright-blue eyes and pale skin. I wasn't a very tall person for my race, only five foot two. People often told me that I was a very stubborn person and how I was very talented in combat despite the idiot that I was, whatever that meant.

While walking home, Jack asked us,

"Hey, did you guys hear about that Dragonborn spotting in the north?"

"Oh yeah, I heard it came from over the mountain range close to the kingdom of Amarabliss," Bolt replied.

"I haven't heard about any of that. Where did you hear about it?" I asked.

"It was in the morning paper. I can read it to you, if you're curious?" Bolt offered.

"Oh, it's fine, you don't have to. It's just interesting because they were usually spotted near us from the west, from their land," I told him.

Charles then said, "It's crazy how those devils can fly so far. They don't even have real wings like birds."

Jack replied, "I know, aren't they fascinating! I wonder how long they can fly for? They say they can fly up for over two hours before taking a rest!" He then pondered to himself, laughing a little while thinking.

"I still don't know how you find those monsters cool. Remember what they did to us?" Charles asked.

"Of course I remember, but I still find them fascinating! Like for example, how their joints can move about thirty percent more than ours!" Jack explained passionately.

"And how most of them have super good vision that can see far away. Some can even see through thick smoke," I added.

"That too! I love their powers and elements! If I had to pick a favorite, it's gotta be electric. Because of the possibilities of all kinds of inventions!" Jack told us.

"Really? Those ones cause blackouts everywhere," Charles said.

"Then I really like the wind! And how they zip around the place faster than any horse or bird can!" Jack said.

"They also push rainclouds to us and ruin everyone's afternoon," Charles added.

"Do you hate ice too? They make the area around colder in the summer," Jack asked him.

"All Ice Elements do is ruin crops and create even more snow for us to shovel up," Charles replied as he crossed his arms.

"Then what about the Fire Elements and—" Jack said but was interrupted.

"Please, Jack, you know how much I hate those devils," Charles told him.

"All right, all right… but what about the Toxic Element and how their sludge can even hurt us a lot!" Jack asked.

"Toxic ones I don't mind too much because they do the least damage to us," Charles replied.

"Oh yeah, how so?" Jack then asked him, and Charles stared back, getting annoyed.

Jack and Charles kept going back and forth on the subject of Dragonborns, and I watched them both, walking next to Bolt.

"It's nice walking next to you, Bolt, unlike these two," I told him, then pointed to the two arguing.

"Well, you know me: I sorta just go with the flow with the topic. I'm kinda in the middle with my options, unlike those two," Bolt replied as he then looked over to Charles shoving Jack aside, who was nagging him more and more about Dragonborns.

"I'm kinda on the same level as you with my options about them. Though it's a little complicated, as you know," I told him.

Bolt then tapped me on the shoulder and said, "The house is right around the corner."

"Oh, it is? Well, see you tomorrow, guys," I said to Charles and Jack.

"See you soon, Aika. Try to read the article about the spotting for yourself. I know Bolt collects stuff like that in his room," Jack told me.

Then Charles said, "See you around, you two—don't forget about tomorrow!" Then the two of them went on their way back to their place.

"Do you actually collect newspapers in your room? I've never seen any," I then asked Bolt.

"No, Jack is just being Jack. Come on, let's go," he told me and headed toward the house. "Uh… all right," I replied and walked with him.

Later that night I developed my master plan on how to never be discovered as a Dragonborn while in the Slayers. First part, become the top of the class. Who would ever think the most talented person at fighting Dragonborns would be a Dragonborn? Most people think Dragonborns were just these heartless monsters that attacked people for no reason. Well... that was half-true: some Dragonborns did attack for no reason, but not all the time. We were a lot more human than people thought we were. Citizens often forgot that we were just a race with powers. Most had no idea about our culture and the different ideas that clans of Dragonborns had. Some wanted to kill others, and then there were some like me who aren't murderers and just wanted to live like any other regular person. So they would never suspect a Dragonborn to hide in the Dragon Slayer army. To them it would be suicide for any Dragonborn to ever try this. Second part, always keep your cool no matter what. When I was in training, I needed to never look worried, because if I started to freak out during one of their speeches on how to kill someone of my race, it would look mighty suspicious, and would look at me weird. Then I shouldn't glare at certain people because some people knew that Dragonborns had a signature glare that beamed into the soul of everyone. They were somewhat right about it, but we only did that to other Dragonborns. But it didn't work on people… I thought.

Then as I was putting together my plan in my room, Bolt knocked on my door. "Hey, you okay, Aika? You've locked yourself in there since we came back from hanging out with the others."

I shouted to him from the other side of the door, "What? Oh yeah, I'm fine! Everything is good, I'm just planning out something!"

Bolt went silent for a moment before he said confused, "You're... planning something? Are you sure you're, okay? I've never seen you plan something... like ever? Is this about what happened earlier?" Bolt asked me.

"Uh... maybe," I replied.

I heard Bolt sigh from the other side of the door. Then he told me, "Well, there's hot brewed coffee out in the kitchen if you want any."

With a loud crash, I bashed against the door, then immediately opened it and asked, "Coffee?"

"Of course that's the thing that gets you out of your room," Bolt said to himself.

"No time for that, Bolt! There's coffee that needs to be acquired!" I said to him as I dragged him off to the kitchen with me.

As I dragged him along, he asked me, "So you gonna explain what you were planning?"

"Nope!" I immediately replied.

"Yep, that checks out," Bolt mumbled, tiredly.

The next day when we all met back up, we signed up and put our name and skills on paper. After we were all done, Jack looked over the forms to make sure everything was all set. While looking over them, he stopped and asked me, "Hey, Aika, why did you put 'Unknown' for your last name?"

I replied, "Well, I don't really have a last name, so that's better than nothing, right?"

He went silent and looked at me stupidly for a moment, but then said, "You could have just written Bolt's last name, but yeah, I suppose it is." He continued looking over everything.

Afterward he told us, "Well, I'm ninety-nine percent sure everything looks good here."

"Yeah, then let's mail these out and get some lunch!" Charles said excitedly as he got up from his seat.

"Lunch sounds good to me," I joined in with Charles.

"Yeah, you get me, Aika!" Charles said back to me.

"I think there's a place that opened up near the post office, you want to check that out?" Bolt asked us.

"Yeah, it can be a little celebration for signing up!" Charles happily replied to him.

"You do know we haven't even been accepted yet, let alone turned in our forms?" Jack asked Charles.

"Ah, come on, Jack! Once they look at Aika's skills, we'll immediately get in!" Charles replied to Jack.

"My skills aren't that good," I told them.

"Aika, our first-ever meeting still haunts me to this day and every time I spar with you," Charles told me.

"Your pride is still hurt from that day?" I asked.

Charles went silent for a moment, then said, "Never mind! Let's just head out!"

So we headed out on our way and joked around with each other some more.

Then about a week later we all got acceptance letters saying we got into the Slayers and would start training in a month starting midspring. And that was how we signed up for the Dragon Slayers, and where this tale of ours really began to take off.

Chapter 2: Venny

It was early in the morning before announcements on our first day of training. We were waiting on the main slayer-training ground for the instructors to tell us everything with around thirty other people who'd signed up. This training ground was a big field with several different areas for practicing all sorts of different things like combat, archery, horse riding, and much more. Then we also had a big cabin house next to the fields to sleep in, which was split up by gender and years and all connected to one big room in the middle, which was the living room, that had a kitchen connected next to it. Then there were also many washrooms everywhere, a medical section, and outside there was a big horse stable, storge units, and a few classroom buildings. Then behind the cabin we had a picnic area to eat at.

Everyone was distant and observing each other quietly, seeing what people they would have to deal with for the next few years… except Charles and Jack, who were both yelling out at each other on how excited they both were about training. Dragging all the attention onto our one little group with everyone watching us. Not a very good first impression for Bolt and me, who didn't want attention from others.

Bolt, filled with anxiety, said to them, "Hey guys, quiet down. Look around you, everyone is staring at us!"

Charles said back to him, "Oh, come on, lighten up, Bolt. It's the first day—no one cares about each other."

I said to Charles, "Oh, don't mind Bolt; he just doesn't want to be marked down on anyone's hate list. But anyways, look at this slut down there," I said as I pointed to the richest, trashiest person I've ever seen.

Charles said to me, "Oh, I heard they're loaded! I forgot their name, but they were popular from where they came from."

So I said back to him, "Huh, interesting... so how much money do you want to bet she'll walk over here and ask why we're pointing at her and making jokes?"

Charles said back with confidence, "I bet twenty bucks that her first words to us will be 'Yo, bro, what are you saying about me' or something similar to those lines."

Jack said to him, "Oh please, do you really think she'll actually come over here and speak to us?"

Charles looked him dead in the eye and said, "Oh yeah, I bet an additional thirty bucks that she will come over here, in a few minutes."

Jack laughed at him and said, "Okay, deal. If she does none of those things, you'll have to give me fifty bucks then."

We were all making jokes and not paying attention to anyone. People around us were talking to each other as well, but then everyone went dead silent, and it was only us talking to each other.

Then behind me I heard, "Um... excuse me. Hey, bro, why did you just point at me laughing and such."

I turned around and saw her behind me. I didn't even notice that she was behind me. "Uh, what?" I asked.

"You were talking and laughing with your squad while pointing at me. Why? Don't you know who I am?" she asked.

I looked back at the guys and saw Jack hand Charles fifty bucks, and all of them nodded back to me. "Yeaaah, of course I know who you are!" I replied.

She just stared into my eyes for a moment, then said, "Okay, obviously you don't, so I'm going to tell you only once. I'm Vanessa, and if you mess with me, I will personally make your life here a living hell."

How naive I was when I replied, "A living hell? From you? Ha! Yeah right, like you could make someone like me feel like that experience."

"You'll see," she replied in a smug tone.

Vanessa made my life a living hell. She was like the queen bee: if you didn't praise her for everything or agree to everything she said, you got put down on her hate list. She looked like every rich, trashy, popular girl put into one person. She was five foot four and had olive skin, blue eyes, a beauty spot on her upper right cheek, and long straight black hair that went down almost her entire back. She wore a black V-neck tank top, with high-rise purple skinny jeans, with brown ankle-high designer boots with a black sole and brown laces. Vanessa had the perfect body that could control any straight man to do whatever she wanted and turn any girl with low self-esteem issues into her yes crowd to agree with everything. This bitch, she would put so much hell into my life. The worst part about it all was that our two squads were matched together to train all the time. By the end of our first year of training, everyone knew who Vanessa and I were because of the fights that would break out between us. But the thing that made everyone know me in particular was what happened after my and Vanessa's introduction.

When the first-year instructor finally came out to make the announcements, everyone's attention was only on me and Vanessa. So they walked over to us and asked,

"All right, what was going on here."

"She started it!" Vanessa immediately told them.

The instructor then turned to me and asked, "What did you do?"

So I explained, "I didn't do anything! I was just joking with my squad here until she came over and started this whole mess."

The instructor said, "Then how about you two just spar it out over there in that field. I was going to make you all do so anyway."

"Oh, gladly! I was top in my district with combat skills. No one can beat me," Vanessa said smugly.

"Where are you from?" I asked.

"Northeast Infinitas, why?" she asked with an attitude.

"Oh, well, I live in the southeastern district area, so it makes sense why you think you're the best," I told her.

Everyone around in the background watching made "Oooh!" sounds after I said that to Vanessa.

Jack in particular was laughing at Vanessa and said to Charles and Bolt, "Oh I can't wait to watch this!"

"This might end up bad," Bolt told him.

"What are you worried about Aika?" Charles asked.

Bolt replied, "What, of course not! Aika will be fine; it's Vanessa who I'm worried about. Aika is going to destroy her pride in front of everyone like she did with you."

"Hey!" Charles replied.

Vanessa overheard their conversation and asked me, sounding concerned, "What the hell do they mean by destroy my pride?"

"Oh, what's the problem, getting cold feet now?" I asked.

"What, no, never! Come on, let's go!" she replied, annoyed.

"Well, if you insist," I told her.

Then we walked to the opposite sides of the field, and the instructor shouted out,

"Okay, let's say the winner will be the person who shows the most skills. Now get ready and COMMENCE!"

Then Vanessa drew her sword from her left side and charged at me. "GET READY FOR THIS!" she yelled at me angrily.

As I stood there watching her charge at me, I looked up to the sky. I remember it was quite nice out that day. The sun was shining, the sky was clear, it was warm but not hot, the birds were flying away scared from Vanessa's yelling; all was pleasant. Then I stepped aside when Vanessa swung at me.

"How the hell did you dodge that? And wait a moment, you don't even have a sword on you!" she shouted out to me.

I told her, "Well, I want to make this battle fair, so I'm not using my sword."

Pissed, she yelled, "Fair? Come on, don't patronize me. Use your damn sword and spar with me already!"

"Welp, I just hope you'll remember... that this is what you requested me to do." Then I reached to my right shoulder and drew out my sword, which I'd hid under my jacket.

"Oh wow, they have a devil sword!" a random person from the crowd called out.

"No way that's real!" Vanessa said in disbelief.

"What idiot would carry around a fake Dragonborn sword?" I asked. Vanessa was silent for a moment before saying, "Good point."

So to end Vanessa's embarrassment, I cut the battle short and swung at her sword and made the two collide, screeching. Then without a second to waste, I twisted her sword and launched it across the field.

"Wow, how did your wrist turn like that?" she asked.

"Oh, it's nothing much. That's just my signature move. Only I can do it," I explained.

"I don't think you're using that word right, but geez, where did you learn how to do that?" she asked.

I replied to Vanessa vaguely, "Oh nowhere. All right, bye."

Then I quickly walked back to my squad to avoid more questions and sheathed my sword. When I approached my squad, I saw Jack waiting for a high five and Charles proudly talking about how awesome I was in combat to some other person in a gray jacket. So I high-fived Jack as I walked by him and looked over to Bolt and saw him looking at me, disappointed.

"Hey, Bolt what's with the look?" I asked him.

"You don't remember the conversation I had with you the night when Charles asked to sign up, don't you?" he replied.

"Before or after the coffee?" I asked.

"After," Bolt replied.

"Oh… then no, not at all," I said.

Bolt sighed and said, "I told you not to flaunt your combat abilities like, well, the way you just did—because of this," he said as he pointed behind me.

So I turned around and saw everyone looking at me like I threatened them.

"Ah yes, I forgot people also get insecure around here about someone being way better than they are," I said to myself.

"Just remember to hold back on them. None of them know what you're like yet," he told me.

"Oh yeah. definitely noted," I told him.

Then other people began to spar, and after everyone got to see each other's skills, it was almost late afternoon, so we all had Dragonborn classes after.

During the first few years of training, Vanessa screwed around with me all day, doing little things to piss me off after that day. For example, she would flirt with Charles, and his dumbass self would mess up on whatever he was doing, and he would mess up our training exercise. Also she loved to steal my belongings such as my sword, which was one of a kind. My sword was very special to me, it was one of the few possessions left from my old life, before I came to Infinitas. Dragonborn swords were made from a mix of steel and our armor plates. My sword, for example, was made from my own plates. Dragonborn swords were doubled-edged straight blades that were around twenty-eight inches in length and had a small furrow engraved on the blade that followed up to almost the tip of the sword. The hilt of the sword was basic: the cross guard was a steel trapezoid, with the top connecting to the blade shorter and the bottom connecting to the grip longer. Then it had a black round-cornered *X* engraved into the middle on both sides of the cross guard. The grip of these swords usually consisted of white wrappings that covered the handle to make a stronger hold, so it didn't slip from our hands for any reason. Then the pommel at the end was a smaller version of the cross guard, with the smaller side connecting to the grip. The cross guard and pommel were usually the same color that was a darker color than their aura, with of course the tint of the sword being determined by the color of the plates it was made from. My sword was tinted blue, with a navy-blue cross guard and pommel with white wrappings. Then the scabbard had a golden locket and chape with a leather body, which was either dyed blue, green, red, white, or black depending on what Dragonborn clan they come from. My scabbard, for example, was blue for the body.

People couldn't make these swords; they could only obtain them by stealing them from Dragonborns. People were allowed to have them, but they were worth a lot of money. So normally civilians wouldn't have them, only rich people or Slayers mostly had them. So whenever people asked how I got one, I always told them 'I got attacked by a Dragonborn years ago' to convince people I stole it from a Dragonborn. I had deep scars on my arms from a bad Dragonborn scratch, too, so I had some sort of evidence if people didn't believe me. Dragonborn swords were usually carried on the backs. They were connected by multiple black leather belts that connected to the scabbard, which went across the back and chest in a loop from shoulder to waist, depending on which hand we wielded our sword with. That belt connected to a second belt around the stomach to secure it in place. For example, I wielded my sword with my right hand, so the way I wore my belts that attached to my scabbard allowed me to draw my sword with my right hand from my right shoulder. Our scabbards were made to be worn on our backs so we could move around more freely in battle, having no fear of losing our sword within the chaos of the fight. In Infinitas, though, people usually carried their swords at their hips. Sometime after I met Charles and Jack, some people had gotten suspicious of me. To them I was some random kid who randomly showed up at Infinitas, carrying some Dragonborn sword on their back all the time. So Jack suggested to me one day, "Hey, why don't you just hide your sword under your jacket, so people don't look at you weird when they see you carrying your sword on your back." After I tried that, it stuck with me. No one would notice I had a sword on me because my handle and scabbard were blue like my jacket, so when I pulled it out, it would make everyone go silent if they had no idea about me.

When I was forced to spar with Vanessa one day, I thought of the nickname Venny for her. Let's just say I pissed her off... bad… when I first told her.

"So Venny, how are you doing today? Have you messed with anyone yet?"

Her immediate reaction was "What did you just call me?"

"Oh, do you like my little nickname?" I asked.

"How the hell did you come up with Venny?" she asked, pissed.

"Well I overheard you talking down to one of your 'yes' people. And I heard them call you Ven for short. So I thought to add n-y to Ven and make it Venny," I explained.

"Don't you dare call me Venny!" she demanded.

"What's wrong, Venny? Feel embarrassed about the name?" I asked.

"No!" she shouted.

"What, do you think everyone is gonna call you Venny?" I asked again.

Then she yelled out at me, "Shut up! Stop calling me that! If you continue I'll—!"

"You'll what?" I said, cutting her off. "Make my life more hell with your annoying little tricks? They get on my nerves a lot, but I can endure them. You, on the other hand? You care too much about your reputation and stuff, while I'm over here not giving a damn what others think. You should rethink, Venny."

After that she stormed off, and later, while I was talking with my squad, I was doing a few simple practice hits on a wooden dummy, chipping cuts into it.

Jack from behind tapped my shoulder and said with much enthusiasm "Hey, Aika! Guess who's here?"

"Who?" I asked as I turned around and saw Vanessa. "Oh great." I muttered to myself then asked her in a up liftering voice "Hey Venny, what do you want?"

She replied, "Nothing much, I was just thinking of what you said to me earlier, and thought you were right about a few thinks, and wanted to say thanks for opening my mind."

"Huh, wasn't expecting that... well glad you agree with me on one thing! Now let's just put everything aside and start over!" I told her and stabbed my sword into the dirt to my near right and opened my hand for a handshake.

"Of course, let's start over!" Vanessa said as she shook my hand.

She let go, I told her "Glad we can settle this with no big—."

"DON'T YOU SAY THAT ABOUT THE GODS!" a person screamed in the background which grabbed my attention and glanced over at the chaos in the distance to my left, then back at Vanessa and saw her running off with my sword.

"Hey!" I called out to her and chased her around the place till she ran inside the cabin and out of sight.

I spent an hour looking for my sword with the help of my squad after... lots of convincing, then finally found it on a shelf that I couldn't reach. Charles helped me out after he and the others watched me for a good minute trying continuously to reach it. All he did was simply reach up slightly to grab it, and I embarrassingly took it and thanked him. Then the next day and forever after that, I continued to only call her Venny.

The people in Vanessa's squad were... something. In Vanessa's squad she also had her boyfriend, and he was the most stereotypical Chad in the world. Even his fucking name was Chad! His personality was exactly what you would expect it to be. He was six foot three and had jacked muscles, brown pretty-boy-styled hair, and blue eyes. He always had a suntan, and he wore thin tank tops with ragged jeans and work boots like Charles. But to be honest I never paid any attention to Chad; he was always doing his own thing in the background. Chad only ever did one thing to me.

"Question... how are you so good at wielding a sword while being this short?" he asked me.

"Excuse me?" I asked, a bit pissed with an attitude.

"Well, it's quite impressive seeing someone as short as you be so good.

I half expected you to be like an archery person like Blonde over there," he said again, and pointed at Bolt.

Jack then hollered to him in a panic, "Chad! CHAD! Run away… NOW!"

"Why?" he asked, confused.

Then he looked over to me, cracking my knuckles.

"Geez, you got a short fuse too," he added.

Bolt then noticed the situation going on and ran over to us.

As I took a step toward Chad, Bolt held me back and told me, "No, bad Aika! You will not beat up Chad!"

"Oh, come on, Bolton… let me at least slug him across the face once," I asked him.

"CHAD, RUN!" Bolt and Jack called out to him at the same time.

Chad, finally realizing that I was about to kill him, said, "Oh… OH, you're being serious! All right, I'm out. See ya, thanks, my dudes," then walked away.

"Why are you still holding me back, Bolt?" I asked him.

"Because if I let go, you're going to kill him," he told me, then looked over to Jack. "Dude, help me out with her?"

Jack crossed his arms and thought to himself for a moment, then suggested, "Wanna get some coffee for her?"

"Great idea!" Bolt replied as he dragged me inside the cabin, far away from Chad.

While they were dragging me back, I was still laser focused on Chad.

Charles walked by us and asked, "What in the world is happening over here?"

"Chad called her short, protect him with your life," Jack yelled to him as he opened the door for Bolt as he dragged me inside.

"Oh goodness," Charles said to himself as he ran after Chad to make sure I wouldn't kill him.

Another person was Peter, and he was in one of those religious groups who worshiped Dragonborns as gods. He was the complete opposite of Jack's personality. He was five foot ten and was always dressed up formally, definitely not looking like he was going to fight at all, wearing a white collared shirt, black dress pants, and very nice-looking black loafers in training, which I had no idea how he managed. He had blondish-brown styled hair, green eyes, darker-brown skin, and he always looked terrified for no reason. All he ever did in training was shout out stuff like "The gods are watching!" or "No one should ever question how the gods work!" For some reason Jack also really hated this guy; I didn't know why till a long time after. Jack and I had so many conversations about how crazy his logic was. I know Jack was crazy about Dragonborn knowledge, but he seemed to despise Peter whenever he had an opinion on something. He was a background character for me as well, though, he bothered me way more than Chad.

One day while we were out training, Peter randomly screamed out, "EVERYONE, EVERYONE! I JUST LEARNED THE GODS CAN TALK OUR LANGUAGE!"

"You didn't know that they could speak Infinitan?" I asked him.

Jack turned to me and said, "Oh please, Aika, he's from one of those religious groups. They don't teach you anything about Dragonborns."

"Really? That seems like nonsense. Why would they not learn about their own god?" I asked.

"They're all idiots, that's why," Jack said back.

Then Peter shouted at Jack, "HEY, WE DO NOT QUESTION THE GODS!"

I had no idea how bad these groups were until I met Peter. All I knew was that they thought we were some mighty, powerful gods or some stuff like that.

And finally there's Niki. You see, Niki was a bit... different. To get an idea about who Niki was, just imagine the craziest person you know… now put them on crack, then you'll get something close to the level of craziness that was Niki. She was five foot five and had olive skin, short straight black hair that ended before her shoulders with spiky bangs, and brown eyes. She wore a gray hooded jacket, which she could zip up but always kept open so she could take things in and out of her inner pockets; a dark-blue long-sleeve shirt; black jeans that were cuffed; and combat boots almost like mine, but they were black and slightly shorter; and she always had a black backpack on her or near her at all times with basically everything you could imagine inside. Niki always talked about conspiracy theories and stuff about how there had "always been Dragonborns in this world" and "they live among us people in secret." I mean, she's not wrong, but the part that was very worrying to me was that she ranted about her theories on who was a Dragonborn within us. She had made many theories on multiple people, including me. She was the only person who could see right through my lies. The only person who had just looked at me and immediately knew I was a Dragonborn. She had made the most theories about me out of all the other people she had accused. Some of them scared the hell out of me, because they were right. Others were the funniest things in the world for me.

My favorite theory of hers was how I had an accent to her.

"Read this!" She said to me one day, shoving a recorder in my face.

"Um… why?" I asked.

"I'm seeing if you have an accent," she said.

"You think I have an accent?" I asked.

"I don't think you do, I know you do. So shut up and read this," she said, shoving her recorder in my face again.

I looked over at Bolt and asked, "Are you seeing this shit right now?"

Then she hollered over at Bolt, "Hey, you, Bolton! Do you think she has an accent!"

Bolt just looked at me nervous and said, "Uh… I don't know?"

I then shouted out at him in confusion, "You don't know? Come on, Bolt, we've known each other for years, and you can't just say I don't have an accent to the crazy person!"

"Well, you sorta have one," he said.

"Oh please, you definitely have an accent," Jack said beside us.

"When the hell did you show up?" I asked.

"I walked over here at the first 'shut up and read this' part," Jack explained.

Then I said out loud in confusion, "Wait, why the hell does everyone say I have an accent?"

"It's the way you talk sometimes?" Bolt said to me.

Jack then scoffed at Bolt and said, "Sometimes? Please, she had this accent since we first met. I will say, though, it's a lot less defined from when we all first met, but you do hear it once in a while," Jack explained.

All I could think to myself was "Why did they need to say this right in front of Niki?" and you want to know what she was doing while Bolt and Jack were talking? She was writing this entire conversation down in her notebook that says on the cover of it "Notes For the Board."

Niki also loved to spy on everyone. No one was safe from her. She wrote notes on everyone she met and wrote down everything she knew about them into her pocket-size notebooks, which she kept in her jacket or backpack. Because she was this crazy, no one ever thought her words were true in the rants she made. Niki had almost exposed me multiple times throughout the years of training. If people actually listened to her rants, I would be dead without a question. Because at times she would scare me beyond imagination from her finding out all the little things I do to keep my powers hidden. Some of her theories were stupid and funny to laugh at, and then there were the ones that were actually true. One time, though, she did something that really scared me. One day while I was having lunch with my squad, she asked me, "Hey, Aika, why do you always wear gloves?"

"That's private information," I immediately told her.

"What are you hiding, an element birthmark on one of your hands?" she asked, looming over me.

All Dragonborns had a birthmark of their element symbol on the top of one of their hands. It was a round-cornered *X* with different line patterns around depending on what element it was. Dragon Slayers found these marks on their armor form to find out what element a Dragonborn had without them using their powers. On their armor it glowed the color of their auras, but on their regular skin, it was a simple birthmark.

"What do you mean, am I hiding an element birthmark? I just like wearing gloves, that's all," I told her.

"Then why do you never take them off? You only use the private bathrooms, and whenever you don't wear them, you wear wrappings instead," Niki asked.

"I…uh… Bolton, help me out!" I asked him.

"Well… uh… Aika has a problem with her hands and wears gloves because of it," Bolt told her.

"What kind of problem?" Niki asked.

"Again, private information!" I told her.

"Well, all right, but I will find out soon," Niki said ominously.

Niki was my biggest threat.

Dragon Slayer training was nothing really special, though. They taught us how to master basic combat with real and fake swords, and we dueled each other constantly in the fields. So I ignored Bolt's words, showed off my skills too much, and destroyed everyone so frequently in these duels that everyone eventually became too afraid to train with me. So I spent most of that time screwing off and doing whatever, watching everyone train.

"Hey Aika, whatcha doin'?" Jack asked me playfully as he walked by me chilling in the shade on a hot day during summer.

"Oh nothing much, just watching everyone suffer while eating some protein bits… want some?" I asked as I showed him a clear bag of crushed-up protein bars.

"Sure," he said as he sat next to me. "So why are you sitting in the shade all by yourself?" he asked as he grabbed a handful of bits.

"Oh, it's just because I beat everyone in a duel within ten minutes and because it's too dang hot and I'm overheating," I told him.

Jack then said as he was eating, "I still don't understand why you just don't take off your jacket like how me and Bolt did. I know that you talked about having a bunch of scars, but I doubt anybody would push you to talk about how you got them," he told me.

"It's… I have my reasons why I do some things," I explained.

"Okay, I'll shut up… so you got any more bags of protein bits?" Jack asked.

"Oh, do I?" I questioned as I showed him my inside jacket pockets overstuffed with bags of protein bits. "Take your pick, my friend. I got peanuts, almonds, cashews, chocolate, mint, and much more."

"Oooh, how do you have this many?" Jack asked.

"I stole a whole bunch from the kitchen yesterday when I skipped training. Just don't tell anyone because Bolt will get disappointed again," I told him.

"Again?" he asked.

"Last week I did the same thing, and I offered him a bag, and all he did was sigh and said 'You really shouldn't steal like this.' So I asked him what he was going to do about it," I explained.

Jack then asked, "What did Bolt say after?"

"Nothing, he just looked at me dumbfounded and walked away without taking a bag," I told him.

"Wasted opportunity," Jack said as he pointed to a mint bag.

"Yes indeed," I replied as I handed him the bag.

At that moment Bolt walked by us and saw all the bags I had on me, then yelled, "You gotta be kidding me, you stole more?"

"Hey, I was hungry!" I replied as I crossed my arms proudly.

Bolt then looked back at us and asked himself, "You know what, why do I even bother?" then walked off to where he was heading.

Jack asked, "Is this the good brand? It's not as dry as some of the others."

"Of course it's the good brand! Why bother stealing the crap brand when the risk of stealing either one is the same," I said.

"Nice," he replied as he put up his fist.

"You know it," I said as I fist bumped him.

As months passed quickly, winter came faster than ever for me and I had to slack off a bit differently. The basic living area had tables set up for people to chat or eat at, and fireplaces with couches and chairs set up around to relax next to on cold days. In the back of the living room there was a kitchen that served free breakfast, lunch, and dinner for everyone. And I took full advantage of it.

"Where the hell were you all day?" Charles asked me as he stood next to the chair I was sitting in taking off a thin dark-red sweatshirt.

"Relaxing next to the fire," I told him as I munched on some protein bits with a soft blanket over my lap.

"You were here all day doing nothing?" Jack asked as he walked over, laughing.

"Yep," I replied without hesitation.

Bolt asked them, "Oh, come on, guys it's like twenty degrees outside. Did you really expect Aika to leave the building?"

Charles said, "Good point. She never did before."

Bolt said to the others, "Come on, let's get some dinner. Do you need anything?" he asked me.

"Oh, I'm good right now, thank you," I replied.

"Did you just offer to do something for the person who's been doing nothing all day?" Jack asked smugly.

"I… uh…" He looked away, embarrassed, and said, "Whatever, let's just get our food. Don't ask me why I did, I don't know." Then he walked away.

After that moment I asked the other two, "So you guys want any protein bits?"

"Hit me," Jack replied.

I reached into my jacket and placed a bag down on the table in front of me and grabbed my coffee.

"Damn, you must have had a good day," Charles said to me.

"Mm-hmm," I said as I drank my coffee. "Caught up on some sleep… polished my sword… drank a lot of coffee… you know," I said as I put my coffee back down.

"Well, come on, Jack. Let's get some food with Bolt. See you in a few minutes again," Charles said as he walked off and Jack followed.

"Have fun," I told them as I looked over to the long dinner line that had already formed and watched the two of them push each other around... Charles won.

Our winters aren't too horrible here, I usually just wear a thicker long-sleeved shirt like my usual one, a dark-blue scarf and hat, and nothing more because my normal outfit is already warm. Bolt has a thicker hoodie with soft fluff inside, Jack has a thicker dark-green long-sleeved shirt with thicker brown boots, and Charles just had his thin sweatshirt he wore sometimes with his normal clothes underneath.

But I couldn't slack off all the time, sadly, because we also had to practice other things that didn't involve swords, like archery, which was okay for me. I wasn't the worst, but lots of people were better than me. The best person at archery was Bolt.

"How do you always hit the bull's-eye?" I asked Bolt, who had shot a bull's-eye five times in a row.

"Well, it's quite easy for me, but I know you will have a hard time with it. All you need to do is become left handed or just relax for a moment and think of where you need to shoot," he told me.

"What is this thing that you call... relax?" I asked playfully.

"Well, relaxing is when you stop trying to be better than everyone and just focus on what you want to accomplish," he told me in the same playful tone.

"Hmmm... I don't think I can do that," I told him.

"Welp, your problem," he said as he aimed his bow to shoot another bull's-eye.

"What's happening over here. Is Bolt showing off his skills again?" Charles asked as he walked over to us.

"Yeah," I said as I watched Bolt pull back on his bow, close his right eye, and effortlessly shoot another bull's-eye, creating a faint breeze as the arrow whizzed away.

"Hey, just remember, Aika... we can both beat him in any sword duel," Charles said.

"You know what, you are right about that part," I replied.

"You two are so petty," Bolt said to us.

"I'm not that petty, it's that one who's petty when someone is better at something than them," Charles said as he pointed at me.

"Hey!" I yelled back.

"Then prove to us that you're not petty," Charles said as he crossed his arms and gave me his full attention.

"Well I…" I said, then went immediately quiet, having no responses to prove him wrong. "I am not… that petty," I told them.

"Wow, you even admitted that you were a little petty, dang," Bolt said to me.

"Well, at least we can all agree we're not all as crazy as Jack," I replied.

"I… you know what, you're actually right about that," Bolt said as he thought to himself.

"I heard my name! What are you all talking about?" Jack said, walking over, excited.

"Oh, we're just talking about how crazy you are," I told him.

"Hey, at least I'm not as crazy as Niki," Jack told us.

"Now that's something we can all agree on united," I said.

"Absolutely," Charles agreed.

Also during all the years of training, many people came up to me and asked,

"Hey, uh… how do you say your name? My friend saw your name written down on a piece of paper, and we got into an argument on how to pronounce it. I think your name is pronounced *A-kaa* and my friend thinks it's pronounced *ahh-kii*. I think I'm right, but I just want to make sure," some person asked.

"Oh, it's no problem. My name is pronounced *I-kah*. It's a foreign name around here. I get asked a lot," I told them.

"Ah cool, nice to meet you, *Ah-kah*," they said cheerfully.

"Oh, uh, you said it wrong again, but it's okay. My name is pronounced *I-kah*," I told them again but slower.

"So it's *I-kee*, right?" the person asked again.

"I… no, it's *I-kah*, understand it?" I asked.

"Okay, it's *E-kaa*. I'm right for sure this time!" they said, confidently.

"My name doesn't even have an *E* in it… I… you know what, call me whatever you want," I said, giving up on them.

"What a cool name you got there, *A-kee*. What does it mean?" they asked.

"You don't deserve to know what my name means after this conversation," I told them before I walked away, not answering another question from them. I then sat at a nearby table next to my squad.

"You look defeated, what's wrong with you?" Charles asked me.

"Some guy was trying to pronounce my name and completely butchered it," I told them.

"Really, your name is quite easy to pronounce. It's just *I-kah*. Was it really that hard for them?" Jack asked.

"You have no idea, dude… no idea. Let's just say one of them was *E-kaa*," I told him. Jack and Charles then hysterically laughed at me, and beside me Bolt even cracked up a smirk and did a small giggle.

"My name has no *E* in it. How the hell did they come up with *E-kaa*, like how?!" I asked, confused.

"Maybe they were just being a jerk?" Bolt said, while trying to hide his smile.

"The worst part is that I think they were being genuine about it when they pronounced it… in fact they almost got it right when they asked me the first time," I said in disbelief.

"Hahahaha, this is way too funny!" Jack yelled in his laughter to me.

"You don't need to laugh that hard at it," I commented.

"No, I have to, Aika. It's way too funny!" Jack shouted, wheezing in his laughter now.

"Wow," I replied as I watched him struggle for air.

During training, we also learned how to ride horses because we used them to travel about outside of Infinitas, from place to place quicker, and to help us transport people and materials to different places. To the right of the main cabin was the stable, and there were about fifteen horses, one for all the instructors and a couple of trainees. But when it came down to me riding a horse… let's just say I was banned from ever riding one again in my life because of the events that went down when I first tried to ride one. My memory of what happened was basically a blur, but all I know for sure was that I gave some unknown PTSD to some people who would never forget that moment next time they saw a horse. Alongside the stable there were a couple of storage units that held basic equipment for everyone, most of the stuff though were for the horses.

Then finally they taught us all about their different methods of fighting Dragonborns and what to do during an attack, basic information about Dragonborns, and about the work Slayers do in the crime officers part of our job. To the left of the main cabin there were five different classrooms separated by training tiers that were big lecture rooms with big chalkboards in the front that our instructors would use to teach everyone. The classes about how to be an officer were just the laws of Infinitas and how to deal with people and their needs and problems, such as taking down outlaws and helping solve crimes around the kingdom. None of it was interesting or special; it was all basic crap we all already knew in the back of our minds. But I was never around during those classes on Dragonborns, so I had no idea what they were like. Jack also would never attend these classes, so we would screw around during the whole lecture and would sneak off outside and chat for a bit on nice days. Then when I was forced to attend because it was too cold out to sneak off, I would just sleep in the back of the classroom and had Bolt wake me up if anything happened. Jack also did the same as me and slept because we all had to wake up early in the morning for training, then classes would always be in the later afternoon, then it would be dinner. Neither of us needed to attend these classes at all. We both already knew more information than most of the pros—hell, we even let Niki hang out with us two sometimes because she also normally slept in class like us. So all three of us would talk about

Dragonborns and do a little bit of training of our own where nobody had to watch us be pathetic at our worst fighting skills. Then when any test rolled around, Niki and Jack would complete them in seconds and ace them like nothing, and I sat there looking at the paper like an idiot because I didn't pay attention to the information they said about Dragonborns and knew only the correct information. So I had to always ask Bolt to help me read everything and copy off Jack secretly. Then after the test, all our sleep-deprived minds would proceed to fall asleep in seconds for the rest of the class.

Chapter 3: The Curse of My Power

No big event ever happened in training—sure, Venny always messed with me a lot, and Niki existed, but nothing majorly bad ever happened... well, not until the end of our fourth year of training, that is. Everything up until that point had been peaceful with nothing drastic ever happening. We had been training for a while, and it was near the end of our fourth year. It was the end of winter season, just a few more weeks till it was officially spring, and we'd just been blasted by a big blizzard during the night. The snow was almost frozen and was blown into uneven piles from the wind, so we were forced to shovel up the training grounds. Everyone was decked out in winter uniforms with thick black coats, pants, and heavy snow boots. Some people, including me, wore a few extra things to keep themselves warm because it was freezing out, such as scarves, thick gloves, and hats. For me I just wore the uniform and snow boots they gave us. The uniform coat was so thick I had to wear my sword over the jacket for once instead of hiding it underneath, like how I did with my jacket. Then I wore my full-fingered thick tactical gloves, had my dark-blue scarf wrapped around my neck, then had my hair tied back and stuffed in my coat with my matching drak-blue beanie hat.

Even Charles wore the winter uniform with the coat over his tank top. It was rare for Infinitas to get this much snow, especially with spring right around the corner. Infinitas was built in a warm region where it snowed little to none.

Everyone's breath was visible from the cold as they all worked. Some complained, some joked around and threw snowballs at each other, and some just did their work as fast and sloppy as possible to get inside. But as I was out there digging up the snow, barely doing anything as I stood there in the cold shoveling up some ice, I could feel my strength weaken as the day went on. I had great powers, but these powers came at a price. Because of my powers, the cold could be deadly to me if I got stuck out there long enough, because it drained my stamina, making me unable to move well. I didn't have the same warmth as regular people because of my powers. My powers took that warmth and used it to make power. So if it was cold like this outside, I was more likely to get frostbite, hypothermia, you name it. This was the side effect of my powers. I liked to call it my curse because I was forever stuck like this with no way to remove it. But it also had its benefits, too: I was almost never horribly hot, and I very rarely got a fever. Unless it was like a hundred degrees outside—then I would be sweating my back off. This helped me be able to wear my jacket, gloves, and boots all year long without sweating to death, especially in the summer.

It was around sunset when we were finishing up. Everyone was tired and weak from being outside in the cold a lot. Most of the pros were away at the main town area to help the civilians clean up the snow everywhere. The pros often visited the training grounds to help us out or for new supplies. But even though most people were exhausted, everyone had high morale because we were told we would get the day off tomorrow to let the ice melt a little. As everyone was talking about what they were going to be doing tomorrow on their day off, it started to snow a little. No one thought anything of it and continued to finish up.

"So, Aika?" Niki said as she walked over to me. "What are you gonna do tomorrow?" she asked.

"Oh nothing, I just want to relax inside and drink coffee... I hate the cold," I told her.

"Oh really. Why do you hate the cold so much? You never explain why you do and always hide inside," she asked.

Bolt said to her, "I told you before—Aika has always hated the cold. Whenever we would get snow this bad, she would never leave the house," he explained.

"Ah, interesting. Could you explain why you hate the cold, though?" Niki asked, coming closer to me with a face of innocence.

"Hey, don't give me that face! If I tell you why, you'll put it on one of your weird creepy boards you made about me. Anyways, the only reason why I'm out here is because they caught me doing nothing inside… so they threatened me with no coffee, if I didn't help," I explained to her.

"And your coffee addiction is as strong as ever," Jack commented in the background.

"Maybe I can blackmail her with coffee to get her to explain," Niki then said to herself.

I then gasped and told her, "Don't you dare!"

"Hmm, maybe with that reaction, it will at least work a little," Niki then said, watching my reaction.

"How did the instructors threaten you with coffee?" Bolt asked me.

"Uhh…" I replied as the memory ran through my mind.

"Hey, what are you doing!?!" one of the instructors asked me.

"Uhh, shit!" I panicked as I threw my blanket and coffee to the side. "I was uhh…. cleaning! Yes, cleaning!" I told them.

"Uh-huh, and what were you cleaning?" they asked me as they looked down at the coffee table in front of me with all my stuff scattered everywhere.

"I was… dusting," I replied.

"Dusting what?" they asked.

"Uhh… the chairs!" I told them confidently.

They then stared at me dumbfounded before saying, "Yeah, listen, if you don't get suited up and start helping your squad and everyone else out there, then I'll pour all your coffee down the sink and throw away all the grounds and pods, and take away all your coffee coupons," they demanded.

"No! Nooo!" I yelled, defeated, as I dropped to my knees and clenched my fists above me.

"I'd rather not talk about it," I replied to Bolt.

"Uh… okay then?" Bolt said with a confused yet accepting face.

Suddenly a bit of wind picked up.

"Oh, you gotta be kidding me. What, are we getting another storm or something?" I asked.

Bolt answered back, "Who knows, we'll probably won't get another day off if it does."

The snow started to come down a little bit harder, but we were nearly done with work. I looked down at my hand and squeezed it. It had gone completely numb from the cold. All I could think about was how much I hated the cold and this stupid weather. Then as I was looking at my hand, I noticed some weird-shaped snow. There were no snowflakes; instead the snow was a crystal-like shape. Then it hit me.

"Bolt!" I called out to him.

He looked over and saw my concerned face "What's wrong?" he asked, worried.

I said to him nervously, "This snow! It's from a Dragonborn!"

"What?" Bolt asked, surprised.

The wind around us then picked up hard.

Niki asked, "How do you know this is Dragonborn snow? It looks the same as normal… unless only you can see the difference?" she asked with a grin on her face.

Panicking a bit, I shouted back, "There's no time to explain! If we don't tell anyone now, there will be—"

Then the wind spun like crazy all around us, making my hat fly right off my head, and the snow came down on us like an avalanche. Within the chaos of the snow, a Dragonborn unlike any other suddenly dropped from the sky onto the middle of the field.

Everyone ran for it with a look of horror because many of us had no weapons on hand, so there was no way to immediately fire back at it. In a panic the instructors called out, "Everyone year three or younger go back to the cabin! Everyone else, grab a weapon and stand guard!"

The Dragonborn just stood in place and made the wind go crazy while it watched all of us run. Everything was a mess. The pros were gone, and Dragonborns had never just randomly attacked a Dragon Slayer camp before, so all chaos had broken out. Never had I watched something this chaotic immediately break out so quickly.

This Dragonborn was nothing like these people had ever seen before. One of the fifth-year trainees launched a flame arrow at them, but before it hit them, they created an ice barrier in front of them. As soon as I saw their eyes, I knew exactly what kind of Dragonborn they were. They were more powerful and scarier-looking than any normal Dragonborn the Slayers had faced before. These Dragonborns were almost nonverbal; they could only yell and had no control over their own movements, and they attacked without knowing what was happening. No one here was prepared to fight someone like that.

The instructors and fifth years were the front lines, and us, the fourth years, were the backup. The only problem with the fourth- and fifth-year trainees was that there were only a few of us left at this time. By the time the third year came, most people dropped out of training, usually because it was too much for them. By the time the fourth year of training came by, there were usually only about three groups with four to six people in them. The instructors had also contacted the pros, but they weren't going to be here for a while.

After some time passed, most of the fifth years were out of weapons or unable to fight from injuries, so they gave us the okay to fight. Everything around us was freezing from the snow and wind this Dragonborn made. As I was watching everyone trying to attack them, I was stumped, with no idea what to do at all. Beside me throughout all of this mess was Bolt, setting up his crossbow.

"Are you doing okay there, Aika?" he asked me.

"What? Oh yeah, I'm fine," I said back.

"Are you?" he asked again. "I figured you would have charged at it by now like all the others have. Even Peter tried going near that… thing? I'm not really sure what kind of Dragonborn that is," he told me.

I told him, "Hey, really, I'm okay. I'm just cold. That damn Dragonborn made my hat fly somewhere, and now my ears are frozen… that's all. I've been watching this Dragonborn for a little while too, trying to think of an idea, but I got nothing."

"Can't blame you, no one has a clue on what to do. I bet Jack is probably going crazy, thinking of all sorts of ideas though," Bolt told me.

Then right as he was done talking, we heard someone yell, "THE MIGHTY GOD HAS COME! WE HAVE ANGERED THEM! IT'S USELESS FIGHTING THEM! WE'RE ALL DOOMED!"

We looked over to see who screaming all of this out, and of course it was Peter. Chad was holding that crazy moron down, trying to make him stop yelling. "The mighty god, huh," I thought to myself.

This Dragonborn here was an Ice Element. The Ice Element's symbol was a round-cornered X inside a perfect square. With their powers, they could freeze almost anything, such as rain, rocks, the ground, etc. Anything but something that was too warm to cover over in ice. They could also create things with their power as well, such as weapons, paths, walls, and platforms. They used their power by taking the water in the air and freezing it. They had a weakness to the Fire Element because their ice attacks melted away or couldn't freeze properly from the humidity the Fire Element brought when attacking. And finally their aura colors could be gray, white, any blue or green except the darker shades, purple, and a light yellowish green.

Then from a distance Jack came running to us with Charles following behind.

"There you guys are! I've been looking for you both. You see, I thought of a plan on how to help. It's sort of risky, but I know it'll end up fine," he said confidently.

"What are you thinking we should do?" I asked.

Then Vanessa said beside all of us, "I bet it's probably stupid."

Jack said to her, "Oh, good thing you're here, we'll need your help for this!"

Vanessa asked, "What, really? Me?"

Jack explained to us, "You see, I've been watching them, and the entire time everyone has been near it or shot at it, it's been deflecting all the attacks using its sword about sixty percent of the time. So I figured we should probably at least knock away their sword so the pros have an easier time battling against it. What do you guys think?"

Vanessa then scoffed at Jack and asked, "How are we gonna knock away its sword?"

Jack said to her, "Oh, we're not going to knock away its sword. Aika is gonna do that."

"What?" I immediately asked.

Jack explained, "You see, the plan is, I need three people to district it by running around it and taunting it, and then there will be four backups to support them if anything goes wrong. Then while we're all doing that, Aika can sneak around then and find a blind spot to jump out at them and attack them, sending their sword flying."

"Why me, though?" I asked.

Jack then replied confidently to me, "Oh please, Aika, you're the best person in the entire kingdom when it comes to dueling with swords. You're the most likely to succeed out of anyone here with your awesome skills and reaction timing."

"I know I'm skilled with my sword, but I wouldn't say I got 'awesome' reaction timing," I told him.

Then in the distance, I saw some random object flying toward us at sonic speeds.

"Oh dear, look out!" I shouted out as I pushed Bolt to the ground with me. Then right as we hit the ground, a shovel flew past us, barely hitting us, and sliced halfway through the ice on the ground from the impact. All right in front of Vanessa, who looked a little mortified from almost being hit. Everybody then silently stared at me.

"All right, I'll admit it: I do have really good reaction time," I confessed.

Bolt then quietly said to me, "Uh, Aika?" I realized I'd been hugging Bolt on the ground for about a good awkward minute.

"Oh uh, sorry about that!" I said embarrassedly as I let go and helped him back up.

"Don't worry, it's cool," Bolt replied, also looking a bit embarrassed.

"How the hell did a shovel fly that fast?" Vanessa asked, breaking the embarrassment between us.

Jack then explained, "The wind is blasting around all crazy from that Dragonborn's powers, so objects are flying all over the place. Be careful—if Aika hadn't pushed Bolt down in time, his head would have split open like nothing."

Charles added, "Which means we should probably start this attack now before it gets even worse."

Then Bolt, filled with anxiety, asked, "So what if any of us gets hurt or fails to do their part during the attack?"

Jack casually replied, "We'll probably just die or something," and Bolt stared back at him, dumbfounded by his response.

So I then told Bolt, "Don't worry, I'm sure everything will end up fine. Anyways, someone needs to take the risk to help the pros—look at those fools over there. None of them have the strength to do anything."

Charles then shouted out beside me, "Hey, I say we do it! I want to make that devil feel hell! To think people worship that monster as a god or something. All I see is a devil that wears a human disguise. Everyone always says they're a race of people, but how can someone like that have humanity! So how about we give them hell for coming here."

Charles's little pep talk gave everyone some sort of motivation to do this plan... except for me, and since everyone agreed, I was forced to also join in with them.

As everyone was either getting their weapons ready or telling other people what was about to happen, I was left there by myself thinking about what Charles had said, sitting on the ground behind a pile of ice to block the wind from hitting me. The words "a devil that wears a human disguise" spun around in my head like an endless loop echoing over and over again, until I felt someone touch my shoulder.

"Hey, Aika, are you sure you're doing okay?" Bolt asked me.

"Uh, what?" I asked back.

Bolt was still beside me setting up his crossbow.

"When did you sit beside me again?" I asked.

"I've been here for about three minutes trying to talk to you, but you weren't answering or even saying anything at all, so I shook you a little to see if you were all right," he explained.

"Oh yeah, I'm fine, I'm just colder from... well, everything," I told him.

"Well, all right just don't push yourself too hard, understand? I know you have a hard time doing things like this in the cold," Bolt told me.

"Hey, don't worry—I'll be fine, okay," I told him. Then I noticed everyone around was almost prepared for battle.

"Well, no going back now, I suppose," I said, sighing a bit as I got up.

Bolt also got up and told me, "Hey, you got this. I know you do!" trying to give me some motivation. I smiled back at him, then I raised up my scarf a bit to cover my mouth and nose to keep me warmer, then ran off to get in position.

When everyone was ready, we began our attack. Charles, Vanessa, and Chad were the distractors. Then the support were Bolt, Jack, Peter, and Niki. Then I was the one who would sneak attack on the Dragonborn, then knock away its sword, then run for my life before it fired off its attacks. As the distractors began to run around them and the supports took aim, I got in position and snuck around the chaos behind ice spikes that were scattered over the field. When I got behind the pillar nearest to the Dragonborn, of course something had to happen. For some stupid reason Charles started charging at it, forgetting what he was supposed to be doing. When he swung his sword at them, instead of the Dragonborn just regularly reflecting his attack, they attack back and sent his sword flying. Then a couple of arrows flew by, causing the Dragonborn to look away for a second to see where they came from. Then came my chance to attack. As I ran out of my spot and jump toward them, they turned toward me to block my attack. As I landed back on the ground, I swung at them again, and our swords met, screeching together and making sparks. As they did, I heard people around me cheer my name as I fought.

"Look at you, Aika, stealing the spotlight for yourself!" Charles commented, as he stepped back and grabbed his sword.

"Oh, of course I am, you know me by now!" I replied as I took my sword away and stepped back.

The Dragonborn glared back at me and jabbed their sword toward me. I then blocked the motion with my sword and banged it back to them in a swing. The Dragonborn stepped aside and created an ice pillar that spiked to the side of them that pointed toward me. I jumped out of the way just before it hit me and felt an icy breeze as I saw Charles slash the Dragonborn again, this time succeeding and hacking into their back.

Our back was our biggest weak spot because we only had armor plates on the front of our body. The back side of our entire body had no armor for some reason; instead, there were thicker black scales that connected from one side of our plates across our bodies like straps for our plates. These scales were located on the backs of our calves, triceps/biceps, inner forearm, the soles of our feet, and across our back. These scales protected us better than our regular scales but not the best. Because of that, Charles's sword severed right through their scales and into their back.

In pain they roared out and swung hard against Charles's sword, almost knocking him down, causing him to take his sword away from them.

"Hey, get your ass back over here!" I yelled to them as I got up and swung at them. The Dragonborn turned back around and swung back at me.

Vanessa dragged Charles back and said, as she gestured to me, "Be careful—you're not as crazy as that one!"

"Oh thanks, Venny!" I called out as I took my sword away from the Dragonborn and dodged their next swing by taking a step to the side.

Then Jack shouted to me from behind, "Aika, try to twist their sword out of their hand like you do to us!" Then as the Dragonborn took a step forward to me, arrows flew by me to the Dragonborn, who created an ice barrier and a huge ice spike toward us that almost hit Chad.

"Come on, at me! What, are you afraid? You're like a foot and a half taller than me!" I taunted them as I stepped forward to them. The Dragonborn then covered their sword in thick compacted ice and swung hard at me. I deflected their attack with my sword, which slid against the side of their sword.

"Heh, clever… but what can you do against this!" I yelled as I twisted their sword in a struggle, making sure that mine wouldn't slide off. As our swords were locked together, even more arrows flew by me that stuck into the Dragonborn. They were too busy with me, and as they were unfocused from getting shot, I took this split-second opening and twisted their sword all the way, loosening their grip the best I could, then sent their sword flying into the distance.

I heard everyone cheering in the background, calling out my name in victory as the sword went flying.

Charles then said as he ran, "All right! Way to go, Aika! Now let's get out of here!"

Vanessa, on the side of him, said after, "I can't believe you actually did all of that! Let's just say I underestimated you a bit."

Then she ran off with Charles, and Chad followed behind her. I looked up at the Dragonborn's face to get a good look at who this idiot was before I ran away, and it was exactly what I figured they were. I already knew what kind of Dragonborn this was, but I hadn't seen one in many years. The iris of their eyes were black with tiny red spots sprinkled within, with the rest their aura color, which was a light blue with a teal accent. Their claws and horns were sharper and longer than normal. And their armor had pointier and thicker plates. The rest of their characteristics were quite normal: their horns were just a bit longer than usual, but they looked normal, smooth and curved back like a demon's, and their armor didn't look much different despite it looking sharper. They had the same classic chest, shoulder, forearm, shin, hand, and foot plates as normal. Then they had their elemental symbol on their left hand, which they wielded their sword with. Then finally their scabbard's body color was green.

Suddenly it hit me: time around me seemed frozen, and my body was shaking. I gripped my sword hard and clenched my teeth. My body was telling me to fight, but my head was telling me to run away with the others. Whenever this happened to me, it made every second feel like a minute. I could see every movement around me, from the slight movements of people before they swung to predict their next move, to the arrows flying toward me to make us dodge them like nothing. This feeling only hit me while I was in intense moments: I got stuck in this trance, losing track of everything around. It left me trapped in this intense feeling of knowing everything around me. In this state I could barely feel pain, and background noise was deafened. The only thing on my mind was the danger before me. The only thing that could break this time trance was a sudden strong emotion or attack. I have this sudden feeling a lot right before someone's actions, but it never last more than a half a second. Although when I was in the trance like this, it hit differently with much greater duration and power. This was my greatest curse.

As I was stuck in my trance, I lost track of time right away. Had it only been a few seconds, or had it been minutes? Alongside that, I was yelling at myself to run away: "Don't fight, you can't fight it in front of everyone." I hadn't been like this for a long time, and I had forgotten how to fully control myself. Then in the distance outside my mind, I heard people yelling out my name; the cheers from before had turned into cries. People were shouting out around me,

"Run!"

"Get out of there!"

"What's happening?"

"Is she hurt or something?"

"Hey, snap out of it!"

I couldn't recognize any of the voices. Between me yelling at myself and everyone around me, I was basically frozen in place trying to control myself. Then unexpectedly I had a late reaction, and the Dragonborn grabbed my arm. I immediately broke out of my trance out of sudden fear. Then before I could react, it tossed me in the air and released the fury of its element at me. I got blasted by its ice storm. This attack had wind so powerful it blew me away far into the distance. The cries from everyone before vanished into nothingness. As I hit the ground hard, I started to go in and out of consciousness. I felt completely numb from the cold and wind hitting me.

Unknown time passed as I lay on the snow struggling to move or see. I forced my arms to keep me up as I looked around for anyone until I saw some lights up ahead in a far distance, flashing around. So with the last of my strength, I reached out my arm and flashed a bit of my fire for a split second as a signal, before I fell into the snow. As I lost consciousness, all I could think of was Bolt and the things he told me right before the battle and how I should have listened to him.

Meanwhile, what happened to the others was very different...

"Bolt! BOLT! BOLTON!" Charles called out.

"What? Oh wait, what happened? Where are we?" Bolt yelled out, sitting up from a couch next to one of the fireplaces near the entrance of the cabin.

"Hey, hey, it's okay, we're in the cabin's living space. How are you doing?" Charles asked.

"My head is killing me. What happened outside?" Bolt asked.

Charles took a deep breath and started explaining. "So... we did our attack on that Dragonborn, and it was a success. But things didn't end up the way we wanted. After Aika knocked away that devil's sword, she like… froze or something. Then that devil tossed her up in the air and blasted her away into the distance to who knows where. Then we all went running in the direction she got blown away to make sure she was okay. Then, well—"

Bolt interrupted him and said, "Oh wait, I'm starting to remember now. When we went after her, the Dragonborn released a frenzy of winds all around, throwing people and ice chunks everywhere. Then that must have been when I passed out. How did I pass out, though? I can't remember."

Charles told him, "Oh, you passed out because of the wind tossing everyone around, and let's just say that Chad basically... crushed you. But something good did happen during that time. The pros finally came right after you got knocked out!"

"Really?" Bolt asked.

"Hell yeah, they did! Look at them out there kicking that devil's ass!" Charles shouted out.

"Just in time too," Jack said, walking up to them "I've only ever heard of a Dragonborn being this strong in stories about the GDW Two," Jack said.

"The what?" Charles asked.

Jack explained: "You know, the Great Dragonborn War Two. We learned about these types of Dragonborns only a little bit, but I've done my own research on them. They say those Dragonborns appeared at the end of the war. They say because of them, the war ended. They were some weird mutation of Dragonborns that makes them go crazy and lose all their human characteristics. And... hey, wait, how the hell did you forget about the Dragonborn war? A whole clan of Dragonborns got destroyed. Bolt first met Aika about two weeks after the big final battle that destroyed lots of their land?"

Then Bolt asked, "Hey, speaking of Aika, where is she?"

Charles and Jack just give each other a silent stare, not knowing what to say to him.

Charles then said to him calmly, "Okay, so dude, don't flip when I tell you this, okay... Aika is still out there, and we have no idea where she is."

"What?" Bolt shouted nervously.

Charles explained, "We've told the pros what we did and what happened. They thanked us and said they'll look for her when the devil is gone. But it's been almost fifteen minutes, and they're still out there fighting it. Also, it's like less than twenty degrees outside, and we have been out there all day, but now it's even colder with the wind and darkness. And I'm a bit worried about Aika. She's been acting off all day from the cold and now this."

"Then we gotta go out there ourselves and find her!" Bolt said as he got up and tripped. Charles caught him by his shoulders and sat him back on the couch and told him,

"Whoa there, man! Me and Jack can go, but you gotta stay here and rest. When Chad landed on your leg, he must have twisted it somehow."

"Sorry, dude," Chad yelled out from across the room, fixing Niki's leg up.

Niki said, "Both of us got our legs messed up, so we aren't going anywhere. Mine was slashed by an ice spike during the chaos of the wind, and yours was crushed by this dumbass." She pointed at Chad.

"Want me to get some ice for you after I'm done helping Niki?" Chad asked.

"Oh, uh, sure, thank you," Bolt replied to him.

Vanessa, who had been listening to their conversion, demanded to them, "Hey, let me come and look for Aika too."

"What? Why?" Charles asked.

"Oh please, it's not like I care about her. I just want to rub it in her face that I helped save her for next time she pisses me off."

"Fine by me," Jack replied.

"Wait, really?" Vanessa asked.

"It's still snowing badly out there, and it's pitch black out now. It'll be easier to find her with more help," Jack explained as he looked for extra lanterns.

"Oh okay, we should also bring Peter with us to help. I don't know how, but he's pretty good at tracking stuff. What do you say, Peter?" Vanessa asked him.

"Only if we don't go near the god. I don't want to disturb them again after what happened," he said quietly.

Bolt looked over at all of them and asked, "Please, find her quickly."

Charles said to him, "Hey, don't worry, man, we'll find her. Just calm down and relax—she's going to be fine. I know you like her and you're worried," he then said smugly at the end.

Bolt shouted back at him, flustered, "Hey dude, don't say that in front of them!"

"Oh, come on man, the way you're acting right now makes it look obvious, just chill. Anyways, I bet she feels the same about you—look at the way she saved you earlier from that shovel." Charles laughed at him as they all left.

Bolt just sighed to himself after.

"So you got a crush on Aika, huh?" Niki asked him.

"Oh no, now you know," Bolt said.

"Well, you know me by now, so let's just get right into the questions, can we?" she asked.

"You're not going to leave me alone until I tell you everything, are you," Bolt asked.

"We both know the answer to that question," she replied.

While Charles, Jack, Vanessa, and Peter were retracing their steps to find me, a conversation started among them.

"Hey Vanessa, can I ask you a question?" Jack asked.

"What?" she said back with an attitude.

"Why are you always a jerk to Aika? Usually, you're always the one to start up fights. I know she pissed you off on the first meeting, but why always go that far?" he asked.

She said back to him smugly. "Aren't you supposed to be the genius around here? It's because she's better than everyone here. She's a natural. Hell, she's better than the pros, I bet. That's why you sent her out there to knock away that thing's sword and how she was able to fight that thing for as long as she did. She always holds back on everyone when she fights. It's like they had years of practice before she even signed up for training. What was she like before you all joined the Slayers?" she asked.

Charles replied to her, "Well, she did go to military school for a little bit before we met her. Back when we first met, she was quiet and didn't talk much. She was like that for a little while until she finally started to open up after an incident. After she did, we started hanging out all the time and sword dueled with each other in our little hangout spot. She would always accept the challenge and kick my ass, but it would always end very quickly like she didn't want to show off all her skills like she does to all of you."

Jack then said, adding onto the conversation, "I personally think she just doesn't want to draw attention to herself. If everyone knew how good she was at combat, people would ask her all sorts of questions that would be hard to explain, without going into personal stuff, that is. She barely tells us anything about her past. All we know is that she had absolutely nothing at all when we first met. All she had was her jacket, sword, and… that's about it. So when Bolt let her stay at his place, she didn't have any other place to go, so she went," Jack explained.

"What happened to her?" Vanessa asked.

Jack replied, "Well, we're not the ones who should be sharing that info, but it wasn't the best, let's just say. We don't know most of the details, though. Not even Bolt knows what exactly happened to her, and they're the closest to each other," he then explained.

Charles then firmly told her, "Oh yeah, also, whatever you do: Don't tell her any of this, because she will kick our asses for telling you."

"Oh yeah, don't worry, I won't," Vanessa promised.

Future Vanessa then proceeded to tell me this entire conversation, unknown to any of them except me, her, and Niki, who was eavesdropping on us.

After their conversation, a sudden faint blue light flashed in the distance from the path they were following. "The hell was that?" Vanessa asked.

"No idea, but let's check it out. It might be Aika—who knows,"

Charles said, traveling to the area.

As they followed the light's path, the storm finally started to lighten up a bit, and after a bit of walking they finally found my crippled body face down in the snow.

"Oh, hey, there she is," Jack said casually.

Vanessa snickered at Jack's comment as Charles yelled, "Dude, really?" as he ran over to me. He asked, "Aika! Aika, you idiot, you good!?" as he flipped me over and patted the snow off my face.

"Oh yeah, she's out after getting hit with that attack," Jack told him.

"Oh great," Charles said as he unequipped my scabbard, then threw me over his shoulder.

"Wait, is she okay?" Vanessa asked, unsure.

Charles told her, "She doesn't seem majorly hurt, thank goodness, but she's freezing cold, so we should hurry back. Jack, could you pick up her sword and hang on to it? I'll pass you her scabbard."

"Sure thing, man," Jack said as he picked it up, then looked away for a second and gripped the handle.

Then Charles carried me off to the cabin to get fixed up with Vanessa, Jack, and Peter, who followed behind him.

When I woke up, I found myself in the medical section of the cabin, where they brought all the other injured people. This was a section within the cabin located next to the entrance stocked with medicines, badges, and medical tools. It was a big open area with many beds separated by privacy curtains, for injured people to rest in. Within this section, nurses worked there full-time so they could immediately help anyone if an accident happened. As I looked around the place had injured people everywhere and no nurse had any time to slack off. Then I noticed Bolt sitting in a chair beside me reading a book while fidgeting with my scarf. I muttered to him, "Bolt?" and immediately he looked over to me and said,

"Aika?" His voice was full of concern, and he closed his book.

"Hey, what happened to you?" I asked, pointing at his leg elevated on a chair. I then looked back at my hand and saw that my gloves were gone, but the bandages I wore were still on. "Thank goodness," I thought.

Bolt replied to me, "Oh, my leg is fine—it's just a bit swollen because Chad crushed me and twisted it up a little. Everyone just sorta dumped me here next to you because there was no space left at all, and we are in the same squad after all. But enough about me, how are you doing? Do you need anything?" he asked.

"I'm... fine. Just a little cold and tired. Why, what happened? How long was I out for?" I asked.

Bolt then told me hesitantly, "So you were out for about... a half a day."

"That long?" I asked, a bit surprised.

"Yeah… you see, let me explain what happened. So after we did the attack, you sorta froze up. And when we ran after you to pull you back, we got hit with an icy wind attack. Me and Niki got hurt a little, but we're pretty much fine now. But you were stuck outside in the snow for a good while. And when Charles finally found you and carried you back. Let's just say your temperature was not the best. In fact, it was almost in the deadly zone of hypothermia," he told me.

"Yeah, figures I would get that again after being out there all day," I told him.

"So after we… wait, what? Again?" he asked.

"Oh yeah, I got that before back in the day," I explained.

"Uh... all right. Well, anyways, after you were inside, all we did to you was remove your snowy uniform and your boots. Your normal clothes underneath were dry, luckily. Oh, also your gloves because they were covered in ice, but we left your bandages underneath because they were still dry. I know how you are about your hands, so I asked the nurses not to do anything with them," he explained.

"Oh yeah, thanks for that," I said.

Bolt sighed and said back, "Man. You have no idea how worried I was. I couldn't stop thinking about bad things as I waited for them to find you. I… I just—" Bolt then started stuttering, trying to talk.

I stopped him and said, "Hey, I'm fine now. Stop worrying so much about me."

"Are you?" he asked. He then explained, "You lie a lot about how you're doing when you're hurt. I know you hide a lot of things about yourself, but you don't need to lie to me about how you're doing. Back at the battle you told me you were fine, but I knew you weren't doing good—that's why I checked in with you again after Charle's little talk."

Seeing Bolt confess all his worries, I told him, "I'm sorry, Bolt. It's just... well... I don't think I can tell you just yet why I keep so much to myself. You don't need to worry about me, though. Right now, I'm doing okay, promise."

Bolt replied, "All right, I'll take your word for it."

Then after a moment of awkwardness I asked him, "So what happened with the pros?"

Bolt's eyes then lit up a bit as then told me cheerfully "Oh yeah, of course! So after we told the pros what we did, they thanked us and rewarded us with some credit for taking it down alongside Vanessa's squad. We saved them quite the time by knocking their sword away. All they had to do was figure out a way to make it leave," he explained.

"Well, that's one good thing to come out of this," I said.

Bolt then got up off his chair and told me, "Anyways, I'll let you rest and think about the things I told you. Ask the nurses if you need anything. I'm going to tell everyone you're all right and such because they were also worried about you."

Then he placed my scarf around my neck and said, "Don't worry about any paperwork from the incident—I'll take care of everything. All right, see you in a bit. Rest up, okay?"

Then he waved goodbye as he walked away to another room.

Then not even a minute later I heard Charles yell out, "Hey, everyone! Aika's all right!" then a roar of "YEAH!" that sounded like it came from a big group of people.

But after the uproar I saw Jack walk over from the entrance, nervous.

"Hey Jack, what's with the face?" I asked.

"Well… I just came over to apologize about what happened. I had no idea you would end up like this from my plan," he told me, looking away.

"It's no trouble, dude, I'm already doing better. It wasn't your fault anyways. Blame that crazy Dragonborn," I told him.

"Thanks for understanding, Aika, though I gotta say I want to learn more about that Dragon we saw so bad!" he told me in his usual carefree attitude.

"Welp, after what happened, we're bound to come across another one eventually," I told him.

Jack then pointed to the corner table next to me and said, "Oh, looks like you got a letter."

"I do? Bolt must have forgotten to show me. Could you read it to me please?" I asked him.

"Yeah, it's no prob," he told me as he walked over and grabbed it. Then he opened it up and said in a playfully stoic voice, "To Ms. Aika. We Dragon Slayers are very sorry for not arriving sooner to prevent you from getting hurt. We hope you will not publicly discuss the events of this incident for a long period of time. We hope you agree, and if not, we will pay a sum of money to not speak publicly about the events and people who were involved. Thank you and we bid you a fair day!" He suddenly stopped and stared at the letter for a moment, then handed it to me.

"What's the matter?" I asked.

"Uh… you can read numbers… you can discover this for yourself. But I'll visit again soon, Aika. Bye-bye!" he told me then walked away.

Confused about what he'd seen, I looked over the letter, then realized why he'd handed it to me. The money they would give me for keeping quiet was a really good amount.

"Damn, the Slayers just bribed me with money… and I'll gladly take it!" I said to myself happily as I put the paper back in the envelope and put it aside. I then sighed to myself and got comfy in bed to think about all the stuff that had happened. As I did, something crossed my mind. I started to think about what Charles said back at the battle: "They're a devil that wears a human disguise." This made me think of how he would react if he ever found out I was one of those so-called devils. It made me think of how everyone else would react if they find out. Would they try to kill me? Would they use me to fight? Or would they be cool with me? Then I thought, can I trust anyone to know about me? The only person I could think of was Bolt and how he was the most likely to understand out of anyone.

Chapter 4: Upon the Hill of Flowers

It had been about two months since the attack from that crazy Ice Dragonborn. The pros decided to call those types of Dragonborns "War Dragonborns" because they first appeared during the second Dragonborn war.

It was the spring season. The fifth years were graduating from training and were the new pros, while we became the new fifth years. Everything had finally calmed down from the attack, and it was spring break, so Bolt and I were staying at Bolt's uncle Clay's house. Clay looked a bit like Bolt, but he had olive skin, short faded blond hair going a bit gray, a bushy beard that was a bit blonder than his head, and gray-blue eyes. He wore long white-sleeve shirts with old black overalls with a beige belt, and wore thick faded brown steel-toe work boots. The house he owned was a big two-story place that had rooms for all three of us, a big living room was on the bottom floor, where our squad would hang out or sleep on the couch and chairs. Then outside there was a big forge outside near the side because he'd worked as a blacksmith for many years.

We had been there for a few hours talking and such.

"So are you sure you're both okay from the attack?" Clay asked us for the third time now.

Bolt had been getting a little annoyed by him asking repeatedly, so he said back, "Hey, we're both fine now, Uncle. I know you were worried when you first found out we both got hurt, but we're both here in front of you talking now."

"Want me to do a backflip off the roof to show him?" I asked.

"No, don't," Bolt replied.

"Why not? I did it before we left the training grounds, and the cabin is taller than this house," I asked.

"Aika, you jumped off the roof so you could prove Vanessa wrong," Bolt said.

"Hey, I nailed that landing perfectly," I told him proudly.

"You barely nailed the landing! After you took a step forward, you almost tripped and fell on our face because your legs were shaking," Bolt explained.

"Almost, Bolton... almost," I replied.

Clay then said, "Okay, I understand. I'll stop asking. I'm going to do a bit of work in the forge. You two can hang out someplace. Just be back by dinner—you don't want to eat supper cold, now."

Then he got up and grabbed his hammer hanging from the wall and walked over to the side door to his forge. Bolt looked over at me and sighed in disappointment.

"Hey, after I walked over to Vanessa, she said she was actually impressed that I could do that," I told him.

"Aika, everyone was impressed that you could still walk fine after you did that," Bolt replied.

I said back, "Well, whatever… so what do you wanna do now?" I asked.

"No idea… uh, you wanna walk around for a bit?" Bolt suggested.

"Yeah, sure we got nothing better to do right now," I replied as I stood up and stretched my arms out. "Maybe we could find out if Charles and Jack are busy," I said.

"I doubt they'll be free, knowing Charles's mom," Bolt replied as he stood up and grabbed his bag. "She'll probably be questioning all the events that happened since the last time they spoke," Bolt said as he walked to the door.

"You're probably right about that one," I replied as I walked to him.

Bolt held the door open for me and said, "After you, my crazy lady."

"Why thank you, Bolton," I said proudly as I walked by.

"Wow, and you don't even deny it," Bolt said as he shut the door behind him; then we went on our way.

We stopped by Charles and Jack's house, and as predicted they were busy. It was early afternoon, and it was a relatively nice day out with a few clouds all around, the sun hitting our backs for warmth, and a slightly chill spring breeze in the air that blew our hair in the wind. I had no idea where we were going—I was just following behind Bolt as he led the way—but he turned weirdly quiet, not talking much after we left the house.

"What are you thinking about?" I asked.

"Oh, uh, nothing!" he replied, sounding a little startled.

"Really nothing? You can't trick me, Bolt. I've known you for long enough to know that's a lie," I replied as I walked up close beside him.

"Uh, well... all right, I was thinking of what we could do together today," he admitted, looking a bit embarrassed.

"That's all? It seemed like you were thinking about something way more intense. But anyways, what did you have in mind?" I asked.

"Well, not much… Do you want to look around the market plaza and get some coffee maybe?" he asked.

"You're asking me if I want to get some coffee? Please, you've known me long enough to know my answer," I told him.

"Yes, to feed your crippling coffee addiction," Bolt replied confidently.

"Well, of course!" I said back playfully.

Bolt laughed and asked, "Oh geez, why did I give you your first cup of coffee all the way back then?"

"Because I had insomnia from my nonstop nightmares," I told him.

Bolt asked, "They're still better now, right? I haven't asked you that in a while."

"Oh yeah, they're fine right now. I haven't gotten them in a little while," I replied.

Bolt said happily, "That's good that they're gone. I remember back in the day you could never sleep because of them. I remember one random night when I woke up and went to grab some water, and I saw you polishing your sword out in the living room at like two in the morning. When I stopped to see what you were doing, you just casually said 'Sup' to me, then continued working on your sword."

I laughed back and told him, "To be completely honest, I barely remember those early days from back then. The only things that I can remember are the stupid things we did together with Jack and Charles. But that story did remind me that I should pick up some of that good polish for my sword—the stuff Clay has is horrible compared to the good stuff."

"Well, let's head to the plaza now, then, before it all gets sold out," Bolt suggested.

"Hey, good thinking, and after that we can get some coffee and relax for a bit," I said, then looked at the plaza down the road.

The market plaza was a large gravel field with shop stands everywhere for people to visit and buy whatever they needed. There was a shop for almost anything here such as food, tools, clothing, etc. Most of the time there were no big outbursts from people, but when they did happen, it was fun to watch the fights that broke out.

Then when we arrived, we did a bit of shopping, got our coffee, and we sat on a bench and watched people come in and out of the market plaza. At the time there were many people there and it was quite packed with travelers, guards, children, and just people passing by. As I sipped my coffee, I watched smiling children who were loudly causing chaos for their elders, and lots of people from all over working their jobs, who were getting bothered by merchants selling as they walked by. But my attention was mostly at the café where a Slayer complained about the coffee he'd ordered, then walked back and forth in a hurry.

"How much money do you want to bet that the coffee he ordered was made wrong on purpose because he acted like an ass," I asked Bolt, who was still a bit quiet.

"Oh uh, well the all the pros have been busy a lot recently. I bet they are in a rush to get to work." he replied.

As then I heard the guy said as he received his coffee, "Finally! Now I can go home and sleep, darn it"

"Uh... yeah busy." I replied Bolt.

Bolt then asked me, "Hey, you want to go someplace else? It's a bit pack here today."

"Where do you feel like heading to next?" I asked him.

"Oh uh… I know a place. You can just follow me!" Bolt said, sounding more confident.

"You going to tell me what place it is?" I asked.

"I'll let it be a surprise. Come on, let's head out," he told me.

"All right, you better not disappoint me then," I replied, then finished off my coffee.

So I followed behind Bolt, who was leading me to who knows where. Time had passed since we went to the market plaza, and it was sunset. The sky was in different rays of yellows, oranges, and reds as the sun began to disappear. I wasn't sure what Bolt was planning until I noticed he had walked to the place where we'd first met.

I asked, "Hey, isn't this—?"

"It's where we first met, remember," he said back to me before I could finish talking. It was a training ground with a small hill behind the field where people would hang out sometimes and watch the people below practice combat.

"What are we doing here?" I asked.

"Well, I've been planning to tell you something all day, and thought I should tell you here, where it all began," Bolt said, as he gestured to me to sit with him on the hill.

"Oh no," I thought to myself. I knew exactly what he was going to tell me and was not prepared. So I followed him up the hill and sat down with him on grass facing him, with the sword ground to the right of me. The hill we sat on was covered in lush grass with patches of violet and orange flowers.

"So what's up? You've been weirdly quiet all day and brought me here out of all places," I told him.

"Oh, well, I guess there's no beating around the bush, huh. I figured you would catch on right away," he said, a bit shy. Bolt took a deep breath, looked at me right in the eye, and told me, "So for the past few months, I've uh… I've had a crush on you! The way you act and the things you say give me motivation and courage to do things I would never normally do. Without you, my life would be totally different. I love you and all your strengths and flaws. I love how you have the courage to do all these scary things even when you don't want to. I love how much you care for everyone in your own way. When you lie and say you're okay even though you're not, it makes me worry a lot, but knowing you, I know I don't always have to be."

As Bolt was confessing all his feelings for me, a horrible guilt formed within me. As it continued to build up every second, I silently let him finish talking.

"I just need to tell you all of this. Because if I don't… I know I'll regret it one day. So how do you feel about me?" he asked.

"Well... I uh..." I said, unsure, then took a minute to organize my thoughts. "Bolton, I also love you… but you don't deserve someone like me," I told him.

"What do you mean?" he asked, confused. I finally decided to finally tell him the truth… the truth about me.

"Bolt, I'm not like any other person," I said as I held his hands. "I've been keeping a big secret." I told him.

"Oh, I bet it's not as dramatic as you think," he said.

"I'm not a normal person, Bolt," I told him.

"Wha… What do you mean you're 'not normal'?" he asked.

"Bolton… I'm a Dragonborn," I told him.

"What?" he asked, surprised and confused.

So I told him again: "I'm of the Dragonborn race. I'm not a normal person like you... I'm cursed!"

"This is just some sort of prank, right? Because I've known you for like seven years now," he said. I stayed silent and didn't answer him. "I would have found out earlier if you were one, right?" Then he went silent for a moment until he said softly, "You are one, aren't you," with the face of realization.

Full of guilt for never telling him, I cried out, "I'm a monster! A devil! I tricked all of you into thinking I was like you… normal."

Bolt was silent.

"Someone as kind as you doesn't deserve a devil like me to be by their side," I told him, then took my hands away from him.

But before I knew it, Bolt grabbed my hands back, looked back at me, smiled, and asked, "How can someone as kind as you be a devil?"

"What?" I asked.

Bolt told me, "Devils are cruel, hateful, destructive. But you? You're kind, courageous, and emotional. How can someone like you be considered a devil? You probably call yourself a devil because you're a Dragonborn. You hear people constantly call you some sort of evil monster all the time. It must be hard to hear that all day long. But you're no devil. Not to me at least."

That's when I realized who I was talking to. He wasn't like Charles, who hates Dragonborns, or like Jack, who would ask a million questions. Bolt was the kindest person in the world, and if he didn't accept me, then no one probably would have. He's the guy who let me, a complete stranger to him, sleep in his spare room all the way back then. He's the one who sat beside me for over half a day to make sure I wasn't alone when I woke up after the attack. He's my best friend who had always stuck beside me through my stupidity. He knew me better than I could ever know myself.

Unable to look him in the eyes, still in tears, I told him, "I'm sorry I never told you. I'm sorry I keep secrets from you all the time. I was going to tell you way earlier in the past, but then that incident with Charles's family happened. After that I became too afraid to ever tell anyone the truth about me. I was even afraid to tell you because I thought it would affect the way you felt about me."

Bolt turned my head to him, kissed me, and said, "Why would my feelings change because you're a Dragonborn? Sure, it's quite a surprise to suddenly learn, but that wouldn't change how I feel about you."

"Wow… that was smooth. To be honest, though, I have no idea how none of you realized it back when I first met all of you. I sucked at keeping my powers hidden back then," I admitted.

Bolt explained, "Well, back then I was too pure and thought nothing bad of anyone, so I would have never guessed. Charles can be a big idiot at times, and I think Jack had some suspicions, but I think they all got pushed aside after that incident with Charles."

I wiped away my tears and asked, "You won't tell anyone about me, right?"

Bolt immediately replied, "Of course I won't tell anyone. What was your plan anyways for if you did get revealed?" he asked.

"Oh uh... well to be honest… I had no plan at all," I admitted.

Bolt looked back at me, dumbfounded by my response, and said to reconfirm to himself, "You had no plan?"

I replied, "Well, I had a plan: to make sure no one would ever learn I was a Dragonborn!"

All Bolt replied with was "Wow, I forget how much of an idiot you are sometimes." Then he sighed and asked, "So what was this brilliant plan you had to never be discovered?"

So I explained, almost back to my regular self now, "Well you see, the main reason why I even agreed to become a Dragon Slayer with you guys was to help fool everyone into thinking I wasn't a Dragonborn. Everybody always thinks 'No way would a Dragonborn ever join an army of people that fight Dragonborns, that would be suicide' or something like that. I've just worked so much on making sure no one would ever think of the possibility of me being one. My strategy had always been just giving everyone a vague answer that's true, then immediately changing the subject, hoping that they would go along."

The only thing Bolt said was "That is very you."

I explained, "For example, people ask me from time to time occasionally where I'm from. I always just give everyone a vague answer by saying I'm from the western lands. I am from the western lands, I'm just from the far west, from the destroyed Eastern Dragonborn Land."

Bolt asked, "How did you even travel to Infinitas from lands that far away?"

"Oh well, that's a whole entire story itself. I should probably start from the very beginning before I tell you about that. But I'll wait for that tale another day because that's a pretty heavy story, and you should probably process it all slowly. Besides, I don't want to ruin this moment even more than I already have," I told him.

"What do you mean by that?" Bolt asked.

"Oh, please Bolt, you confessed your love to me, and I responded with 'I've been hiding my real identity from you all this time.' I'll explain more to you tomorrow, though, because it's a lot to hear it all at once," I explained.

"Oh yeah, it's no problem. But could you promise me something, Aika?" he asked.

"Like what?" I replied.

"Promise me you won't lie to me about anything anymore. Because if you do, how would I be able to help you out when things go wrong?" he said as he smiled back at me.

I said back to him, "I promise I won't lie to you anymore. I don't want to keep on lying to you. To be honest it's hard keeping it all together. Also, could you do something for me?" I asked.

"What is it?" he replied.

"Could you keep our relationship a secret from the others for now?" I asked him.

"I can keep it a secret, but why?" he asked.

I explained, "If I ever get revealed that I'm a Dragonborn to everyone... I don't want you to get hurt. If everyone found out about me and if they all knew we were dating, the Slayers will go crazy on you for obvious reasons. If they think you were only my friend, like Jack and Charles, maybe they won't be as cruel," I explained.

Bolt sighed and told me, "Well, I've got to say that's going to be quite a challenge trying to hide it because, uh, well... everybody already knows we both like each other," he said quietly at the end.

"What?" I asked, confused.

"Yeah, so I've had a crush on you for a bit and told Charles and Jack about it, and they sorta blabbed about it in front of Vanessa's squad and… wait, are the rants Niki makes about you accurate?" Bolt stopped midsentence and asked.

"To be honest, here and there during her rants, she does say things that are true about me. You have no idea how scary Niki is sometimes to me; she is the only person to have just watched me and instantly picked up that I'm a Dragonborn without a question. I'm just glad everyone thinks she's insane during her rants and doesn't give it another thought. If they did, I would most likely be dead, to be honest," I explained.

Then a bit of wind picked up around us and made a chill in the air. Bolt turned to me and said, "Well, the sun will be fully down soon. How about we head back? It's getting a little chilly out now, and I bet Clay made some dinner."

"Oh sure, I hate the cold anyways," I replied.

"Why do you hate the cold so much? You never really gave me an answer for that," Bolt asked.

"Oh, don't worry. You'll find out when I tell you about my powers," I told him playfully, then kissed him.

"Well, uh. All right then, let's head out," he told me.

Then he and I walked back to Clay's place together.

It took till the end of the break to tell Bolt everything because I told new information a little bit at a time every day so he could process it all correctly. I had finally told Bolt about what truly happened to me in the past. I told him who I was, what my life was like, and why I even came to Infinitas in the first place. After he knew most of the information, we started making all sorts of plans on what to do if I ever got revealed. Bolt learning about me was only the start of what was to come later down the line.

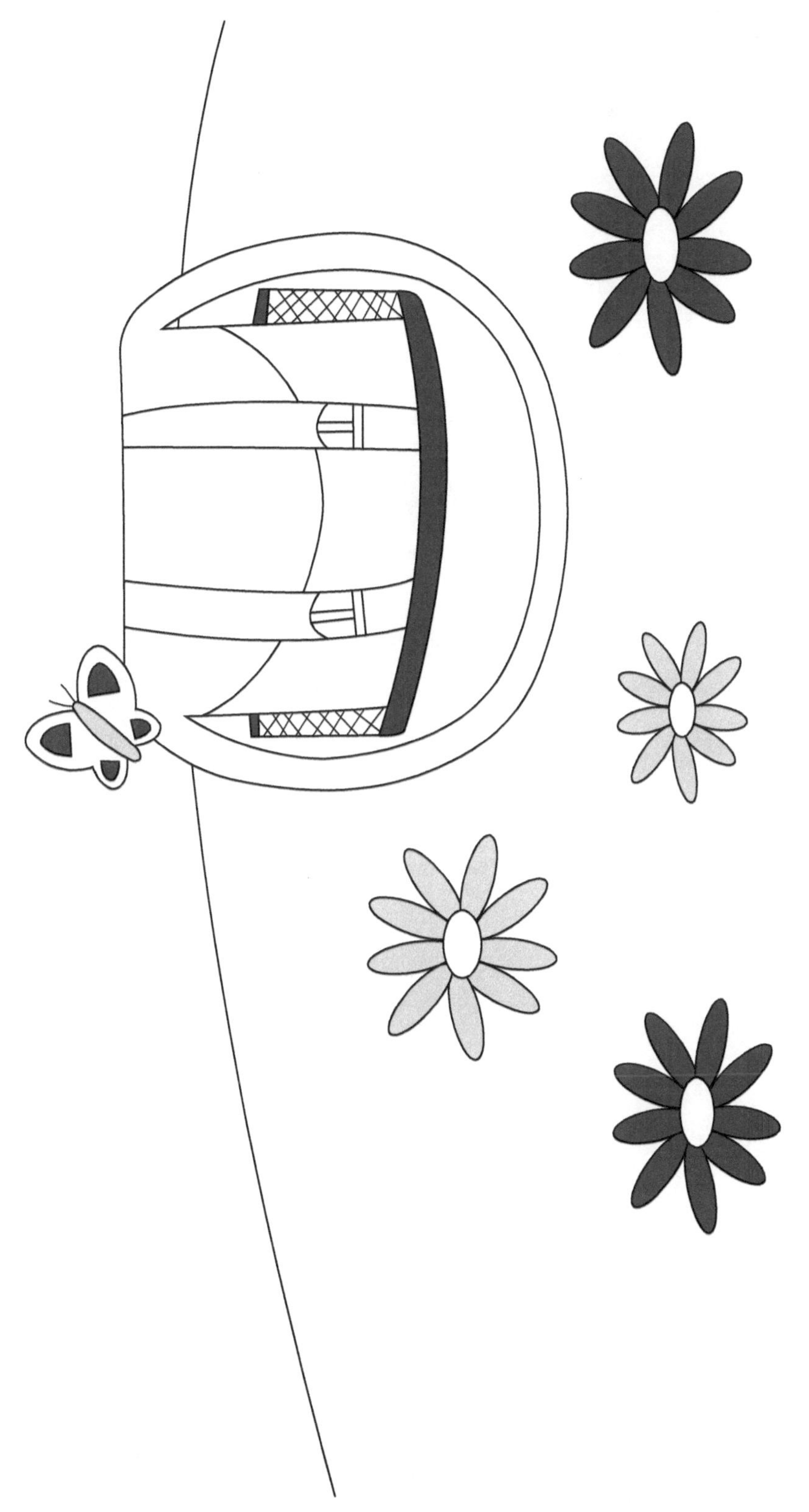

Chapter 5: The Sparks of Fury (Bolton's Origin)

Throughout my entire life I never really understood why people called Dragonborns devils. When I learned Aika was a Dragonborn, that's when I realized people had never given them a chance to just be people. They gave them the label "devil" and talked about them like some mighty gods that felt no pain or emotions, but they were none of those things. They're all just regular people with hopes and dreams, that feel pain and sorrow like everyone else. We were taught to hate and fear these devils throughout our lives and were given many examples to be afraid of them. But never were we taught about who they really were as people and about their culture. But the truth that no one wanted to accept was that we were all exactly like them… human.

I was always a little bit more self-conscious about everything than any other kid. My parents were Dragonborn Hunters that traveled the land. They visited every kingdom and village on our map doing their job. I lived with them until I was seven, until they dropped me off at my uncle's place and he took care of me from then on. I had very little memory of my parents from when I lived with them. The most I can remember was them trying to train me to become a Dragonborn Hunter like them, but I could never fulfill the expectations. They were the ones who taught me how to use a bow and aim perfectly, how to make traps and upgrade weapons from resources around me, and much more, but I couldn't remember. I can barely remember their personalities, but I knew they were kinda messed up a bit in their head. They were always ready for the next job and collected new weapons that were faster and better. They were very harsh people who never took no for an answer. They had the charisma to persuade anyone they met into doing what they wanted. They could manipulate people into helping them with jobs and giving them free supplies.

My dad had messy dark-blond hair with a darker-blond beard, olive skin, and brown eyes. I got most of my physical traits from my mother. She had brownish-blond hair, light-blue eyes, freckles, and the same pale olive-mixed skin. Whenever I was forced to go hunting with them, I could never willingly kill anything and cried every time I did. My dad figured I had gotten it from his side of the family because my uncle was the same. So they dumped me off to my uncle and went to the Eastern Dragonborn Lands, and it ended up being the last time anyone ever saw them. I know nothing about what happened to them after, but whenever the topic of them was mentioned or Dragonborn Hunters in general, I got a weird shiver down my spine.

But after that my uncle took care of me. I always used to help him out with his work until he retired. He was a blacksmith who forged swords for the Slayers. We would always talk about all sorts of things like weapons, life advice, and dumb stories. I learned a lot from him that made my views on things different from everyone else my age. Every guy my age would always play some sort of sport and want to be strong like the soldier men in the Slayers. I didn't really want to do any sports or look like one of those strong men. I liked weapons and such from my uncle, but I mostly only liked to practice my sword once in a while because it was a good skill to know. My uncle even helped me make my own custom sword from scratch. It was usually on display, but I used to practice with it a lot when I was younger.

I never really made any good friends until I was twelve. One day some bullies were playing monkey in the middle with me, tossing my bag high in the air. I'm not a strong or tall person. I got most of my height when I was sixteen, so back then when I was even smaller. I could never jump up and catch my bag at all. When I would get close to one of them, they would push me to the ground and call me "bolts of nothing." I always would stand back up and keep on trying again and again to get my stuff back. But on this fateful day everything changed. When I got back up, some other kid started chasing the bullies suddenly. Then when they scared everyone away from me, some other kid walked up to me and asked,

"Hey, are you all right?"

"Uh... yeah. Who are you?" I asked.

"The name's Jack, and the one who's chasing all those bullies is my pal Charles. He told me we should help you out because he thought it was cool how you 'continue to fight on, when they pushed you down' or something like that," he explained.

Charles was bigger and stronger than most of the neighborhood kids— nobody could beat him up. Jack looked basically the same as he was now, and the only difference in Charles was that he had no facial hair at the time. He only let it grow out a bit after he was seventeen. After that day we became good friends. They showed me their secret sword ground that became our usual meet-up, and they taught me how to better speak up for myself. Whenever I hung out with them, no one would mess with me, but when I walked back home, I was always alone, and sometimes they would just come back.

The worst time I was ever jumped was when I was fourteen, and it was the end of the spring. I was walking home after hanging out with Charles and Jack. Little did I know that I was not alone on that walk home. I saw a group of people who liked to mess with me often, so I looked behind, and there was another group of bullies. Then I noticed another sword-training ground nearby, so I ran there to escape them. But there was nowhere to go— it was a trap. It was already too late. The gang of bullies had followed me in.

"What do you want from me?" I asked.

The leader of them said to me, "I want your sword, pal."

"What, why?" I asked.

"I saw how bad you were using swords, and your sword looks pretty nice. So I want it," he demanded.

"What, no!" I yelled back.

"Come on, bolts of nothing. Just make it easy and give up your sword," he said.

"No, I can't! My uncle helped me make this. You already have your own. Leave me alone," I told them.

"Give me your sword, scrub, or we'll just take it by force," he demanded.

"No, you can't!" I shouted out.

Then he snatched it from my scabbard and pushed me to the ground.

"Give it back!" I hollered.

"What are you gonna do about it?" he asked.

With a little bit of hesitation, I stood back up and punched him in his face while he was laughing with his friends.

"I'll stand up for myself! That's what I'll do. I can't let you take that sword from me, it's mine!" I shouted out.

He looked at me for a minute, then said to his friends, "Hold him down."

Then his gang jumped me and held me down in the dirt, and the leader started to punch me repeatedly in my face. He had a sharp ring that busted my nose as he punched me. He kept on punching until we all heard someone yell out, "Hey, assholes!"

Everyone looked over to see who it was, and that's when everything changed. There was some kid standing in front of the entrance with their hands on their hips. The sun was hitting their back, which caused a shadow to appear over us.

"Why are you beating the shit out of this guy? You all taunt him for being weak, and when he stands up for himself, you do all of this? Why?" they asked.

"Who the hell do you think you are, dude? Come on closer and… hold up," the leader said as they took a closer look at them. "Hey, wait, you're no dude… eh. whatever. I don't care if you're a chick—I'll beat your ass if you get in my way!" the leader shouted out at her.

She took a step closer and said, "Ah yes, I'm a 'chick,' you say. Well, I'm not like other chicks, and threats don't work on me. Try again," she told them.

Pissed off, he pointed my sword at her and said, "Oh, really, threats don't work on you."

She just stared at him blankly for a moment, then at the sword, then back to him, and said, "That's it? That's your threat? Oh, that's cute."

Angered, he yelled "What the hell do you mean by cute? You don't even have a sword to fight back with!"

"Are you sure about that?" she asked as she reached behind her and drew out her sword a little.

"Is that a… d-devil sword? How'd you get one? Who are you?" he asked nervously.

"Who am I? I'm about to be your worst nightmare, if you don't give his sword back to him," she demanded.

Terrified of what she'd do, the leader dropped my sword and yelled out to the rest of his gang, "Run, you fools!"

Then everyone scattered away as fast as they could. After everyone left, she put her sword back and walked over to me.

"Need a hand?" she asked.

As she helped me up, I was still in disbelief about what happened.

"Hey, you doing okay there? Your nose is all bloody," she asked me.

I said back, "Oh yeah, I'll be fine. Thanks a lot for helping. I have no idea what would've happened if you never showed up."

She replied to me, "Oh it's nothing. I saw the whole thing go down. I was walking down that path and saw those assholes following you, then I saw you run in here in a panic. That's when I got a bad feeling."

I said back, "Well, thanks so much again. My name is Bolton—you can just call me Bolt though. Who are you? I've never seen you around here before," I asked as I reached my left hand out.

She looked like she hesitated for a minute but replied, "My name is

Aika, nice to meet you," and shook my hand.

The outfit she wore back then was a lot different than the way she was now. She of course had her jacket on, but it looked a tad bit big on her because she had fewer muscles. She wore a gray T-shirt underneath that was tucked into her pants, which were some beaten-up black tactical cargo pants with her usual black belts around her pants, waist, and chest. Then well-worn black army boots, and full-fingered armored gloves. She didn't look too different back then either, the only difference from now was her hair. She still had her classic bangs, but the rest was a whole lot shorter, being a midlength guy style. She was the same height, though; she never grew an inch over the years, but she also looked younger, of course.

As we shook hands, I barely noticed below her wrist there was a horrible animal-like scratch.

"So where are you from?" I asked.

"Oh, you know, from here to there. I'm a traveler," she replied.

"Oh cool, who do you travel with?" I asked.

"Uh... I travel alone," she explained.

"Really, you do? You look like my age," I said.

She didn't reply and kept quiet. Aika had always been an awful liar, but back then she was an even worse one. I had immediately figured out that she was probably a refugee from the recent Dragonborn attacks. I'd been told over and over to not associate with any of them, but I didn't care at the time. I was just some dumb kid who saw another kid my age who was going through something bad.

"Hey, be honest with me. Do you have a place to go? Is it because of the recent attacks in nearby towns? We've been getting some of the refugees here recently from them," I asked her.

She was silent for a minute but then said "Yeah" back quietly.

"Are you okay? I saw a bad scratch on your arm," I asked.

Aika was silent again for a moment but then said, "Those aren't the only scratches."

Then she pulled up her sleeves and revealed the marks going halfway up her left arm, then on her right arm, the marks began where the left one's ended and continued to almost her elbow.

"You got a good eye. I'm surprised you even noticed those scratches. I guess there's no hiding it," she said as she pulled her sleeves back down, then said, "My village was… sorta attacked by Dragonborns. Let's just say those scratches are from me running," she explained.

A part of me wished I hadn't asked because I knew I was pushing her to explain personal stuff even though I just met her. But the other part of me was glad I'd picked up on it, because the reason she even told me all of that proved that she needed serious help right then.

"Hey, want to stay at my place for a bit?" I asked.

"What?" she asked, confused.

"My uncle won't mind if you stay. We got a guest room you could sleep in if you have no place to go," I explained.

"Are you sure? I mean, I'm a complete stranger to you. Why would you do this much for someone you don't even know?" she asked.

"You didn't know me at all, yet you still helped me out and told me all this information," I replied.

"Uh, well... you asked me and… I haven't talked to anyone 'nice' in a… let's just say a long time. It felt good to finally talk to someone. No one else around here seems to care about any of us," she said as she walked back a little.

So with a smile I told her, "Hey, it's no worries at all. It won't be a problem after I explain the situation to my uncle; he'll help any kid like you in a situation like this. So come on, I'll show you where it is."

With a bit of hesitation, she said, "All right," quietly, then walked beside me back to the house.

As we walked back, I told her all about my uncle, Infinitas, and about the general area. She quietly listened and didn't ask any questions.

When we got there, I told my uncle what happened, and he gladly let her stay the night. We talked for a bit, and she explained a little bit more about what happened, but all she said was "I was attacked by Dragonborns about two weeks ago and lost everything. My parents died and my entire village got burned down. For the past two weeks I've been running from village to village trying to escape them. But no matter where I went, they came and burned down every place I ran to." Then she thanked us so many times for letting her stay. After dinner we talked for a bit, and she ended up falling asleep on the couch. Clay carried her off to our guest room so she had a bed to sleep in. She proceeded to sleep for about fifteen hours straight, and that alone concerned us both greatly. After hearing her story and seeing her so messed up on top of having almost nothing at all, my uncle offered to let her stay for as long as she needed and made a dumb joke, saying I needed more friends other than Charles and Jack. My uncle had immediately recognized that Aika was no threat, especially when she asked us, "Wait, you actually meant it when you offered me breakfast?"

She was in disbelief at the offer and kept on asking if it was okay for her to be there repeatedly, which proved even further that she wasn't going to do anything to us. It took her the whole first week to realize that we were being serious and that she could stay with us and how we weren't going to kick her out.

After that first week, Charles and Jack met Aika, and it was an experience to remember. After Aika finally accepted that she could stay here, she wanted to contribute to something and "not be a freeloader" in her words. So my uncle told her she could help us out in the forge… but she wasn't very good at helping us. Sorta making it harder for us to work when she did help. So she became the delivery person, dropping off the finished products and running to the market to grab supplies for work. Once afternoon though while I was hanging out with Charles and Jack, they kept asking me questions about Aika because they hadn't met her yet. All they knew was that this mysterious person that helped me was staying at my house because of the Dragonborn attacks. I told Aika about them, of course, but she still needed some time to adjust to everything that happened to her.

"So Bolt, when are you finally going to let us meet this new mysterious person?" Charles asked.

"I already told you, it's too early for you to meet her," I said back.

"Dude, we're almost at Bolt's house. He said she's probably helping Clay with work, so we'll just see her then, right?" Jack told him.

"Wait, is that the reason why you're walking home with me?" I asked.

Then around the corner, we arrived at my house and saw my uncle working.

"Hey, what's up, Clay!" Charles shouted.

"Oh hey everyone, what are you all doing here?" my uncle asked.

I explained, "They followed me home, hoping to see Aika."

He said back to us, "Well, you're all too late for that. I sent her out to get some supplies at the market plaza. You may see her on the way back."

Charles said, "Well, shucks... okay, Bolt, come on. Let's go and find her."

"Wait, what?" I asked, surprised at his immediate response.

"Come on, let's go find her. I want to meet this new friend of yours," Charles said playfully as he dragged me off with him and Jack.

As we were walking on the path toward the plaza, Jack asked me,

"Hey, what does Aika look like again?"

I told him, "She has shorter brown hair and wears boots and a blue jacket with a sword on her back, why?" I asked after.

Jack pointed off to the right side of the path and asked, "Is that her?"

I turned to see what they were on about, and to my surprise it was Aika walking. She was slowly walking down the opposite path back to the house carrying a bag full of supplies over her shoulder, looking off into the distance of the main town to her left. This specific path we were on was on a hill. At the bottom there was a tiny field, and farther up led to the main town, where lots of people lived. My uncle's house was more in the suburb area of the kingdom, so it was always a walk to get there.

"Maybe," I said back to him.

Charles overheard me talking with Jack, so of course he suddenly shouted out to her from across the road,

"Hey, you, person with the sword on their back!"

She stopped and looked over to us and saw Charles waving his hand in the air trying to call her over like a goon, while Jack laughed at me from getting embarrassed by Charles. Aika just sighed and walked over to us slowly.

"Are these the friends you told me about?" she asked me.

So I said back to her, "They've been waiting to meet you since I first told them about you, so they went looking for you and dragged me along. But anyways, here they are, Charles and Jack. I already told you a bit about them, so yeah," I explained, full of embarrassment from the situation the other two put me in.

Charles shoved me out of the way and greeted her, saying, "Hey, what's up, I'm Charles!"

Jack, on the side of him, just said, "Hey, nice to meet you. The name's Jack," normally, remembering what I told him about her.

"Uh… hello, I'm Aika?" she said awkwardly.

"Hey, so, I heard how you helped Bolt with those bullies, and I'm curious: do you know how to use that sword?" Charles asked.

"Yeah," Aika said, blankly.

"Well, I want to see how strong you really are. Want to test your skills in that field over there?" he asked.

"You don't want to battle me," she told him immediately.

"What, why?" he asked.

"You'll just end up embarrassing yourself," Aika replied with no remorse.

Jack laughed at Charles and said, "Damn dude, she just destroyed you! I'm surprised you're just taking it."

Charles of course got annoyed at him, so he said back to her, "Oh yeah! Just you wait, I'll destroy that confidence of yours on the field. You haven't even seen me battle yet!"

She thought about it for a minute, then said, "You know what... sure. We'll battle, and when I win, you're gonna get laughed at by that guy there for an hour I bet," Aika said confidently.

"Oh, you're on!" Charles said, hyped up, then ran to the field at the bottom of the hill.

"Hold this, please," she asked me.

"Oh sure," I said as I grabbed the bag of supplies, then she walked down the hill where Charles ran off to.

Jack asked me, "Do you know where she came from? She has a bit of an accent that makes every word sound slightly… off, if you know what I mean. Kinda like this is a second language to her."

I told him, "My guess is close to the west because that land has been being destroyed by Dragonborns recently, but they also speak Infinitan, so I'm not really sure."

As we walked down to the field to watch, Jack asked me, "Hey dude, I have another question. Have you seen her fight with her sword yet?"

"No, she doesn't really use her sword that much. But I did see her swing it out in the yard once or twice, and it looked like she knew what she was doing," I told him.

"What do you mean by that?" Jack asked.

"Well, the way she was practicing her stance was nothing like the way our soldiers train. It was... unique, to say the least. I asked her about it, but all she told me was 'Oh, it's nothing special from where I'm from.' I don't really understand what she meant, but I think she definitely has some experience using swords," I explained to him.

"Interesting, I guess we'll just watch what happens then," Jack said as he looked over at the field where they were about to begin.

Aika and Charles stood across from each other with lots of space between them. The sky was cloudy with specks of the sky spread apart from each other.

"You can swing first," Aika said to Charles.

"I was about to say ladies first, so you're gonna regret that," Charles said as he drew out his sword excitedly and readied himself

"Oh, you sure about that?" Aika said as she drew out her sword normally and slowly readied herself as she watched Charles's actions.

"Nice sword... But do you know how to use it!" Charles asked, as he swung his sword. Then instantly his sword flew off into the distance near us and banged into the ground near us causing a dirt cloud.

"Wow, what the hell was that?" Jack asked.

"I don't know, it all happened so quickly!" I said back, also surprised.

Over in the field Charles asked, "How did you send my sword flying like that?"

"I told you, you'll just embarrass yourself," Aika said back, putting her sword away.

"Hey, let's spar again! This time I'll beat you!" Charles requested.

"Are you sure?" Aika asked.

"Hell yeah, again!" Charles shouted out to her.

Minutes later Charles's pride was completely destroyed. He was on his knees in the dirt. "H-how?" he muttered to himself.

"What was that?" Aika asked.

"How did you send my sword flying twelve times in a row?" he asked in disbelief.

"Again, I told you, you'll just embarrass yourself. Didn't you listen before?" she asked.

"Who are you?" Charles asked.

"I already told you my name, didn't I?" she questioned as a cloud above us moved, making sunlight hit her back. "It's Aika," she said as she offered her hand to help him up.

As Charles got helped up, he asked, "Where did you learn how to fight like that?"

"Oh, you know... you uh… pick up on things here and there," she said vaguely as she put her sword back in her scabbard.

"How did you get a Dragonborn sword like that?" Jack asked, as he and I walked toward them.

"Oh, uh, yeah, I got attacked by a Dragonborn and stole it from them," Aika explained.

Jack gasped and asked, "You met a real-life Dragonborn! Oh, tell me what happened?"

"Uh well, that's private. You're not ready to hear about that stuff," Aika said as she backed off a little, looking nervous.

Since the tension was building, I asked everyone, "How about we all go back to my place and get something to eat?" trying to brighten the mood back up for Aika.

"Yeah, food is the best!" Charles shouted out immediately after I suggested that.

On our way back, Charles talked about how he couldn't wait to eat and such to me, but behind me, though, Jack and Aika started to talk about Dragonborns and stuff.

"You're the one who loves Dragonborns, right?" she asked.

"Yeah, I love them, why?" Jack asked.

"You wanna know a cool fact about them?" she asked.

"Oh yeah, what's that? I know so much about them I probably already know it," he said confidently.

"Well, did you know it's very rare for a Dragonborn to have the same exact aura as another Dragonborn? Sure, some Dragonborns have the same color auras, but each Dragonborn has a different value light from their aura. Some auras are brighter, and some auras are dimmer. So for a Dragonborn to have the same exact brightness and color is rare," she explained.

"Oooh, I've never heard about that! What other cool facts do you know?" Jack asked.

Aika said, "Well, you see, some Dragonborns are—"

They started talking about all kinds of things that flew right over my head. Stuff I was not smart enough to understand. I had no idea about how she knew that much about Dragonborns at the time.

It took her a while to fully open up to all of us. It wasn't until after Charles's incident that happened about two months after we all met her. But now I know what truly happened to her and how much she lost. She had some sort of PTSD from the whole experience for a while when we first met. It was a bit weird out of context because I thought "How can someone so knowledgeable about Dragonborns be so afraid of them coming after them," What a fool I was back then. But we were all fools for thinking that was the case.

But now I finally know why I wanted to be a Dragon Slayer. Before I was just following Charles because he hyped everyone up, but I never had a true reason why I joined. But now I knew. I want to be a Slayer, not to fight Dragonborns or anything like that, but to protect people. To make sure no one ever had to experience what happened to Aika. So no one would see the horrors Aika saw, so no one would get hurt like that again.

Chapter 6: White Noise

It had been about three months since our fifth year of training had begun. Nothing had happened. My and Bolt's relationship was still a secret to everyone, and we continued our regular training. But one day like any other day, we were unexpectedly visited by the commander of the Dragon Slayers.

The day he arrived was a very interesting day. Everyone was telling rumors about the commander, all morning:

"He's killed more Dragonborns than everyone combined!"

"You better say 'sir' every time you talk to him or else."

"Or else what?" I asked them.

No one would explain where they heard all of this. I even asked Niki why people were saying these things, but of course she didn't help. All she said was, "Oh, I don't care about the commander. The thing I care about are the Dragonborns themselves, or should I say you?" As soon as she said that, I walked the hell away and tried to forget that conversation. So I asked a bunch of other people, but they didn't explain either. Instead, they told me even more rumors such as,

"There has never been a Slayer smarter than the commander before" and "He's the scariest man you'll ever meet."

I asked my squad about him, but they didn't even know anything useful. Having no idea what to think of this guy, I just waited till I met him to see who he really was.

When he arrived in the afternoon, we were all told to gather around to meet him. When I saw him, he looked like one of those typical army guys. He was tall like Charles at six foot two and dressed in a formal navy military outfit with black army boots. His entire head was shaved, and he had a deep voice that echoed in people's ears as he talked.

"Greetings, soon-to-be Dragon Slayers!" he said to everyone. "I, as you all know, am Commander Zane. I remember when I was like all of you, training to become a Slayer and..."

He started going off on a rant about how it was for him in his training days. But it was nothing interesting and didn't answer my questions arising from the rumors I'd heard. But what was interesting to me were his movements as he talked. As he talked, he kept walking back and forth in the same way repeatedly, very similar to how fights Dragonborns have with each other. Then at the end of his little speech, he told everyone to follow him to the Experimental Factory. Beside me I saw Jack's eyes light up with excitement when he mentioned the place. "Oh no," I thought, realizing why he was excited. This was the place where they developed weapons to fight Dragonborns. This place had lots of information kept private from civilians and us in training still.

As Zane explained what the place was, Jack turned to me and said, "Aika, help me out here! Charles won't, so please help," he asked.

"Uh, what is it?" I asked.

"I finally have the chance to sneak into that place and steal a bunch of documents about Dragonborns! But I need help hiding all the papers. If I had a bunch, it would be suspicious. So if you helped me hold some, I could get away with it!" he explained.

"No way!" I immediately told him.

"What, why?" he asked.

"I'm not gonna help you steal government documents right in front of everyone!" I told him.

"Then you leave me no choice, Aika," he said, then walked toward Niki.

"Oh no," I said out loud when I realized their plan.

Before we walked into the building, Jack looked over at me in disappointment.

Zane gave us a tour around the factory, and I saw Jack and Niki sneak off to who knows where at every part of the tour. He showed us where they made weapons such as arrows and new bows. Then the supplies they used such as metals, ropes, and toxic sludge gathered from Toxic Elements. And then where they tested the weapons for their effectiveness. Finally, we arrived at the end of the tour at the entrance of a certain room that was different from everything else we had seen. He said to everyone, "Now this brings us to the end of the tour. There is something I would like to show everyone in this room before you leave."

As we all walked in, we all saw this weird, tiny device. It was a small mic that was a rectangle shape but had a rounded smooth top. Zane said, "Now everyone, this is our latest and greatest weapon we have made. We call it the Sound Radiator or the SR for short. We have finally made the finishing touches on it so it's more usable for people to use. We want to show you all this because soon you'll all be using it. You see, this weapon works by creating a certain wavelength of noise that stuns Dragonborns, making them temporarily paralyzed. This device has this effect on Dragonborns because they have such good hearing that the sharp noise that this device creates overpowers them. This device makes a sound so powerful that it even hurts our own hearing if we're exposed to it for a long period of time. How do we know all of this, you may all think? Well, this device was first tested during that Ice Dragonborn incident. When we were fighting, we were having a hard time getting it to flee from the grounds. Because its sword was knocked away, we thought we could just launch flame arrows at it till it got tired of the constant attack. But no, it did not work. Then we got an idea to use the SR in battle. Surprisingly it worked great, but the noise caused some people to have short-term hearing loss. And we were afraid that if activated for a long period of time, it will cause permanent hearing loss to people with sensitive hearing. So tomorrow we are putting everyone through a test to see who would need a special device that we have named the A-wave, short for anti-wavelength. This device helps the user block out the wavelengths that the SR creates and helps prevent this hearing loss. They are tiny little devices that go into your ear to block out the waves. We only have so many extra, so we want to see who really needs them the most. Any questions?"

As everyone was talking and discussing the new things we all heard about the SR, I was spacing out into my own head trying to process everything. I would've never imagined this tiny little thing could affect a War Dragonborn that bad. This thing was either going to help me or be my future doom. As everyone was about to leave, Zane said to us,

"Oh, one last thing, everyone. The SR is not out to the public yet. So if you talk about it, be careful who you talk to and where you talk. To be honest with all of you, the only reason why the Ice Dragonborn left was because of the SR. If we had not brought that with us, it would have taken us a lot longer than we already did. We do not want to scare the public. If it were to get out, there would be mass panic about the War Dragonborns. We do not want the public to feel unsafe if we get another attack like that. Understood!" he demanded.

"Yes sir!" everyone shouted out. I was still stuck in my head thinking about all the possibilities of this device, then suddenly Bolt shook me a little and said, "Hey, Aika! Aika! Are you doing okay there?"

"Uh, what?" I asked.

"Come on, everyone is leaving," Bolt said as he took my hand and dragged me off with everyone else. The only thing I could think about was the sound radiator and what to do with it.

Later that night Bolt and I discussed what to do about tomorrow and what could possibly happen to me.

Bolt asked me, "Uh, Aika, are you doing okay? Earlier I had to drag you out of the factory cause you froze up looking at that device."

"I've been doing some thinking," I told him as I walked back and forth across the room.

"Do you have any ideas on what to do for tomorrow? Cause I got nothing right now," he asked.

I stopped in front of Bolt and told him, "After thinking about it for a while, I have thought of some different possible outcomes that could happen."

"What do you think?" Bolt asked.

"Well, it depends on how loud it is. If it's not too bad, it would probably most likely just give me a bad headache based on the information we know so far. But if it's at full blast, I have no idea how extreme it would be for me," I explained. We were both silent after that.

"The only thing I can think of is, if we turn down the volume on the SR system before it activates," Bolt said. That's when he gave me a horrible idea.

"Hey, Bolt, that gives me an idea."

"Oh yeah, what's that… wait, no! No, we are not going to do that!" he said worriedly.

"Hey, hear me out," I told him confidently.

"No, I know exactly what you're thinking! We are not going to sneak into the Experimental Factory and turn down the volume on the SR—it's far too risky!" Bolt demanded firmly. We snuck into the place later that night and lowered the volume on the SR.

The next morning we all gathered back for this test. Some people were excited to see how it worked, and some were nervous knowing their bad hearing would affect them. Out of everyone in the crowd of people, of course the loudest person was Jack next to us as he ranted about how cool the SR was and how genius it was. The night before he'd ranted all about it to Charles, showing off all the papers that he and Niki stole about the weapons the Slayers had been making. I wasn't around to hear it, though, so Charles had been listening to him nonstop for probably nine hours straight. After some waiting, the time arrived. Bolt and I nodded at each other silently and I took a deep breath to get ready for what was about to happen, but suddenly felt sick to my core. My ears popped instantly, and they rang loudly in my head. I fell to my knees from the overwhelming feeling that I unexpectedly got. I had no idea what was happening, it felt like I was about to lose my mind. As I held my head with my left hand and looked down at my other hand shaking, the only thing that crossed my mind was, "Is this the power of the sound radiator?" I noticed Bolt was kneeling beside me trying to talk to me. But I couldn't hear his voice; all I heard was the ringing in my head. He looked over with a dumbfounded face at something that was happening. But I couldn't move my head to see what was happening because of the pain.

This was what was happening outside my head: When the SR activated, it was activated at full blast for some reason, and made all of that happen to me. Everyone else just complained and covered their ears. But when they all saw me fall to the ground shaking from the noise, everyone was shocked and looked over at me, concerned, because everyone knew what I was like by then. Bolt immediately got down next to me to see if I was okay. Charles and Jack had no idea what to do in this situation.

"Excuse me, everyone! Is everyone okay? We had a system error. Apparently, someone turned the volume to… max?" they said, a bit confused.

Everyone just glared at each other, thinking someone did it as some dumb prank. As everyone around started gossiping on who it could be, Charles turned to Vanessa and asked, "Hey, Vanessa, why are you suspiciously quiet?"

"Wha-what do you mean?" she asked nervously.

"Usually, you would be going off complaining about how childish this was, but you're kinda quiet right now," Charles explained.

"Yeah, he's right. You are really quiet," Jack said, backing up Charles.

Vanessa, trapped, said to them, "Okay, okay, I'll tell you! Just don't tell the pros, okay. So last night I was walking around because I couldn't sleep. And during that walk I saw some people running out of here. So I thought that it was a little suspicious, so I checked it out. When I got here, I saw the volume on the SR lowered to almost nothing. So I thought I would fix it, so I kinda… accidently set it to max," she explained.

"You what!" Charles yelled at her, with Jack holding him back to stop him from strangling her. This was what Bolt was dumbfounded by, just watching them in disbelief. This was when my hearing started to come back to me ever so slightly. The ringing was still loud in my ear, but I could hear the muffled sounds of yelling in the background. When I looked up to see what was happening, I witnessed pure chaos, with Charles yelling something at Vanessa and Jack using all the strength he had to hold him back. Jack turned to me and saw me watching all of this happening. He shouted something out that I couldn't hear, then Bolt helped me up and brought me outside.

After we got outside, it took a minute to start hearing things right. When I could hear everything again, I asked, "Bolton, what the hell did I just witness?"

Bolt took a deep breath and then told me everything that happened. "...and that's when Jack noticed you were starting to come out of your daze. So he yelled at me to get you out of there, before you realized what Vanessa did and started trying to strangle her too," he explained.

I was silent for a minute and just stared at him in disbelief. "You're kidding?" I asked.

"Nope. It's all true, sadly," he said, sounding discouraged.

"Wow," I said to myself, in disbelief still.

"But anyways, are you doing okay? Because you did not look good at all during all of that," Bolt asked.

"Oh yeah, I'm doing fine now. I just got some stupid ringing in my ears and a wicked headache. But damn, I really underestimated the power of that thing. I didn't expect it to do all of that to me. There was no information told about how it affected the War Dragonborn," I explained.

"Well, at least you're doing better now. I felt kind of useless watching you fall like that. I wasn't expecting that to happen, either, so I had no clue of what to do or how to help," he said, disappointed.

"Hey, don't feel useless! There was nothing planned, and neither of us knew what was going to happen. We had no idea Venny saw shadow people, a.k.a. us, leaving the place and decided to turn the volume to max," I told him.

"Yeah, I know. It just feels like I let you down because I said I'll watch your back when something went wrong, then that stuff happened," he said quietly.

"Hey, don't be like that! When the time comes and total chaos happens, I'm relying on you to help explain how I'm not a bloody murdering devil that's going to kill everyone. Also, you'll be there to hold me back when I lose my mind, while fighting other Dragonborns," I told him.

Then I noticed in the distance Zane was walking toward us.

"So this is where you two ran off to," he said as walked up.

Bolt stepped ahead and said to him, "Sorry, sir, I was the one to bring her here. Sorry for the inconvenience I have caused for you. I just had to get her out of the chaos before it got worse and—"

Zane put his hand up to stop him from talking and said to us, "Now, now, no worries. I understand, don't apologize. I should be the one to say sorry for the trouble I caused. We should have double-checked the actual device instead of just the speakers and systems—"

"Wait, you're telling me you all forgot to check everything before blasting that thing?" I asked, interrupting him.

"Uh w-well…" Zane said, stuttering, "Well, here is a set of A-waves for you, Aika. You had the worst reaction to it. You don't need to come to the retest. I bid a good day to you both!" he said awkwardly, then walked away quickly.

We were both silent about the event that just happened.

"Wow, Bolt, your people surprise me every day. No wonder why no one knows I'm a Dragonborn," I casually told him.

Bolt just sighed back in agreement, not knowing how to respond.

Later that night, I asked Jack if he had stolen any documents about the SR and the events of the Ice Incident.

"You want to look over the documents?" he asked, confused.

"Yes," I replied confidently.

"All right, sure," he said all cheerfully as he handed me the documents. "Niki and I both already memorized everything there, so it's cool."

"Oh, uh, thanks," I said back.

"So why do you want them?" he asked.

"No reason," I said.

Jack snarkily said, "I know why—you want to look over them because of what happened earlier, huh."

"Maybe," I replied.

"Eh, no sweat. Just don't lose them or Niki will kill me," he told me.

I proceeded to have Bolt read me every last detail on those documents and found some pretty juicy information on what happened to the Slayers the night of the incident. Apparently the SR wasn't even meant to come with the Slayers that day. Some random guy just thought, "Huh, we should test this on a real-life Dragonborn, maybe," then proceeded to blast everyone's eardrums out. After that night, they discovered how useful it might become, so they decided to add different volumes, then compacted it to make it even smaller to control where the wavelengths would hit. After a month of retesting it, they officially said screw it and made it one of the newly created weapons to fight Dragonborns with and called it the Sound Radiator because it would blow up people's eardrums on the regular. I sorta wished I did help Jack steal more documents after Bolt read it to me.

That day was very interesting, though. I was shown something that would become very important to me later. Then Vanessa did something that almost revealed me to everyone. But what she did that day was nothing compared to what she would do to me a few months later.

Chapter 7: The Jacket

This was the worst event to happen during all five years of training. The day where all of Vanessa's come-uppances finally took place. The day everyone called the Photo Incident.

It was the beginning of fall of our fifth year. It started to get a little chillier out at the time, but on that day, it was still quite warm. After a long day of training, I decided to freshen up and took a shower before I joined dinner with everyone outside in the picnic area. The washrooms were all around the building, containing showers and baths, sinks, and toilets, which were separated into groups of men's, women's, and a few single rooms that anyone could use and have privacy. But I mostly used the privet ones because of my hands. As I finished up, I put on my gloves, got dressed, put on my boots, equipped my sword, and put down my hair, which was tied up to prevent it from being soaked, then went to put on my jacket. Turned around to grab it off the hook and... it had disappeared. "Oh goodie," I thought. I noticed a random sticky note on the door, and the words I could make out were *"Took... jacket... you won't mind... Vanessa."* after a minute it clicked, and pissed off, I ran out of the bathroom and threw the outside door of the cabin open and looked around for Vanessa. Everyone sat at wooden benches and tables casually chatting with one another, Throughout all our time here, Vanessa had never been able to take my jacket from me once, until that day she finally did. I saw her showing off my jacket to everyone and describing how she took it. "Venny, you bitch! Give me back my jacket!" I called out to her.

Vanessa, not caring, mocked me back and shouted, "Why should I give it back? What are you hiding something in here? You always wear it, so maybe?" She started to dig through my jacket's pockets, trying to find something.

"Hey!" I hollered as I ran to her.

Meanwhile as I was chasing Vanessa, my squad was just watching us fight from a distance.

"What's happening over there?" Bolt asked as he sat down with a tray of food.

Charles, with food in his mouth, replied, "Oh, just the usual fighting. This time Vanessa took Aika's jacket."

"Shouldn't we stop them? You know how Aika is with her jacket," Bolt asked.

Charles just shrugged and said, "Heh, we'll step in if Vanessa does something extra stupid. Well, at least one of us would have to step in to hold Aika back from beating her to a pulp."

"Hey, thanks!" Vanessa shouted to him as she ran by their table.

"The hell, man!" I yelled out to him as I ran past their table chasing after Vanessa.

Vanessa was surprisingly fast, almost as fast as me. Whenever I would chase her, most of the time she escaped me, and lead me into place I would lose her. As I ran after her, she searched around through the pockets of my jacket and yanked things out, such as extra wrappings, spare gloves, handkerchiefs, and bags full of protein bits.

"Wow, you got a lot of different random things in here!" she said, surprised.

"The stuff that is inside my jacket is none of your business!" I shouted as I almost grabbed my jacket back.

Vanessa questioned excitedly, "Oh, what's this?" as she took a flat black container out of my jacket.

"Vanessa, no! Don't you dare take that out!" I yelled in a panic and froze in place.

"Oh no," Bolt said worriedly as he watched us.

"Okay, that's the signal to go over there," Charles told Bolt and Jack as he stood from the table. As they walked over to where we were, Vanessa said,

"Wow, I've never heard you yell like that before! What the hell even is this?" she asked.

Vanessa opened up the container and pulled out a small photo.

"Oh my goodness! Is this a picture of you when you were little with your parents?" she asked. My squad then looked at me, shocked. I had never shown anybody that photo, and I never talked about my past, so it was even more mysterious to everyone.

That photo she was holding was from when I was fourteen. It was taken about a month before I met Bolt. It was a picture of me and my parents together. My parents stood beside each other and I stood in front between them. I wore the usual military outfit I always used to wear. To the left of me in the picture was my mom. My mother had long black hair, gray-blue eyes, pale skin, and was way taller than me at six foot one with the same slim, muscular body type as me. I looked identical to my mother—the only difference between us was our hair and eye color. In the photo she wore a long white V-neck strapped sundress that had a blue flower pattern all over, with black fingerless gloves, and casual black rounded flat shoes. To the right of me in the picture was my dad. My father had midlength curly hair with a stubbly, spiky beard. Then he had bright-blue eyes and pale skin. My dad was quite short compared to other men of my race; he was only five foot three. My dad wore his usual military outfit, which was a thick blue sweatshirt that was tucked into his pants and a black belt. His pants were black cargo pants that had zip-up pockets all over, which were stuffed into his boots, which were black combat boots like mine but bigger. Then he had his sword, which he wore on his back set up exactly like mine, because our auras were the same. He also wore black armored gloves. Then his scabbard had a blue body. My mom was my dad's partner in the military; she just knew when to get out of the uniform, unlike my dad, who always wore his. Behind us there was a large tree with stones around the trunk on the ground. The tree was in the center of our village, and around the tree were paths that traveled north and south of the town.

"Wow, you look exactly the same from when you were small, but with a military getup and short hair! And man, you look identical to your mom and—" She continued talking about my parents and comparing me to them, all while looking back at me periodically. Charles and Jack had no idea what to do or how to help; they just stood there overwhelmed by everything Vanessa was shouting out. Then Bolt was in front of the two, standing beside me, looking like he was slightly glaring at Vanessa during her little spew, almost clenching his fists. When she started provoking me to explain why I never showed anyone this picture, things went down real fast.

"Damn, Aika, why do you keep this picture of you and them a secret? Like, what happened for you to never show anyone this?" she asked.

"Just give me back my things," I asked her, defeated.

"Geez, what's the matter? Do you have some hidden trauma about your parents?" she asked jokingly. I went silent; I didn't know what to say back to her. Charles and Jack stared back at each other, unsure. But luckily, I had someone who knew about all my past trauma and knew how hard those words hit me.

"Vanessa, you need to stop talking right now!" Bolt said angrily as he stepped forward.

"Oh, wow that's the first time I've ever heard you talk like that!" she said, a bit surprised.

Bolt said, even angrier, "Quit mocking me, Vanessa! All the things you have been saying are private information about her life! I won't stand to hear you say another thing!"

Vanessa asked, "Oh yeah, what are you going to do about it?"

"This," Bolt said as he carefully snatched the photo out of her hand.

"Hey!" she yelled at him.

"Oh shut it, Vanessa!" Bolt shouted back and gave another small glare, directly at her.

Vanessa stepped back and clenched my jacket in her fist and said, "Fine then... if you're joining in too now, I actually have a question for you both. Are you two like... finally dating or something?" Vanessa asked.

"What?" Bolt and I both asked at the same time.

"Like are you two both secretly... 'doing it' outside of training? You two have been awfully close with each other," she asked, playfully.

Before I could reply, Bolt blurted out, "What, no, we wouldn't do that stuff with each other this early!"

Everyone went silent.

"Uh... dude. Do you know what you just said?" Charles asked.

"Uh... wait," Bolt said, realizing as he turned to me and I just glared the "You idiot for once" look at him.

Vanessa was heavily laughing at all of us as she watched this conversation go down. Charles said to me and Bolt, "To be honest, Jack and I knew that you two were secretly dating. For the past few months you two have been a lot closer than usual and well... other reasons," he explained.

"Wait, so you both knew about us the whole time?" I asked nervously.

"Well... we could tell that you two got together during spring break. But that information seems a little too private for all of us to know," Charles admitted.

"Did you guys seriously think no one would notice that you two hooked up?" Vanessa asked all smugly.

At this point I was getting tired of Vanessa's comments. I just snapped and yelled out at her, "Venny, can you just shut up! I'm sick of all your damn comments. Your squad isn't even here to back you up—they're watching all of this from a nearby table," I shouted at her and pointed toward her squad. "Look over there, Niki is even waving at us now!" I hollered. Then I realized Niki was just watching us and not writing down everything. "Wait, why are you just watching us over there, Niki?" I asked her.

"Oh, I already saw that photo a long time ago, back when I first met you. I already looked through your jacket, so I'm not that interested in your current drama," she said casually.

I stared back at her blankly, and asked myself, "Why am I surprised by this?" then just sighed and turned back to Vanessa, still pissed off. I asked Vanessa, "So let me just ask you, why do you start all of these fights? I know I purposely start them sometimes, but you always take them to the extreme. Just why do you start most of the fights? You take my sword on a daily basis! You took my jacket! And you spilled a lot of private information out loud. I haven't even shown Bolt that photo yet! Just why do you even—!" I suddenly stopped in my rant and looked around in the sky.

"Even what? Why did you stop yelling?" she asked.

"Something doesn't feel right," I replied back nervously as I looked around more.

"Why the hell do you always have to pause like this sometimes? You do it randomly all the time. And why did you get weird when I asked if you had some secret trauma. Did you watch your parents die or something?" Vanessa asked. That last thing she said struck a chord in me the wrong way.

Pissed off, I shouted back at her, "Listen you bitch, I—"

Then a burst of wind blew around us, and before anyone could react, a Wind Dragonborn dove down and dragged me into the air. With the sudden appearance of the Dragonborn, my time trace overwhelmed me, causing time to look much slower as I watched everyone freeze up and watched the realization form in their faces.

As I was dragged up high, on the ground, everyone was paralyzed and scared. The only person with almost a clear mind of what was happening was Bolt, who grabbed the closest crossbow in a panic, then aimed it up at us to shoot down the Dragonborn. But he started to shake and brought down the crossbow.

"Dude, what's wrong? Shoot it down already!" Charles hollered at him.

Bolt shouted back, stuttering, "I-I can't! She's freaking f-fighting it up in the air!"

"What?" everyone yelled confused, at him.

I immediately knew this fella was a War Dragonborn because of their iris color: red with white and black spots sprinkled within that area, along with their out-of-control actions. They had a Wind Element with a forest green aura with a dark-green accent. This Dragonborn in particular had oval-spiked armor that was super thick, like the other War Dragonborn. Their horns were also longer and sharper; they were smooth, curved down, and spiraled like a mountain goat's. They had their element symbol on their right hand, and their scabbard's body was green.

What had happened while I was in the air for about a minute was chaos. I had completely fallen into my trance and everything was in slow motion. I escaped its grasping claws but scratched my arms, but in doing so, I got an opening to strike. As I held on to them with one hand, I took my other and bashed them on one of our weak spots—between our clavicles, above where our armor chest plates begin. The Dragonborn flinched and disappeared their wings, causing us to immediately drop back down to the ground. As we fell, I held them head down at a slant with all my strength, as they tried to move back. What Bolt saw me doing was struggling to pose them like that while falling at a fast speed downward.

The way we flew was by flapping our wings to create wind for us to fly up, then glide in the wind. While gliding, we turn our bodies to the direction of the turn, then while gliding down, we open our wings out and up to glide slowly. But when we needed to pick up speed, we could dive down to gain momentum, then summon our wings to gain a burst of speed. Usually when we flew, we always had some sort of trace of aura or particle from our element such as small flames, ice sparkles, droplets of sludge, or slight electricity sparks. Only the Wind Element had no trace of anything, so they became deadly in the sky flying with their powers, speed, and stealth.

I watched the ground as we fell, waiting for when it came close enough for me to jump off. As I did, I noticed everyone watching in horror as I tried to control them. When I came close, I struck them in the same spot as before and made them summon their wings at the last possible moment before hitting the ground. Right when we flew up a little again, I jumped off in a flip and landed back on the ground, sliding back a little as I did. The Dragonborn also landed for a brief moment and disappeared their wings to regain its balance again.

This Dragonborn had a Wind Element. The Wind Element's symbol was a round-cornered *X* with a horizontal rectangular dash on the top and bottom of the *X* and a vertical rectangular dash on the left and right as well. The Wind Element had the weakest power compared to the rest, but it made up for that with its speed. They were the fastest-moving element. Almost no one was as fast as them when it came to flying, running, and fighting. With their powers, they controlled the air around them. With this they could create strong breezes that could blow people and objects away. They could also use this on themselves to make themselves fly faster at extreme speeds in the sky. They had a weakness to the Electric Element because their powerful winds picked up their electricity as they moved, making them more prone to being shocked. Their possible aura colors could be mostly any color except any darker shades and black.

When the Dragonborn turned around to see me, it summoned its wings once again to fly away. Right before it could make some air, I ran up and grabbed their foot and was still stuck in my trance a bit, I yelled out at them, "Hey, you! You're not getting away that easily! You're not the only devil here!" Then I slammed them down on the ground and shouted out, "I'm so done with everybody's shit today!"

In distress the Dragonborn got up with the help of their wind, and drew out their sword and tried to swing at me. My trance changed from every moment to right before every attack, allowing me to predict their every attack, so immediately I drew out mine and averted the attack. My hair flowed in the breeze caused by the Wind Dragonborn's presence; they deliberately made the wind flow right at my face to slow me down. The Wind Dragonborn swung again at me but this time with great speed. I stepped to the side and dodged the attack, then swung my sword back at them. As the Wind Dragonborn deflected my sword with theirs, an arrow flew by us, and they caught the arrow before it pierced their scales. I glanced behind me to see who shot it and saw Bolt lower his crossbow to reload. Everyone else around was panicking or frozen with fear. People in the background started yelling many things as our swords collided again and again after, such as,

"Oh no, it's happening again!"

"Hey, it's the same crazy chick who fought the last War Dragonborn!"

"Yeah, they are the same person, they're like the War Slayer or something!"

"You go, War Slayer!"

"Yeah, kick that devil's ass!"

They kept on yelling all kinds of random stuff after that chanting out "War Slayer" as I battled this Wind Dragonborn. A few people helped by launching arrows at it, distracting it for a moment. During the chaos Vanessa said to my squad, "Geez, she's fighting that thing basically by herself!"

"To be honest I'm surprised she hasn't tackled them to the ground," Jack told her.

"She can't tackle them… well, not yet at least," Bolt told them as he fired off more arrows, this time using his bow to launch more quickly. "She doesn't have her jacket, so she could risk getting burned if they cover themselves in fire," Bolt explained as he shot out more arrows at the Wind Dragonborn, who made the wind blow them in a completely different direction.

"Damn, dude, those arrows you're firing off are flying as straight as me to that Dragonborn," Jack commented.

"Hey, I'm doing everything I can! And …wait, why am I the only one out of all of us doing anything to help?" he asked.

"Because of that," Jack said, pointing to everyone giving up as they watched the Dragonborn dodging the arrows like nothing by them controlling the wind around to send their arrows flying back around like crazy and sending paths of fire to anyone approached us dueling, all while swinging at me with its sword, causing me to deflect it and making the whole process repeat itself.

"Hey, Aika, get the Dragonborn to turn around so we can hit it from behind!" Charles called out to me.

So I swung at the Dragonborn again, screeching our sword together, and stepped to the side to turn them a bit. Then as I took my sword away, then swung again, Bolt fired off more arrows to the Wind Dragonborn's back. Because they were occupied with me slashing my sword into theirs, the arrows hit them, piercing into their scales, so they roared out and backed away from me. I ran at them with everything I had and swung at their sword again. With them being weakened, I twisted their sword and caused it to fly out of their hand across the field. Angry, they sent out a path of fire toward me, then tried to run away to fly off in the distance. I dodge-rolled out of the way of the fire and chased them. Probably a bit frightened by me, they released a burst of wind at me to blow me back. I stuck my sword into the ground to hold me back against the wind and glared back at them. As everyone finally tried to go after it, they summoned their wings and flew up to the air, blowing everyone back. As I watched them fly up, I yelled out at them, pissed, "Don't you dare run away! You finish this fight, you goddamn coward!" But my yelling was worthless. They glared back at me for a moment before flying off into the distance. After they flew far enough, the wind around me calmed back down. Everyone around was silent, not knowing what to do. I looked back at the others and saw them all frozen in place, not saying a word. Even Bolt was frozen, still holding his bow and arrows and my photo visible in his hoodie's pocket. The pain from my arms being scratched finally hit me. I looked down at them and saw that they had bled down to my hands and a bit on the side and front of my shirt. The scratch wasn't bad, but it was still decent enough for me to bleed a lot. I walked back toward everyone; they were all still silent from what happened. So without stopping, I snatched my jacket from Vanessa's hand and walked off to an empty area where no one would see me.

Having no idea what to do with myself, I sat against some nearby building and hid my face in my jacket to try and calm down some more. While doing so I heard Bolt yelling about something in the background to everyone. After a minute or two went by, I heard footsteps nearby, so I looked up and saw Bolt slowly walking toward me.

"Hey, can I sit next to you?" he asked softly. I nodded back to him silently, and he sat beside me. "Are you okay?" he asked. "That was quite a mess back there."

Before I answered him, I asked, "Hey, Bolt, did anyone see anything of my… you know."

Bolt told me, "Oh, don't worry about that—I didn't see any glimpse of it, and everyone was freaking out about that War Dragonborn so much that even if there were, no one would notice… except Niki. She would have. But there were no signs, so you're good. Everyone is probably going to ask you how you got their wings to disappear like that in the sky, but that conversation will be for later. But besides that, show me your arms," Bolt ordered.

I showed him my arms, which were hiding under my jacket, and told him, "I just got these scratches from their claws from when I was snagged. It doesn't hurt too bad, but now my arms are all bloody."

Bolt said, "Well, that's good at least. I told the others to inform a nurse about your arms, so whenever you're ready, we can head on down to the medical section of the cabin."

"All right, we can go now then. Can I just have my photo back—you have it, right?" I asked.

"Oh of course. I'll put it in the case to make sure you don't get blood on it," he told me.

"It's in one of my inside pockets here," I told him as I passed my jacket to him.

As Bolt dug through my pockets and pulled out the case, he said, "I know you've talked about that photo once or twice but didn't expect you to always have it in your jacket. When Vanessa pulled it out, it surprised me."

"Well, to be honest, I always carry around the things I have left from the past. My dad helped me make my sword, and I got my jacket from my mom. This photo is a combination of the two, I guess. Whenever things get tough and I'm by myself, I pull it out and think about them. It gives me the little motivation I need to keep on pushing myself to go on and do my best. That's what they would have wanted me to do," I told him.

Bolt had put the photo away as I was talking, so after I finished, he stood up and said, "Come on, let's go and fix your arms up." He helped me up, and we walked together toward the cabin.

As we walked, people all around looked over to me and started saying stuff to each other. I remembered some words my dad told me once. "Aika, life is short. You never know when something might happen and it will all be over. So listen closely and remember this: don't bother thinking of what people might think about you. Just focus on what you want to do, and only care about the people close to you." Those were the last words my dad told me before he died in battle. My dad was an okay dad. He taught me how to use my powers, he made me laugh and feel good about myself, and he loved me.

When we passed Vanessa, she said to me, "Hey, Aika, I-I'm sorry." She speed-walked away awkwardly.

"What was that about?" I asked Bolt.

"Well I… you see, I sorta… well… I told her if she ever did anything like that to you again, I would ask Niki for a favor," he explained.

"What does that mean?" I asked, even more confused.

"Something happened a little while back between us, so me and her made a deal. As a result of that deal, she owes me a favor," he told me.

"What the hell did you have to do to make her owe you one!" I asked, a little scared.

"Uh, well… that's not important right now," Bolt replied.

"Bolt, you're avoiding the question. I'm scared! What did she make you do?" I asked again.

"Nope, not saying what I was forced to tell her, let's go!" he demanded. Then I saw Charles happily smiling at us, then Jack on the side of him smirking.

"Oh, look at you two, finally out about dating each other," Jack said as he pointed to us holding hands. "And here I was thinking that you two were going to keep this secret till you got married," he smugly added.

"I wonder why we kept it a secret from you," I replied in the same smug attitude as him.

Bolt said, "Guys, not now. A lot just happened and you're doing this to each other."

Charles said to him, "Oh come on, dude, you have no idea how long we've been waiting to say this kind of stuff to you two. You were that one pair that acted like a couple but not actually together. It was kinda funny watching you both secretly dating each other like if you were breaking the law."

"Well, that is kinda true for where I come from," I said quietly.

"What?" Bolt asked.

"Oh nothing, come on," I replied as I dragged him with me away from Charles and Jack, who turned to each other and laughed.

As I got my arm treated, Jack asked me, "Hey, Aika, how did you knock the Dragonborn out of the sky?"

"Bash them in their weak spot, and any Dragonborn will flinch up and stop what they're doing. I just know where all the sweet spots to hit them are," I replied.

"Where's the spot you hit them? They have no weak spots on their front, I thought," Jack asked me.

"It's a secret Dragonborn fact I have," I told him.

"No, Aika, tell me—don't do this to me!" he begged.

Charles told him, "Don't worry, dude, you'll find out when the pros arrive to interrogate her."

Then the nurse finished wrapping up my arms and said, "That should do it for now. If something happens, you know where to find us. Take it easy for a bit in training until you're healed up." she then left to do other work.

I asked as I took my jacket from Bolt, "So when are the pros coming to see me?"

Charles replied, "Oh, you know… right now."

Then two soldiers came walking up to me, and one asked, "You mind explaining the details of the devil and your fight with them?"

I sighed as I put on my jacket and told them about the Dragonborn and what I did in the sky and how I fought them on the ground, but I purposely left out where I struck them to knock them down.

They said, "Thank you for your time. We'll report this all to the commander. We bid you a good day and essay recovery," then they walked away.

"You're so goddamn petty, you know," Jack told me.

"Yeah, I know," I replied. I stood up from the chair I was sitting on and said, "All right, I'm going to get some food. I was too busy trying to kill Venny earlier to grab some." Then I walked out of the clinic like nothing ever happened as everyone watched me grab some food and sit down at a table inside with my squad next to me. Watching everyone panic in a search for the Wind Dragonborn, I ate my food in peace.

Two days after the Photo Incident, a Slayer came up to me and gave me an envelope and said, "We are once again so sorry that this happened and hope you will agree to not talk about what happened in public." Then they walked away before I could ask any questions.

As I opened up the envelope, Bolt walked over to me and asked, "What do you got there?"

So I answered "Not sure yet?" I pulled out a folded paper inside, so I unfolded it and realized it was another apology letter with a check for a large sum of money. "Oh my Ultimus," I said to myself.

"What is it?" Bolt asked, concerned.

"Just… look at it," I said as I handed him the check.

Bolt looked down and said, "Holy shh…oot."

"Oh my Ultimus, again. You almost swore," I said as I watched his reaction. "Hey, we should look at buying a place to live after we graduate from training," I suggested.

"With this much money, including the last check you got with all our savings, then absolutely we can," Bolt said as he read the entire paper repetitively.

"Where do you think we should live? In Southern Infinitas next to where everyone else is like Clay, Charles, and Jack?" I asked.

"Oh, uh sure," Bolt said as he leaned against a wall, still in disbelief at what they gave me.

"Probably something small because it's just the two of us and we don't need a big-big place," I suggested to him.

"Uh, yeah, whatever you want, Aika," he said as he handed me the check again, still looking shocked.

"Oooh, we should check out that place next to that coffee shop!" I told him excitedly.

"Yeah, that sounds about right for you," Bolt replied. Then he did calculations in his head of expenses as I ranted about where we should live.

The scratches on my arm luckily didn't scar at all, so that was good. The pros went out to try and find that Wind War Dragonborn, but they couldn't find any clues on its whereabouts or where it flew off to. But after that day, people started to call me the "War Slayer" for some reason. I asked people why, and they all gave me different answers, such as "I had fought the most War Dragonborns" and "I single-handedly defeated a War Dragonborn." People had even started to call me a hero for some reason. Also after that Vanessa messed around with me a lot less, to the point where she had some respect for me.

This was the last of the important events that happened to me in training. But none of it would compare to what happened to me within the first month and a half that I was a Dragon Slayer.

Chapter 8: A Night to Remember

When springtime rolled around it was graduation day at last, when all of the fifth years officially became Dragon Slayers.

At the ceremony, we received new official slayer armor, a new slayer sword, and our identification badge. At the end of training, we returned any old armor and swords we got at the beginning and got our own new personal gear for free. The identification badges were black fireproof armbands that had a white embroidered Slayer logo, which was just a round-cornered *X* with a Dragonborn sword through it. Our names were also embroidered in white under the logo. All of our badges were black, besides Zane's, which was navy blue.

As I watched my squad go up and get their stuff, I overheard some of the other Slayers talking.

"Hey, isn't that the War Slayer?" one of the guys said.

"No way, dude, they can't possibly be them. I heard the War Slayer was like the strongest person there," the other said.

"Hey, looks can be deceiving. I heard that they fight like one of those devils. They even got a devil sword."

"A devil sword?"

"Yeah, I'm pretty sure it's like a blue tint or something. They hide it behind their jacket to make it unnoticeable. It's almost the same color as their jacket, so it camouflages with it."

"No way, man, how old even are they?"

"I think they are only like twenty-two, dude. I heard they first signed up when they were like seventeen."

"Damn, I'm surprised they didn't drop out early. How many new guys are we getting anyway? Like fourteen or something like that, if I recall."

"Yeah man, we got four squads or something this year. Last year I think we only got like seven people. All I know is that a lot of people dropped out when the ice devil appeared on the grounds and attacked people."

I fight like one of the devils, eh. The irony of that statement. The two Slayers continued to talk about different things after that. But I started to think about the last thing I paid attention to.

I looked over back at the others and noticed that it was my turn to go next. I watched Jack grab his stuff and leave, so I stepped up next. Zane was there passing out everyone's rewards.

"Congratulations, Aika, we're all expecting great things from you," he said as he handed me everything, then fixed one of his pins on his uniform.

"Yeah, I bet you all are," I said before walking away and joining the others.

I saw everyone either showing off their armbands, equipping their sword to their sides, or trying on their new armor. The slayer armor looked almost like Dragonborn armor: it had the same shoulder and forearm plates but slightly different leg plates because they had the shin, knee, and thigh armor in one set of plates, which were all secured by a belt, and the armor was made of silver. The Slayers made everyone's armor identical so everyone would match in the uniform. Then the Slayer swords were single-edged blades with a saw on the bottom to the middle on the other edge, and it was made from silver. Then the hilt of the sword consisted of the cross guard, which was silver rectangular shape with a knuckle guard connected to it that was long and curved; the grip, which was a brown leather wrap; then the pommel, which was similar to the Dragonborn sword, where it was a small squarish trapezoidal silver metal piece.

As everyone showed off their stuff and chatted, Bolt came up to me and said excitedly, "Oh, there you are, Aika. Come on, let's go with the others. I heard all the other graduates are throwing a party at the training grounds to celebrate our achievement!" He grabbed my hand and brought me to the others talking. All the other graduates around talked about having a party and begged Zane to throw one at the training fields.

"Training fields, training fields, training fields!" everyone chanted to him.

"Fine! Just throw a party there, geez!" he yelled out at everyone, and they all cheered.

Then everyone made plans to meet up later that night, including me and my squad.

For the rest of the day, everyone just relaxed, but after we all got back together later that night at the fields, everyone decided to throw an even bigger party than planned. It was originally just going to be the graduates, but some people brought all their friends, some people brought family, and some brought their significant others, bumping up the number of people to almost sixty. Most people that joined usually did so alone and then had to meet others who signed up to form a squad. But if you and three or more of your friends signed up all at once, they just placed all of you into a squad, like what happened to us when Charles signed us up.

The party was filled with loud music and all different food and drinks that people brought with them. There was so much food it was like a feast. A couple of crazy people even opened a bar at the side of the food and served all kinds of beer and wine for people to buy. While some people danced, sang, or filled their faces with food, me and my squad were at a table chilling and talking about all the stuff that happened to us during training.

"Man, we've been through hell these past five years," Charles said.

"Oh please, you had hell? I got made fun of by Venny for almost five years straight and was attacked by a War Dragonborn twice. Well, the first attack was my fault, though, I will say. I did decide to charge up at them and attack. But the other one, full on, only attacked me," I told him.

"Oh, come on, it wasn't so bad. People gave you the title War Slayer because of all the things you did," Charles said to me.

Jack, not listening to our conversation, suddenly shouted out, interrupting us, "Bolton come with me! We need to get to the bar, pronto! This isn't a party until there's alcohol!"

Bolt turned to me and asked in the most worried voice possible, "Oh no, Aika, don't make me go with him! We all know what happens when Jack's drunk!"

"To the bar!" Jack shouted, dragging Bolt off with him toward the bar.

"Save me!" Bolt called out toward us as Jack dragged him away.

"Welp, we're screwed when they come back," I said to Charles.

He looked over at me and said, "There's only one thing more terrifying than when Jack goes on a rant about Dragonborns."

I stared back at him with the most serious look and asked, "Him drunk going on a rant about Dragonborns?"

"What else would it be?" he asked.

We had a good laugh after that, and the party around us started to take off with people and music.

"It's funny how when I first asked if you wanted to become a Slayer, you hesitated to join us, even though you're the most skilled fighter out of all of us," Charles said.

"Well, I had my reasons why I was hesitant," I told him.

At a distance I noticed Jack and Bolt coming back, carrying lots of drinks with them. When they arrived, Bolt nearly dropped a bottle trying to place the armful of drinks Jack had forced him to carry.

"Geez, how much did you spend?" I asked.

"He bought way more than he needed. Almost the entire bar, in fact—one of the guys went on a beer run because of Jack here," Bolt said, out of breath and sighed, as he sat back down next to me.

"Woow! Got the beer, the music is blasting, let's get drunk!" Jack yelled out.

"Oh no, you're the ones who took all the beer," a voice said behind Jack.

He moved over, and of course it was Vanessa standing there.

"Look who's here to ruin our night," I said.

"Oh please, I'm not here to cause trouble. I was just wondering if you all wanted to join my squad and talk a bit?" Vanessa offered.

I thought about it for a minute but said, "You know what? Sure. But I'm going to stay partly sober so if you get drunk, I'll remember all of it so I can mock you till the end of time about it."

When we joined Vanessa's squad, they had just opened up their drinks. So we opened ours up, and we all talked about funny things that happened during training.

"Hey Bolt, you should try this!" I offered a beer to him.

"Oh really, what's this?" Bolt asked as he checked the label, then turned to me. "I see what you're planning now," he told me.

"Wha... what do you think I'm planning?" I asked him.

"You're trying to get me drunk, aren't you?" he asked.

"How do you know?" I asked him.

"Because there's a label in red saying seventeen percent, and I know you know what that means," he told me.

"...Okay, I just want to see you drunk," I admitted.

"Nu-uhh, you know I won't get drunk," he said.

"Oh come on, Bolton, drink drink drink drink!" I chanted.

"Yeah, Bolton, drink drink drink drink!" Jack chanted along with me.

Bolt stared back at us with a blank expression and simply replied, "Yeah... no. Try Vanessa?" he told us.

"Oh please, I told you before I wasn't," Vanessa replied.

"Welp, there you have it," Bolt told us.

"You disappoint me sometimes, Bolton... you really do," I told him.

Jack asked Vanessa, "Hey, remember the time that Niki and I got the highest score ever recorded on a test, and it only took us two minutes to complete it?"

Vanessa asked, "How did you even read the questions that fast? There were fifty questions on that test!"

"Because I'm a certified genius in Dragonborns, and Niki is Niki," Jack told her proudly.

"You're not the only ones," I told him.

"How did you take so long on your test? You're as smart as them in Dragonborn knowledge, yet took forever," Vanessa asked.

"Well, uh… I sorta… can't read…" I admitted.

"You're kidding?" she asked.

"Hehe…. uh… I wish," I told her.

"That… makes quite a lot of sense now… still how, though?" she asked.

"Well, I know two different languages," I told her.

"Wait, you know another language?" Vanessa asked.

Charles told me, "Oh, you should totally speak in it to her!"

"Yeah, Aika, speak that crazy talk no one can understand!" Jack cheered for me.

"All right, give me a moment to switch," I told them as I cleared my throat and mind. I said in Dragonborn to them, "Please, for the love of Ultimus, don't let Niki, understand any of this."

"Oh you are so speaking Dragonborn!" Niki said as she wrote stuff down in her notebook.

"What kind of language is that? You never tell us," Jack asked.

"That's a secret," I told them as I spoke back in Infinitan.

Charles asked everyone, "Remember when Aika first tried riding a horse!" and made everyone then groaned sadly.

"So what exactly happened? My memories of that event are like a blur," I asked them.

"There's a reason why your memories are a blur," Jack told me.

"Do you think she's ready to hear the full story?" Bolt asked.

"Oh yeah, it's been long enough since then," Jack told him.

"What in the world did I do?" I asked, a bit scared.

"Okay, so who's going to tell her?" Vanessa asked.

"I can," Niki said as she flipped through her notebook to a certain page. "I wrote down every last detail on the events that happened. I can tell it in the most accurate way possible," she explained.

"I'm so sorry for this, Aika, but Niki, do it," Jack told her.

"Oh geez," I said to myself, worried.

Niki told us, "So it all began with Aika skipping the one important class that explained everything about horses and what we would be doing the following day if it was nice out. The next day it ended up raining, so we rode the horses the day afterward, but the rain from before made the area we were supposed to ride in muddy, so we practiced in a nice dry grass field instead. Aika, barely awake, who was also almost late for attendance, didn't pay attention to anything the instructor was explaining, which was what we were going to be doing with the horses. So everyone got into groups, and ours ended up being all of us here. As we were waiting, Aika was flirting with Bolt a bit, and she wanted to show off to him while riding a horse. So our lovely Aika here stepped up first to get on a horse when one became available. She climbed on top of it and sat there like a goon, having no idea what to do next. That's when Jack commented to her, 'You have no idea what to do, do you,' and Aika scoffed it off and said, 'Of course I know what to do.' Then she bashed the poor horse's rib cage with her boots to make them walk. But of course as you all know, the horse flipped out, went on its hind legs, and Aika being Aika, forgot to properly secure herself on the horse. So when the horse jumped up, Aika fell headfirst to the ground, knocking herself out. The horse ran off into the muddy area freaking out for ten minutes and running around in a circle. It took fifteen people to get it to calm down because everyone kept on slipping and sliding in the mud. In the process of that, two other horses were injured, four people were injured, and all fifteen of the people who helped calm down the horse and most people around got PTSD from the event. So everyone agreed to never let Aika touch a horse again… oh, and also, Aika was knocked out for five minutes from a minor concussion that gave her doubled vision for a few minutes, an hourlong headache, and forever forgetting the events of that morning till evening when dinner rolled around."

"Damn, that's what happened? It was only an accident, so why did everyone go to the extreme to immediately ban me?" I asked. Everyone stared over at me silently. "Okay, then I'll just shut up," I said after.

Jack told me, "Let's just say nobody ever wanted you to be near a horse ever again after that day."

"What year was that in?" Bolt asked.

Vanessa told him, "It was in the third year, so you and that genius there were either nineteen or twenty."

Bolt said, "Oh, we were nineteen then. My birthday is in the early spring, and that one's is in the midwinter," he said as he pointed to me.

Then a question came to mind, and I asked Vanessa, "Hey, how old are you guys? You never really did anything when it was your birthday."

"I'm twenty-four, Chad is twenty-five, Peter is twenty-five, and that one is twenty-three," she answered as she pointed to Niki at the end.

Charles asked Vanessa, "What made you guys join the Dragon Slayers?"

My interest was immediately piqued, and I joined in with Charles. "Yeah, why in the world did you join? Aren't you rich, Venny?"

Vanessa told us, "Well, my dad is rich, but I decided that I don't want to be rich because of my parents—I want to be rich on the money I made for myself. So I decided to get the highest-paying job here in Infinitas, and Chad here wanted to go with me, and Niki joined me because she can gather more government information if she's a Slayer."

"Wait, so how did you know Niki before this?" I asked.

"Oh yeah, I guess I never really told anyone, and I blackmailed her to not tell anyone, but I guess I'll tell you lot. Niki here… is my sister," she told us.

"No way!" I said as I started comparing the two.

"Now that's the highlight of my night!" Jack said, laughing.

"Yeah, us two look nothing alike except our skin and hair and our last name, Myers. Oh yeah, I also forgot to mention Peter before. He was randomly put in our group, but he's here because his parents forced him to come after he was convinced Dragonborns are gods."

"But they are gods!" he said after her. "Do people not know of the mighty five Ultimates?" he asked.

A chill went down my spine as he mentioned the Ultimates.

Niki clarified to us, "To the people who don't know, they are basically some super powerful Dragonborns with an abnormal aura color and supposedly have the blood of Ultimus, the god of the Dragonborns. For example, this one worships the Red Ultimate, who is an Ice Element."

Peter stood from his seat and screamed, "They are the great gods who rule over each section of the Dragonborn lands! One for each section! Mine rules the north because they're the best of the best! Avery the' Unetnal! Who then sided with the most powerful of them all the Back Ultimate, Connor the' Undertaker!" He pronounced the word *the* in the middle of the names with a long *e*, drawing out the word.

"The what?" Charles asked.

"Not just '*thaa*' its '*th-eee*' idiot!" Peter yelled at him.

Niki dragged him back down to his seat and said, "Oh shut it, none of us have ever seen these so called 'Ultimates.' Before the GDW Two, the Dragonborns who resided near us in the eastern land blocked anyone from traveling into their land. Then after the war, anyone who traveled over the lands was never seen again, probably killed or something, I bet you. So no one has ever seen or met one of these Dragonborns." She looked at me and Jack, who were weirdly quiet. "What's with you two—did you guys not know about them?" she asked.

I had no fake story prepared to explain how I knew about them, so I told her, "I never heard of the Ultimates. Are they just a made-up thing from the religious groups?"

Before Niki could answer, Jack said, "They are… they're a story they tell to convince people that they're gods. They made a whole-ass prophecy too that goes along with them… it's all so stupid," he said a bit quietly at the end.

Niki said, "I have no idea myself if they're real or not, but I'm not totally surprised that you knew about them," she said as she closed her notebook and put it away inside her jacket. Then she said, "The mood is a bit depressing now… how about we have a challenge? Let's see who knows more about Dragonborns once and for all!" she said with a smirk.

Jack laughed a bit and said, "Oh, you want to one-up each other on facts about Dragonborns? Heh, you're on!" He finished his beer and stood up.

"This is going to be fun for me to watch, Bolt," I said to him as I watched the both of them walk over to the side of us and start throwing facts at one another.

Charles suggested to us, "Hey, we should have a drinking competition to see who can drink the most!"

"I'm in!" Chad said as he opened another beer.

"Anyone else in?" Charles asked.

"No," we all said at the same time to him.

"Geez… okay, Chad, bottles up!" he said cheerfully to him.

Then the two of them started their little thing.

"Bolton!" Jack called.

"Uh, yeah?" Bolt asked.

"Get me some more beer so my brain can dig out more useless facts about Dragonborns!" Jack demanded.

"What?" Bolt asked, confused on how it would help.

"You heard the man, Bolt, get him another beer," I said to him.

Bolt got up and passed him a beer. Jack chugged half of it in one go and continued to yell out random information about Dragonborns. Then right as Bolt would sit next to me again, Jack would call out to him to get another beer, so Bolt passed him another, and the same process repeated again. This made Bolt just stand up and watch him and Niki yell at each other until either he passed out from alcohol poisoning or until their argument was over.

This went on for quite some time with me, Vanessa, and Peter watching this mess until there was no beer left at all because Jack drank it all.

"BoLtON! HanD mE mORe bEER!" he hollered at him.

"Uh, Jack, I can't. You drank it all," he told him, but to no avail, because Jack paid no attention and continued to yell random gibberish at Niki about Dragonborns.

"Guys, I don't know what to do," Bolt told us in a bit of a panic.

Vanessa ordered Peter, "Hey grab someone's unfinished drink and give it to Jack."

"I don't think he should have another," he said quietly.

"Just do it," she demanded.

"Okay," he said as he got up.

I said to Vanessa, "I don't think I've ever had a full-on conversion with Peter or Chad, not once in my life."

"Don't bother, they're both idiots," Vanessa said.

"Well, I got idiots of my own," I said sadly, as I gestured to Charles, who was blackout drunk next to Chad, who was also out. I looked over at Jack, who got his beer and continued to argue.

"Hey, at least you got Bolton there. You got one person in your squad who's not a total idiot," Vanessa stated.

"Venny, Bolton is the only one who's not an idiot," I told her.

"What, are you calling yourself stupid?" Vanessa asked.

"Oh please, you seriously think I'm not an idiot too?" I asked.

"Well, you act smarter than all of them," Vanessa replied.

"Venny, I'm an idiot with confidence," I clarified to her.

Bolt collapsed in the chair next to me and said, "At last I'm free from Jack," then picked up his head and asked, "So how are you ladies doing?"

"Oh, you know, me and Venny are just talking about these idiots here," I told him.

"That's cool. I'm just going to rest here for a moment. Hope you don't mind," he said tiredly.

"Hey, wait, are we still allowed to sleep in the cabin, or do we need to carry these drunks home?" I asked.

"Oh geez, I didn't even think about that," Vanessa said.

"Do you wanna just ditch them here?" I asked.

"Absolutely!" Vanessa replied with no hesitation.

"Do you wanna head out, then?" I asked.

"Sure," she replied.

So I shook Bolt and asked him, "Wanna head out?"

"Please..." he muttered back to me.

So we all got up to start walking back. As we walked away, I looked over back at Jack, who was still arguing with Niki. So I shouted at him, "Hey, Jack! Bolt and I are leaving with Venny! Don't do something stupid and get yourself in trouble! Oh, and don't forget about Charles too!" Still arguing with Niki, Jack gave me a thumbs up. I sighed, then told Bolt and Vanessa, "Okay let's go."

We left the party together, leaving all the drunken idiots behind.

It was around two in the morning when we walked back home together.

"So where do you two live?" Vanessa asked.

"Southwest Infinitas. We recently moved into a new house we bought," Bolt replied.

"You two got your own house?" Vanessa asked.

So I told her, "The Dragon Slayers like to keep a 'good name' with the public, so they paid me extra to keep me quiet about how I almost died twice in training. Also we had been saving our money for something like this for a while now. It's nothing spectacular, it's more shack than house, but it's nice having our own little place without Clay. Back when we lived with him before training, we were just housemates, and now it would be kinda awkward."

Our house had just a single floor with two bedrooms, one for us and a guest room, then a single bathroom. In the main section it was just a small living room with a fireplace and a small couch and two chairs and matching coffee table. Then behind the couch an open kitchen connected to the living room with just the appliances and a basic wooden table and chairs.

Vanessa replied, "Damn, that sounds nice to have your own little place. I just live with my dad in his big house in Northeast Infinitas. Niki moved out and lives in her own little place my dad bought her because she would make a mess with everything and creep out anyone who visited with her boards. I still have nightmares about waking up to see her stuff everywhere, but that's a story for another day. Down there is my path back home, so I'll be seeing you guys around on the job," Vanessa told us.

"See ya, Venny," I said.

"Have a good break until we begin our new jobs," Bolt said.

We waved goodbye as she walked down her path, and I told Bolt, "All right, let's go home."

Bolt and I walked together down our path home.

"You two seem to be on better terms," Bolt said to me happily.

"Eh, I don't want to strangle her every time I talk to her now," I replied.

Bolt asked me, sounding a bit serious, "Hey, Aika, do you have a feeling of anything going wrong now that we're officially Slayers?"

"Not really. As long as no explosive events happen, it should all be fine. Why, you worried about something?" I asked.

"Well, we're probably going to be dealing with a whole bunch of new situations now, and to be honest I was a little worried, but if you have no bad feelings, then it should be fine," he explained.

"Don't worry too much—it's only the beginning of this. Look at what happened during training: we made it out with only a few scars to look back on. I'm sure everything will be fine in the end, right?" I told him.

"Well, all right, if you say so," Bolt replied.

When we reached the house later, I immediately collapsed onto our bed and proceeded to sleep for the next twelve hours to process all the things I'd witnessed that night. That night was fun. Everyone had a good time, until they all woke up the next morning with a hangover, except Bolt and I, who were mostly sober. Vanessa and I actually got along for once and had a nice conversation that night. But of course two weeks after graduation, we began our jobs as Slayers.

Drink
Drink
Drink
Drink
Drink
Drink
Drink
Drink

Chapter 9: The Monster within Us

It had been about three weeks since our first official day of working as Dragon Slayers. Nothing big had happened; we did the usual Slayer jobs. We had to go on patrols around the kingdom, help the civilians with problems, and observe the skies and outer land beyond Infinitas from the outer wall to look out for Dragonborns. But this was about to change very quickly for us on one fateful day.

Bolt and I were just chatting outside the main Slayer headquarters while waiting for Charles and Jack to finish getting ready so we could go on our patrol. We were secluded from noon until after dusk. The main Slayer headquarters, or what we like to call "the main base" for short, was a fancy mini castle with three floors made from gray brick that was basically just a big office that contained all of our own business mailboxes, lockers combined with bathrooms separated by gender, and Zane's office, which was at the very top floor, with other smaller offices and closets around that stored many government documents about past events that were never made public and top secret information on weapons, Dragonborns, and certain people.

"What the hell is taking them so long?" I asked Bolt.

"Well, I was already prepared, so that's why I was ready first," he said.

"I wasn't prepared at all, and look at me," I told him.

"Hey, who knows. Jack probably stole more government documents and is trying to hide them somewhere in the locker room," he told me.

I sighed and said back, "Yeah, that sounds like something he'd do."

As we were waiting some more for them, I suddenly got a horrible chill from nowhere.

"What's wrong?" Bolt asked.

"I… don't know?" I said as I looked up to the sky. "I thought I felt someone's aura, but no one's here," I told him.

"Maybe it was a Wind Element flying fast above the clouds?" Bolt questioned.

"No, it can't be that," I said back. "They would be far too high up to sense their presence like I did. They would have to be as powerful as a bomb if I could feel them from up there," I explained.

Finally Charles and Jack came out of the locker room. Charles said to us, "Sorry we took so long… Jack here stole some documents and made me help him stash them somewhere," he explained.

"Look at that, it was exactly what I told you," Bolt said to me.

Charles noticed how uneasy I looked and asked, "Hey, you okay, Aika? You look like you saw a devil."

"Oh yeah, I'm fine. I just got a bad chill for no reason," I explained.

Charles asked, "Well, whenever I feel bad, know what makes me feel better?"

"Yelling crap out about Dragonborns?" I answered.

"Nope!" Charles said.

"Having a duel?" Bolt answered.

"Guess again!" Charles said back.

"Act like a fool?" Jack answered smugly.

Charles just looked over to him and silently flicked his forehead, then said back to all of us,

"Good food always makes me feel better! So how about this, after we finish our patrol, I'll treat you all, except Jack, to some good grub. This new bar just opened up. I heard the food was pretty good, wanna check it out?" he asked.

"Oh cool, that'll be fun," I said back.

"Yeah, let's check it out!" Bolt said cheerfully.

"Thanks for including me," Jack replied.

"Hey, that's what you get for making me partners in crime with you," Charles replied to him.

"Well, the last papers got found, so I need to find better hiding spots for them," Jack explained.

Bolt told us, "Come on, guys, we'll get in trouble if we don't get to work."

Jack sighed, then complained, "Fine, all right, I'm going."

So we headed on our way and continued our conversation. On the way, though, I still felt that same shiver follow me from when I was waiting.

During our patrol, we helped a few people here and there with their problems—nothing too crazy, thankfully, except one of them. While the guys were trying to fix something, some lady was yelling nonsense at me trying to prove herself innocent by telling me all about her "poor, poor angel kid" who was just playing a game. A game that somehow "accidentally" broke off an entire section of some poor old shopkeeper's shop roof in the market plaza. As I was trying to calm her down, I was questioning, "How in the world did I get dumped with this job?" I looked back at the others who just told the guy, "Yeah, uh, you should be fine. Just get a board, a few nails, and shingles, and you should be good," Charles told him.

The guy said to them, "I feel bad for your friend over there—that lady is a fruitcake yelling about her kid. I already told the kid it was all right, but she freaked and called you guys over anyways."

"You gotta be kidding me!" I silently screamed within me as I listened to this guy while this lady was yelling at me.

As I paid attention to her again, she hollered to me, "That man there is probably going to make you guys throw my child in jail! They're my baby!

My angel! And I think you should—"

Then in the distance, I saw Vanessa's squad. I cut off the lady midsentence and said, "Hey, wait here. I'm going to talk with some other people to see if they want to help us, okay?"

She told me, "Oh good, more help! Now I can let more people help me get justice in my situation and… hello?" she said, looking for me and realizing I disappeared.

I had already walked off to Vanessa's squad and said hello to them.

"Is that crazy woman looking for you, Aika?" Niki asked as she pointed over my shoulder. She was now bothering the guys who were trying to help the shopkeeper out.

"Maybe… you want to take over this job? I know how much you like talking, Venny, and I've been having the worst chill down my spine all day long," I asked her.

"Ah… no," she replied.

"Hey, uh, you, crazy lady! My friend Venny here is going to help you out. You care to talk about your child more?" I shouted out to her.

"Oh do I?" she said as she shuffled over.

"Aika, what the hell?" Vanessa asked.

"Oh sorry, Venny, did you say no? I thought I heard a yes. I'm terribly sorry, but now I gotta go now, bye-bye!" said to her happily as I quickly walked away.

"Aika, no, don't do this to me! I thought we were okay with each other!" Vanessa yelled at me.

The lady said to her, "Why hello, Venny, can you help me out? You see, my child—"

"Aika, why?" Vanessa shouted.

"This is what you deserve after what happened to me after the Photo Incident!" I hollered back cheerfully.

"Did you just make Vanessa take over the job of calming down the crazy person?" Jack asked me.

"Yep," I told him, with no hesitation.

"Aika, you make me so proud sometimes to call myself your friend," Jack told me as he finished fixing the guy's roof.

Charles told the guy, "All right, everything looks good here. Call us over again if you see us if it falls apart again."

"Thank you younglings so much for helping. How can I repay you?" he asked.

"Make sure that crazy lady doesn't follow us, or especially me?" I asked.

"Oh, for sure, miss!" he replied.

"All right, take care now, thanks!" I said as I grabbed Bolt's hand and speed-walked away.

"I have no idea what's worse right now, the feeling that something is going to go horrifically wrong at any moment that makes me want to scream, or that lady?" I told them.

"You still feel like that?" Charles asked me.

"I… I don't know what this feeling is," I said, a bit confused about myself.

"Hey, it's all right, we'll walk around the peaceful areas with few people," Jack said, then patted my shoulder. "Damn, are you actually doing okay? You feel freezing, and it's almost late spring," he asked.

"I'm fine… I'm always cold, you know that," I said as I let go of Bolt's hand and walked ahead of them.

"Oh, she is not doing okay," Jack said to Bolt and Charles.

"Just let her be, she won't even tell me what's wrong," Bolt told him as he walked behind me.

As the day went on, the feeling only got worse, but our shift eventually ended. We walked back to the main base to grab our paychecks. While walking, Charles and Jack had a little brawl, and Bolt was behind them quieting them down a bit because it was night. I watched them all from the very back, pretending like I wasn't associated with them. Then while I was watching them, I suddenly felt the same chill as I did earlier, so I looked around to see if anything was up. As I did, I noticed lots of smoke coming from a distance.

"Hey, guys!" I called out to them.

"What's up?" Charles asked as he pushed over Jack.

"Look over there! I think there's a fire!" I told them as I pointed up to the sky. They all looked over to where I pointed and saw a large amount of smoke in the distance.

"That's no tiny fire! That's someone's house!" Jack told us.

"Come on, let's run to the base and get some help!" Charles said as he ran.

We all followed behind Charles to the base. When we got there, we told the Slayers who were there, then all traveled toward the smoke. As we ran, a horrible feeling whelmed up within me. There was a very powerful Dragonborn nearby.

Bolt hollered to us, scared, "Hey guys, this path leads to my uncle's house!"

As we turned around to see where the fire was coming from, it became Bolt's nightmare. We all saw Clay's house burning up in flames. But this was no normal fire; it had bright magenta flames with a dark-magenta accent. Immediately I knew this Dragonborn was a Fire Element from how bad the fire was. Other elements had fire-like abilities, but they weren't strong enough to do something as big as this. The only element that could do this was the Fire Element. But what was so strange about this fire was how strong it was. Around the house there were several other Slayer squads and Zane. Bolt ran toward Zane and told him, "Sir, this is my uncle's house... w-where is he... have you seen him?" he asked.

Zane said to him, "I'm sorry to say this to you... but your uncle is stuck inside of the house. We've been trying to rescue him, but the flames were too great for us to get inside deep enough to find him," he explained.

As I watched the color drain from Bolt's face, I was left with horrible guilt of not knowing what to do. Then I remembered the guilt I felt from long ago. Bolt was frozen in place, helplessly watching Clay's house burn down. So I walked over to Charles and asked him, "Hey, Charles... can you do me a solid?"

"Yeah sure, what do you need," he asked, still in shock.

"I'm gonna do something stupid. Hold Bolt back for me, will you?" I asked.

"What do you mean?" he asked.

"Just make sure he doesn't follow me, okay," I told him.

As I walked away, I looked back at Bolt and knew if I didn't act now, I'd regret it forever. So I ran toward the house at full speed to the front door, which was slightly open.

"Hey, what's the War Slayer doing?" someone shouted out.

"Someone stop them!" another yelled.

I didn't care what everyone was shouting about around me. I had to save Clay. I never wanted to have the same guilt from before. I needed to save him! For Bolt! For me! Clay was the one who let me stay with him all those years ago. I couldn't let him die like this! I kicked the door open, and a blast of fire came out. As figured, Bolt came chasing after me to stop me from running in.

But Charles stopped Bolt and told him, "Hey, she'll be fine. You know how she is when there's a Dragonborn nearby. Anyways, Aika probably has a plan... right? Like she would just run into a burning building without a plan."

I had no plan. None at all. I just ran into a burning building because I was mad at myself. So I searched around the house aimlessly for Clay. The fire was much greater inside; most of the stuff around me was either broken or ashes. I heard someone call out, "Aika?"

"Clay?" I replied.

Then I saw Clay running toward me unhurt, holding one of his swords.

"Wha... what are you doing here? How did you get in? The fire is too great," he asked.

"Do you really think I was going to let you die like this?" I told him.

"How did you—?" Clay asked, but I cut him off and told him,

"Listen, you need to get out of here now! I made a path toward the front door. You need to run now!" I demanded as I pushed him toward the door.

"What about you? Aren't you coming?" he asked.

So I told him, "Don't worry about me, Clay. I'm going to find the loser who did this to you and beat the hell out of them. Please just run out of here. I'm the only one who can tolerate this fire. I'm cursed."

Clay shouted, "Please be careful!" then ran out of the house.

After he was safe, I ran farther inside to find the jerk who did this. The fire got stronger as I continued farther in, but it didn't really matter. I'm almost utterly fireproof myself because of my jacket and powers. As I looked around, so many memories were flooding in my head as I watched it all burn down. The horrible feeling I had sensed from them was bone chilling. This Dragonborn I was looking for was a Fire Element.

The Fire Element had the power of pure destruction. The Fire Element's symbol was a round-cornered *X* inside of a vertical rhombus. This element was weak against the Wind Element, only because the wind could blow out fire that came toward it. Other than that it had very few weaknesses. Such as how slow they were. They were the second slowest at using their power. They needed to charge up a lot of their power before attacking. Also when they flew, they were the slowest, but the damage they did made up for the time it took for them to charge it up. The power for this element was how they could control their fire. Other Dragonborns could only use their fire to attack or shield themselves with a single flow that comes from their bodies. But the Fire Element could control almost every aspect of theirs. They could control the path of it and spread it to wherever they needed it. Their fire was the hottest and most powerful of all fires. They could melt the plates on our armor right off we were exposed to it at high heat for too long. Another power they had was that they could create this lava-like slush from their hands and burn almost anything it touches. It was three times as hot as regular fire. They could build the slush up within their hands to create an explosion. These explosions were their greatest power. It could be as small as a vibration or as big as a bomb. The more they charged their power, the bigger the explosion would be. The possible aura colors the Fire Element could have were any shade of yellow, orange, red, and some darker shades of purple.

As I looked around the house, I could feel their presence all around me as I searched, but I can't find them. So I called out to them, "Come out, whoever you are! I'm one of you, so just come out and fight me!"

Right behind me felt their presence, so I turned around to see who they were. When I saw them, I stepped back a bit and froze up in shock. This fella was no normal Dragonborn. They were a War Dragonborn, but... different. They were mutated like a monster. Their horns were very long, ridged and curved back like a demon's. They were longer and sharper than the other War Dragonborns'. Their claws had plates on them unlike normal, making them sharper and deadlier. Their armor form looked melted and jagged; the points of their plates were also way sharper than usual. The scales were a dark magenta, and their plates had a touch of red and pink mixed with silver. Then finally the only part of their eyes that had color was their irises, which were glowing a bright magenta. Besides that the rest was black with spots of red, white, and green sprinkled within that area. On top of that, our scales covered over our faces like a mask to help protect us from breathing in anything deadly. But this Dragonborn's mouth had broken right through their mask, and it was wide open. It looked like a dark void, and they had razor-sharp tooth-like scales on the top and bottom that resembled a shark, smiling at me. This Dragonborn was the most messed-up thing I had seen in a long, long time. This poor Dragonborn was barely human anymore. The only human thing left about them was their body figure and how they walked on two legs. Then they started walking toward me, tilting their head and raising their sword up at me. This Dragonborn was just holding a sword; they didn't even have a scabbard on them at all. It probably burned off them as they were setting things on fire. Suddenly they jumped out toward me to attack. I dodged right in time and ran to the exit as fast as I could.

Meanwhile everyone outside had no idea what was happening. Clay had run out of the house coughing, and ran toward everyone. Bolt ran over to him and asked, "Uncle Clay, what happened, are you okay?"

Clay caught his breath and said, "I'm okay, I'm not hurt. But I'm not who you should be worried about now."

"What do you mean?" Bolt asked.

"Aika, she went farther inside to fight the Dragonborn!"

"What?" all the Slayers yelled around the place.

Zane shouted to everyone, "All of you, get your weapons ready! When Aika runs out of the house, we'll do an all-out attack on the devil!"

Then everyone started to run around to prepare the attack. But before they were all ready, I slammed the side door open and ran out while yelling "OUT OF MY WAY!" to everyone. I ran for my life past everyone, knowing that monster would blast out any second. I only stopped for a spit second in front of Bolt. I ran up to him, grabbed his shoulders, and shook him while shouting out, "BOLTON, I PISSED OFF ULTIMUS!" then ran away before he could say anything back. Everyone looked back at me shocked as I ran, not knowing what to think. I had never in my life been this scared in front of them, ever. A huge explosion happened on the side of the house I'd run from. When everyone turned to see what it was, then they all saw the nightmare monster of a Dragonborn that was chasing me. Everyone immediately started to fire at it with all the weapons they had. But to no avail, it did absolutely nothing to them as they dodged all of it while still having their head tilted, staring at me. They screamed out toward me, then started chasing me again. As they ran after me, they sent out a blaze of fire in a path toward me. I barely dodged the fire in a quick slide. They jumped toward me to slash me with their sword. I barely dodged again, with their sword barely missing my arm; then I drew my sword out. It tried hacking at me again, but I diverted it with my sword. As my sword got pushed back, I looked over at the others, desperate for help. But all of them were just as freaked out as me, if not more.

Bolt was frozen in place, and Charles was yelling at Jack, "Dude, what the hell is that thing?"

Jack, also frightened, yelled back, "I... I don't know? It resembles a Dragonborn but... well just look at it!"

While I was looking toward the Slayers, I got distracted slightly watching them all freak out, and fear overwhelmed me and made me weaken my grip for a moment. Because of that, they knocked away my sword across the other side of the road, scary similar to the way I do. Everyone saw the pure terror that came upon my face as I tried to reach out for my sword. As I watched my sword get farther and farther away, time seemed to get slower. I looked at the Mutant, sword ready, as they went to slash me again. When I dodged them, I noticed a gush of blood from my leg when I ran. I looked toward everyone and saw them all terrified with my sword landed over near Bolt, far from me. Having no weapons on me, I ripped off my scabbard and threw it in their face as a distraction to run away. Behind Clay's house it just so happened to also be where a big river flowed throughout Infinitas. So I ran for my life toward there down an open road. As I did, of course the Mutant followed right behind me, with the Slayers following behind them too. But I noticed it was charging up an explosion. Knowing that this was a big one, I threw off my jacket and tossed it right in their face as they set off the explosion. As they did, my jacket glowed with a golden triangle pattern along the edges for a moment, with the symbol of the Fire Element on the back, and the power of the explosion got weaker as it glowed. The Slayers behind were blinded from the smoke, and it was only the Mutant and me. The Mutant threw my jacket to the ground, which made the glow disappear, and stared at me like they were about to rip me to shreds. When they ran toward me again, right before they jabbed at me again, I slammed down smoke bombs to blind them, then jumped to a nearby ditch to sneak away.

As the smoke disappeared, the Slayers arrived and saw the Mutant looking around for me. People started to whisper about the Mutant and what it was doing. As they did, my squad was just trying to find where I ran to. While running, Bolt had picked up my sword and scabbard for me as well.

"See her anywhere?" Charles asked as he looked across the field.

"No clue where she went. That thing looks like it doesn't know either.

Look at it searching around," Jack said as he pointed at the Mutant. That's when Bolt saw my jacket on the ground.

"Aika?" he said worriedly as he picked it up.

Charles and Jack looked over to Bolt, worried, as he held my stuff close to him and searched the field.

"What the hell happened to her? Aika would never throw off her jacket in the heat of battle," Charles asked.

"There had to be a good reason why she did it, though," Jack told him.

Some of the other Slayers watched my squad question what happened to me and also started to get quite concerned.

Zane, hearing all of this, yelled out to everyone, "The War Slayer is none of our concern right now!" he said as he pointed to the Mutant staring at them. The Mutant walked toward them slightly, then stopped. It tilted their head at them, then blasted a path of fire toward them. Having no time to react, they were sure to be hit. But then out of nowhere, right before the fire hit them, a navy-blue-scaled Dragonborn jumped down from a nearby building and blocked the fire from hitting them. As the Slayers watched in disbelief, they shouted all kinds of different things out about it.

"Jack, what kind of devil is that?" Charles asked.

"It's just a regular Dragonborn! I don't know what element it is, though, there's no armor plate on its hands! It's just some regular leather armor glove from our armory!" Jack explained.

Everyone had no idea what to think after Jack said that and were trying to figure out what to do. But while everyone else was freaking out, all of this hit Bolt a lot differently. As the blue Dragonborn stared back at them all, Bolt suddenly realized that this Dragonborn who was protecting everyone was none other than me, Aika.

My aura was a bright yale blue that looked even brighter in the dark. My armor form was basic; I got dark navy-blue scales and ridged, wavy horns like a dragon's. My plates had a blue tint like my sword, then my shoulder plates were smoothed at the end instead of pointed like most.

My forearm plates had the scars on my arms engraved into the plates. The scars on my plates were the same blue as my aura; they glowed slightly alongside my eyes when in darkness. The accent color of my aura was a blue indigo that shone brightly from my irises and fire.

Zane ordered to the Slayers, "Everyone set up your weapons and take aim at the Dragonborns!"

As everyone did, Bolt panicked and shrieked, "Wait, stop! Don't shoot!"

Everyone just turned around and glared at him as they continued to set up their weapons.

"Bolton, why are you yelling out at us not to shoot at the devils!" Zane shouted back at him.

Bolt panicked and said, stuttering, "W-well... uh... we shouldn't shoot at the Dragonborns because… we should wait till they're done fighting one another so we only have one Dragonborn to worry about! That way the one Dragonborn left would be tired and weak, so we would win... easier?" he explained to them.

Zane was silent for a minute, then said, "I actually like your idea, Bolton." Then he shouted out, "Everyone hold back for now, and we'll shoot at the winning Dragonborn in battle!"

"Wait, did that actually just work?" Bolt asked himself in disbelief, as everyone put down their weapons.

I also could not believe what was going on behind me. I just facepalmed myself while listening to this crap go down as I held back the Mutant's fire. "How in the world are these people as stupid as me? No wonder why Niki was always blabbing about me being a Dragonborn," I thought as I pushed back the fire even farther. Realizing their stupidity, I called out to them,

"Hey, could any of you lend me your sword?"

With no surprise, some idiot from the crowd actually threw over their sword next to me into the dirt. "Wow," I thought to myself again. I couldn't believe that actually worked. So I pulled out the sword from the ground and blasted away the fire from me with my own. Me and the Mutant glare at each other for a minute. They charged at me at full speed, raising their sword. This time with a clear head, I charged at it also and swung back at their sword. As they screeched together, the Mutant swirled fire around themselves and tilted their head once again. I created fire around me and swerved their swing away from me. We both stepped back and launched our fire paths at each other. While doing so, my body shook a little. It had been an awfully long time since I used this power to its fullest. I looked over back at Bolt holding my jacket and kinda wished I had it with me. If I did, it would reveal my element to everyone, but it would also help control my power. It was made out of unique fibers that had special properties that absorbed some of our aura and help concentrate it into stronger attacks. But it could be used to surprise others and make their attacks weaker as well. When we used our powers to a certain strength, it activated and glowed a golden triangle pattern along the edges and on the back whatever elemental symbol you had.

After our fires collided for a minute, I ran through mine and the Mutant's and swung hard to their sword, screeching them both together again. As sparks were created from our swords, my time trance formed and I tried to knock away their sword, but their grip was amazing, and they almost knocked my sword away the same as last time. "Who is this person?" I thought to myself as I fought against their strength. Finally, as I shouted out, I twisted my wrist so hard, as much as my joint could move to the left, and knocked away their sword far away, near the Slayers. As they grabbed the sword, they chanted out,

"Yeah, kill them, Blue Dragonborn!"

"Make our job easier, will you?"

And simply just…

"FIGHT! FIGHT! FIGHT! FIGHT!"

The Mutant was angered from all the noise around, so in distress, they ran over and slugged me in the face hard. Pissed off now, I threw back the Slayer sword and suckered punched them back in their face, and thus a fistfight broke out between us, and we started to beat the living hell out of one another in front of the Slayers. My trance was semi broken as I saw some punches slow and others fast, unable to dodge. Some people were rooting for me to win, others for the Mutant. People were watching in shock. And of course, I can never forget… Jack was having a field day shouting about how amazing all of this was.

"Guys! Look at this! None of this has ever happened before! A Dragonborn protecting a bunch of Dragon Slayers from another Dragonborn! My goodness!" Jack shouted as I continuously punched the Mutant pinned on the ground.

"Who do you think is going to win?" Charles asked as the Mutant then pushed me to the ground and started punching me over and over again.

"Don't know!" Jack said very confidently as they heard me yell in anger as I punched the Mutant off me. Then Bolt, in the very back of all of them, was just helplessly watching me get the hell beaten out of me and flinching at every little punch I got.

"Hey Bolt, you doing okay?" Charles asked him.

"Oh yeah… I'm just worried about Aika. You know how much of an idiot she is," he said as he watched me tackle the Mutant while yelling out, "Get your ass back over here!" then watched me get bashed in the stomach so hard that my plate cracked slightly.

Me and the Mutant brawled for about five minutes straight, brutally punching and kicking each other as hard as we both could, not even using our powers anymore. The Mutant looked pretty much the same from when the battle began, but I was a complete mess with my plates covered in scratches from the Mutant's claws and busted up with bruises under my scales. I thought it would never end until it took its claws and horribly scratched across my entire back right through my thick scales while I was trying to catch my breath. I screamed out in pain from the scratch as my scales instantly regenerated, covering over the scratch. Full of rage, I turned around and landed a good slug to the Mutant's face and knocked them to their knees. They screamed back at me, then summoned their wings. Their wings also looked melted like their armor, and then they flew off into the darkness that was the sky. As I watched it fly away, I sighed and finally relaxed because it probably wasn't going to come back. I remembered what was said earlier and turned around to all the Slayers pointing their weapons toward me. In the very back I saw Bolt flailing his arms around gesturing at me to "GET OUT NOW!" Everyone started running and launching arrows toward me. So of course I ran for my life, running away from everyone trying to kill me, after I saved them. The irony of it all.

As I ran, I felt the dizziness hit me from being injured from the Mutant. My leg was screaming with every step from that slash from earlier when I lost my sword. Parts of my plates and scales started to wither away into aura. As I was running, words from my mother rushed through my mind: "Aika, if the world ever chases after you because you're a Dragonborn... don't hurt them, just run away from them. They probably have no idea who you actually are, so please don't ever hurt them. Because if you do, you'll only prove to them that they're right." So I ran with everything I had. I needed to run far enough to lose everyone. If they caught up to me and knocked me down, I'd surely lose all strength and deactivate my armor form, revealing that I was a Dragonborn to everyone. And I know that Bolt was not prepared to explain to everyone at this moment about everything. So I used the little strength I had left and fire blasted a cloud of navy-blue-smoke around me, blinding everyone so I could escape without any trace.

When the smoke had disappeared, everyone was left with no idea where I ran off to. Zane, pissed off, yelled out to everyone, "Search the area they can't be far! Find any trace or clues to where the Blue Dragonborn and... that thing went to! GO!"

Everyone scattered around to find something. Bolt, Charles, and Jack met back together and talked.

"Guys, we need to find Aika!" Bolt told them worriedly.

"I also want to find her. Who knows what happened?" Jack said, agreeing.

"How about we all split up and search the area," Charles suggested.

But as they were all planning where to look, Zane walked up to them and shouted, "Hey Jack, what are you doing? We need you to look for evidence!"

Jack, not wanting to, said back, "But, sir, Commander. I need to help look for Aika. She may be hurt or—!"

"I don't care! Have the other two look for the War Slayer. I bet they're probably fine. You're the most intelligent about Dragonborns. We need you here. Got it?" he demanded.

Jack looked over at the other two, then back to him and said, "Fine," quietly back. Zane walked away. Jack said to them, "Tell me right away if something bad happened to her. I don't want to be in the dark if something did happen."

"Don't worry, man, I'll tell you right away!" Charles said as he followed behind Bolt, who already started looking around for me.

So Zane was completely wrong about me, because while they were having that conversion, I had finally just found a place to deactivate my armor form which fully withered away into aura and took a single breath, then immediately passed out and fell to the ground. When Bolt finally found me collapsed on the ground, I wasn't too far away from the smoke bomb I'd made. He immediately called out to Charles, dropped my stuff, and ran over to me, to check if I was alive.

"Aika! Aika, are you okay!" he called out as he shook me in his arms.

When Charles ran over to Bolt and saw me all messed up, he shouted out, "Oh geez, what the hell did that thing do to her? She looks like she got in a fistfight with a devil!"

Bolt held me for a minute, then told Charles, "I'm going to bring her to the closest clinic around here! Tell the others what happened to her, and run there the first chance you get! Also hold on to her stuff for me!"

Before Charles had a chance to respond, Bolt lifted me up on his back, then ran off carrying me to the closest clinic. Charles grabbed my stuff and ran off and told everyone what happened.

The events from this night would lead to one of the biggest events of my life. This was only the beginning of what was to come. And much later on, this Mutated Fire Dragonborn would become a much bigger deal for me.

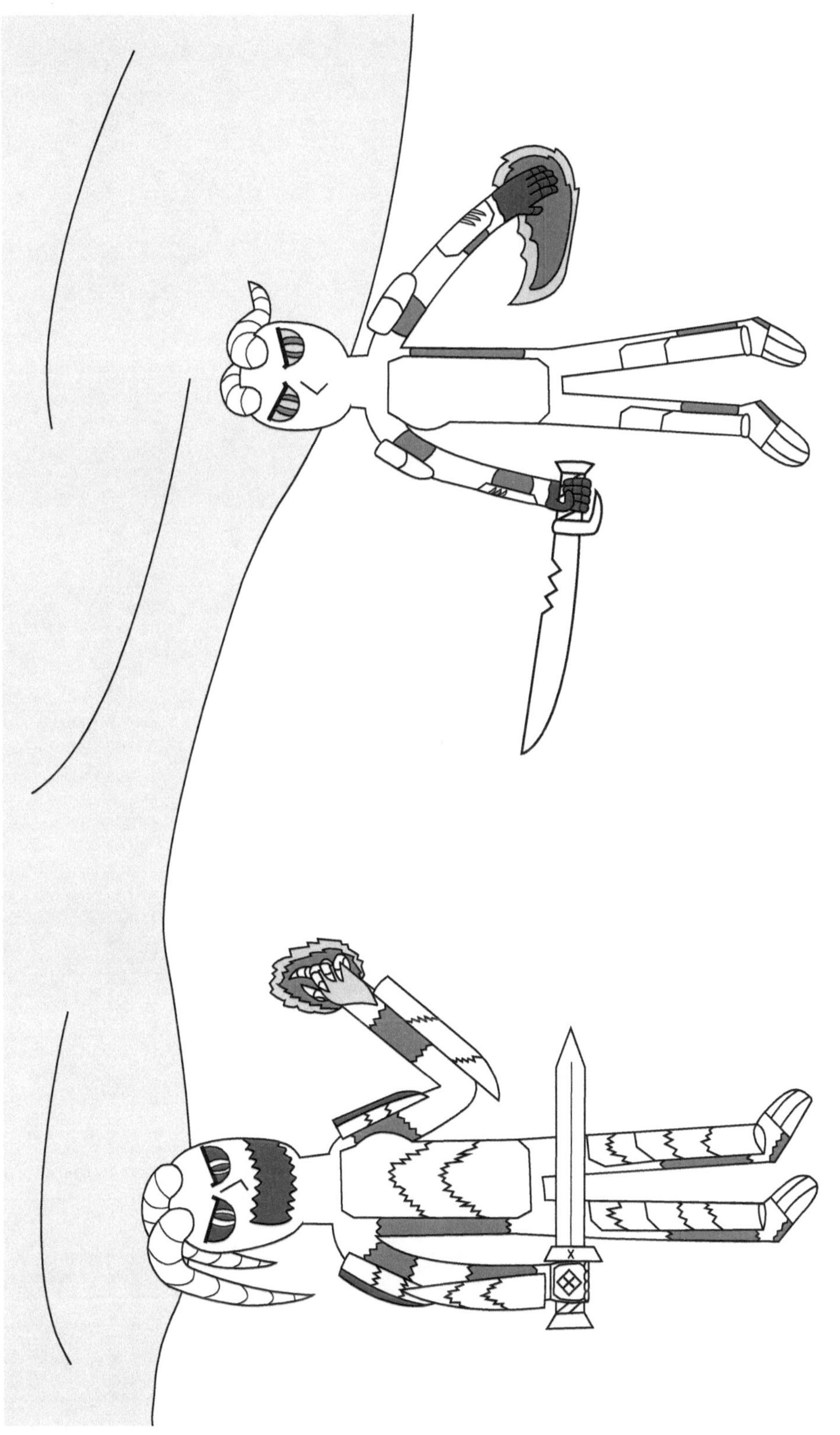

Chapter 10: The Devil among Us

Everything was completely dark. My body felt numb, and I could barely move. I heard a voice here and there but couldn't decipher any of it. It felt like I was stuck in an endless nightmare. The only things going through my head were dramatic memories from my past. I thought I was dead, until I heard muffled yelling in the background that woke me and made my senses come back to me. As I opened my eyes, I found myself in a bed with a thick white blanket on me. I was dressed in hospital clothing, which was just a simple light-blue short-sleeved shirt and light-blue sweatpants, and my entire body felt like it was wrapped up in bandages. I immediately checked my hands and saw that they still had wrappings on. Then I noticed it had writing on my right hand that said, "Don't worry —B." the yelling I heard started to become clearer, so I turned my head over to the left to see who it was. And of course it was Charles and Jack yelling at each other with Bolt trying to quiet them down. It was unclear what I heard Charles and Jack saying, but I did hear Bolt say to them, "Guys, keep it down! Remember we're in a hospital! Aika is also right beside us resting, come on!"

As I watched all of this chaos unfold, I had to say some stupid comment back to them, so I weakly said to them from the bed, "I swear every time we all hang out, someone starts a fight. Then we all yell at each other for like five minutes… then we forget it all a minute later like it was nothing."

Everyone stopped and turned to me silently when they heard my voice. They were all speechless as they just looked at me, shocked, as if they hadn't seen me in years. Until Jack finally said, breaking the silence, "Oh, look at that, our useless argument made Aika finally wake up."

Charles just punched his shoulder and said, "Dude," as he gestured toward Bolt, who had broken out into tears, then run over to me a moment later and hugged me tight.

As he did, he cried into my shirt and softly said, "Oh, thank goodness you're awake."

When I saw his reaction to me waking up, I hugged him back, then immediately asked the other two, "Oh dear, how long was I out for?"

Charles and Jack looked back at each other for a second, then Jack said back to me, hesitating a bit, "Almost... three days."

In shock, I questioned, "What? Three days? But why did I—" I remembered how messed up I got from the fight, and I remembered that I forgot to tell Bolt something very important relating to why this happened to me. So I hugged Bolt back a bit tighter and asked, "So what exactly happened to me? I can barely move—like my entire body is wrapped up, and all I feel is pain throughout my entire body."

Charles told me, "Well, Bolt was the first one to find you, and when he did, he kinda... saw you collapsed on the ground... covered in your own blood… and you looked like you got into a fistfight with a devil, covered in scratches and bruises. Surprisingly no burns though. I thought your clothes would get at least a bit damaged from all the fire, but no."

"Well, most of my clothes are fireproof," I replied.

"Really, why?" he asked.

"Uh well…" I said as flashbacks from me covered in fire getting beat up from the Mutant also covered in fire ran through my head. "Uh, I have my reasons," I told him.

"Uh, okay, well anyways, Bolt ran up to you… you were unconscious.

Then he carried you here in a panic. After a while of waiting, we were told that they stitched up your back because it had a horrible Dragonborn scratch across it. Your upper right calf got stitches from getting sliced by that monster's sword. You were also covered in bruises and scratches all over your body like you fell off a cliff. Finally you had fallen into a coma-like state from the events that happened to you. No one had any idea how long you were going to be like that for. So that's why Bolt was very worried about you and—"

Jack cut off Charles and said, "Very worried? Now that's an understatement! Bolt hasn't slept in days, and he's barely spoken a word at all. Hell, he's had Aika's sword equipped on him the entire time to keep it safe."

Bolt, embarrassed, let go of me and shouted back at Jack, "Hey, come on, dude, don't say all of that! Well, at least not in front of Aika."

"You were that worried about me?" I asked.

Bolt immediately turned back to me and replied, "Of course I was that worried about you, you're my girlfriend!" He sat in a chair beside me next to the bed and sighed, looking a bit embarrassed by Jack.

"Hey, what happened to Clay? Is he okay after what happened?" I asked.

Bolt explained, "Oh, don't worry, he's okay. Some other Slayers brought him to this same place to make sure he was okay after breathing in all that smoke. They did a few tests, and they said he was fine. But of course his house was gone, so I told him he could stay at our place for now until we figure out what to do."

"That's good, I'm just glad he's all right and not messed up like me," I told him.

Bolt said, "He actually came to visit you the first chance he got. He wanted me to tell you when you woke up that he was super grateful for you saving him like that, and if you hadn't done that, he probably would have died in that fire. Then he said a bunch more thank-yous and such," he explained.

"Oh thank goodness he's okay." I said relived. Then with all of that settled, I asked, "So give me the basics on what happened with the Slayers while I was out."

"What do you last remember?" Charles asked.

I was silent for a minute, thinking of what to say. I had no idea what to tell them. I culdn't just say, "Oh yeah, the last thing I remembered was saving everyone's ass from the Mutant, but all the Slayers started chasing after me calling me a devil while trying to kill me because I'm a Dragonborn." So I made up the most believable story I could think of on the spot.

"Well, the last thing that I remember was... uhh… I was running down a path, and the Mutant set off an explosion, blinding you guys. Then me and that thing were alone. So I set off some smoke bombs to blind them, and they scratched my back while I was running away. Then I ran into some empty area then… I passed out, I think?" I explained.

"You don't remember how you got all beat up like this?" Charles asked.

I paused and looked over at Bolt, then back to them and said, "Nope! No idea!"

"Did you see any other devils besides the mutated one?" Charles asked.

So in the most convincing way I could, I asked, definitely confused, "Whaat... of course not! If there were, they probably appeared after I passed out. Why, what happened?"

Jack's eyes lit up with excitement, and he said, "Aika, you're not going to believe this! So after we all saw the Mutant looking for you, it turned to attack us! And when it did attack, some random mysterious blue-scaled Dragonborn came from nowhere and protected us! No Dragonborn had ever protected Dragon Slayers before. It was the most historic moment I've ever watched! And there is a rumor going around the entire kingdom that this Dragonborn is most likely one of our people. The Slayers have been going crazy having meetings every day since that night," he explained.

So I asked, "What do the Slayers want to do with this Dragonborn? It kinda sounds like it saved you guys."

Jack said, "Oh the commander wants us to find this Dragonborn and kill it. In his words, 'WE SHOULD BE ASHAMED OF OURSELVES

THAT WE ALLOWED A DRAGONBORN TO PROTECT US FROM ANOTHER! WE SHOULD FIND IT AND SHOW IT THE POWER OF US SLAYERS AND TAKE IT DOWN!'" Jack shouted as he impersonated Zane. Then said back in his regular voice, "Personally, I just want to watch them fight again because when they did fight, they beat that Mutant so hard it flew away limping. Also they kept their element hidden, and you know I want to see what kind it is," he said as he started to ponder.

"What do the other Slayers say about this?" I asked.

Jack snapped back to reality and said, "Oh, most people want to kill them like Zane. But some want to leave it alone because they have no idea how powerful they are. And others think we should let them be, because it saved us and it is the least we can do to thank them, they say."

Charles said after him, "Well, I say we should kill them! No devil should protect us from other devils! That's just weird to me."

Jack said, "You know what surprised me, though, yesterday during the meeting, Niki said out loud in front of everyone that we shouldn't kill the Dragonborn and should leave them alone. I thought they would have wanted to join the kill train like most people," he explained.

"Well, they probably want to study this Dragonborn, most likely," I told him.

Jack said, "You know what, you're probably right about. See, this is the chaos that happens when you're not here, Aika."

Charles said, "Hey, speaking of meetings, we should probably be heading out soon to one."

Jack sighed and complained to him, "Do we really need to go? All of these damn meetings have been pointless. All anyone ever does is argue with one another."

Charles said, "Oh come on, we're already late and we need to tell them Aika woke up. Anyways, we should give Bolt and Aika some privacy," he said as he dragged Jack away.

"No, don't take me to that place! Aika, save me!" Jack shouted out as he was dragged off.

"Have fun!" I said cheerfully as I smirked at him.

Before Charles went out the door, he said back to us, "Don't worry, Bolt, we'll tell them you're with Aika. Also, of course, see you later, Aika! We'll come by again in a little bit. Until then, rest up."

Then he dragged Jack with him out the door. While Jack was dragged away, he waved bye back to us sadly, then the door closed, leaving us alone.

Bolt sighed, then turned to me and said, "You're so lucky that everyone here is an idiot."

"Oh please, why else do you think I stayed here?" I said back.

Bolt asked, "So, Miss 'Mysterious Blue Dragonborn,' care to explain the chaos you caused?" as he leaned in closer near me.

I replied, "Oh yes, it's about time I explained. So remember how I got that terrible chill in the morning and how I felt uneasy during the entire day?" I asked.

"Of course," he said.

"Well, the reason I did was because I felt the presence of that Mutated Dragonborn flying around all day. Later on that night, I got another chill from when it dropped down, and that's when I saw the smoke in the air," I told him.

"What happened during that fight? I had never seen you that scared in my life when I saw you run out of the house," he asked.

So I told him, "When I found Clay and told him to run out, I had no idea what to expect. I thought this fella was just going to be this regular War Dragonborn. So when I did find them... I ran my ass away because as they walked toward me, they tilted their head at me, then proceeded to run toward me at full speed. You guys saw what happened to me when I ran outside. But what really happened when I threw those smoke bombs was I just ran away and climbed up a nearby building to summon my armor form safely. You saw me save all of you, then of course saw me get my face bashed by them. Then I ran away from the Slayers and collapsed in a nearby area. And that's about it," I explained briefly.

"It's crazy to think about how strong that Dragonborn was. It all makes sense though on how you were able to sense its presence from miles up in the sky. No wonder why it knocked you out for so long," Bolt said.

"So about that... just hear me out for a minute," I told him.

"Aika, what did you not tell me?" he asked as he stared at me with a blank face.

"So I passed out unconscious from the fight, but I fell into a small coma for a different reason."

"What?" Bolt asked, confused.

"Yeah, so, let me explain. So sometimes when a Dragonborn overuses their power too much, sometimes we can fall into a two- to five-day coma for no reason," I explained in a casual tone.

"And you forgot to tell me something this important?" Bolt asked.

"Oh, come on, Bolt, you know me by now," I replied.

"Of course you forgot to tell me something this important," Bolt said.

"Yep, of course I forgot to tell you," I told him.

Bolt sighed and asked himself, "Why am I surprised by this?"

I asked him, "Hey, what happened to all my stuff? I can see that you have my sword equipped on your back, but what happened to my other things, such as my jacket, for example?"

Bolt said, "Oh right!" as he reached into his hand bag and pulled out my jacket. "It was thrown on the ground and got all filthy, so I washed it and kept it in my bag so I could give it back to you when you woke up. Here!" he said as he handed it to me, then said, "Your boots are at home—I'll bring them here for you when you get discharged. Your shirt and pants got torn a bit from the scratches and stained with blood. Finally your gloves were practically destroyed from you… well… from the fire and punching the Mutant… repeatedly. Let's just say it was a good thing the gloves were only your armored work ones, so your casual pair are still fine at home."

I put on my jacket and asked, "So what other crazy stuff happened during the meeting while I was out?"

Bolt made an exhausted expression and said, "Oh, where do I begin?" He proceeded to tell me all kinds of crazy stories of what people were saying around town about the situation and how the Slayers were handling it.

Bolt and I ended up talking for a while after, until visiting hours were closed and he got kicked out. Charles and Jack got caught up in the meetings, so they never showed back up that day. But they came the next day and told me what happened. Then a day and a half later I got out of the hospital after proving to the doctors that yes, I was fine after waking up from an "unknown" coma, and I finally got to go home.

When Bolt opened the door to the house, Clay immediately came over to me as we walked in and hugged me tight and said, "Oh, Aika, it's so good to see you up and moving. You gave me such a scare when I saw you that night."

"It feels good to be back, Clay," I said as I returned his hug.

Bolt told me, "You can sit down on the couch and relax. I'll start up some coffee for you." Then he walked over into the kitchen and started preparing mugs.

So as we sat down, I asked Clay, "How has it been staying here? It's a lot smaller and has a whole lot less stuff than you're used to."

He explained, "Don't worry too much about it. Some of the Slayers helped me go through the rubble, and we found a few swords that still looked good enough to sell. Then tons of clients I've worked with in the past have donated some money, so I should be good on my own in about two months if you'll let me stay here."

I told him, "It's no problem—you're family with Bolt, and I could never repay you for what you did for me back then, so stay for as long as you need."

Bolt brought over the coffee he'd made and placed a mug down for each of us. "All right, everything should be good. Do you guys need anything else?" he asked.

"Hmm, I think you should just bring the entire pot over," I told him.

"You already drank half of it, didn't you?" he asked.

"Yep," I replied as I took another big sip.

"I still don't know why I ask these things," Bolt said as he walked over and grabbed the pot.

"So how long do you have until you need to go back to work?" Clay asked.

"They gave me about two weeks to heal up. By then I should be almost fully healed, and all my stitches should be good to go," I told him.

Then someone knocked on the front door.

"I swear if that's Charles and Jack telling me to go to a meeting, I'm going to lose it," I said as Bolt walked over to answer it.

As he opened the door, Charles and Jack cheerfully smiled at Bolt and said to him, "Hey Bolton, so everyone keeps yelling at us to bring you to the meetings… and they are now threatening us to bring Aika."

"You'll have to drag me out of here if you want me in those meetings! I haven't even slept in my own bed yet since everything happened!" I hollered at them.

Jack asked, "So Bolt, how bad are her stitches? Do you think it will hurt if we drag her out?"

Bolt said, "You don't need to drag her out. I know what to do." He turned around to me and threatened, "I will make Jack pour this coffee outside on the ground if you don't get ready to go."

"You wouldn't dare!" I replied.

"Jack," Bolt said, turning to him, "would you be a pal and dump a cup of this out?" he asked.

"You monster!" I yelled at him.

"You leave me no choice: it's the coffee or an hour of your life in which you tell people stuff that they already know," he told me.

"Damn, that's a hard decision… how long do I have to think about it?" I asked.

"This long," Bolt said as he handed Jack the pot.

I stood up, grabbed my sword, then told him, "All right, ready to go!"

"Wow, you really know how to threaten her," Jack commented to Bolt.

"Coffee is the only thing that will make that one get out of bed," he told him.

"See ya, Clay," I said as I walked over to the gang.

"Take care, you lot," Clay said to us before the door shut.

Charles asked me when I got outside, "What's with this look?" as he pointed to me having my sword equipped to my side with my two upper belts missing.

"Welp, my back is a bit messed up still, so I got this setup for now until it heals up more. It's only until I get my stitches out. What are you guys going to be up to this week since we all got time off?" I asked.

Charles replied, "I'm going to visit all the best bars around and find out which one has the best grub!"

Jack replied, "I just want to sleep and think about all the cool things I learned recently about Dragonborns. Are you two doing anything fun?" he asked Bolt and me.

"I'm definitely just going to lie in bed all day and munch on protein bits," I answered.

"Classic Aika move. How about you, Bolt?" Jack asked.

"Relax and make sure that one doesn't do anything stupid," Bolt said as he looked at me.

"Hey, how stupid can I act when I can't jump off a roof?" I asked.

"Exactly my point," Bolt said to the other two, which made Jack laugh.

"Oh, what? I just said I can't," I asked, confused.

We continued talking about more things we'd do over our break until we reached the main base and headed inside the meeting area. When I walked in, everyone looked over to me and gossiped about all sorts of things about me as I sat down in a chair with my name labeled. The meeting room had a whole lot of chairs set up in a circle that cut off at the wall. Within the middle of the wall there was a big black board with a… chalk drawing of my armor form… but with tiny limbs, a big head, and armor plates that were very tiny.

"What is that?" I asked to make sure.

"You," Niki answered.

"I…" I said, then suddenly stopped as I realized I couldn't say anything because of the story I made up. "What do you mean?" I asked.

"Oh, you're playing this stupid game… I see. I can't tell if you're just acting like an idiot or you are just an idiot," she said as she took out her notebook, and Jack laughed at me as he sat down in his seat.

"Ugh, I already want to jump out a window," I said to Bolt.

"Good luck with that. There is none here," he told me as he sat down.

"That there is supposed to be the Blue Dragonborn that everyone saw," Bolt told me.

"It's insulting to look at," I whispered to him.

"Don't worry, it gets worse," he whispered back.

"What?" I asked out loud.

As everyone sat, Zane stood before everyone and said, "Listen up, everyone! As you can see beside me, the War Slayer is finally awake. So now she's going to tell everyone what she saw," he said as he dumped all the attention on me.

"Wow, wow, what?" I asked.

"Yeah, Aika, tell everyone what happened," Jack told me playfully. I saw Niki stare right at me, smiling, as she grabbed out her notebook and pen.

So I told everyone, "Uh yes… what happened to me was… uh—" Having no idea what to say to them, I told them the same story I told Charles, which he'd already told them. And after I finished talking, I looked at everyone, and they just stared at me, extremely scared.

All Zane said to me after was, "Is that it? Anything else at all after?" all disappointed like.

So I immediately asked my squad, "Why does everyone look terrified?"

"Oh, you'll see," Charles told me as he pointed at Niki laughing to herself.

"Oh no, what's happening?" I asked.

Zane said to everyone, "So because Aika… our last hope… failed us, I'm afraid to say this, but…" Then he paused for a moment before saying, "Niki, you're allowed to investigate this case to find the Blue Dragonborn."

"YES!" Niki yelled out, standing from her seat.

"But on one condition!" Zane blurted out. "You need to… have Jack help you!"

"WHAT, NO!" Jack screamed as he stood up from his seat.

"Jack also has very good knowledge in Dragonborns… plus I need someone to accompany you. None of us trust you enough without someone else agreeing with your facts," Zane said.

Niki laughed and looked over at Jack and said, "Oh, no worries! I've been wanting to explain something to Jack for a while now."

"Commander, please don't make me work with her!" Jack begged.

"I'm sorry, Jack, but you're the only one smart enough to understand the things she says. Also you worked with her during your training, how bad could it be?" he said to him.

Jack looked over at Niki, and all she did was wave to him, and he back said to us "Friends, remember who I was before this. Because after I work with her, I'll never be the same."

Niki said, "Come on, Jack, let's get moving! I got a fresh new board to build up about this case!" And he was then dragged by Niki to work as Jack stared back at us. He looked terrified of what he'd be forced to do. All I could feel was pity for him as I watched from a distance. Jack yelled for us to help him, but none of us moved an inch, and we all watched him get dragged down the halls of the main base.

About a week passed, and the rumor of this Blue Dragonborn had spread to everyone. Almost every person I walked past was talking about it. The story of what really happened had gotten all messed up by people saying "It saved the Mutant" to "They tried to kill the Slayers." Almost no one knew what the truth was anymore. There were also a bunch of lovely rumors about me. The rumors were as crazy as the Dragonborn ones, such as "I thought she died in that battle" and "Didn't she get burned to a crisp?" It just amazed me when I first heard someone call me a zombie because they thought I'd died. I may or may not have laughed in their face until I couldn't breathe and had to cling on Bolt to stand properly from laughing too much. But while this was all happening, there were lots of reports and such being made from Niki and Jack. As much as they did hate each other, they did work scary well together, making rocket progress on searching. Which was kinda terrifying.

But after five days, all progress unexpectedly just stopped, and no one knew why. Neither of them talked about why they'd stopped as well.

But the good side of what happened to me, Bolt, Charles, and I got to have our free mini vacation until I was healed up enough to work again. So after I got all my stitches out a few days after the meeting, we all decided to hang out at that new bar Charles had told us about to celebrate me not dying and to help cheer up Jack after an exhausting day of working with Niki. We all decided to be there by eight. The bar we went to was a big one with lots of people around. The place had a giant bar area with mixing beverages across the entire back of the wall with big tables all in front of it with a stage to the side for people to sing and play music on for everyone to hear.

Eight fifteen, *we were all at the bar waiting for Jack.*

"So how's you back doing, Aika?" Charles asked me.

"Doing good—the doctors were astonished to see it healed enough to remove the stitches from it. They were only going to remove the ones in my leg, but as you can see from me wearing my sword on my back again, they also took them out," I explained.

"Nice," he said.

I asked him, "...So, want to see my new scars?"

"That's the first thing you ask?" Bolt asked me.

"Hey now, I got a killer story to tell with this one. The other ones I have are just from a traumatic experience or from me being stupid in military school," I told him.

"The new scars you got are from a traumatic experience!" he told me.

"Hey, at least you guys were here for that traumatic experience. The other ones are from my mysterious past I never explain," I replied.

"At least you admit that you never explain it," Charles said.

"I… you know, forget it," Bolt said as he sipped his water.

Eight thirty, *still no sign of Jack anywhere.*

"I think I might get this one," I said, pointing to the strongest drink on the menu.

"You are going to get the 'Infinitan Death Destroyer,' are you sure?" Bolt asked me.

"Positive," I replied.

"That is the strongest drink on the menu," Bolt told me.

"Exactly why I want this one," I replied again.

"Oh, I have to get something light so I can remember this night!" Charles said excitedly.

"Goodness, why?" Bolt asked himself as he put aside his menu.

"What are you having?" I asked.

"I'm having water so I can make sure you don't kill yourself or anybody else!" he told me.

"I'm not that horrible drunk," I told him.

"Oh really?" Bolt asked.

Charles told me, "The last time you were drunk, you started a bar fight, and it ended in three people almost dying."

"Hmm, don't remember that," I replied.

"That's because you got blackout drunk that night before all the fighting ended," Bolt told me.

"Oh, that would explain it then," I said, "Wait, how did I start that fight?" I asked.

Charles told me, "Some guy bumped into you and acted like a creep and told you 'Move aside, lass, or unless you want to come with me to my place tonight?' Then you punched them in the face… and threatened to pull out your sword. When the guy's friends came over, you punched them, and when one of the guys tried to punch you back… you dodged them and they punched another person's face and their group joined in… then more people joined in. Then while that was all happening, you sat back next to Bolt and blacked out drunk after you took yet another shot."

"Really, I did all of that?" I asked.

"You sure did," Bolt said, sounding disappointed.

"Uh… how did I get home that night?" I asked.

"I carried you on my back. When you woke up the next morning, you asked what happened. I told you this entire story, and you immediately proceeded to forget about everything that I told you and behold this conversation," Bolt told me.

"How long ago was all this?" I asked them, a bit worried.

"About a month ago in the bar we got banned from," Charles replied.

"Wait, am I the reason why we get banned from so many bars?" I asked in a sudden realization.

Bolt looked right at me and replied "Yes," then took a sip of water.

Nine, *still no Jack.*

"Guys, I think Jack died," I told the others.

"Aika, Jack is not dead. He's probably just late because of Niki," Bolt explained.

"Bolton… since when has Jack ever been late to meet up at a bar to get wasted?" I asked him with my most serious tone.

Bolt went silent and looked like he went into deep thought about the question, until he said, "Oh my goodness, he's never been late in his life. He's always been at least a half an hour early to the bar."

"Exactly my point," I told him.

Charles asked us, "Hey doesn't it seem weirdly quiet?"

Then it hit me. "Yeah, you're right, it is! Usually there would have been a bar fight by now with Jack and the bartender!" I told him.

"Hey, I don't start all the fights! It's only with the bartender. She's the one who fights with everyone else!" a voice said behind us.

We turned around and saw Jack moping to the corner. He collapsed in the empty seat next to me and muttered, "Someone get me the strongest drink here."

"Long day?" I asked.

"Oh, you guys don't know the half of it. I think I was arguing with Niki for… at least eight hours today?" he said, unsure of himself.

After we got our drinks, Jack chugged his the moment he held it. When he put his beer down, he sighed and looked over at me.

"What's wrong?" I asked.

"Oh, it's nothing much… I'm just thinking about the stuff Niki said to me earlier about you," he replied.

"Oh geez, what did she say about me this time?" I asked.

"Well, know how we were gathering suspects on who could be the Blue Dragonborn. Well, we investigated all of the people that were on that list, and they were all innocent. But there's one person left on the list. And take a wild guess who that is," Jack said.

"Me," I answered with no hesitation.

"Yep, and me and her have been fighting about it for the past… two days I think," he said.

"Well, you're finally away from her. Have a couple of drinks and have a good time. We have all been through a lot within the past few days. I've been called a zombie every time I leave the house, Bolt is recovering from sleep deprivation from when I was badly messed up, and Charles has been… you know what, I don't think anything has happened to him. He's been the exact same," I told him.

Jack laughed and told me, "Charles never worries about anything. He just goes with the flow, probably because of how stupid he is."

I said back, "Yeah, that sounds about right. Oh yeah, I got a question!"

"What's up?" he asked.

"What were you and Charles arguing about when I first woke up from that coma? I couldn't recognize a word in my awakened daze. All I heard was muffled yelling, then Bolt yelling at you two to keep it down."

"Oh, it was just a pointless argument about what happened during the events of the chaos. Then some of it was about how I didn't chase after the Blue Dragonborn when they tried to run away," he told me.

"You didn't chase after them?" I asked, confused.

"There was no point in attacking them—they saved us, after all. Who knows what could have happened if they didn't show up. Anyways, Bolt had a face of horror watching the two Dragonborns fight, so I stood by him the entire time to make sure he was okay. Though I wonder why he was so scared watching them fight," Jack explained.

"Oh, I know why he was, but that doesn't really matter now. Let's just get drunk and party until we black out!" I told him.

That night we all had a good time. Jack and I got wasted at the bar, Charles was just normally drunk, and Bolt stayed sober to make sure none of us would start a fight. The next day I woke up on the couch with the worst hangover and could not remember anything after that conversation with Jack.

When I asked Bolt what happened that night, he just said, "Well, let's just say… the stupidity of how you act wasted will be forever engraved into my brain."

"Oh geez, what did I do?" I asked.

"Well, you didn't start any bar fights and do anything to reveal yourself, at least. What I will tell you is that you were singing beautiful gibberish to everyone in Dragonborn mixed with Infinitan, so no one had a clue on anything you were saying for most of the night. Also you forgot how to walk properly at the end of the night, so I had to carry you home from the bar."

"I was so drunk that I forgot how to walk?" I asked, confused.

"Yeah, and while I was carrying you back home, you were only speaking in Dragonborn whispering something to me, with your arms wrapped around my neck with your head leaning against mine as I carried you on my back," Bolt told me.

"Did… did I do anything else to you?" I asked, a bit nervous.

"What, oh no, don't worry about that. As soon as we got home, you blacked out drunk on the couch. You were acting like such a goon last night, I left you there as punishment," Bolt replied.

"Oh uh, all right then," I replied, not knowing what to think.

The day after my hangover, Jack's fight with Niki would finally end… after she dragged me into it, of course. It was a bright and sunny day, and everyone was out and about doing their afternoon tasks. I was just peacefully taking a walk, minding my own business. But this was all soon to be over when I spotted Niki speed-walking toward me. Knowing she was probably going to chase me, I stopped and waited for her. When she approached me, without a word she suddenly started dragging me off to where she'd walked from.

"Hey, what the hell? I thought you were just going to talk!" I shouted at her.

"Shut up. I need to prove something to Jack. If I could make you admit this, there's no way I would be wrong," she said. She dragged me off all the way back to her study.

When we got there, the place was a mess: papers and notebooks were open and spread out everywhere with all sorts of different boards out. Some boards were about different random theories, and others were about random stuff on how they would fix the government. As I was dragged down the hallway, I hit my shoulder on a shelf, and a clutter of notebooks fell to the floor.

I said, "Uh, that just—"

"Don't bother picking those up, the whole place is a mess right now," Niki cut me off.

We entered the living room, which was an even bigger mess with boards out everywhere that she'd made about Dragonborns and different people who could be them. The only real piece of furniture in the room was a matching brown leather couch and chair with a wooden coffee table in front that was also cluttered with notebooks. She pushed me in front of Jack and shouted,

"Look, idiot, she has to be a Dragonborn! We have gone through every single possible suspect there could be. And trust me, I've been keeping notes on everybody who could be a Dragonborn, and she's the only one left that we have not talked about. I know she's a Dragonborn, Jack!"

Jack, angered, yelled back at her, "The hell, Niki, why drag her over here!" Then he sighed and said to me, "I'm sorry about all of this."

In confusion, I asked him, "Jack what the hell is going on?"

Jack sighed and explained, "Well, Niki here won't stop the investigation about who the Dragonborn is. Even though we went through all the suspects. She absolutely thinks that you're a Dragonborn and won't stop yelling at me about it!" he said as he shouted the last sentence out at Niki, who was just glaring back at him.

Until she politely asked, "You really think Aika here is not a Dragonborn?"

"She's not a Dragonborn! I've known her for years, Niki!" Jack hollered at her.

Niki, who was done with Jack, just said, "Okay, let me explain how she's a Dragonborn. I'll give you every little detail on how, and when I'm done, Aika here better be able to counter all of my evidence. And if she can't, I'm going to fucking snap if she doesn't admit that she is one. Does that sound okay?" she asked in the most threatening way.

"Oh, please tell me, how is she a Dragonborn?" Jack asked, sarcastically.

"Jack, this is not a good idea," I whispered to him.

But before he could respond, Niki began her rant and yelled out, "Let me explain how she is a Dragonborn. Where should I start? Oh I know, first of all, she wears gloves all the time! I've asked all the Slayers if they had ever seen her without them. And of course no one has. Second piece of evidence! She owns a Dragonborn sword! It's even tinted blue like the Dragonborn we're looking for! Also, she only uses that sword in battle. Yeah, she's good with a Slayer sword, but have you seen her using that sword? Slayer swords were meant to counter Dragonborn swords, yet she still knocks everybody's sword away like it's nothing. She's amazing at using it! She's better at using it than the veteran pros who work for the king! These people were the best of the best! Your friend Charles's dad was one of these soldiers that served the king—you know who they are, the royal guard. It's common sense around here! Then my biggest piece of evidence is how she interacts with Dragonborns. Jack, we both know that different Dragonborns have a history with each other. You can clearly see the hatred in her eyes as she fights others! Look at what happened during the Photo Incident! She crashed a Dragonborn from the SKY! She single-handedly brought down that Dragonborn with only her hands! Also when she fights these Dragonborns, don't they look a bit scared when they fight her? Remember that Ice Dragonborn who attacked us at training? Aika froze up staring into its eyes; she couldn't hear a thing we were shouting out at her. While she was, that War Dragonborn looked a little frightened, didn't it? Hell, I bet she was too busy fighting her head to hear us! That's probably the only reason why she got messed up like that because she was too stuck in her head. That Wind Dragonborn was the same! They tried to run away from her when she chased after it. That's another piece of evidence for when she fights other Dragonborns—that she chased a War Dragonborn! finally my last important piece of evidence! I know Aika can sense the presence of Dragonborns! Whenever there's a Dragonborn around, she always looks up in the sky before it even appears! Remember before that Ice Dragonborn appeared? She freaked out about a Dragonborn, then one magically appeared! It was almost the same as the Wind Dragonborn! She froze in the middle of an argument and looked around in the sky. But Vanessa distracted her, and she snapped back to it, but then one appeared! Do you want more evidence, or is this enough? I mean, I can just talk about her personality alone, and I'll still have plenty of evidence! For example, no one knows her past? Maybe Bolton, but that's it. I know you don't know everything! And the story I love most is how she got attacked by a Dragonborn. How? How can a young kid survive an attack from them? Were they merciful? Probably not! Have you seen the scars on her arms? They're horrible! In fact, witnesses say that the Blue Dragonborn had very identical scars to the ones she has on their forearm plates. What a coincidence. Oh, also, while I'm going off about her scars, I'll add this in as well! Remember that photo of her and her parents? Well, in that picture of them, you can see that Aika has her sword equipped! And for all the information that I can gather, I can assume that she was fourteen in that photo, and you all met when she was fourteen. So this sword either has to be her own personal sword, or she had to be attacked at an even earlier age for her to have it! Oh, also, her dad has the same exact-looking sword, so I can take a good guess that it is her own sword. I have so much evidence.

Do you want me to continue? Her first language is something that none of us know! But I can take a good guess that its Dragonborn, though. Also witnesses say that the Blue Dragonborn's plate curved slightly out on their chest, so the sex of the Dragonborn is probably female, and who would have guessed Aika has tits, so that's even more evidence for your dense skull. Do you still think that she's not a Dragonborn? Tell me, Jack, do you? And Aika, can you counter my evidence? Please, tell me: I would love to hear your feedback!"

Jack and I were speechless. Everything she said was completely true. I had nothing… nothing at all to say back. I looked over at Jack, and he was clenching his fists, looking down at the ground.

"Jack, you really don't believe in any of this. Do you?" I asked.

"I don't know who to believe anymore," he said.

I was backed into a corner. Niki looked at me as if she had finally won the war between all of the fights we'd had. With Jack finally suspicious of me, I decided that I couldn't lie anymore. There was way too much evidence to escape clean. So I finally admitted it.

"Congratulations, Niki. You are officially the only person to have ever realized that I'm a Dragonborn," I told her.

Jack looked at me silently, not knowing what to say, but Niki stepped back. With eyes full of joy, she shouted out, "YES! Finally after all this time. I… I was right! Everyone would call me crazy and insane, they would never believe me! But finally! Finally I was told I was right! Oh, Aika, I don't blame you for always denying it. If everyone actually did believe me… well, you'd probably be dead. I'm sorry about that," she said to me all cheerfully.

"You're not going to tell anybody about this, right, Niki?" I asked, scared.

"Oh, don't worry, Aika! I won't tell a soul. I want people to say out loud, 'Holy shit! You were right, Niki' for when you do get revealed. That's all I've ever wanted," she said to me.

"How reassuring of you," I said back. I looked over back at Jack, who was still in his head. "Jack, are you doing okay?" I asked.

He looked up at me and said, "I think I knew you were one all along. I think I buried the truth of it in my head after that day," he said.

"What day?" I asked.

"Oh, that doesn't matter right now. To be honest, no normal person could tell you were. I know everyone here thinks that Dragonborns are like… unhuman. But it's just hard for me to process because… well, I've known you for years. It makes me think about what others would think," he said.

"Well, actually, Bolt already knows about me," I told him.

"When did he find out?" Jack asked.

"Not a super long time ago, only when he confessed to me a year ago. Your reaction is quite similar to his."

Then Jack realized, "That's why Bolt was a mess when you appeared in your armor form! Oh geez, that explains why you were so beat up as well!"

Niki asked me, "Hey, Aika, what's it like to be called a devil every day?"

"You get numb to it after a while," I told her.

"Cool… okay, next question, what's your element?" she asked.

"I'm also curious about that. What is your element? There was no sign of it from the battle at all," Jack said.

"Well, you know my aura is blue. That's your hint," I said to them.

"Oh, you won't tell us!" She laughed a little to herself and ran off.

"Hey, Aika, what are we going to tell the commander? If we show him nothing from our work, he's going to be pissed," Jack asked.

"I don't know," I told him. Then I noticed Niki in the background putting together a board about my powers with red string and thumbtacks holding up thoughts and such about what power I might have. "How about that?" I asked as I pointed toward the board.

Jack looked at the board, then said, "Yeah, that'll work. Most of them are idiots up there. They probably accept this."

"Oh, they better!" Niki shouted, looking for more stuff in her closet. Then she came out and dropped a box on the ground filled with all sorts of tools and asked, "So let's get on with all the questions I've been preparing… shall we?" she asked.

"Oh Ultimus," I said to myself.

"So first question… who's Ultimus? I always hear you mutter that name," she asked me.

"Uh, well…" I said, worried as she took out many notebooks filled with questions and smiled.

When I was finally free from Niki, it was about eight at night. I was there at her study for about six hours. When I finally got home, I saw Bolt on the couch waiting for me.

"Where have you been all day?" he asked.

So I plopped down beside him and said, "Bolton… she finally outed me."

"What?" he asked.

"Niki… she finally convinced Jack that I was a Dragonborn," I told him.

"Oh… Does that mean—?"

Before he could finish talking, I said, "She said she won't tell anyone. In fact she can't wait till I get revealed because she wants everyone to praise her or something. But Jack of course won't tell; he's still trying to sort his thoughts out."

"So what's going to happen now?" he asked.

"Don't know," I told him tiredly as I laid my head in his lap.

Bolt sighed and said, "Come on, let's go to bed," then he dragged me half-asleep to our room.

Jack and Niki kept my identity a secret and showed Zane the board of what my powers could be. He accepted the information and put the search temporarily on hold for now. Three days later everyone went back to their regular jobs, including me. But the search for the "Mysterious Blue Dragonborn" was not over yet.

Chapter 11: What Is a God? (Jack's Origin)

One time when I was a kid, about ten or so, my dad brought me to an open field in view of the mountains west and south of our village, and told me about how powerful the Dragonborn gods were. After he was done talking, I asked,

"Hey Dad, what is a god?" He looked at me, confused by my question, so I explained what I meant. "Like, what defines a god, Dad? Is it their power? Their guidance? Their appearance? Or all of those things?"

All he said back to me was "We are not allowed to question the gods, William."

I was born into one of those super religious groups who worship Dragonborns as gods and went to church every day to pray to them. My village was one of five villages that resided north of the mountain range that protected us from the Dragonborn Lands just west of the mountains. I used to always walk to the beach everyday just a little north of my village. From there I could see how big the mountain range was, and to the east of me I could see the kingdom of Amarabliss just a half day's walk away from afar near the coast past all the other religious villages.

The basic rules in all the villages were that we always had to be cleaned up and properly dressed with our hair pushed back, we headed to church every day and prayed, and finally we never said anything bad about Dragonborns. If anyone ever broke any of these rules, the punishments varied depending on how badly you broke the rules. But now that I was away from that place, it felt more like a cult than anything. There was a group of high-status people who controlled everything called the council. My dad was one of the lower council people who helped out but was not in charge. They would preach to us about Dragonborns every day at church, about the power and destruction they caused. They told us if we didn't pray to them, that they would come and kill us. But they never did attack us.

I can't remember much from when I was little or what we talked about during church. But I remember waking up early every day trying to learn everything I could about these gods. This was when I first started stealing all sorts of documents about them. I loved Dragonborns. I loved how cool their armor forms were. I loved how powerful they were. I just wanted to learn more about them. One day I asked out of curiosity during a session, "How do Dragonborns use their power?"

Everyone glared at me, horrified, like I'd committed murder. My dad dragged me out of church and knelt down to me and said, "William, we are not allowed to just ask these questions. If you really want to learn more about Dragonborns, then become a member of the council. I have been taught many things about Dragonborns, and I'm not even at the top yet. Now come on, we were just about to start the prayer." He dragged me off back inside like nothing just happened.

I looked nothing like my dad. He was super tall, taller than Charles at six foot five. The only genes I inherited were his height and hair color, but I'm not even that tall. He had brown eyes with square glasses and black pushed-back hair with a black cleaned-up short beard. He always dressed formally in a black suit and loafers, ready for work at all times. My dad was named Harrison Jackson. He was the most well-mannered person you'd ever meet and was a huge stickler for the rules. He hated when I would get in trouble from trying to learn stuff. He knew I was not like other people and wanted to know answers to everything, but he wanted me to learn everything the right way and slowly become one of the council members like him. So he would always tell me the prophecy of our people, which was, "The five Ultimates are the demigods of our world. They share the same blood as our true god the Ultimus, the immortal god who possesses every Dragonborn power and watches all Dragonborns." I had no idea who the Ultimates were. No one would ever explain who they were or what they were; all I knew was that they were some super powerful Dragonborns that had secret unknown powers, unlike normal Dragonborns. There were five different villages that each worshiped one of the five. My village worshiped the Ultimate Blue. But that's all I ever got to learn. No matter what stuff I collected, I could never learn more about them. I was always left wondering, "Why can't I learn about the gods I loved so much?" To me Dragonborns were like the Guardians of Death.

When I was little, I used to always ask my dad if we could visit Amarabliss. I remember I would always start the conversation with, "Hey, Dad, I learned something new about what it's like outside our village!"

He would ask me, "Oh yeah, what did you learn?"

I would tell him about whatever I learned, but one day when I was eleven, he finally explained while doing some paperwork, "William, we aren't welcomed outside our village."

"Why?" I asked.

"People don't like us for our beliefs. They think not of Ultimus," he explained.

"Really? Why don't they believe in Ultimus?" I asked him.

"Most people think Dragonborns are ungodly. In fact, most people think they're the opposites of gods… they call them devils," he told me.

"But what if we don't mention Dragonborns at all and just look around?" I asked him.

"We're still not welcomed, William. None of us are welcomed. That's why we stay here where we belong, safe in our village."

"But most people here are Amarablin. Can't we just blend in?" I asked.

"William"—he stared right at me—"no," he told me firmly, then went back to his work.

For years I was stealing all kinds of documents and notes and the little information we did have about Dragonborns. I knew more information about Dragonborns than everybody besides the council. I had learned how human they really were. I had completely stopped believing that the Ultimates were even real at all when I was twelve. I had so much evidence that Dragonborns weren't gods from our own religion. My only friend I ever had in that place was my friend Spencer. He was the same age as me, and we had known each other since we were seven. Spencer was very Amarablin and had a lot of the basic traits. Amarablins had black, dark-brown, or light-brown hair and light- to dark-brown skin. They were average height as well, and they had blue and green eyes. Spencer had short light-brown pushed-back hair, the light-brown skin tone, and green eyes. We were all forced to dress nice, but whenever he could, he would always try to dress up like a magician with a black suit and shoes he stole from his dad. He would always show me his different magic tricks he knew and would practice them with me. I would always tell him all the different things I would learn about Dragonborns, and he would make a whole bunch of jokes about them as I talked. Spencer and I would always hang out at the beach away from everyone so no one could question us.

One day while hanging out, I asked Spencer, "Hey dude, can you help me out with something?"

"What's up, man?" he replied.

"I really hate my name, William. It just doesn't ring right with me. I need something cooler, but I'm not sure what," I told him.

"Hmm… what about… Jack!" he blurted out.

"Jack?" I asked.

"Yeah like, hey, Jack! Jack of all trades, what are you up to?" he explained.

"Jack?" I pondered.

"Yeah, I look your last name, Jackson, and I shortened it to Jack. You said you want to change your name, so I thought of that for you. What do you think?" he asked me.

"Jack… yeah, I like that. But what about my last name? Jack Jackson sounds a bit dumb," I asked.

"Hmm, …how about Williams!" he said.

"Jack Williams… it sounds sorta like the same but backward," I said.

"You don't like it?" he asked.

I told him, "Oh, no I love it! Knowing my dad, it'll piss him right off, and you're the one who thought of it, so of course it's perfect."

"Well then, Jack, jack of spades. You wanna steal some more documents and cause chaos?" Spencer asked.

"Oh, you know it!" I replied.

Then we went off to disappoint my father. Of course my dad hated the name I told him, but I didn't care. My name was Jack Williams, and nothing was going to change that. William Jackson was the kid who believed Dragonborns were gods. But Jack Williams was the kid who was going to find out the truth about them, no matter what. My dad refused to call me Jack, but I had Spencer who did, which was all that mattered to me. I was almost thirteen when I made that name for myself.

When I was thirteen, though, everything changed. One day my dad's maid found all these documents in my room while cleaning around the house. When I came home that evening, my dad had already seen everything, and he forced me to the church's council. When the high council looked at all the papers I had stolen, they had a face of fear all over, then told my dad, "Get rid of him. He is a threat to our religion. If this information he obtained gets out, it will be chaos for us all. Will you risk everything for a boy who's only gotten into trouble?" My dad gave in to them and disowned me. He dragged me outside of all the religious villages, and before he left, he told me, "Do me a favor, William: if you ever come back to this village, bring the Blue Ultimate with you. Only then will you ever be forgiven for your sins." Then he threw me a silver amulet that had an engraved symbol of the

Electric Element on it. This was an amulet they gave people for when they became part of the head church.

He told me, "They say the Ultimate we worship here has this symbol on their hand. Good luck."

He gave me one last look then sulked away back to the village. I wore that amulet around my neck and looked away from the villages to the path ahead. In the far distance, I saw Amarabliss and the nearby smaller villages that surrounded it and decided to head out there. But before I left, a voice called out to me.

"Jack, wait!"

I looked back and saw Spencer running over to me.

"Oh hey, dude," I said, a little sad.

"Hey, I heard what happened to you. Is… is this it? You're leaving," he asked.

I told him, "Well, if I don't, they'll kill me. So I guess I must. But don't worry, man, I'll come back one day, and when I do, I'll tell you everything about Dragonborns. I swear to Ultimus, we'll meet again, Spencer! And I'll show you what Dragonborns are really like!"

After I told him that, he said, "Well, I'll hold you to that, Jack." Then he hugged me and said, "And when you come back… I'll be the greatest magician in the area… no, the world, even!"

I hugged him tight and said, "Hell yeah, man… you show the world who you are! Become so big that I'll see posters of your shows wherever I end up."

After our little moment, I took a few steps forward and looked back at him and the village behind him. I stepped forward to the start of my new life. I followed the path that led to the closest village.

It took me till past nightfall to reach the nearest village, and with nowhere to go, I stopped by an inn for some help. When I arrived and asked for help, no one offered, and I was left by myself. I sat at a table alone and pondered to myself on what I should do. I knew nothing of the area and how to survive on my own. As I was thinking, I got tapped on the shoulder by some fancy-looking soldier guy with red hair.

"Hey, you doing all right there, kid? You look puzzled."

"Oh, uh… no, I'm not okay, actually. I'm kinda… out of money, and looks don't pay for a room and food around here," I told him.

The guy mumbled, "Yep, it's as I figured."

"Huh?" I said, confused.

The guy said, "You came to the right inn, lad, because I can help you out."

"Really, what can you help me with?" I asked.

The guy pulled out a chair and sat next to me and explained, "The name's Christopher Collins, call me Chris. I saw you earlier asking people for some directions and money, but the people around these parts aren't too nice to outsiders. I can feel the same. I'm Dominari, and I'm wearing a Infinitas royal guard outfit, so I look twice as mysterious to them."

"Infinitas?" I asked.

"Oh yes, I live there with my family. Right now I'm out on a business trip. Today was our last night here, so we decided to rent a room at this inn before we set out on our way. The road home is quite long, even on horse. But where do you come from? You don't look like you're from around these parts," he asked.

"Oh I'm from… Amarabliss. Yeah, I come from near the coast, but my dad threw me out of the house, and now I'm out on my own. My dad is an awful man. I still don't know why he was so harsh to me," I told him with all honesty.

Chris patted me on the back and told me, "I know what it's like to be out on your own a bit. Me and my wife are immigrants from the kingdom of Domitori. We moved to Infinitas because of some… civil problems, let's just say, and for a while it was hard for us until I decided to become a Dragon Slayer because of the pay. My wife owns a restaurant that serves food from our culture. At first it didn't do so well with most people being Infinitan looking at us as outsiders. Kinda like you right now, which is why I wanna help."

I told him, "I'm actually seventy percent Infinitan. I'm thirty percent Amarablin, but the only thing I really have from that is my hazel green eyes. Is that why people look at me differently?" I asked.

"A lot of people look at you differently if you look different, but I choose to ignore them when they talk about me. The only people who I don't care for are Dragonborns… those people are something else, I'll say. Hell, they're the reason why I'm on this hell-forsaken trip to deliver information from the front lines on what's been happening down west," he said, annoyed.

"What's been happening with the Dragonborns?" I asked.

"You haven't heard? Well, can't expect much from your situation right now, so I'll explain. You see, about a few months ago, two of the Dragonborn clans started a war with each other, and it's been quite a struggle making sure none of them harm our land," he explained.

"Which ones?" I asked eagerly.

"It's the Defender and Conquest clan. Those two have always been fighting a bit we've seen, but we never expected another war," he told me.

"Another war? There's been one before?" I asked him another question.

"It's not talked about too much, but back hundreds of years ago when they first appeared, they said all the Dragonborns were at war with each other. And at the end they separated into five different groups based on beliefs they had. That's all I know—I fell asleep during the class. My instructor talked about it during training," he explained.

"Wow! What else do you know about Dragonborns?" I asked him.

"You sure like Dragonborns, kid," he commented.

"Oh I don't just like them, I love them! Dragonborns are the coolest, most powerful, most amazing things I've ever learned about! I wish I could meet one someday," I pondered.

Chris laughed a bit to himself, then said, "Well, maybe you can. Sometimes Dragonborns appear above my kingdom for a split second while flying by. You can come along with me if you like, and I'll introduce you to my family. My wife Carol, my daughter Cloey, and my son Charles. I got a feeling you and Charles will get along great with each other," he offered.

"Really?" I asked excitedly.

"Sure, you don't seem like a bad kid, and I can't just leave you all alone after listening to your story," he told me.

"I… this is amazing, thank you! I can never repay you for your kindness!" I said happily.

"Don't sweat it, kid, though what's your name? You haven't told me yet," he asked as he chuckled at my reaction.

"My name…" I said, then gave him a smile and told him enthusiastically, "The name's Jack Williams, my good sir! And I promise I won't be a nuisance to you!"

"Hehehe, come on, let me introduce you to my squad over there." He pointed to a group of people in similar armor to his.

"Yeah, totally!" I said as I stood up, excited, from my chair.

The next day I joined him and his squad on their wagon all the way down southwest to Infinitas to meet his family. During the way, I completely changed my looks and went from my clean proper look to my casual look today by messing up my hair and getting some new clothes along the way to Infinitas. During the travel on the wagon, I saw the world with my own eyes. It wasn't just the details on a document like hills, plants, people, villages, and so much more than I could have imagined. I even saw a glimpse of Domintori during the ride. The kingdom was huge from afar, and I could see the east coast surrounding the kingdom similar to Amarabliss. After a few days of following the trade paths, we finally arrived at Infinitas, the place with infinite possibilities and the place with some of the most groundbreaking information about Dragonborns, though it felt bittersweet to me for some reason.

Chris looked exactly like today's Charles with his hair, skin, eyes, height, muscles, personality, everything. The only thing that was different about him was his facial hair because he had a full beard, and Charles only had a goatee. He was one of the strongest Slayers that Infinitas ever had. While traveling to Infinitas, he told me all about his stories of his battles against

Dragonborns. I had no idea that people even battled against Dragonborns at the time; everything he told me was like a dream come true. When I got to the house, I finally got to meet the family he told me about. The first person I met was Carol, who, after greeting Chris, happily she turned to greet me while he explained who I was to her.

"My goodness, you've been through a lot, haven't you. It's a pleasure to have you here—come on in," she told me.

She was super caring and polite, an awesome person. She had black hair, hazel eyes, and tan skin, and was tall at five foot eight. The second person I met was Cloey, who ran to Chris at first, then stopped and turned to me and said, "Who's this kid?" with an attitude.

She was a bit immature and liked to cause chaos. She was a year younger than me, Bolt's age. She looked almost exactly like Chris as well, with her having the same hair and eyes as Charles. She was also pretty tall especially for her age, at five foot six. finally I met Charles, who walked over and asked, "Who's this, Dad?"

Chris explained, "This here is Jack. I met him during my trip to Amarabliss. He was in a difficult situation, and I offered to let him stay here for a time."

Charles said, "All right, my name's Charles. Nice to meet you, buddy." He greeted me and put out his hand.

"Buddy… huh. Well, nice to meet you too, mate!" I said to him as I shook his hand and smiled.

 Chris said to Charles, "Jack here really likes Dragonborns if you wanna talk all about them with him for a bit while me and your mother talk."

"Oh yeah, I know all about them, if you like Dragonborns," Charles said to me.

"Oooh, you do!" I replied in excitement.

"Wow, you really do like them! I think I just saw your eyes light up from the mention of Dragonborns," Charles said to me.

"They do? Eh, anyways, what do you know about Dragonborns?" I asked him, hyped.

"Uh, well, I know that—" Charles told me some of the information he knew about Dragonborns, and we ended up talking for a bit about them, while Cloey watched me suspiciously and Chris and Carol talked for a bit. All four of them were of the Dominari race. Their traits were brown hair with a tint of red, orange, or blond and tannish skin that could be dark or light. They were usually tall people, and they had brown or blue eyes.

Later on at dinner, I made up a story about my dad and why he threw me out of the house, and afterward they kindly let me stay there with them because Chris and Carol knew all about the troubles of finding a place to stay after moving to another kingdom. They even admitted that they were rich and had plenty of space for me to live with them in their house, which was a huge three-story building with all kinds of fancy furnishings. Charles used to be very rich because his father was part of the royal guard, which were paid greatly, and that's how I ended up living with Charles.

That first night I spent there, Charles and I spent the entire night talking about Dragonborns. He told me lots of stories about them that I had never known. He taught me so much. Charles was like an older brother to me that guided me on how things actually worked in the world outside of the village.

About a few months later after I met Charles, we both met Bolton. Charles and I became really good friends with him. We would always hang out and duel each other at our usual sword grounds area or at each other's houses. And they would always let me rant about cool facts that I learned about Dragonborns. It was just us three always hanging out. It was like that for almost two years. Until the Great Dragonborn War Two ended. During the war, a very special individual came out of the shadows to us people. They were a Dragonborn that had powers like no other we had ever seen. All we knew about them was that they had a powerful Electric Element like no other with a strange aura color. They were one of the commanders in the Dragonborn war. But they died at the end of the war alongside their entire army and clan. Hearing about that Dragonborn made me remember what my dad told me and made me wonder if I'd ever be able to meet the Ultimate. About two weeks later after the war ended, Bolt met Aika. When

Bolt first told us about her, he refused to tell us anything about how she had nothing and said, "She'll tell us what happened to her when she's ready." I didn't understand what he meant until much later. During the first two months when we first met each other, Aika was always quiet. She did not open up to us at all, maybe Bolt a little, but she kept to herself a lot. She was very suspicious to me because she said she got attacked by a Dragonborn and seemed to have some sort of PTSD about stuff, yet she knew so much information about Dragonborns and seemed very cool about the topic of them being mentioned. What made her even more suspicious was her military-like outfit and Dragonborn sword. It made me doubt her intentions here in Infinitas. I had no idea what to think of or say about her. But all of that disappeared after she finally started to open up to us after the incident with Charles's family: the moment that changed Charles's life forever, and the incident that made Charles believe Dragonborns were devils.

Around this time Dragonborns were invading our villages and kingdoms. They came from the Dragonborn Lands from the west, from the fields of the great war. Aika was terrified of them; she kept on saying, "I can't let them see me. If they do… it will be all over for this place." None of us had a clue about what she meant, and she barely went outside. So one day when we finally convinced her to go out, we decided to go have dinner at Charles's house and hang out for a bit. Charles's mother was still out at work, so it was only his dad and sister there with us.

While eating dinner we had quite a few conversations, but the only one I remembered was the one Cloey started with Aika.

"Hey, what's with your scars?" Cloey asked rudely to Aika, while pointing to her right wrist.

"What?" Aika asked, quietly.

"I asked, what's with your scars? They kinda look like my dad's scars, plus they look super new," she repeated, being rude to her again.

"Hey, be polite to her!" Chris shouted at her.

"I was just asking her a question, geez," she said back in an attitude.

Aika told her, still quiet, "I got my scars from an attack."

"What kind of attack?" she asked bluntly.

Aika was silent for a moment but then told her, "That's private."

"Uh, whatever. You're no fun anyways," she replied with an attitude toward her still.

"Well, you seem like no fun as well," Aika commented quietly.

"Whatever you say, bitch," Cloey replied to her.

"Wow, where did you learn that language?" Charles asked her.

"Her," Cloey replied as she pointed to Aika, and we all stared at her.

"Ah, shit… ah, I mean! Ah uh, no, what do you mean you learned it from me? I never say language like that, not at all!" Aika said.

"Oh really?" Bolt asked her.

"I know Aika is pretty quiet, but we should tape her mouth shut near Cloey," I suggested.

"That… is not a terrible idea," Charles replied.

"No, guys. We can't tape her mouth shut!" Bolt told us.

"But why?" I asked him.

"No wait, I—" Aika tried to speak, but Charles cut her off and said,

"What if we just had a profanity button and whenever we know she's about to swear in front of her, we can just press it?"

"…I kinda like that idea," Bolt said, thinking.

"No, wait! Please, guys, I'm sorry!" Aika said, speaking at a regular-volume voice.

"Hey, look at that, Cloey—you made Aika finally speak normally," I told her.

"Wha?" Aika said, turning to me.

"Yeah, I did," Cloey said proudly.

When it got darker out, we decided to walk together back to Clay's house. Before we went out, Cloey asked Charles, "Hey, can I walk with you?"

Charles said back, "What, no! You were being rude earlier, and it's way too dark out already."

Cloey just pouted and yelled out, "Meanie! It's because of her!" then pointed at Aika.

"She just doesn't like all the Dragonborn sightings all over so I'll be safer in a group if anything happens," he told her.

"Fine," she replied, then ran away to her room.

"Why does she act like that?" Aika asked Charles.

He just told her, "Oh, she's always like this. Just because we're rich, she thinks she's a princess or something stupid like that. But don't worry; she'll mature soon enough, like you and Bolt."

When we left the house, we were only half way down the road from Charles's house, and Aika suddenly told us, "Something's not right!"

"What's wrong?" Charles asked.

"Somewhere around here… there's a Dragonborn nearby in the sky!" she said, worriedly.

I think Charles was getting aggravated from her saying this kind of stuff constantly for the past week.

So he said, "Oh, come on, there's nothing in the sky. Look up, there's no one here. I know you're scared of them or something, but there is nothing to worry about right now."

Then she said, frightened, "No! There was one nearby flying around. I know there is, trust me!"

Charles looked sick of her acting like this and became a bit of a hypocrite to his own words from earlier and immaturely started a fight, asking her, "Oh yeah, how can we trust you? We have only known you for two months. And how in the world would you know that there's a Dragonborn in the sky? Is this some sort of joke? Because it's getting old real fast! The sky is almost completely black, so how would you see them in the sky?"

Aika said quietly, "You have never seen one before. So you don't know—"

Charles cut her off and said, "Dragonborns are not that strong! My dad has been fighting them constantly recently, and he's always fine! No Dragonborn would ever step into Infinitas. We are the most powerful army in the land."

Aika said, "That doesn't matter to them when they have a mission."

"Mission? Them? Who are 'them' and what do you mean by 'mission'?" Charles shouted at her.

Aika was silent.

"Anyways it's not like we're randomly going to get jumped by a Dragonborn, they freakin' glow in the dark," Charles said.

Aika quietly said, "They don't glow in the dark."

"What?" Charles asked.

Aika explained, "Only their aura glows. And they can somewhat control how much aura is released from them. Because of that… sometimes they can disappear within the dark. I've seen this happen many times. Trust me," she told us, a bit ominous.

Charles scoffed it off and said, "Whatever, you sound like Jack. Anyways, how does someone like you know so much about Dragonborns? It's weird because you're not obsessed like he is, so why?" he pressured her to answer.

Things were getting bad, so I said to Charles, "Hey, dude …how about we just calm down. Okay? She probably has a reason why she knows all this stuff. Just let her tell us when she's ready, like Bolt said to us before. Right?" I asked Bolt at the end.

Bolt had no idea how to respond to any of our fighting. We had always messed around with each other, pushing and mocking each other. But never had a fight like this. All Bolt did was nod back at me.

Charles hollered at us, "No, she's going to tell us right now!" He turned to her and shouted, "Who are you? You tell us nothing about your past! What are you? You don't look like anyone around here—what's your race? How do you know so much about Dragonborns? Why are you staying at Bolton's place, don't you have a family you should be with? How did you get attacked by a Dragonborn? Where do you come fr—"

Before he could finish his last question, we heard an explosion in the sky from somewhere. Suddenly a Dragonborn flew through the air and blasted Charles's house, then disappeared into the night, exactly as Aika described. It all happened so fast it was a blur to watch. The fire spread rapidly and covered the house. The fire was a bright red, clearly from that explosion the Dragonborn made flying by. Aika had immediately drawn her sword and ran to the house and looked to where the Dragonborn flew off to. Charles was speechless and ran toward the house in shock as he watched the fire. Bolt and I followed behind Charles, but it was already too late. All the entrances were unusable, covered in flames. Charles tried to run in and save his dad and sister, but Bolt and I held him back. He kept yelling at us to let him go over and over again, but I kept holding him back with all my strength to stop him. Bolt had no idea what to do and was in tears holding Charles back with me.

I looked over at Aika, who was just staring into the flames, clenching her sword and mumbling to herself, "Damn, I'm a coward."

Other people started to appear soon after they saw the flames. When enough help finally arrived, it was already too late for Charles's dad and sister. They died, burned to death in the flames. Alongside that their house was completely destroyed. Charles watched the entire thing without looking away. His eyes were wide open, and filled with tears as Bolt and I pushed him back as he yelled and tried to run back to the house, but we wouldn't let him. Eventually he stopped struggling and let us drag him back.

While we were all waiting for his mom to arrive, Aika said to him quietly, "I'm sorry I never tell you anything about me. There are some things that I can never tell you about."

Charles replied, "It's okay. I shouldn't have pushed you to tell us. I should have just trusted your judgment. Now look at what happened."

I said to her, "You don't need to tell us everything. I also have secrets about my past I've never told anyone. Everybody has a secret or two hidden deep within their minds."

Carol finally got there and she saw Charles and immediately ran up to him and asked in a panic, "Charles, where's your father and sister?" Charles looked away and didn't answer. Carol went pale and asked, "How… how did this happen?"

Charles stayed silent again, so I told her: "A Dragonborn came from nowhere and blew up the house for no reason."

Carol shouted in confusion and sorrow, "Dragonborn? W-why would one come here! Jack, why would one do this?" she asked me.

"I… I don't know, honestly," I told her.

She dropped to her knees and hugged Charles, crying out, "Dammit! Why! Why did it need to be this house!"

I noticed Aika silently standing in the back watching everyone. "Aika, you okay?" I asked.

"I don't know… it's all too much," Aika said as she gripped the belt across her chest. Bolt was silent throughout most of this. He would watch the house burn, then turn to us, then back to the house, having no idea what to say or do to help.

As soon as Clay heard the news about what happened, he offered to let the three of us stay at his house for the night. All of us couldn't go to sleep after what happened. We all just had coffee and chatted in the living room till the morning came. The only one who had some sort of sleep was Aika, but she woke up yelling from a night terror. The next day Carol and Charles went to talk with some people about where they would live and the money situation, and to discuss things about funerals for Chris and Cloey. I stayed behind because it was more personal family matters with them, so I hung out with Aika and Bolt all day. During the afternoon that day, I saw Aika sitting outside by Clay's forge, holding some sort of picture. Then I saw her stand up and put the photo back into her jacket and walk back inside.

"You doing okay after what we saw?" I asked.

"I could ask you the same. At least I fell asleep for an hour yesterday, unlike everyone else," she replied.

"Yeah, but you were having a nightmare, then woke up yelling. What kind of sleep is that?" I asked.

"My regular sleep," she replied.

"Oh yeah? What was this nightmare about this time? Dragonborns?" I asked.

"It was about what happened to me. Right before I met Bolt," she told me.

"Oh… that doesn't sound too pleasant. Was it because of yesterday?" I asked her nervously.

Aika told me a bit coldly, "Let's just say… it was very similar to what happened to me, but I lost everything, unlike Charles. It kept on happening to me over and over again wherever I went until I arrived here."

I was silent; I had no idea what to say back. That kinda reminded me of how I got here traveling from a far way place. But I knew hers was because of a much bigger situation than mine. To get a better idea on who she was, I asked her, "Hey, can I ask another question? Why do you wear military clothes?"

Aika replied, "Right before all hell went down, my parents sent me off to military school because it was the only safe place away from the attacks. But no matter what, no place I was at the time was safe from them. The only reason why I still wear these rags is because new stuff would be expensive and I have too much pride to ask for money," she admitted.

"Man, and here I was thinking that you were some sort of spy or something. How foolish I am now," I admitted to her.

"Hey, I don't blame you. If I saw someone looking like me, I would also be suspicious," she joked. Aika then asked me, "But on a serious note, what do you think is going to happen next for you and Charles?"

I told her, "Not sure, but I hope everything will work out fine and we'll all be like what we were before… right?"

Then the doorbell rang, so I walked over and opened the door.

"Oh hey, Charles, how did everything go?" I asked him.

"My mom is still busy, she sent me off because there was nothing else I could do to help her," Charles said as he sat on the couch. "I… I really hate Dragonborns. No wonder why my dad was a Slayer. They're the worst! Dragonborns are the worst!" he shouted out.

"Hey dude, come on, calm down. You don't mean that, right?" I asked.

"Jack, I really hate Dragonborns! Look at what they did! They killed my father and little sister by blasting my house! All of them… all of them are devils!" Charles yelled loudly in anger. I was silent; there were no words that could convince him to change his mind. When I looked back at Aika, she was standing in place and looking down at her right hand.

"Great, now I need to be extra careful," I heard her mumble to herself after.

Before I could ask her what she meant, Charles then asked Aika, "Hey, do you hate Dragonborns, Aika? Your village got attacked by them right? Those bastards, I tell you."

Aika never replied to him, but Charles took the meaning of her silence as an agreement to him.

Bolt came out of his room and asked tiredly, "Oh hey, you okay?" Bolt had been taking a nap in his room for a bit, and probably woke up when he heard Charles yell.

"My mom is trying to get a place to crash at with our savings. I did all I could to help. But with all the calculations done, she learned we don't have enough money to hold a funeral. I hate them so much!" he yelled again after he answered Bolt.

The three of us sat near him on the couch and talked for a bit. Aika then told Charles what she told me and about herself and her situation and told him the same stupid joke about her outfit, which made him laugh a little.

After that incident everything changed forever with us. Bolt did not change at all, really. The only thing that happened with him was he was a bit horrified of Dragonborns for a little while, until he got over it a month later, after he watched Aika arm lock someone because they stole her coffee, which proved to him that he should probably be more scared of Aika's coffee addiction than Dragonborns.

Aika finally began to open up to us. Then she started to show her true sarcastic, stubborn self that refused to let anyone be better than her. We saw how skilled she was at fighting and how stupid she actually was. Plus after a while she learned how to hide her accent decently so it was not as noticeable right away. Nowadays I only hear her accent once in a while because she copies the way we speak.

Charles had grown very vengeful toward Dragonborns. He used to just think Dragonborns were cool because of his dad fighting them, but now he called them devils and thought of them as some inhuman monsters that randomly killed people.

I always loved talking about Dragonborns with him, but whenever I talked about them around Charles after that day, he always looked a little annoyed. So when I hung out with Aika and talked about Dragonborns, we would have full-on discussions about them. It was a bit scary how much she knew about Dragonborns. But it all made sense to me now on why they knew so much. Aika taught me so many things about Dragonborns. We became good friends by just talking about Dragonborns alone, not even including everything else that happened. Her being a Dragonborn made everything she did make sense finally.

Carol ended up getting a place for the three of us to stay at, but things were never the same in the house. Carol got depressed after and worked so much to regain the money that they lost so that they could live a peaceful life later in retirement. Because of that us two would always hang out at Clay's or in our little meet-up spot where we would duel each other.

Before Aika left Niki's study the night we found out about her, she told me she had a bad feeling about what was going to happen next. I'm not sure if it was her Dragonborn senses telling her this or not. She told me she'd tell me everything when the time was right. Right now it would be too much for me to handle or something, she told me. And after she did tell me everything I needed to know, she'd tell me about the plans she and Bolt have. I don't understand what she means by plans, but it was probably to do with when she got revealed.

I didn't understand everything just yet. But that was okay. All I hoped for was that Charles wouldn't completely freak when he learned the truth.

Chapter 12: The Devils of the Devils

One night back in training, Bolt and I were stargazing on some random roof. I was telling Bolt about all kinds of stuff about Dragonborns. Afterward Bolt asked me, "Hey, Aika, what kind of characteristics do Dragonborns have? Like their normal selves, not their armor form. I've only ever met you, and we don't talk about it a lot during lessons. I know they're a bit different from Infinitans because we can have any hair color, blue or brown eyes, then most of us have olive skin, and finally most of us are decently tall. I don't know why my skin is a bit lighter, though—it came from my mom's side of the family. It's kinda like yours in fact, but mixed with the Infinitan olive color," he explained.

I looked up to the stars and told him, "Well, most Dragonborns are pretty similar to me. The most common feature that we all share is we have darker hair, either black or dark brown, then our skin is usually pale. We're pretty tall compared to you guys, but I'm one of the short ones. Finally, we all have blue eyes."

"All of you have blue eyes?" he asked.

"Well, almost every Dragonborn has blue eyes—it's a very dominant gene. All Dragonborns have blue eyes, except for a few," I said.

"Who are they?" Bolt asked, confused.

"Don't know. There have only been a few Dragonborns that had different-colored eyes, but I did meet one of them once. They were a Toxic Element."

Bolt said, "Wasn't that the one who—!"

Before he could finish talking, I said, "Yeah, he is. I bet he's still looking for me out there. Who knows… maybe he thinks I'm dead, like all the others do," I told him.

A week after I told Jack and Niki what happened, a mysterious thundercloud appeared outside the outer walls of Infinitas toward the west from the Dragonborn Lands. This cloud was unnatural. It did not produce rain or move fast; it seemed to be slowly moving toward Infinitas. Jack, Bolt, and I were watching it spin around slowly from the walls.

"What is that thing? Is it from a Dragonborn?" Jack asked.

"Oh, it's definitely from a Dragonborn. Most likely some War Dragonborn who has an Electric Element," I told him.

Bolt told us, "I heard that yesterday they ordered a few Slayers to investigate that cloud thing, and most of them got struck badly by lightning. Because of that we were all ordered to stay away from it."

I blurted out, "Oh, then it's absolutely a Dragonborn. Lightning strikes would not just hit five people like that. I bet you they're spinning around like crazy producing large amounts of electricity, and that's what's making a large amount of clouds circle around."

After I noticed Charles running toward us from a distance.

"There you guys are!" he said, out of breath.

Jack asked him, "Dude, what took you so long? You knew we had lookout duty. What, did you forget?"

Charles caught his breath and said, "I was talking with some other Slayers, and apparently some guy came to Infinitas and said they have been hunting that cloud thing for some time."

"What did he look like?" I asked.

"Don't know, but I was told to bring you guys with me to the main plaza. I was told that the commander had some sort of announcement," he explained.

So we all decided to head down to the plaza to check out what all of this was about.

When we got there, almost all of the Slayer squads were gathered around. Everyone was also questioning what was happening. We were waiting for about a minute until Zane finally showed up and shouted out to everyone, "Thank you all for coming here this afternoon. I know you all know about that thundercloud outside our walls. We have confirmed that it is caused by a Dragonborn. As some of you know, we sent out two squads to investigate this cloud. These people did get injured, but they are all okay now. Even though those people got injured, one good thing did come out of it. The person who brought them back safely to us was this man here. He is a Dragonborn Hunter from a faraway land, who wanted to make a deal with us all. Would you care to take over, sir?"

Zane backed off, giving the stage to this guy. I looked over at Bolt, who looked a little sick, then back to the stage.

"Ah yes, I'll explain," the guy said with an ominous voice that had a bit of an accent that gave me a cold chill. The guy said out loud to everyone, "As you all heard from your commander, I am a Dragonborn Hunter. My name is Blank. For some time now I've been tracking that Dragonborn, and it keeps on escaping from me whenever I get close to capturing it. It been a real nuisance, you can say, so I have a deal for you people that would help us both. I've heard rumors around that there's a hidden Dragonborn somewhere in this kingdom. If you people capture this Dragonborn for me, in return I will find this devil and reveal them to all of you. What do you all say?"

Everyone around started cheering and yelling out, "Deal!" all motivated and excited.

Meanwhile I was standing in the very back of the crowd panicking to myself having no idea what to do, because this guy would definitely discover that I'm a Dragonborn. Beside me Bolt looked pale at the mention of this guy's title, and Jack looked over to me, concerned for me and Bolt.

Beside us Charles shouted out, "Hell yeah! Now we can find that devil and bring them down!"

Jack turned to him and asked, "Uh, hey, why do you want that Dragonborn dead again? It did save us, remember."

With no hesitation, he replied to Jack, "Who cares that it saved us, they're still a devil. And they're gonna pay for thinking they could just live here like any other person."

Jack secretly whispered to me, "Sorry, I asked."

I whispered back to him, "Hey, no worries, I'm numb to it by now."

Charles said to us, all filled with excitement, "Hey, I got a good idea! We should sign up to be one of the groups to take down that Dragonborn! Aika has the title of War Slayer, so we can use that to get the job."

Bolt and Jack looked over to me silently, not knowing what to think.

"Well, it doesn't really matter to me what we do," Jack said back to Charles.

Bolt said, "It's up to Aika. I don't really know what we should do." He gestured to me to make the call.

I thought about it for a moment, then said to them all, "Yeah, sure, we can go out and get them."

Charles cheered out in excitement, "All right, I'll go and sign us up then!" then ran off into the crowd.

"Are you sure about this?" Jack asked.

I sighed and explained, "If we don't step in, people might think we're a little suspicious still after that whole thing with you and Niki."

Bolt told us, "We should be careful about the way we act in public too. Back when you were hurt, everyone would constantly be talking about you. Some people do have their suspicions about us now, so it would be best to act normal."

So we all agreed to not do anything extra stupid out in public and to continue acting like nothing happened with Niki.

Later on that day we were told to head down to the main base to set up for battle because we ended up being picked to be sent out to capture this Dragonborn. As we were getting ready, we heard, "Oh, you gotta be kidding me," by a very familiar voice from behind.

When I turned around to see who it was, of course it was none other than Vanessa and her squad behind us. When they were picking out which squads to go out, they chose two, which turned out to be ours and Vanessa's.

"I'm surprised that you signed up," I said, irritating her.

"Oh shut up, Niki forced me to. She wouldn't stop bugging me about that cloud thing and how she wanted to see it up close or something," she explained.

I looked over at Niki, who was staring right at me, unmoving. That's when I realized, "Ah shit, she rigged the pickings."

Jack said beside me, "They probably put us together because we trained together. I bet they think we're buddy-buddy or something."

I said back to him confidently, "Ah yes, we are buddy-buddy... hey, Vanessa, remember the time when you almost killed me?" I asked as I turned to her.

"Which time?" Charles added in.

Vanessa, getting pissed off, yelled out, "Geez, all right, I get it! Talk about something else, would you!"

Niki cheered out excitedly, "Oh, I know! Have any of you heard about what happened to the Sound Radiator" she asked.

"Uh… no?" I said back, a bit confused.

"Oh, then you're gonna love this news! It went missing this afternoon!" she shouted.

"What, really?" I asked.

Niki walked up to me and explained, "Yeah, the news just got out an hour ago! My theory is that the new hunter guy, Blank, stole it!"

I said back to her, "Hey, he probably did steal it. Before I even saw what he looked like, I got a bad feeling about him."

Charles shouted to us, "Hey, I think Blank is pretty cool! Especially his sword and armor. He has this purple tint on them that makes them super cool!"

I looked over at Charles for a moment, then asked, "Wait… he has tinted-purple armor and a purple-tinted sword? Does his sword look like mine?"

Charles casually explained, "Oh yeah, it did look exactly like yours now that I think about it. It had the same type of handle, scabbard, and well, everything!"

Dumbfounded by him, I looked over at Niki, who was writing all of this down in her notebook, so I asked her, "Hey, Niki, what kind of notes do you have on this guy?"

As Niki finished writing, she told me, "Not much… yet. What, do you guys think he's a Dragonborn too?" she asked.

Charles laughed and said, "Ha, you think Blank is a Dragonborn? Please, he's way too cool to be a devil. That's like saying Aika is a Dragonborn."

Bolt, Jack, Niki, and I awkwardly stared at each other, then back at him.

"Uh… yeah, definitely," Jack agreed awkwardly, laughing a bit.

Vanessa shouted at Niki, "Oh please, stop with your stupid theories about people being Dragonborns. Look at the mess you've already caused Aika. Also, when the hell did you become friendly with all of them? Last week you were about to kill Jack and hide his body," she asked, sounding a bit concerned.

Niki cheerfully told her, "Oh, I had a lovely conversation with Jack and Aika about something, and I can't wait till our little secret gets out and everyone's reaction to it when they find out!"

"About what?" Vanessa asked.

"Don't worry, you'll find out soon enough!" Niki told her with a smile.

"Uh… okay, I guess," she said, sounding a little scared.

As we were about to head out, we heard a voice by the exit, "Ah, so you're my team of Slayers who are going to attempt to capture my Dragonborn!"

I felt a shiver down my spine as I turned around to see who it was. That's when I first saw him, Blank. He was very tall at six foot seven and was lanky but muscular, with black hair, spiky bangs, and a black thinly shaved beard with no mustache. His skin was as pale as mine, not like anybody else's around here. He had a black military-like uniform with black combat boots. Then sharp purple-tinted armor that looked like plates from a Dragonborn's armor, with black armored gloves. He also had a plain cape that went down to his knees, which was a vibrant purple with golden laces that tied around his neck. His scabbard's body was black with the sword Charles described before stored inside, which was hidden under his cape with the hilt of the sword sticking out, like how I did with my jacket. Then finally his eyes were emerald green.

"I came to warn you all about something," Blank said as he walked into the room slowly, looking at all of us. He stopped in the middle of the room and told us, "For the past few weeks a certain Ice Dragonborn has been following me around. You may see them during or after your battle. If he shows up, do give him a hell of a time for me." Then before we could ask any questions, he walked away out the door. As he turned around, I saw him glare into my eyes for a moment, then he left us there to think.

"He doesn't look like a Dragonborn Hunter," Bolt told us quietly. "He wears a cape and is dressed like a soldier. Dragonborn Hunters usually wear a sleeved hooded cloak with ragged clothes," he explained.

"That gives me an even worse feeling about this guy. Let's just finish preparing, okay," I told everyone quietly, and we all finished up.

It took us a little while to travel to the cloud. We traveled there by horse and a big open wooden wagon that could hold around three squads of Slayers. By the time we had reached it, the sky was already black. The field around us was empty, depleted of life; the only thing alive was the grass on the ground. The cloud above us was a deep gray with flashes of bright yellow bolts on and off repetitively. There were sounds of thunder banging all around us from above. They were so loud it sounded like they were striking right next to us.

As we all watched the cloud for a moment, Jack said to us, "According to the reports, the Dragonborn only came down only after they shot at the cloud, so we probably have to trigger the fight. So let's figure out what we're going to do before we do that."

As everyone was trying to think of ideas on what we were going to do, I was staring up at the cloud watching the lightning flicker in and out. Then an idea popped into my head of what I could do to distract it while everyone sent out their traps.

"Hey, Bolt, over here!" I called out to him.

"What's the matter?" he asked.

"I got a good idea on how I could distract them, allowing you to capture them. Remember what I told you about my sword?" I asked him.

"Of course," Bolt replied.

"Well, I'm pretty sure I can reflect back their electricity back at them and stun them in place for you guys to launch your nets," I explained.

"What about the electricity all around you? Would you get shocked by it?" Bolt asked, concerned.

"What, that? Oh, don't worry about me getting shocked. I've spent years electric proofing myself," I told him.

"Well, that's the best plan for distracting them so far. Jack has already thought of the set-up for us to launch at the Dragonborn, but he had no idea about how we were going to distract them," Bolt told me.

As I was explaining how I was going to do everything to Bolt, Niki suddenly appeared up behind us and asked, "So what are you two planning?"

Bolt and I both backed up, surprised by her.

Bolt told her, "Oh, uh, Aika had a good idea on how she could distract the Dragonborn, while we launch the nets out."

Niki smiled back at me and told us, "Oh, all right! But don't disappoint me, Aika. I'm expecting a great battle from you." Then she walked back to the others all carefree.

"Come on, let's tell them all the… actually decent idea," Bolt said proudly as he walked back to the others as well.

"Oh yes, we should and… wait, why were you impressed that I came up with it?" I asked as I walked with him. He stared at me without answering, then joined everyone's conversation.

After a good minute of trying to explain my idea, Bolt asked if we should try this to everyone.

"Is it even possible to do that with your sword?" Jack asked me.

Confidently, I said back to him, "Jack, have faith in me. I know what I'm doing. And let me tell you, this is nothing compared to what else I can do with my sword."

With no other comment, we unanimously decided to do this plan, so everyone started to get into place.

"Why are you talking off your Slayer armor?" Charles asked me.

So I explained, "When the Dragonborn drops down from the sky, it will surround the field around me with electricity, to try and trap me in place. Most of the stuff I wear is already electric proof, but the armor might cause me some issues, so it would be best to take it off beforehand."

"How do you know it would do that?" Vanessa asked, in her usual attitude.

So I explained all smugly, "They are out of control right now, so they want to eliminate any threat around. So if I stand alone in the middle of the field, they will think I'm the only enemy and target me. I would be the ultimate bait for this fella because they will never expect what I'm about to do to them."

Vanessa stared at me for a moment before saying, "Your death wish."

"Heh, you wish," I replied confidently as I crossed my arms smugly.

When everyone got their launchers ready, I walked to the middle of the field right below the vertex of the cloud. When I shot an arrow into the center, everything around went silent. All the thunder and lightning stopped, the wind blowing around disappeared, and time itself seemed to completely stop. Suddenly lightning started striking all around the field. Before I could hear the sounds of thunder, the clouds opened up slightly, and the Electric Dragonborn dropped from the sky with lightning following behind them. When they dropped to the ground, all the crashes of thunder were finally heard. When they looked up at me, they spread a field of electricity out around in a circular path as predicted. When the electricity came at me, it deflected off my boots and jacket, covering the ground near me. I drew out my sword and pointed it toward them while shouting, "Hey, come at me with all you got!"

They sent out a ray of electricity toward me. I shielded myself with my sword, and the electricity averted off it, spreading everywhere in front of me. I looked over at this Dragonborn's face and saw that they were a War Dragonborn with a light-yellow aura with a dark-yellow accent, and they were completely losing it. Their irises were black with green spots. They had ridged spiral horns with their armor spiky on their shoulders, forearms, chest, and shin plates. I saw their element symbol on their right hand, and finally, they had a white scabbard.

The Electric Element had the power to generate electrical waves and manipulate them to their will. The Electric Element's symbol was a round-cornered *X* with rectangular dashes at each corner of the *X*. They created these waves by converting their body heat from their limbs into electricity they could control. Because they converted their body heat, they had a severe weakness to cold temperatures and the Ice Element. They used these electrical waves in many different ways. They could create rays or beams of electricity to attack others and stun their opponents in place, or gravitate their weapons back to them from far away. They could cover themselves in their electricity for a power and speed boost, which left a trail of electricity behind them as they moved around. Electric Dragonborns could also absorb electricity into their scales and plates and charge up this electricity into an attack to blast back at their opponents. Sometimes they could charge too much electricity, so they created these tiny electrical crystals that shone the color of their aura that were only half an inch long. They could use these crystals at a later time to recharge if they ran out of electricity, and the crystals also gave them a temporary power and speed boost. Finally, they could send down bolts of lightning onto their opponents and paralyze them for up to two to six minutes. Their possible aura colors were any yellow, orange, red, or greens then white.

I veered away all the electricity and ran over and swung again at the Dragonborn. They stepped aside and blasted a path of fire at me, which I barely dodged by jumping to the side. They ran through their fire path and tried to swing at me again. I blocked it with my sword and stepped back, waiting for it to use a certain move on me as I readied my sword.

"Come on at me, pal! Come on, send out another ray of electricity at me! I dare you," I taunted them as I backed up slowly. They angrily sent out a powerful ray of electricity at me, so I raised up my sword, and the ray bounced, off spreading out all over the ground near our feet once again. As I was deflecting the electricity, I looked over at everyone else. They were all looking back at me, waiting for me to make an opening to attack, except for Niki, who was writing every detail of this fight down in her notebook. With a bit of hesitation, I used my powers to start absorbing the electricity into my sword. Doing this made my eyes slightly glow yale blue. I just had to hope that the people who didn't know about me won't notice my eyes.

As my sword filled with electricity, I heard in the background, "Look at Aika over there showing off her skills like usual in battle against a Dragonborn," Vanessa said smugly as she watched me.

"Oh please, it's Aika, what do you expect? I bet you any money she'll yell out a swear within the next two minutes," Charles replied to her statement.

"Good point," Vanessa said.

"Hey, the question is, what swear will she yell next?" Jack added.

"Oooh, that's a good question! Knowing her, she'll yell out the f-bomb," Charles replied.

"Hey, you guys, come on already. Save the dumb talk for later!" Bolt told them as he watched me battle.

"Boo! Where's all the fun in battling without the dumb talk, Bolton?" Jack asked.

"After the battle—now look at what you're missing!" Bolt hollered as he pointed to me on the battlefield with electricity swirling around the Dragonborn and me absorbing tons of electricity. My sword had quickly filled up with electricity while they were talking, so I looked around for a place to escape where I could safely blast my attack back at them. As I looked around, I saw someone fly though the sky, leaving a trail of teal sparkles that disappeared in a seconds. But before I could think about it more, my sword created a bright blue light that blinded me and the other Dragonborn. With my sword glowing bright with the other Dragonborn's aura, I knew it was fully charged up. The War Dragonborn was disoriented from the light and had stopped attacking me, leaving me the opening I needed.

"Fuck you!" I yelled as I slashed my sword from the air to the ground, creating a wave of electricity back at them. They screamed out in pain and tried to grab at me, but they were too stunned to move close enough to get me. Without a second to waste, everyone else sent out their nets to contain them in place. Not even a minute later the Dragonborn was stuck in place, paralyzed from my attack and the containments. My sword had stopped glowing and went back to normal. As I start to calm down from everything, I looked back at the others, who were all cheering, celebrating the success of it all. "For once everything worked according to plan and we won very quickly," I thought, until I remembered the other Dragonborn I'd seen flying up in the sky before. I looked up in the sky to try and find them, but they had seemed to disappear.

As I was searching, I heard Bolt call out to me, "Hey, you doing okay over there, Aika?"

I looked over at him and shouted, "Don't come over here, something's not right! I think there's another Dragonborn some—" Then before I could finish talking, that Dragonborn flew out of nowhere and grabbed me and the War Dragonborn into the sky above the field. As I was dragged, I dropped my sword and watched it fall to the ground while I heard everyone shout orders from below, but I was too high to hear any of it.

This Dragonborn had a teal aura with a shaded greenish-blue accent with darker blueish-green scales. Their horns were smooth and short like an imp's and curved ever so slightly down at the ends. Their armor was similar to mine, but their shoulder plates were sharper, with scars similar to mine on their biceps that looked like they were caused by a claw scratch. And they had a blue scabbard. Then finally they had black scale-like leather across their eyes that went around their head like a mask. These were accessories to a Dragonborn's armor for those who needed glasses to see. Not a lot of Dragonborns had this because our eyes were usually super good.

"Who are you? What do you want?" I spoke to them in Dragonborn. They were holding me by the collar of my shirt, dangling me away from them. I was basically helpless. I couldn't use my powers in front of Charles and the others, and it was too risky for me to drag them down from the sky, like I had with that Wind Dragonborn.

They said back to me also in Dragonborn, a bit smugly, "Who I am is not important right now, but what I need to tell you is this. I'm sure you've met that Dragonborn Hunter guy down there, right?" they asked me. They had a bit of a deep voice that echoed slightly because of their armor form.

"What about him?" I asked as I struggled trying to keep myself secure in their grasp.

"Well, earlier I flew down there to see what he was up to this time, and I saw him snooping around gathering information about you and your other friends down there. I also heard quite a bit about you as well," they told me.

"Like what?" I asked.

They said again all smugly, "Oh you know, like how you're really good at taking down War Dragonborns and such, how people call you the 'War Slayer,' and how you're always targeted by Dragonborns. But it all made perfect sense to me. I mean, you are a Dragonborn like me, after all. You even speak Dragonborn like me, which is quite rare for people around these parts. Although your powers are quite a mystery to me—they remind me of an old friend of mine," they said as they closed their eyes and shrugged.

Then an arrow flew by us very close to our heads.

"Why are you telling me all of this? Why warn me about him?" I asked, concerned.

They told me, "I don't have much time left, so I'll just tell you this. I need your help saving someone. You've met them before, so you'll know what I mean once I explain. But for now, watch out for him! He plans to reveal you very soon. I'll be watching you both from a distance for now. But if anything goes super bad, I guess I'll help you out. Oh, and don't worry about the fall—there's someone down below to catch you,"

Then before I could say anything else, they dropped me from the sky and flew off into the distance, still carrying the War Dragonborn with them. As I watched them fly off, I saw a trail of ice particles follow behind their wings, creating the path I'd seen before in the sky.

Not knowing what to expect, I closed my eyes and braced for impact before I hit the ground. But when I landed, it was a lot softer than I thought it would be. When I opened my eyes, I found myself in Bolt's arms.

Out of breath, he asked me, "Hey …you okay?"

"Fine now, thanks to you. I wasn't expecting to be caught in your arms all romantically like this, though," I said back playfully.

"Oh, well you know," he said, blushing a little, as he put me down on my feet. "I saw you up in the sky like that and knew that you were in a bit of trouble, but, uh, anyways what was that all about? I couldn't understand a word either of you were saying," he asked.

"Oh, we were just speaking in Dragonborn—you know how different it is from Infinitan. But anyways, they were that Dragonborn Blank mentioned before. They seemed okay to me at least. They acted all smug-like, though, when talking to me. But they gave me a warning about Blank. Apparently he's been gathering information about us in particular and how he's planning to reveal me real soon," I explained.

Bolt sighed, then told me, "Well, we'll discuss this at a later time. Come on, let's walk back to the others," he said as he held my hand and walked back to everyone.

As we walked, I said, "Jack and Niki are going to give me hell on how I did all of that with my sword. Where is my sword, speaking of it?" I asked.

Bolt told me, "Oh, it got dropped near the others, Niki probably already picked it up by now, examining it. Hey, when are you going to tell them about your powers and such? They should probably know before everything goes down, right?" he asked.

"Oh yeah, I should probably do that soon. They would definitely help us out big time when I get revealed," I told him.

When we got close back to the others, their reactions were what I expected.

"How did you do all of that?" Niki immediately asked, holding my sword.

"Geez, not even an 'Are you okay' or anything?" I said back to her.

She whispered to me, "Oh yeah, Aika, I got a good idea on what kind of element you might have!"

"You can interrogate me all you want later about that. For now shut up," I told her as I grabbed my sword from her and sheathed it back in my scabbard.

"What was that all about with Niki?" Charles asked.

"Long story, not important right now," I replied.

Jack asked me, "What the hell was that all about up there?"

"Oh, just the Dragonborn that Blank warned us about. They just told me they were taking the War Dragonborn and left." Then I gestured to him that I'd tell him the real story later.

Vanessa asked, "Why are you always being dragged up to the sky by Dragonborns?"

"Not sure!" I told her confidently.

Vanessa said, "Well, we should probably head back to the main base before they yell at us for being gone for so long."

I replied, "For once I agree with you, Venny. Before we left, they put us on a time crunch for no reason to get back by tomorrow afternoon, even though we were ordered to capture a War Dragonborn."

"So who's going to drive the horses?" Jack asked.

"Uh, traveling back… I forgot about that part," Charles complained.

"What's wrong with driving the horse back? Want me to do it?" I joked.

"Noo!" everyone told me firmly all at the same time.

"All right, I get it, geez," I said.

Peter said, "I guess I'll do it."

Vanessa patted him on the back and said, "Ah, good, make yourself useful finally."

Peter questioned, "Did… did you not see me help shoot out the nets back while fighting the god?"

But we all ignored him and hopped in the wagon.

On the way back, everyone was having their own little conversations with each other to keep themselves up just in case that Teal Dragonborn came back. But everyone's exhaustion was nothing compared to mine; I was well spent after using some of my powers I haven't used in years. So I leaned against Bolt's shoulder and looked up into the sky at all the stars above.

"Are you sure you're okay?" Bolt asked me, concerned.

"Yeah, I'll live, I'm just tired from…you know. I'm just gonna rest beside you for a bit," I told him quietly.

Bolt smiled and told me, "Rest all you want, you've been through a lot today," as he put his arm around my shoulders and brought me closer to him. As I dozed off looking at the stars, I noticed that the thundercloud was completely gone now with the Electric War Dragonborn gone. That teal Dragonborn was probably long gone by now in the distance. When I thought about it, that Dragonborn also reminded me of an old friend from my past.

Chapter 13: Nothing Stays Forever

By the time we got back to Infinitas after fighting the Electric War Dragonborn, it was early morning right before sunrise. Everyone was either sleeping or barely awake.

"Aika… Aika," Bolt said, waking me up.

"Uh, what?" I asked in a tired daze as I opened my eyes to see us passing through the southern entrance gate that was a part of the outer wall.

"We're back at Infinitas. It's time to explain what happened," he told me.

"Oh five more minutes," I told him as I closed my eyes and leaned my head back against him again.

Bolt told me in a playful tone, "We'll get a coffee before heading to the main headquarters."

"Uh, fine I'll get up," I said as I sat up straight next to him and looked over to the others, still sleeping.

"Hey, why did you wake me up first?" I asked.

"Because you take the longest to wake up, and the only thing that will make you get up is the mention of the word *coffee*," he explained.

"So when will we get some?" I asked.

"Calm down, in a few minutes we can once we arrive at the nearby stable," Bolt said as we traveled. Then we hit a big bump, and the whole wagon shook.

"Ah shit, is it time to get up?" Jack asked as he woke up. "Oh good, you already got Aika up," he said to Bolt.

"See, told you," Bolt said to me.

"Oh, come on, I don't take that long to get up," I said.

Niki, who had been awake the entire time, said to us "Almost every day during training you showed up almost late to morning attendance. Many times I have knocked on your door to warn you, and I heard the sounds of you yelling 'Wha? Oh shi—!' right before I walked away."

"That was you?" I asked, surprised.

"Yeah, it was fun to hear the panic in your voice. It made my morning every time I heard you," she said.

"You hearing this right now, Aika?" Jack asked smugly as he looked at the pure confusion on my face.

"I… whatever, let's just get going and grab a coffee," I told them as the horse parked at the stable.

We all stopped to get a quick coffee in the market plaza, then we all headed on our cheerful, happy, wonderful way to get yelled at by Zane for basically failing the mission. When we reached the main base, it was surrounded by Slayers guarding the place with people entering and leaving the building.

"Oh, this looks like it's going to be fun," Jack said as we walked to the entrance.

"There are definitely more people on duty than usual. What day is it again?" Bolt asked.

"Today's Thursday, which is usually a lot of people's day off," Niki said.

"Oh, so the place has tight security today, goodie!" I said as I walked to the front entrance.

As we passed through the doors, which were made of iron, there were crowds of people walking from room to room with documents and books.

"What in the world is going on here?" Jack asked.

"Let's see what's up then," I said as I tapped a security guard's shoulder while walking.

"Yes, can I help you?" they asked in a rush.

"Hey, can we ask what happened? We've never seen the place so crazy."

They told me, "I'm sorry, I don't know. I was called into work to find all data on anybody who could be a Dragonborn. If I were you, I would watch everything you do and say." Then they ran off to an office down the hall.

"Damn, Blank is really tearing the place apart for answers," I said, a bit nervous as I held Bolt's hand.

"Hey, don't worry about any of them right now. We got our own situation to focus on," Bolt told me.

"Yeah, you're right, let's keep on going," I said, then continued walking to Zane's office.

As we slowly walked down the main hall, fewer and fewer people were around and made the place a whole lot quieter, like how it usually was. But we all had one other thought in mind.

"So what do you think they're gonna say?" Vanessa asked as we walked to the office.

Jack replied, "I bet they're all just going to be flabbergasted by how a regular Dragonborn up and took on a War Dragonborn for no reason."

Charles said, "The commander is gonna be pissed when he finds out that we basically failed."

I told him, "Commander is not who I'm worried about."

Charles asked, confused, "You're not worried about what the commander is gonna say? Who's worse than the commander? The king?"

Then we arrived at the entrance to Zane's office, which were nicely engraved double-sided doors with a golden frame around. So with lots of hesitation, we pushed them open and saw Zane and Blank talking. When all of us walked inside, Zane turned to us and asked, "Ah, you have all returned unhurt. How did it go?"

We all looked at each other for a moment and nodded. Then Bolt stepped up and told him, "Sir, we had successfully captured the Electric Dragonborn, which was indeed a War Dragonborn. But something else happened after we did. You see, sir, after we secured them, a… uh, another Dragonborn… sorta came from nowhere and basically… stole them.”

“WHAT? How in the world did you let that happen?” Zane shouted at us, confused.

Bolt told him, stuttering a bit while doing so, “Well, you see, sir… we, uh, w-were attacked by an Ice Dragonborn after we had secured them, and it snatched the War Dragonborn into the sky for unknown reason and, well… flew off faster than we could react, so it got away.”

All Zane did was look back at us dumbfounded, just standing in place silently, processing how stupid this whole situation was. He asked, “Did anything else happen?”

“No sir!” Bolt replied.

Zane and we were both quite unsure of what to do, but behind Zane, I heard Blank say to himself quietly, “So he did interfere with me again, interesting,” then chuckled slightly.

Blank stepped up toward everyone and said, “You all have no need to dread anything that has happened. Like I told you before, they had been following me for quite some time, and recently they have been messing with my work too now. But anyways, rest for now, and you’ll receive more news later on the matter. I need time to think about what I should do.”

Without a second to waste we were all kicked out of the office, with the door slamming shut behind us echoing down the hall. Immediately a second later after the echo faded away, Vanessa said to me and the others, “Well, that was something. I’m going home.” Then she walked down the hall with her squad following behind.

“Bye, Aika, see you soon!” Niki said back to me, waving as she followed Vanessa.

Everything had happened so fast within the last few seconds that I just sighed and asked the others, “So what are we going to do now?”

Bolt immediately replied, “Let’s just get out of here for now. We’ll think about that after we get away from here—this place makes me nervous.”

Charles said excitedly, "Oh, I know a good place to head out to that will calm everyone's nerves, follow me!"

So with nothing to do and so much to process, we followed Charles, who was just going with the flow.

We all followed Charles, not really knowing where we were heading. On that particular day it was beautiful outside. The sun was bright, and there were only a few clouds were in the sky and a slight breeze. The birds were chirping away peacefully, and it was the perfect weather to walk around and hang out.

"Here we are!" Charles said proudly. He had brought us to the old training ground we all used to hang out in almost every day. The same place where he'd first asked us to become Dragon Slayers.

"What are we doing here?" Jack asked.

Charles turned around and said, "Oh, come on, we got the day off. Let's just hang out and chill."

So we walked through the entrance and saw that no one was around.

"Ah good, we got the place to ourselves. So does anyone want to spar?" Charles asked.

I replied, "I'll sit this one out. I'm too tired, and you all know what happens when Charles and I spar."

"Someone loses their pride?" Jack answered as he pointed to Charles.

"Hey, I'm not that pathetic! Am I?" Charles questioned.

"Bolt, you should spar with him," I suggested as I sat down in my old spot and pulled out a bag full of protein bits.

"You got another bag of that?" Jack asked.

"Jack, who do you think I am?" I asked as I opened my jacket and threw a bag at him.

"A crazy person," Jack answered as he sat down next to me.

"Come on, Bolton, let's duel!" Charles said to him as he ran across the field.

"You go, Bolton! Show off to me!" I cheered to him.

"Yeah, you got this, Bolt!" Jack shouted at him too.

"Oh, Charles is going to destroy him," I whispered to Jack.

"Oh please, the only person Charles can't beat in a spar is you," he replied also in a whisper.

"Yeah," I said softly as I smirked, and I grabbed a handful of bits.

After we watched them spar with each other for a bit… Charles won. We all hung out and reminisced for a bit about the events that had happened.

"Hey, remember the first day of training when we all met Vanessa, and Aika straight-up laughed in her face on how stupid she was?" Charles asked.

"What do you mean? I still call her dumb and laugh in her face at everything," I told him.

Jack laughed and replied, "Yeah, you do."

Bolt said, "And I'm the one you hide behind every time Niki runs after you when she spots you after making fun of her."

Charles asked excitedly, "Remember that party at graduation!"

I laughed at him and said, "Please, you probably don't remember any of it."

Bolt said beside me, "Oh geez, I will never forget that night. What happened to me that night is engraved into my brain."

Jack asked, "Hey, what exactly happened that night again? I was so hungover the next day that I forgot we even graduated from training."

"Are you sure you want to know?" I asked, sounding a bit mischievous.

"Damn, what did we do? You sound like Niki," Charles asked.

I told them, "Oh, nothing much… Charles, you just got wasted and passed out after having a drinking contest with Chad, and Jack got drunk and argued with Niki—who was also drunk, might I add—about Dragonborns and stuff. But you and her were both just saying gibberish all night trying to one-up each other on whatever the hell you we saying. While Jack was doing all of that, he kept forcing Bolt to fetch him more beer, even though he drank it all already and there was none left. And in the background of all of this, Venny and I were having a lovely little conversation about how stupid everyone was," I explained.

"Yeah, that does sound exactly like us," Charles admitted.

"Hey, remember right after the Ice Incident where Aika jumped off that roof?" Jack asked.

"Oh geez, not this again," Bolt said to himself.

"What? Venny was saying shit to me, so I had to prove her wrong," I told them.

"Do you even remember what she said?" Charles asked.

"Charles… Charles, my dude… of course I don't remember what she said to me. What did she say?" I asked.

Charles laughed and told me, "Let me tell you! So it's like the day after you woke up from being out all day, and us four were just casually having lunch together. Vanessa walked by us and commented with her smug tone, 'Aren't you supposed to be in bed still resting?' And you said back in your usual smug tone to her, 'I'm not like other people, Venny, I recover a lot faster than others.' Then she said, 'Oh yeah… prove it then.' Then you stood up and yelled, 'Oh yeah? Watch me, Venny, I'll…' Then you looked around the place then said back to her, 'I'll jump off the roof of the cabin to show you.' So Bolt here immediately freaked out and said, 'If you do that, you'll overstrain the little energy you do have!' Then you said, 'No no no, I'm going to prove to Venny that no little frost can hold me back.' Then you got up and walked to a ladder that was hanging beside the cabin. We all tried to stop you, but you being your idiot stubborn self, hollered back, 'Venny is going to regret waking up this morning!' back to us. You got to the top and shouted some random insult to Vanessa, then did a flip of the roof. You barely landed okay, and when you stood up straight, your legs were shaking. Vanessa said, 'Damn, I'm actually surprised you landed at all.' You yelled 'Fuck you' to her and took one step forward and almost tripped on a rock that would have made you fall on your face."

"Hey, I did prove myself at least," I told them.

"If you ever try to do a flip when you're injured like that again, I will hold you back with all of my strength," Bolt told me.

"The question is, do you have the strength to hold me back?" I replied to him.

"You're unbelievable," Bolt said back.

Charles asked Bolt, "If you can't, you want me to hold her back? I know how scary powerful you are, Aika, but my strength is close to yours," he said as he flexed his arm, showing off his muscles.

A thought came across my mind. "Hey, Charles, can I ask you a question? It's a bit off topic," I asked.

"What's up?" he replied.

"How would you react if you found out someone you know really well turned out to be a Dragonborn. Like one of us, for example," I asked.

"Hmm, let's see… well, I don't really know how I would react. I mean, it's not like any of us are devils anyways, so I don't see any point in really thinking about it. What brings this question up?" he asked.

Jack and Bolt silently stared at each other, then looked back at me.

"Oh, no reason. I was just wondering because there was a lot going on. Who knows, this Dragonborn might be someone we know well. Everybody has a secret side to themselves that they never reveal. Some are ugly and bad, then some and good and sweet," I explained.

Everyone was silent after I was done talking, probably thinking about all the stuff I'd said. The noise around was the wind blowing, which had grown quite strong since earlier. When I looked up to the sky, I saw a flagpole with a Slayer flag flowing strongly in the wind. The Slayer flag had the Slayer logo with a black background, like our badges. I heard heavy footsteps behind us and turned around.

"What's wrong?" Bolt asked.

"I hear someone walking nearby," I told him. Not even a second later, some fancy-looking soldier from the castle came walking up to us. They had silver armor and boots with a white uniform buttoned-down shirt with a purple collar and sleeve cuffs, and white trousers stuffed in their boots. This uniform was worn by all royal guards that served the king. This one in particular must be a messenger royal guard.

"Excuse me, are you the War Slayer and their squad?" they asked.

A little bit weirded out from their greeting, I replied, "Uh, yeah, I'm the 'War Slayer,' but just call me Aika. That's my name, and this is my squad. What's, uh, wrong?" I asked.

They stepped forward to us and said in a very proper tone, "You four have been ordered by the royal guard to come to the Royal Sword Ground this evening. Here are the directions to the location," they said as they handed me an envelope. "I bid you all a fair day," they said, then walked away to the exit.

"That was… weird?" I said uncertainly.

Charles, a bit angry, said, "I don't like how they just addressed us three as the squad of the 'War Slayer,' They didn't even say Aika's name at all."

Jack also joined in with Charles and said, "Yeah, I don't like how they addressed Aika either. The way they said it made her sound like she's a weapon for the Slayers. Also they must have been looking for us because this place is very hidden from everywhere else; that's why we would always hang out here."

I told them, "Oh, it's all right. I've been called a weapon more times than I can count in the past before I met all of you, but them finding this place is quite concerning for the amount of time they must have been looking for us."

"Check what's inside the envelope," Bolt told me.

"Oh, right!" I said as I opened it up. Inside was a map of the area around the biggest castle of Infinitas that was located in Central Infinitas. The map showed directions to follow to find this Royal Sword Ground, which was hidden to the northeast of the castle on a field on top of a hill.

"Wow, this place must be fancy! I wonder how much money they wasted on this field for it to be so hidden?" Charles said.

Jack told us, "We should probably start traveling there. If we leave now, it would most likely be almost evening by the time we arrive. We're at the bottom of South Infinitas. It's quite far from that castle in Central Infinitas," he explained.

Bolt joined in and said, "I also agree with Jack, and plus we have no idea what this is all about, and we don't want to get any higher-up people mad at us. Look at the mess we've been in recently with the commander."

I sighed and replied to them, "Well, all right, let's get going," and I put the map back in the envelope for now until we got close, and I gave it to Bolt so he could put it in his bag.

As we walked out, Jack questioned, "Huh, I wonder if any other squad was given this map or if it was just us?"

"Eh, we'll see," I replied.

After a bit of walking, we approached this fancy sword ground. We hiked up a hidden trail that led up the hill it was supposedly on.

"Uhh, how long is this damn trail?" Jack complained.

Bolt told him, "I think we're close to the entrance. The map says it's right past this big tree up ahead."

This hill we were forced to walk up turned more into a hike more than anything, with the map being weirdly confusing to follow with a whole bunch of extra routes that led to nowhere. This giant tree was also weird; it looked like it was purposely placed to help hide this big, fancy place. After we passed the big tree, we saw a stone path that led ahead to a gray brick wall with a fancy silver gate that blocked us from going farther. In front of the gate there was a royal guard with the same outfit as the other guard we saw earlier.

Bolt walked up to them and asked, "Excuse me, is this the Royal Sword Ground?" sounding a bit uncertain in himself. "We were ordered to come here by another guard. Here's the map as proof," Bolt explained, showing them the map.

"Why yes indeed, come on in," they replied in a proper tone like the last guard and allowed us by. So we walked through the gates and into the field, and what we immediately saw was a chaotic mess. There were squads of Slayers all around the place, chatting with one another and asking why they had been summoned here just like us. The sword ground was as expected, though, with stone paths all around the dirt field and two fancy bleachers that rose high so a bunch of people could watch like it was a tournament arena. Then there was a long bench at the bottom of both bleachers, for a team of people to sit next to each other like at a sports game. Finally the stone wall we saw before enclosed it all together, making it even more private than it already was. Everything about this place was elaborate and made no sense compared to the field we were just in that had one small bench and a tiny dirt field with uncontrolled grass everywhere around. Hell, it didn't even look like the Slayer training fields that were just a bigger field of dirt with at least the grass cut around the area.

As we were taking in this chaos, I heard someone say to us, "So you guys were called here as well?" I turned around and saw Vanessa and her squad here, just as confused as us.

"Oh, hey, Venny. What's uh… happening?" I asked her.

"No idea, we have the same confusion as you. Some royal guard guy came up to us earlier and ordered us to come here. I thought it was just some elaborate prank, but look how many other people are here," she explained.

Jack said to her, "It's the same as us, some royal idiot came over to us and said the same. I wasn't expecting this many people, though."

"No one was expecting this many people to be here," Niki said right after Jack was done talking.

"What do you know about the situation?" I asked her.

Niki explained, "I've talked to a whole bunch of other squads, and they all say the same thing: none of them know why they were called here, and they were all summoned by members of the royal guard for some reason. Also, might I add, 'the Royal Sword Ground' is a very horrible name for a place as fancy as this. It could have named it much better than that—it is very unoriginal."

Before we could continue talking more, we all heard a voice call out to us, "Greetings, everybody!"

Immediately I knew who it was and turned to the direction I'd heard it from. Everyone around stopped talking and turned around as well to listen.

In the very front of the crowd of Slayers before us, I saw Blank step up on a mini stage in front of the battlefield. Beside him there was a soldier with orange-tinted armor that resembled Blank's armor. Blank yelled out to everyone, "I have called you all here for a very special reason! I am here to cut off all the suspects I have who could be the Blue Dragonborn. With the evidence I have gathered, I suspect the Dragonborn to be one of the Slayers here in this crowd. To go through everyone here, I'm going to test you all in a quick battle to test your strength, speed, and reactions. I'm going to go all out on you in battle in a matter of seconds to test these skills. So one person from each squad, come over and sign your squad members' names below on a list to determine who fights when. The first squad to sign is the first to battle; the last to sign is the last to battle."

Everybody around roared in excitement because more progress was going to be made in this case. Charles was one of the loudest ones as well. When people started stepping up to sign their names, he said, "All right, he wants to fight us thinking one of us is a Dragonborn? Then let's do it! I'll sign our names up right now to fight him immediately." Then he took a step forward to the crowd.

In a panic of not knowing what to think, I grabbed his shoulder and shouted out, "No, wait!"

Charles turned around, confused, and asked, "What's wrong? You sound frightened."

"Oh, uh, well…" I said as I took my hand away and froze in place for a minute, unsure of what to say. "Uh, well, we should… wait a minute and sign up close to last instead of early!" I blurted out.

"Why?" he asked.

"Oh, uh…" I mumbled, trying to think of a reason.

Jack patted his other shoulder and told him, "We should wait to fight in a later battle so we can see how he fights and such, so we have a better advantage and give them a nice fight!" he said, matching Charles's excited tone.

"Oh, now I get it, sure!" Charles replied.

After a minute we sent Charles up to sign our names and after he left Jack asked me, "Hey, you doing okay there, Aika?"

"I just have an extremely bad feeling about all of this, and I don't really know why, but I'm terrified for no reason right now," I told him.

Bolt told me softly, "Hey, just calm down. Everything is all right now. If anything goes wrong, I'm right here to help you."

I nodded back, and we waited until Charles returned.

We ended up being the fourth to last squad to go up, so we followed behind all the other Slayers and took a seat at the bleachers to watch the battles. On the bleachers I sat with Bolt sat to my left and Jack to my right with Charles on the other side of him. Vanessa's squad was a bit below us, and Niki kept on looking over to us from time to time.

After everything was organized, the first person stepped onto the field to begin the sparring. As the first battle commenced, not even a second later, Blank sent their sword flying across the field immediately. I heard Blank say to himself, "Had no immediate reaction time. Next!" he shouted out. Everyone was stunned at how quickly he'd battled the first person.

Charles, amazed by Blank's movements, said to me, "Wow he sorta moves like you in battle!"

I said back quietly, "No, he moves exactly like me."

Everyone around was fascinated with Blank's movements and fighting skills. As one person after another came up, the more nervous I got. He was only using two moves during all the battles: a regular swing with his sword, then a sudden surprise swing that usually knocked away everybody's sword, like I did. As I was thinking all these questions to myself, I saw Vanessa's squad come up to him. They all got immediately destroyed by Blank, but surprisingly, Niki lasted a bit longer than anyone else I'd watched. I was too far away to see what was exactly happening, but it looked almost like Niki reached out for something as she was fighting. Her sword was knocked away like all the others, but for some reason when she walked back to the bleachers, she looked weirdly happy, making me think she'd done something or found something out about Blank. As she walked back, I noticed that the soldier who was beside him earlier was crossing off names of people on some sort of list they had. They wore a similar uniform to Blank.

As more and more squads came and went from the field, my mind was dizzy with thoughts. I sweated every time I saw a sword fly across the field, causing my body to flinch at the same time. My vision was fixated on the battles, with every second feeling like a minute.

Bolt held my hand and told me, "Hey, Aika… Aika, look over to me," so I did and saw Bolt look at me with concern.

"W-what's wrong?" I asked, breathing hard.

"Hey, it's going to be all right. I'll be right beside you if anything goes wrong," he told me.

"I-I'm fine, why y-you saying this?" I asked.

Jack said to me, "Because you look terrified."

"What? N-no, I'm n-not!" I told him.

"Then describe exactly how you're doing right now," Jack said.

"Well I… uh," I said, realizing.

"What's making you this nervous anyways? He's just some guy," Jack asked.

I told him, "They're not just some guy… they're a Dragonborn. I can tell by their movements alone, never mind their armor and fighting style."

Jack looked over to the current battle and said, "Oh... now looking at it... yeah."

"Also when you two do battle them, try and notice if you can see their aura at all. Sometimes you can see a bit of it when we move a lot," I told them.

Bolt asked, "How are we going to last long enough on the field to even see any of it?"

I told them, "Oh, that's easy! Blank has only been using two moves, and I've pinpointed his movements to see what he does next. When his shoulders are tensed up, he does a surprise attack, and then when his shoulders are relaxed, he does a regular swing," I explained, pointing to the field as he did said movements in battle.

"Oh yeah, I can see them now," Jack said as we watched some poor fool's sword fly across the field, and another group was ordered to come up.

Eventually after watching lots of people suffer, it became our turn to step up. As we walked to the bench to fight Blank, I saw Bolt and Jack discussing something in front of me as we were walking, then the three sat on the bench as Charles stepped up to be the first of us to fight. When the battle began for Charles, he lasted not even a second, like everyone else. Of course Charles just walked back to us all cheerfully, blissful in his ignorance. Then Jack stepped up to battle. Jack was able to take a good few swings, but he wasn't fast enough to handle a bunch in a row and got his sword knocked away like everyone else. No sign of Blank's aura from his fight. Then it was Bolt's turn. Blank had to talk to his henchman for a minute before Bolt's battle, so we also talked for a moment.

"Watch out, that guy does not hold back for a moment," Jack told us. He looked around and asked, "Hey, where did Charles run off to?"

Bolt told him, "Oh, he ran off to talk with Vanessa's squad over there. Niki is keeping him distracted so if anything goes wrong during Aika's battle, Charles won't see."

I said, "I'm a little surprised she's being this cooperative in helping us."

Bolt got the cue to head up to the field. "Looks like it's time to go. Wish me luck," he said as he walked away.

Jack sat down next to me and said, "After this, you need to tell me more about your powers. Time is speeding quickly in these final hours of peace."

As I watched Bolt's sword immediately flying across that field, I replied to him, "Yeah, I know." Then Bolt walked back to us, and I walked over to the field silently. Behind me I saw Bolt and Jack discussing something again, but none of it mattered. It was time.

"Well, well, well, it's the mighty War Slayer I've been hearing so much about! I haven't had a proper one-on-one discussion with you yet, huh. I've been looking forward to this!" Blank told me ominously.

"Let's just get this over with," I replied.

As soon as we got the okay to start, Blank immediately tried to pull a fast one on me and surprise attacked me immediately. I deflected it and stepped back a little, keeping distance. Blank said to me in Dragonborn, "I knew you were the Dragonborn everyone was looking for when I first saw you getting ready for that fight. I got to say, though, I wasn't expecting you—the War Slayer—to be this short."

I spoke to him in Dragonborn, "Oh, shut it about my height! Why the hell did you do this big sword duel with everyone?" I asked.

He bashed against my sword and replied, "Because it gave me time to dig through everyone's data and because it was the only other way for me to talk with you without any Nons around. You're always around that blond one especially. What's the deal with them?" he asked.

"That"—I said as he swerved his sword back—"is none of your business!" I told them as I swung out at him.

"You won't tell me? Eh, I already know, you filthy Non-lover. I heard some people in the office talk about you two. But that doesn't matter, I'll just kill you both," he said.

"You touch a single hair on him, or any of my other friends for that matter, I'll turn all your fucking bones to dust!" I threatened.

He laughed back at my remark and said, "Yeah, sure. Like you, a kid, could do that to me. I'm a veteran at this stuff, kid. I've been fighting for longer than you have been alive," he told me. He did a few casual swings at me until he screeched our swords together and said, "You told the other two about my attack pattern, didn't you. That's why they lasted a little longer." I separated my sword and backed off again. "That red-haired guy—Charles, was it? He knows nothing about the situation, doesn't he. He smiled at me blissfully, hoping for a good fight like everyone else, while the other two were nervous and gave it everything they had," he said as we walked in a circle, both keeping our distance. Blank ran up and swung at me again. As our swords clashed together, he said, "What I'm most curious about is what your battle against the Mutant was like. I saw them recently, and they gave me a great fight. I also want to know what your element is, but first I need to see if you are the Blue Dragonborn!" Blank screeched his sword hard against mine and stared into my eyes intensely. As I held his sword back, I did the same to see if I could get any glimpses of his powers.

Suddenly time around me completely stopped. I heard no noise. Felt no wind. The background of everything around me turned to white, leaving Blank the only visible thing. That's when I finally saw it, the thing I'd been trying to see from Blank… his armor form. I saw his armor slightly visible around him with the little aura I did see also flowing around him. His aura was a bright violet with a dark-purple accent, and in his armor form he had dark-purple scales with ridged spiraled-out horns like a demonic figure. I already knew his plates were sharp, but they looked completed with the scales next to them. Then on his right hand, the same hand he held his sword, I saw a Toxic Element symbol on it. This guy, Blank. His name wasn't just Blank, I suddenly realized. Everything around me suddenly went back to normal in a blink, and I heard everyone's voices roar out with the wind hitting me once again.

In shock at who I realized it was, I froze up in place from the initial realization of it all. During this state, Blank knocked away my sword, and it flew across the field close to Bolt and Jack at the bench.

I said, stuttering quietly, "Wha-what was that! It c-can't be real! No no no!" I looked over to Blank. "It… It can't be you! No, it c-can't be! You're—"

Blank cut me off and said, still in Dragonborn, "I don't know what you saw, but I saw a glimpse of your blue aura glow in your eyes, and that's all I care about. Tomorrow, kid, I'm gonna reveal you to everyone. I expect a great fight from you. Better use all your powers. I can't wait to see what kind of element you have. Until then," he said as he gestured for the next squad to come up.

I was frozen in place, unable to move. Thoughts were rushing through my mind at the same time as a bunch of flashbacks from my past. This guy

Blank… his full name was Seath De'Blank. He was one of the most dangerous Dragonborn generals back in the war. He was the one who destroyed everything from my past. He was the one who burned down my home village, the one who killed my parents, the one who gave me the scars on my arms, the one who chased me all the way to Infinitas, the one who had been haunting my dreams for the past eight years. I only saw his face once long ago, so I couldn't recognize it. All I could remember from them was that they had green eyes and a purple Toxic Element, but their armor form, on the other hand, was deeply engrained into my brain.

While I was stuck in my head, everyone around was wondering what was wrong and gossiping all around.

"Uh, Bolt, what's wrong with her?" Jack asked.

"She's frozen in place. I'm going to drag her out of here, do our emergency plan!" he told him, then ran over to me. As Bolt ran to me, he picked up my sword. Then he stood in front of me and shook me a bit and asked, "Aika… Aika, what happened? What did you see?"

He heard me mumbling to myself over and over, "It's him… I'm dead… I'm so dead."

Bolt, seeing me like this, put my sword back in my scabbard and grabbed my arm and dragged me away in a panic, with me barely able to walk as he guided me.

The event of Bolt dragging me away was a blur, with different lights and voices that I couldn't recall, but Bolt had dragged me out of the arena into the wood area from where we entered from. He let go of me and placed his hands on my shoulders and told me reassuringly, "Hey, it's all right now, I'm here. Just try and relax. You're away from everyone, okay?"

Jack came running down to us from the arena and said, "Bolt! I told Niki what was happening to Aika, and right now she's doing her part and distracting Charles, then told the guards an excuse, saying that Aika was suddenly sick."

"Oh good, thanks for that," Bolt told him. He turned to me and softly asked, "Now, Aika, please tell me what you saw."

Still overwhelmed from the realization, I told him, stuttering a bit, "I-I saw his armor form for a brief moment. That guy Blank... he's… he's Seath! The one who destroyed my life all those years ago."

"No way he's the guy!" Bolt said, shocked.

"Who's Seath?" Jack asked, confused.

Bolt hugged me close and explained to him, "Don't worry, you'll probably understand in less than a second. You already know who he is, Jack. I bet you've studied him greatly in the past. He was one of the Dragonborn generals from the war, the general that destroyed a whole clan of Dragonborns. They have the Toxic Element. I'm sure you know who that is."

Jack said a bit unsure of himself "Wait… they are Seath De'Blank? The general that won the Dragonborn war! The one who destroyed the Defender Dragonborn clan! That Seath!" He elevated his voice as he spoke more and more. "But that's impossible. Why would someone like that be here to hunt down random Dragonborns in hiding?" he asked, confused.

I quietly said to them, "He's probably here just for fun and games, but I bet you he probably came all the way out here to hunt down runaway War Dragonborns."

"What do you mean?" Jack asked.

"Don't worry. You'll understand later after I tell you about him. Because right before he walked away, he told me he was going to reveal me tomorrow."

"Tomorrow!" Bolt said, surprised.

"Yeah," I said quietly back to him.

Bolt, not knowing what to say, just sighed and said to us, "Well, we'll have to discuss this all later when we have more time. For now let's just head back before anyone realizes we're gone. Okay?" he asked me.

"Yeah, it's fine… I can pull myself together until it ends," I told him.

We all snuck back into the arena and sat on the bleachers to watch the few remaining fights left.

Seath here was a Toxic Element. The Toxic Element was probably the strongest element out of the five. It even had the nickname of the

Anti-Element because it was resistant to all of the other elements and had no major weaknesses. The Toxic Element's symbol was a round-cornered *X* with tiny triangles that pointed toward the center on the top, bottom, left, and right of the *X*. The power of the toxic affected all other elements the same; only other Toxic Elements were immune to their toxicity. They created sludge that was highly toxic to Dragonborns, but it barely stung regular people, so Slayers often used this sludge in weapons and traps. This sludge caused Dragonborns to feel totally numb and slowed us down a lot in our movements and reaction time. This sludge was created from their hands, and they could cover themselves in it for protection and shoot it out of their palms like a hose and cover the nearby area with sludge or hit people hard. Their only other powers were their fire, which was decently powerful, and their flight, which was the slowest compared to all the other elements. They were also the only Dragonborns who could have a black aura. Their possible aura colors could be almost anything except anything light or whitish colors in general; all their colors had some sort of darker tone to them.

Finally when all the battles were done, Seath shouted out to everyone, "Thank you all for coming here this evening. Now I have a very important announcement! I have been collecting a lot of evidence about people, and I finally found who your mysterious Blue Dragonborn is. I plan to reveal them tomorrow evening before sunset, so get plenty of sleep and get ready for a great battle!"

All the Slayers roared with excitement, talking with one another.

Charles, beside us on the bleachers, cheered out in excitement, "You hear that, guys, that devil is doomed!"

Jack said to him, "Hey, Charles, I'm going to be a bit busy after this. How about you hang out with Vanessa's squad for a bit?"

"Oh, uh, okay, what are you busy with all of a sudden?" Charles asked.

"Oh, uh… I just realized I forgot to grab a few documents from a certain place and needed to run over and grab them and hide them someplace else, before the other Slayers find them," Jack told him.

"Well, all right then. I'll just hang out with Vanessa for a bit," Charles said back. So when we all finally left, Charles went over to Vanessa's squad, and Niki joined us, and we all walked together back to her study.

When we all got settled down in the living room of Niki's study, it was finally time for me to tell them who exactly I was.

"Jack… Niki… it's about time I finally told you who I am. But before I do, I'm curious about something. What kind of element do you think I am?" I asked.

Niki's eyes lit up, and she said, "Oh, Aika, I can't wait to tell you what I thought of!"

Jack said, "To be honest, I'm stumped on what it could be. Everything I thought of had a counter for it not to be that element."

I said to Niki, "What did you think?"

Niki began her rant and said, "Oh, yes, I'll begin! First of all, you can't be a Fire or Electric Element because your aura is blue. You can't be an Ice Element because fire attacks are super powerful, so I heard. Also you can't be a Wind Element because you were like electric-proof the other day back in that battle. Then finally you can't be a Toxic Element because back in training, you looked sick after touching any toxic sludge at all. So I think you either have a power none of us has ever seen before, or I've completely lost my mind trying to figure it out."

Jack said to her, "That's why I can't figure it out! Whenever I think of something, there's always a counter for everything, which doesn't make any sense."

Niki said, "I remember there was a Dragonborn back in the war that had some kind of special power, though. We never got the chance to see much of their power, but I heard it was unlike any other!"

Jack replied, "I'm pretty sure I know who you're talking about! I think they were the commander of the Defender Dragonborn clan. It's too bad they died in that war; I would have loved to study their powers."

Bolt and I looked at each other for a moment. Then I turned back to them and said, "Well time to finally tell you and give you your answers. Jack, remember what I told you about my last name?" I asked.

Jack answered, "You always say your last name is unknown?"

I asked him, "Jack, do you recall the full name of that Dragonborn commander you just mentioned?"

Jack replied, "Their name was Adem the' Unown, why? Wait… wait… wait, what?" he questioned.

"Wait, was I right about you having some unknown power?" Niki asked, astonished for once.

So I finally told them, "My name is Aika the' Unown. I was the heir to the destroyed Defender clan. I am a Dragonborn with powers unlike any other alive! My element is the Ultimate Blue Electric! People often call me the Blue Ultimate. You may have heard it once before; people have created a whole religion from it."

Jack said, "The… the Ultimates are real? And you're the Ultimate Blue! I… this is a dream come true, but I would've never expected you to be them. I thought it was all just a crazy thing that the religions made up?"

"To be honest, I just thought Peter was even more crazy than me, so I never took what he said to heart," Niki said.

"I now respect you because of that statement," Jack replied to her.

I told him, "Well, most of it is fake… but some of it is true. Because I do have some sort of hidden power that I don't even know—I never got told what kind of power the Ultimates have or how it activates. I know I have my own special one compared to the rest; I may have never used it before, or I might be using it all the time. I don't know. But the rest is all quite normal. I have the same kind of powers as any old normal Electric Element, but they are much stronger than normal. My speed is a lot faster than the normal speed—it's the same as a Wind Element. Then my fire has the same strength as a Fire Element. Finally my electricity is way stronger than any Electric Dragonborn. Normal Electric Dragonborns have a weakness to ice, but my weakness is much more severe than normal, though I'm pretty sure it's because I'm always producing electricity, and that uses my natural body heat to create it. That's why I hate the cold so much: it drains all my body heat to nothing."

Niki asked me, "Hey, Aika, you haven't gone all out with your powers in years. Can you still use them all properly?"

I told her, "Well, the honest truth about that is yes. Back in the day I was forced to train my powers every day, so it all became muscle memory. Though I'm a bit unsure about summoning my wings. I haven't done that in… a long time."

"Oooh, do it right now?" Niki asked.

"I'd, uhh… rather not. I'm too mentally exhausted. But don't fret, you'll see it tomorrow," I told her.

Jack asked me, "Aika, you said you're from the Defender clan, right? Then how did you get all the way here? What… what happened to you?"

So I replied, "Well, I'll just give you the short version of my story. We don't have enough time for the whole story, okay?" I told them, "I am from the Eastern Dragonborn Lands, the Dragonborn land closest to yours. We the Defenders were the reason why you had very few Dragonborn attacks. Our army were the Dragonborns with the blue scabbards. They were blue to represent the east land, which was ruled by the Blue Ultimate… my father. But as you all know, it was completely destroyed years ago. For the past eight years, I've been hiding from Seath and all other Dragonborns because of something that happened to me in the past." I then pulled the photo of me and my parents out of my jacket and gave it to them. I told them, "My father was Adem the' Unown. He was the greatest Dragonborn warrior in history—he made many allies and enemies. You see, at the end of the war, the Defender clan and Conquest clan were battling with each other constantly for a good while. The Conquest clan's army were the Conquerors; they are the Dragonborns who have black scabbards. They were black to represent the south land, which was ruled by the Black Ultimate. One day toward the end of the war, a strange man showed up at our village. He told us he knew how to make our army impenetrable and how no one would ever defeat us. No one believed him, so he left for the Conquerors. That man was Seath. Seath was the one who created War Dragonborns. After he made them, Seath became one of the war generals for their clan. His creation worked wonders and wiped out most of our army in a single week. So one day my dad came to me and gave me a task. It was to sneak into Seath's lair and find out how he was creating all these War Dragonborns and what his next plans were. So I followed his orders and snuck inside, as my dad told me to. When I reached his office, I saw this weird vial filled with black goop on his desk with a large map of the war field with red marker writing all over it, with arrows that represented the troops that would attack. All of this was a giant, all-out attack that was to hit us in a few days. As I was looking over this map, though, Seath walked into his office and caught me. So of course he ran after me because I was some intruder, so right when our eyes met, I grabbed the map and vial, then ran for my life. It was all so quick I never got a chance to memorize his face, only his eyes, which were green. I ran so fast to the exit with Seath following close behind me. When I got outside, I ran to my dad, and he saw Seath after me, so he summoned his wings and flew over and lifted me to the sky. Seath was an inch away from catching me. After my dad got me away, he stuck down Seath, stunning him in his movement so we could get away. When we got to safety, I showed him everything I'd grabbed and explained what I thought he was planning. But it didn't matter because the next day him and his armies came early and destroyed everything in their path. My dad, in a last-ditch effort, battled against Seath to try and protect everyone. But it was worthless. Seath killed my dad, then flew over and burned down my village to ashes alongside almost all of my people. As he was doing so, they saw me with my mother in my village and flew down to attack us. I'm not sure if he wanted me dead because I stole his stuff and got him in trouble or if it was because I was Adem's daughter. But when he attacked, he killed my mother, who was trying to protect me and the others fleeing in a heroic last stand, then tried to come after me. Let's just say I barely escaped. The only damage he did was the scars on my arms. Thus the story 'I was attacked by a Dragonborn' was born. I ran away from everything and started over here at Infinitas. I have no idea if he has been, but there's a good chance that he's been looking for me for the past eight years. But for everybody else who knew me from back then… they all think I'm dead. The only one who knew I could still be alive… was Seath."

Jack and Niki were silent, not knowing what to say after my story.

Jack quietly said, "Geez, I want to punch my younger fifteen-year-old self for never realizing how much you were going though."

Niki said after, "Wow, I knew you had some past hidden trauma, but I never expected this much. I kinda feel bad for letting Vanessa say all those things back then during the Photo Incident."

I told them, "Hey, if you think that was a lot, it's nothing compared to the whole story from the very beginning of my childhood. This was only the short version of it, but that's for after this mess is over."

Bolt patted me on the shoulder, then started explaining the plan to them. "Tomorrow when Seath reveals Aika, all chaos will break loose. We have no idea what he plans to do, so Aika and I came up with a few different plans to use depending on what he does. I'll explain the more complicated ones later, but these are the simple ones we have. If Seath only cares about fighting Aika, it would be the best-case scenario. Us three would just watch the fight and intervene when necessary if anybody tries to attack anybody. But in a worst-case scenario, we would have to evacuate everyone and fully help Aika in battle, because if something does happen in the middle of battle to Aika, we'll be in trouble. And that leads into the next subject: we need to make sure the Slayers don't try and kill Aika. We need to protect her from them during battle because somebody might try and pull a fast one and try to shoot at her in the middle of her fighting. Hopefully I can convince them to hold back from shooting at her and only make them shoot at the others."

I told them, "Seath is at least going to have a few henchmen to help him fight during battle. One of them is already here—they were the person Seath was talking to earlier at the arena. I bet a few more are coming; that's why Seath is waiting till tomorrow evening to reveal me."

Bolt grabbed a quiver of arrows and gave a couple to Jack and Niki and said, "To help prepare for tomorrow, we're going to be making something a little special. As you know, the Electric Elements can create these electric crystals with their powers." Then I created some in my hand and dropped them into Bolt's hand. He continued talking and said, "Aika's electric crystals are supercharged, and we can use them to make a special arrow that can stun Dragonborns for a moment, like if Aika struck them down with lightning. It would be a good weapon to use against the other Dragonborns to help Aika. We already have a few quivers at our house, but it will be better to make a few more just in case."

"Wow, these are like Dragonborn Hunter arrows, man. How did you think of making this?" Jack asked.

"I, uh… know a bit about Dragonborn Hunters and their weapons. I just decided to put my own twist on it. I can show you how I did. Though it's a shame my uncle's forge was destroyed—I could have sharpened our swords and armor," Bolt said.

"Sometimes I forget you have decent blacksmith skills. It's that one who doesn't," Jack said as he examined one of the arrows, then pointed it at me.

"Hey, at least me being the delivery gal made me familiar with the towns around!" I replied, annoyed.

"Really, familiar?" Jack asked.

"Well… know how to get to the market plaza quickly," I said.

"Yeah, that's a more accurate answer coming from you," Jack replied.

"Hey, guys, can we get back on track please?" Bolt asked us.

"Oh yes, sorry, Bolt. Your idiot just forgot how things used to work," Jack told him.

"Jack… please don't right now?" Bolt asked him.

"Oh, what?" he asked.

"Because of that," Bolt told him, then looked over to me glaring at him.

"Oh yeah… all right, sorry to keep you waiting. Go on and explain," he told him.

Bolt sighed, then began his explanation.

So Bolt and I showed Jack and Niki how to make the arrows, which involved gluing the crystals below the tips of the arrow carefully, and how to use them which involved tapping the crystal ever so slightly for it to glow. Then when you shot it out, it would stun whatever target that was hit.

A few minutes into making a whole stack of them, Niki said to us, "Oh, I forgot to tell you guys something important!"

"What is it?" I asked.

Then in the most carefree way possible, she casually said, "I forgot to tell you guys that I stole the Sound Radiator from Seath."

"What?!?" we all shouted at her.

Niki asked, "What are you all so surprised about? I told you yesterday that Seath probably took it, and I was right."

"When the hell did you steal that back from him?" Jack asked in pure confusion before Bolt and I could.

Niki replied, "Easy, during my duel with him earlier. As soon as I swiped it, I purposely lost, so he wouldn't expect anything suspicious."

"You lost to him purposely?" I asked, flabbergasted.

"Yeah, I did, why?" she asked.

Dumbfounded, I just replied, "You know what, never mind! Just hand me the SR, please."

"Okay, here," she said as she handed it to me.

I sighed as I looked down on it and said, "Well, at least I got an emergency backup plan if things go to hell."

Bolt asked me, "Would you be okay if you activated it? Remember what happened last time?"

I told him, "Hopefully I don't have to use it, but if I do, I got those earplugs they gave me, so maybe that will help. If not, I'll just have to put it on low and endure the noise."

"Do you know where your earplugs are?" Bolt asked with a blank expression.

"Of course I do, they're…" I said but suddenly stopped.

"You lost them, didn't you," Jack replied to my silence.

"Maybe," I said.

"Yep, that's what I figured," Bolt said to himself as he placed an arrow into the done pile. "I told you to keep them in a safe spot. None of us got any because we all passed the sensitivity test. What did you do with them once we moved?" Bolt asked me.

"Put them in a place that I immediately forgot about," I replied.

"I'm taking a wild guess that they're gone forever," Niki said as she watched us.

"Not gone forever, I'll find them when I get home," I told them.

"I can see you losing the only thing that helps your greatest weakness besides your pride and pettiness," Jack replied.

"I... am not that petty!" I told him, annoyed.

"Oh really? Try shooting a bow better than me or Bolt," Jack teased.

"Oh, you're on, then!" I told him as I stood.

"Aika, no!" Bolt told me as he grabbed me by the end of my jacket and brought me back to my seat.

"Oh, come on, Bolton!" I replied.

"Finish the arrows first, then you can," he told me.

"But it's going to take us all night to do so!" I told him.

"Exactly," he simply replied with a blank expression.

"Fine," I said as I started working again.

Throughout the night we discussed our plans and worked and made a few good quivers of arrows, then decided to call it a night, and Jack and I did our bet... I lost. We decided to go back home, but before we all went our separate ways, we agreed to meet up at our house the next day to collect everything we were going to need for the battle. As Bolt and I walked back to the house carrying the quivers of arrows we all made, Bolt asked me, "Do you think everything will end up okay? I'm ready for tomorrow, but at the same time I'm not."

I replied to him, "I'm not sure. After tomorrow, things will never be the same."

And never did find my A-waves that night, even after I tore the place apart looking for them.

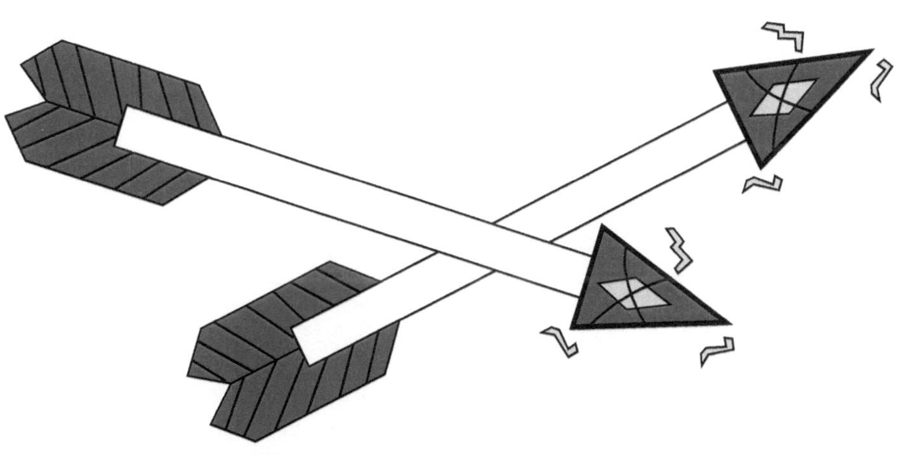

Chapter 14: Revealed

I suddenly woke up in a cold sweat from my sleep. I was having some sort of nightmare from my past but I couldn't remember any of the details. I felt a horrible chill for no reason afterward. Beside me to my left, Bolt was still completely asleep in bed, so I checked what time it was and saw that it was four in the morning. Everything was still pitch black outside. So I tried to fall back asleep, but to no avail. I was wide awake. Bolt, Jack, Niki, and I had worked late into the night making those arrows, and even with my indescribable exhaustion from the last few days, I still could not fall asleep from all my nerves. So I decided to take a walk around Infinitas to clear my head.

I moped out of bed and got ready for the day, made myself a coffee to go, and went on my way to walk around for a while. I ended up walking all around Infinitas, down all the paths we did patrols on, to the sword-training ground we all used to hang out in, the place where I first met Bolt, Clay's burned-down house, Charles's old burned-down house, the market plaza, by the Slayer-training grounds, then on top of the outer wall around Infinitas. While I was on the outer wall, I watched the sunrise coming up from the open plain that was east of Infinitas. As I did, I thought of all the events that had happened within the first month and a half that I had been a Dragon Slayer.

I watched the sunrise for about five minutes until I heard someone walk toward me. When I looked to see who it was, it was none other than Seath.

"It's a lovely area to watch the sunrise, don't you think?" Seath asked me all friendly-like. "Ahh, a sunrise… the start of a new day with endless possibilities," he said again, sounding a bit ominous.

"What are you here for?" I asked, tired of his facade.

Seath said happily, "Oh good, you like to get right to the point! I also hate wasting time, so I'll just begin. You see, I am very impressed with how long you've been here. Then again, the people are impressively stupid to the point that I have no idea on how they have a stable economy. How can you endure them calling you a devil all the time?" he asked.

I asked him, "Why are you talking to me? Why don't we just jump over this wall to the other side and begin this fight now? Why bother to make small talk with me?"

Seath told me, "Oh please, it's way too early in the morning for that. I can see the sleep-deprived look in your eyes anyways. I came to talk to you for a reason. I want to know your opinion about these people—you've been here long enough to have some kind of emotion for them," he said with a sinister smile on his face.

"What are you planning?" I asked.

Seath said, "Well, you see… I really hate the people here. So after our little showdown, I was going to… you know… burn down Infinitas along with all its people," he explained.

"Why are you just telling me all this? You think I'm a complete fool or something?" I asked.

"Oh, I'm telling you all of this for a very special reason! You see, I want to watch the hope drain from your eyes when you see your own people attack you after all you've done for them," he told me.

I told him, "They won't attack me… I got my trump card to help me out."

Seath replied as he walked away, "Just wait and see, kid: once people learn that you're a devil… they won't care about anything you say. I learned that the hard way."

He walked away and left me alone. I sighed and looked over to the sunrise again. The sun had risen over the mountains by then. I was left thinking to myself, "If I lose this battle… everybody in Infinitas will be killed, just like what happened to my home village." I suddenly felt another chill. It was the same from this morning. I looked up into the sky and searched around. The sky was empty, though, but that was what made me realize this aura presence was definitely the Mutant. The chills I had were exactly the same from that day. This battle was going to be far bigger than anything I'd experienced before.

When I got back to the house, I shut the door behind me and leaned against it, sighing. I saw Bolt finishing up breakfast, and he looked over to me and asked, "Hey you doing okay? You look a bit… dead inside?"

I was silent for a moment until I finally told him, "Bolt… I was talking to Seath before I walked back here. It's plan absolute worst-case scenario."

Bolt put down some plates on the table, then walked over to me and asked worriedly, "What's he planning to do?"

I told him "He's planning on burning down Infinitas alongside everyone who lives here."

Bolt was silent for a moment, and all he replied was "Geez… that's going to be trouble later. Come on, let's just have breakfast for now and… we'll think of something later when Jack and Niki come."

While we were at the table eating, Clay woke up and entered the kitchen. He asked us, "What's the matter with you two? You both look distressed."

Bolt asked him, "Hey, Uncle Clay… can I talk to you for a moment?"

Clay replied, "Yeah, sure, what's the matter?"

Bolt told him, "We are going to be busy with work-related stuff this afternoon. Could you run out to the market plaza and grab a few things and come back before evening? Something big is going to happen later, and I want to make sure we're plenty stocked up with supplies in case something really bad happens."

Clay told him, "Oh yeah, sure, and you want me to be out all afternoon?" he asked to make sure.

"Yes, please… Jack and Niki are coming over to help plan out something for later," Bolt replied to him.

Clay asked, "Is this about the reveal of the Blue Dragonborn today?"

Bolt answered, "Yeah… it is."

"Okay then. How about I go out for breakfast, then do the shopping you wanted. Does that sound good?" he asked.

"Yeah, thanks, Uncle Clay," Bolt replied.

After Clay headed out, I lay on the couch and said to Bolt, "I'm so tired right now. All I can think about is what's going to happen later… it's driving me crazy."

Bolt told me, "Relax for now, I'll handle all the preparations. Just try and get some sleep if you can. You're going to need all the energy for later."

"Yeah, you're right," I replied as I closed my eyes.

I proceeded to fall asleep for a while until I smelled a fresh pot of coffee brewing. As I sat up and looked behind me to the kitchen, I saw Jack laughing so hard that he cried slightly, and Niki looking at me dumbfounded as she said, "Oh my goodness, the smell of coffee actually woke her up!"

"See, what did I tell you guys?" Bolt said to the two.

"I'm not even going to question what the conversation was," I said as I got off the couch and stood. "So what were you guys talking about while I was asleep?" I asked as I stretched out my arms.

"Just discussing last-minute plans on what to do because of what Seath told you this morning," Jack told me.

"Oh yeah," I said tiredly as I walked over to my sword lying behind the couch and grabbed it. Around the place there were piles of arrows and bags of my electric crystals together. When I looked over at the time, it was almost time to head out so I walked toward the others.

Bolt asked me, "So how are you feeling? You were out all afternoon."

I told him, "Eh, a bit better than how I was this morning. After I make myself a cup of coffee and put on my boots, wanna head out?" I asked.

"Sure, we're already prepared for everything. We were actually about to wake you up in a few minutes if the coffee didn't," Bolt told me.

"Oh really?" I said as I poured myself a cup.

After I finished my coffee, I got suited up for battle. Then we all headed out to the area we were told to meet up at for the fight. It was finally time to end all of this. Within the next few hours I was to be revealed to the world, whether I wanted to be or not.

The place we were all supposed to meet up at was beside Infinitas's biggest castle. Next to the castle was a flattish hill that was completely empty, perfect for a battle between Dragonborns. On the side of the hill to the right, in front of the castle, Seath and three of his henchmen stood and watched everyone gathered around just before sunset. Me and my squad were the closest to the hill with Vanessa's squad beside us. To the right of us, all of the other Slayers stood and roared with excitement about them finally being able to get rid of this hidden Dragonborn. Behind the Slayers, quite a lot of the civilians showed up as well to watch the battle happen for some reason. Finally Seath stepped up to everyone, and the crowd was chanting louder than ever, waiting for the reveal.

"Greetings, everyone! So glad all of you can make it here this evening. Today is finally the day where I will reveal this hidden Dragonborn within you. During my time here, I've met some very interesting people and heard many interesting stories. After a lot of thinking and finding evidence, I've finally figured out who this Dragonborn is. To some there is an acquaintance, to others a friend, or a rival maybe, even a hero to some. Well, your hidden devil is none other than your very own War Slayer, Aika!" Seath hollered as he pointed over to me through the crowd.

Everyone looked over at me, shocked and in confusion. Luckily, though, beside me Charles was laughing hysterically at what Seath had said.

He, not knowing anything, shouted back to Seath, "Oh man, that's priceless! You think Aika is a devil? Please, I've known her for eight years now, and I can say with complete confidence that she's not a devil. How in the world can she be? I mean, for crying out loud, she's a Dragon Slayer. Why would a Dragonborn join an army that specializes in killing devils like them? That would be suicide!"

The crowd started agreeing with Charles and shouted back at Seath, "Yeah, how can they be a devil?"

"They look like any other person, so how?"

"Yeah, they got emotions and everything!"

Seath scowled at everyone, disgusted, then glanced over at me for a brief moment and saw me staring back at him silently. Seath glared back at everyone and walked forward, angered. As he did, the crowd of people backed up, creating an empty circle around Seath.

He shouted out to everyone, "All of you people disgust me! What do you think Dragonborns are? Demons? Monster? Parasites? Well, let me tell you the hard truth that you'll regret! Dragonborns are just a race of people who have supernatural abilities! That's it! Hell, most Dragonborns don't even know how to activate their powers, let alone use them properly!"

The crowd was dead silent in response to Seath's yelling.

Seath, now royally pissed off, yelled, "All of you people are such idiots! Are you all really this blind? For crying out loud, I'm a Dragonborn! This entire time I've had my armor plates summoned over my clothes right in front of you all! I've been hiding all the traces of my aura so none of you will notice!" He showed them his eyes, glowing their bright-violet aura. "My armor is tinted purple, my sword is tinted purple, my cape is purple! What kind of Dragonborn Hunter wears a cape anyways? I just made up that story off the top of my head to fool you all! If none of this convinces you, want to see my birthmark on my hand? I can rip off my glove right now and show you!" Seath screamed out at them, looking unhinged.

The crowd had backed up even farther from Seath as he was talking. Everyone looked a bit afraid of Seath after he told them this.

Seath calmed down a little and said, "Don't you all know the old saying 'A person of the same kind can recognize another of their own'? I knew Aika was a Dragonborn from the first moment I saw her. All I needed was evidence to convince you all that she is one. So let me explain three undeniable pieces of evidence that I've picked up from my short time here. First of all, I hear they wear gloves all the time and never show their bare skin on their hands. I wonder why? Oh wait, I know! Maybe to cover up their element birthmark all Dragonborns are born with! Second, they have a blue Dragonborn sword. Isn't the Dragonborn you all wanted me to find also blue? Also on top of that, I heard they disappeared when the Blue Dragonborn appeared. It's either a lovely coincidence or they have to be them! Third, don't you think it's strange that Dragonborns tend to target them? I mean, it's not like we can sense each other's aura and feel the need to fight each other. Oh wait… we do! Our powers were made to kill one another!" Seath yelled out as loud as he could at the end.

He stopped, turned to me, and smiled menacingly.

Seath shouted out, "Oh, I know how I can prove they're a Dragonborn right now! You see, only a Dragonborn has super-sharp reaction time to take action before anything bad happens," he said as he summoned the armor form on his right hand and stretched out his claws.

His element pattern glowed brightly on the plate on top of his hand, with his aura flowing all around him. Seath began to scan the crowd of people until he looked over by me again—looking right at Bolt. He took a step forward toward him and smiled. That's when I realized what his plan was: he suddenly dashed forward toward Bolt with his claws ready.

Time around me felt like it completely stopped for a moment. I saw Seath about to tear Bolt's face apart right in front of me. So with no hesitation, I did exactly what Seath wanted me to do. So I pushed Bolt out of the way from his claws, and I glanced right to Seath. His claws shredded through my skin like nothing, from the top right to the bottom left of my right eye. I screamed out in pain as he took his claws away, covered in my blood. Everyone around was silent, frozen in place from the sudden event, not knowing what to do or say.

Seath shouted to everyone, "You see! What kind of normal person could have reflexes and reaction time like that!"

Bolt had fallen on the ground from my push. As soon as he caught his breath, he immediately got up and ran over to me and asked, "Aika! Are you—"

I put my hand out in front of him and stopped him from talking and told him quietly, "Bolton… it's time." Then he backed off a little, knowing what I was about to do.

Today was the day… no matter what happened. I was to finally reveal who I was to the world. So why not do it in the most me way possible, to show everyone who I really was? I was covering my face with my arms and hands, preventing anyone from seeing me. When I tried to speak to everyone, I couldn't and started laughing to myself a little.

Confused, Seath asked, "The hell are you laughing at?"

I stopped and silently put my arms down and looked up at Seath. When I showed my face to everyone, the entire right side of my face was drenched in blood. Everyone saw the power I'd been hiding for years in my eyes, which glowed yale blue.

I shouted out to Seath, "After eight years of hiding my powers, I am finally revealed. And of course I am revealed by another Dragonborn that snitched me out to everyone. Just my luck."

I started to walk around Seath in the circle everyone made around him. As I did, my aura followed behind my movements.

I asked Seath as I walked around, "So, you revealed that I'm a Dragonborn—whoop-de-doo. What are you going to do now? Earlier you told me you were going to burn down Infinitas alongside all its people after you were done with me. But what are you going to do with me? You gonna spew toxic sludge at me till I drop from blood poisoning? You gonna electrocute all my neurons out till I go brain dead? You gonna explode my head off like a pinata? You gonna wind blast me down to a stain on the ground? Or are you going to freeze me solid and shatter me into millions of pieces all over the place? WHAT? What are you going to do with me? Nobody has a clue about what my element is or how powerful I may be!"

Seath ordered his henchmen, "You three, get them!"

Then his henchmen summoned their wings and flew to the clouds above. The crowd around shirked a bit as the three of them flew up.

I shouted out to Seath, "Come on, bring me your best! I've been preparing for this moment for a long time now. I'm ready for anything!"

I stopped walking when I came in front of the hill again. Vanessa's squad and Charles moved aside, and Bolt, Jack, and Niki stood behind me ready. From the sky I saw Seath's henchmen drag down the Mutated Dragonborn, the one that had started this entire mess. But for some reason the Mutant had a weird collar around their neck. They landed in front of Seath and held down the Mutant, who was trying to charge at me.

"Bring it on!" I hollered back at them as I put out my arms.

"Release them!" Seath commanded his henchmen.

As soon as they did, the Mutant charged at me and summoned their wings, then dragged me to the sky above the hill. As they dragged me, I began charging up my power to unleash a heavy attack. Behind us the three henchmen followed in the sky.

While I was being dragged up into the sky, everyone was freaking out on the ground.

Charles ran up to Bolt and grabbed the front of his hoodie and yelled in confusion, "Bolton, what's going on? What the hell is happening right now? How... how long have you known that she was a Dragonborn? Tell me!"

Bolt pushed Charles away and told him, "I'm sorry, Charles. What's about to happen right now is way more important than our own personal drama." He looked over to Jack and Niki and shouted out to them, "Get into positions and set up your launchers, guys. Time to do plan absolute worst-case scenario."

As they got into position, Charles asked Jack "Even you knew? Was I the only one who was left in the dark?"

Jack looked away and replied, "I'm sorry, man, but you need to get away from us. Shit is about to go down fast."

Charles stepped back and joined Vanessa's squad. When they were in position, they all looked up to the sky and waited for me to do my thing.

When the Mutant dragged me high enough into the sky, they set off their explosion, and the three henchmen combined their attacks within the Mutant's attack and created a giant explosion with electricity, ice, and even stronger winds that flowed around everywhere in the sky. But before the smoke cleared away, the sky went dark blue, and navy and black clouds formed above us. The smoke suddenly disappeared around us, clearing the view for everyone to watch. With my aura violently swirling around me, I released the fury of my powers and released four bolts of blue lightning down on the Dragonborns who attacked me, striking them down from the sky. While I did so, my jacket fully activated from blasting my element attack. The edges of my sleeves, collar, and around the sides of my jacket glowed with a golden zigzag triangle pattern. On the middle of the back, my element symbol also glowed in gold, and of course that symbol was for the Electric Element. A second after I released my power, I started falling down fast downward, with a trail of my electricity following me. As I tried to summon my wings after not using them for so long, flashbacks from my childhood ran through my mind of when my dad trained me to use my powers. Then as I was falling, I remembered the day he taught me how to fly.

I was ten years old and my dad wanted me to learn how to summon my wings and glide in the air. So we went to a big deserted field away from everyone, and he lifted me high in the sky.

I asked him, "What are we doing?"

He told me, "Today I'm going to teach you how we fly, Aika. This is the way I learned how when I was a kid, although I was a teenager when I learned... eh, it doesn't matter much."

When I looked down and saw how high we were, I asked, "What if I can't summon my wings?"

My dad told me, "Don't worry about that, Aika. I'll catch you if anything bad happens. Anyways, I know that you'll be able to summon your wings with no problem."

"All right, I guess," I replied.

He gave me a countdown and dropped me down. As I fell, my anxiety went crazy. I had no idea on how to even summon my wings. When I looked back up at the sky and saw the clouds above, I felt this unknown feeling that made me want to reach out to the sky. For the first time I summoned my wings and glided through the wind.

As I did, I saw my dad glide down toward me, and he shouted out, "See I told you could do it! What you're doing right now took me twelve attempts to do so, and I was sixteen years old when I finally figured it out."

He and I glided through the wind together all afternoon practicing.

As I continued to fall, I suddenly felt that feeling again from all the way back then. When I tried to summon my wings, this time I succeeded, and a swirl of electricity swooshed around me as they appeared. When I went to glide upward, I shot up into the sky from how fast I'd been falling. With all the momentum that I had built up, I circled high above the field where everyone stood. A trail of electricity followed me, and my wings and aura glowed bright in the darkness from my attack being unleashed. Time slowed for a second as I analyzed how many people were around and needed to get out of here, I flew back down to the ground near the top of the hill. As I glided, I saw Seath laughing hysterically as he watched me use my powers. I landed in front of everyone with Bolt, Jack, and Niki directly below me on the hill and stopped my attack on the four. The sky above went back to normal, which had turned to sunset.

Having everyone's attention, I shouted out loud for everyone to hear, "Throughout my entire life I've always been asked 'Who are you?' or 'What are you?' Well, let me tell you! I'm Aika the' Unown, the daughter of the greatest Dragonborn warrior to have ever lived! I am the one and only holder of the Ultimate Blue Electric Element! I am a warrior, cursed with powers unlike any other in this world. But listen here, everyone, I am not your enemy! Dragonborns are not your enemy! The real villain here is that monster down there. You may know them as just Blank the Dragonborn Hunter, but their real identity is Seath De'Blank, a powerful Dragonborn general from a faraway land. He is the devil of the devils! Eight years ago that monster destroyed my entire life and almost single-handedly destroyed the most powerful Dragonborn clan to have been built. Please people of Infinitas, listen to me. Seath is planning on destroying your home alongside all of you. If you want to save your home and protect your people, please help me defeat this devil! And I promise you all, after this is done, I'll tell you everything about me and what Dragonborns really are."

From behind me, the Mutant flew down and tried blasting me with an explosion. So I turned around and made a fire shield to protect everyone.

As I did, I heard Seath yell out behind me, "I can't believe it, after all this time you really did survive my attack! Well, good news for me, I didn't kill all of the Unown bloodline." Then he ordered to his henchmen, "Listen, you fools, attack them with everything you got!"

As I turned my head to him and everyone, I saw Seath activated his entire armor form and fly up into the air above us. When he transformed into his armor form, his cape combined with his armor form and glowed a zigzag triangle pattern on all the edges, just like my jacket, and glowed with a golden toxic symbol on the back in the center. Before he flew up too high, Seath quickly blasted me with a spout of sludge from his hands at my back, causing me to step forward from the impact. Then he flew up higher and said, "You better give me a good fight down there, Blue!" before he flew up even higher to the top of the castle to watch me fight. The toxicity wasn't bad because I had gained some immunity from it during training, but it was definitely going to be painful later, making my body more numb as time went on. When I looked at the others; they had successfully backed everyone away from the hill, so with the area cleared, I pushed back the Mutant's fire even farther and struck a good-size bolt of lightning at the Mutant to temporarily paralyze them, then ran down to Bolt and the others.

Some of the Slayers were confused and scared, not knowing what to do. Some others were angry at what was happening and how they couldn't do anything to intervene. They cried to Bolt, Jack, and Niki for answers on what was happening and if they knew about me this whole time.

"Bolton!" I called out to him.

As Bolt ran to me, Jack and Niki blocked the crowd from us so we could talk.

When I got close enough, I stopped in front of Bolt and told him, "I paralyzed the Mutant for a moment to give us some time. Bolt I don't know when I'll be able to talk with you again, so I'll just say this… thank you. Thank you, Bolton. For everything that you've done for me. You know what to do next. I'm counting on you. Show them all your bolts of fury!"

Bolt replied, "Hey, don't worry about a thing down here. I got this! Just get out there and kick all their butts for us, and I'll be down here backing you up at every moment!"

The Mutant started walking down the hill slowly, leaving a small trail of fire as it did.

"Well, that's my cue to get out there. Good luck, Bolton." I kissed him goodbye and stepped away.

Then I activated my armor form in front of everyone for the first time and ran over to the Mutant. When I activated my armor form, my jacket integrated with my arm plates, my forearms, and shoulders, and thick scales all appeared over my jacket with my scales under with the rest normal. At the time I had no idea, but when Seath scratched my right eye, it had scarred my armor form like my arms. The scales on my eye had a bright-blue claw-shaped scar exactly the same as the ones on my arms. As I was running toward the Mutant, I grabbed out a handful of electric crystals from a pocket in my jacket and threw them up in the air around me. The crystals immediately activated and withered away into aura that combined with the aura around me, supercharging my powers. I stopped about seven feet from the Mutant and struck a huge bolt of lightning onto the Mutant, to knock them out immediately so they wouldn't hurt anyone.

While I was doing all of that, Bolt walked up to Zane and sternly told him, "Sir, I demand to be put in charge of the Slayers right now! I am the only one who knows exactly what's currently happening and what's going to happen if we do nothing. Aika and I have been planning on what to do if this ever happened, and now it has. Trust me, look at your army," he said as he pointed to the Slayers freaking out behind him.

Zane sighed angrily and turned around to the Slayers behind him. He yelled to them, "Everyone, listen up! Bolton is being put in temporarily in charge of the Slayers until the battle is over! You will follow his orders with no complaining!"

Then he gestured to Bolt for him to take over.

Bolt stepped forward to them and ordered, "Okay, everyone, listen up! Jack, Niki, and I have been preparing like crazy for the past twenty-four hours like there's no tomorrow for this battle! We have made this new type of arrow from Aika's powers that can stun Dragonborns in place to help back her up in battle. You will be receiving these arrows to help her and defend yourselves. If any of you try to attack Aika at any time, just remember this. You could risk everyone in the kingdom's life. Why? Well, if Aika gets seriously hurt during combat... let's just say you better start praying to whoever you believe in because it will turn into anarchy real fast after they're done with her. Because when they are done with Aika... we're next. And Seath is way too powerful for our army to handle while protecting the citizens. Anyways, now everyone take some arrows and pass them around!"

Jack and Niki handed out quivers of arrows to the Slayers.

As they did, Bolt continued to give commands. "After everyone gets a good amount, split into two groups! Group one needs a quarter of the Slayers to stay here and help us back up Aika in battle, then group two needs the rest of you to go and help the civilians to evacuate to the natural disaster chambers! We have no idea what the outcome of the battle will be, so take all precautions! Make sure that no one will get hurt and keep them safe! Got it?"

As Bolt finished his speech, the Mutant dropped to the ground and collapsed from the amount of electricity I was striking them with. After they hit the ground, I stopped my attack and stepped back for a moment. I was shaking a bit from my attack; I hadn't used that power like that in such a long time. It was overexerting to use it for as long as I just did. I would have to take a break for a good while until I released my next electric attack. I looked up to the sky and saw Seath's henchmen flying around in a circle watching me fight the Mutant. So I pulled myself together and summoned my wings and flew up into the sky while the wind around me was still crazy from the Mutant's fire. When I flew up to them, I shouted out at them, switching to only speaking Dragonborn so they could understand me. "What's up, losers, ready to start the real fight?"

None of them responded; they all backed off and drew out their swords from behind them.

"Eh, rude," I said to myself.

All these Dragonborns were different elements. The first was the original henchman that arrived yesterday at that sword ground. They were an orange Wind Element with a dark reddish-orange accent that had smooth wavy horns. The other two were new henchmen that just showed up. One of them was a green Ice Element with a forest green accent that had ridged imp horns, and the other was a greenish-yellow Electric Element with a dark-yellow accent that had smooth demonic horns. All three of them had black scabbards and spiky pointed armor.

They all stared at me for a moment until they charged at me with no warning. I deactivated my wings and fell downward to dodge them, but the Ice still flew down after me. So I summoned my wings again to fly up to dodge them and flew up high above them all. But below me there were only two of them, which were the Wind and Ice. Then I felt the presence of the Electric charging behind me. So as I turned around and dodged them, I kicked them on their back, pushing them away farther from me and deactivated my wings again and fell. As I did, a Slayer arrow flew by and shot the Electric Dragonborn who had tried to charge at me again. They stopped midcharge and glared at me, as they were shocked slightly from my electric crystals on the arrow.

"Wow! Hell yeah, they worked!" I cheered to myself as I summoned my wings again and flew up a bit. But I stopped once I saw the Electric Dragonborn silently rip out the arrow from their shoulder.

"Hehehe… uh, hey, friend?" I said to them as I flew back a bit and saw all three of them were staring over at me, pissed. "Ah shit," I said to myself as they all charged toward me. I flew high in the air to dodge them and reached into my jacket, then threw electric crystals all around me and struck down the three of them with my lightning.

As I did, the Wind Dragonborn hollered to me in Dragonborn, "Why can't you let us kill you?"

"Uh, easy answer, I don't want to be murdered," I replied.

They shouted, "Listen, kid, we weren't ready to fight an Ultimate today, okay? And if we don't kill you, then that madman will kill all of my family! My wife! My children! My brothers and sisters and their kids! My two coworkers here will also get their families killed!"

"Oh yeah, why do you follow his orders then instead of rebelling?" I asked them smugly as I stopped my attack and watched them paralyzed, still flying in place.

"Of course I want to rebel against them! But…"

The Ice Dragonborn cut off the Wind Dragonborn and said also in Dragonborn, "Our Lord has put them in high order, so I must follow them till our end. Stop talking and fight… before he sees you disobeying orders."

"Oh come on at me, then!" I said to them as I drew out my sword. "Just because you told me your sad backstory doesn't mean I'll let you kill me. Sure it's a sad predicament you're in, but if I die, a lot more people will die. I'd rather have your families killed than an entire kingdom of people to die. You have no idea how many people are dead because of me anyways, so just try and guilt trip me all you want," I replied as I flew back, leaving distance between us.

The Electric Dragonborn shouted, annoyed, "Oh my Ultimus, you're all wasting time here! Come on, let's get this over with before Seath kills them all anyways!"

They raised their sword and charged at me angrily. I flew to the side and jabbed at them with my sword.

The Electric Dragonborn ground their sword against mine to deflect my attack and yelled, "I'm going to kill you if it's the last thing I do! For my Lord Connor! For my family! For respect for being the one who actually killed the Blue Ultimate!"

I sensed the Ice Dragonborn flying behind me, so I suddenly flew down below, and the Ice Dragonborn flew right into the Electric Dragonborn, sending both of them back. As I flew down, I saw the Wind skydive after me, but a cluster of arrows shot them and paralyzed them before they could reach me, causing them to miss me and fall to the ground. As they fell, the Ice Dragonborn flew to me with their sword ready to slash, so I flew up to them and swung against theirs before they had the chance. But as I was doing so, the Electric Dragonborn came from the side and tried jabbing at me. I kicked the Ice Dragonborn on their chest plate to push them back and swung against the Electric Dragonborn's sword. But as I was slashing my sword against the Electric's, the Ice Dragonborn then threw an ice spear toward me, and the Wind made his wind current push the spear with stronger force. I kicked aside the Electric Dragonborn and leaned backward into the wind to dodge, but I wasn't fast enough, and the spear sliced through my scales above my knee plate. I continued to fly backward through the breeze the Wind Dragonborn made as my scales regenerated and saw the Electric Dragonborn chase after me again. As they came close, another cluster of arrows shot into the Electric Dragonborn's scales and plates, and they glared at me, pissed, as they were shot. As I watched them fall, the other two flew up and dodged the rest of the arrows, but the effects from the arrows didn't last too long. As arrows stopped being fired, the Electric Dragonborn flew down and landed on ground in front of the Slayers and prepared an attack on them. I quickly flew down after them when I saw them light up the sky slightly in preparation for their attack. I landed behind the Electric Dragonborn and threw my sword above the Slayers into the building above them. When the bolt came down onto them, I absorbed the bolt into my sword.

I yelled out at the Electric, "Hey don't you dare hurt them!"

They turned around and asked, "These people are worthless, why save them?" then released a powerful blaze of electricity at me, to stun me in place.

But luckily for me, this would be their worst mistake ever because as soon as it hit me, I immediately absorbed all the electricity that hit me into my scales and plates, fully recharging my electric power. But while I was busy draining this loser, I was left practically defenseless, and the other two

Dragonborns flew after me.

I heard Bolt yell, "Fire now!"

A big cluster of arrows fired over me at the two, which made them fly back up, and the Slayers followed them, making a trail of arrows in the air for them to dodge. As all of that was happening, I became fully charged with electricity, and the Electric Dragonborn looked like they were on the brink of collapsing. So I stopped draining their electricity, then ran over to them and sucker punched them to the ground, to finish the job.

"Ultimus damn you!" they said as they fell.

I had absorbed a little too much electricity from them, and it was swirling around me uncontrollably. My head started to spin as my senses got fixated on the active auras around. Then the electricity swirled around me violently. To my luck, though, the Wind Dragonborn came at me from the sky after avoiding all the arrows.

"Oh, what beautiful timing!" I said to them as I struck down a blaze of lightning onto them.

They screamed out in pain, "Ahh for my family! I will—" They cut off their sentence as they crashed to the ground and fainted and slightly shook, paralyzed by my attack.

Finally all that remained in my way was the Ice Dragonborn. They had successfully dodged all the arrows and landed from above as they watched me take down the Wind Dragonborn. When our eyes met, they unleashed a path of ice spikes toward me. So I ran toward them and dodged the spikes appearing before me as I ran. When I got close, I prepared my claws to attack them and slashed with everything I had at them. The Ice Dragonborn dodged my attack and swung at me with their sword. I slid down to dodge their sword and tried to attack them again, but before my hand got close, they blasted me with an ice wind attack, and I was blown back a bit. I had shielded my face from the attack with my forearm plates. When I put down my arms and looked back up, I saw a huge ice wind blast come toward me. With no time to react to the oncoming attack, I was hit hard and blasted against the nearby castle's stone wall and fell to the ground. As I got on my knees, picking myself up, I got hit with yet another ice wind blast and crashed against the wall. But this time when it happened, my head hit hard against the wall, and everything went blank.

When I opened my eyes, I found myself sitting up against the wall across from the area the Slayers stood. I looked around and saw all the Slayers firing out at the Ice Dragonborn almost nonstop.

I heard a voice call out, "Hey, Bolton, she's awake!"

I looked over to see who it was, and Vanessa was there.

I switched my language back to Infinitan and asked, "Venny? Wha… what happened?"

She asked me, "Seriously in the middle of this intense battle you still call me Venny?"

I told her, "Oh, come on, Venny, do you really think that makes a difference to me?"

She sighed and said, "Geez, I still can't believe that Niki was right about you. But, well, that doesn't matter. You mocking me right now just proves how you're just Aika being Aika."

I said back, "Aww thanks, Venny, you're one of four people who know I'm just an idiot."

Vanessa said, "Well, here comes Bolton. See yeah, Aika." Then she walked out of the way, and Bolt came rushing to my side.

He knelt next to me and asked, "Hey, you okay? Can you still move?" very concerned.

"What, oh yeah, I'm fine! Why, what happened—" I abruptly stopped at the end of my sentence when I saw a whole bunch of blood-soaked handkerchiefs at my left side above my hip right next to where my jacket was under my chest plate. "Oh geez! When the hell did this happen?" I asked.

"You didn't even realize you were hurt?" Bolt asked, shocked.

I asked him, "So remember when Seath doused me in toxic sludge at the very beginning?"

"Yeah..." Bolt replied, unsure.

I explained, "Well because of that, I can't feel anything at all, and my entire body feels like it's covered in pins and needles."

Bolt sighed and said, "I think you were also stuck in your trance too while battling the Ice Dragonborn."

"I was, how so?" I asked.

Bolt explained, "Well, after you drained the Electric Dragonborn's power, I shouted out to you if you were okay over and over, and well... you just sorta looked down at your hand and didn't answer me. Then you shot down the Wind Dragonborn and charged crazily at the Ice Dragonborn. Then when that was happening, an ice spike went clean through your armor at a weak spot and sliced through your side."

"Really, that happened?" I asked as I looked over to the field. "Oh wait... yeah, never mind, I see it all now," I told him as I spotted the ice spike covered in blood in the middle of the field.

Bolt continued explaining and told me, "Well, anyways, after that you were ice blasted three times back to back and crashed against that wall over there and got knocked out," he said as he pointed to the wall. There were cracks in the stone from when I had crashed into it, with my plates taking the impact.

"How long was I out for?" I asked.

Bolt said, "Only for about five minutes, but we're almost out of arrows from stalling to make time for you to wake up."

I told him, "Well, I'd better get out there again. Help me up?" I asked him.

"Are you sure you're okay enough to continue fighting? You're not too hurt or anything?" he asked as he helped me up.

As I stretched out my arms and activated my armor form again, I told him, "Don't worry—my scales block out infection and debris from our wounds. That's why our scales automatically regenerate right away. Anyways, it's only this guy left before Seath, I got this!" I told him confidently.

Then I noticed the plates around my injury were crumbled, and there were only normal scales in the place where I was hit by that ice spike.

Before I ran off into battle again, Bolt told me, "Just please don't do anything too reckless, Aika. You're already injured enough now, and who knows what Seath is planning. Okay?" he asked.

I told him, "Hey, don't worry, I know."

I saw my sword still stuck in the wall above, so I sent a ray of electricity out and brought my sword back to my hand, then ran off into battle.

When I ran toward the Ice Dragonborn this time, they sent out another ice spike path at me, but this time I successfully dodged their attack and drew out my sword. When I got close, I swung my sword, and they blocked it with theirs. Our swords screeched together for a brief moment until I knocked their sword away across the field.

"Oh, Black Ultimate, be merciful," the Ice Dragonborn said as they watched their sword fly in the distance, then looked back at me.

I released a blaze of electricity at them, stunning them for a moment. As they were stunned, I sheathed my sword back in my scabbard and ran behind them. I put my fists together and bashed them on the top of their back below their neck and knocked them out. That spot was one of our hidden weak spots of our armor form. When hit there, our armor forms malfunction and make us unable to use our powers. If hit hard enough, it overwhelmed our brain, and we got knocked out from the stress. After they lay on the ground for a moment, I stepped back, deactivated my armor form, and caught my breath. I looked around the place for anyone else while walking back to the others.

When I got over, I told them, "I think that's it for his goons, but I have no idea where Seath is."

Bolt told me, "We got no idea either. Before while you were fighting, we saw them watching the fight from the roof of the castle. But when you got knocked out, all of our attention got turned away from him. They probably flew off someplace else while we were distracted. But for now we should regroup with the other Slayers to figure things out. It's only him left, so maybe it won't be so bad, right?" he questioned a bit at the end.

Right when we were about to head out, Niki tapped me on the shoulder and said, "Hey, Aika, your friend over there is moving again."

"What?" I asked, confused, as I turned around.

From across the field, I saw the Mutant stand back from where it was lying. They just stood in place glaring at me as they tilted their head.

Terrified, I held on to Bolt's arm and screamed out while pointing to the Mutant, "BOLTON! BOLTON! HOW IS THAT THING STILL MOVING? I BLASTED THAT FUCKER WITH EVERYTHING I HAD! HOW… JUST HOW?"

In the distance I saw Seath fly up into the sky and travel over to where the other Slayers were.

"Oh dear, I just saw Seath fly to the others!" I told Bolt.

"What?" Bolt shouted, shocked.

Having no choice left, I told him, "Bolton, you and the others go rejoin the other Slayers! I'm going to stay here and hold off the Mutant."

"You sure?" Bolt asked.

Not very confidently, I told him, "Don't… don't worry, I'll be fine. I'm going to try and knock them out as fast as possible, and if I can't… I'll stall them for as long as I can. Just be sure that Seath doesn't hurt anyone, got it!" I said as I let go of him.

"All right, just… please be careful," Bolt replied.

"I'll try my best," I told him, unsure of what would happen, giving him a thumbs up with my hand shaking.

I ran toward the Mutant and summoned my armor form once again while doing so.

Bolt turned around to the Slayers and shouted, "Everyone, changing plans! Aika is going to stay here and fight off the Mutant. Before she ran off, she told me she spotted Seath flying toward the others, so all of us are going to regroup to defend the emergency chambers! Now let's go!"

Bolt and the others left, leaving me and the Mutant alone to fight.

I didn't notice until now, but it had turned completely dark out, which showed how long this battle had been going on. Me and the Mutant were just glaring at each other for a minute, until I ran my ass away as quickly as I could with the Mutant immediately following behind me as I did. There was no fucking way that I could knock out this guy! I just lied to Bolt to make him feel better because I didn't want him to worry about me. I had barely any strength at all to run; there was no way I could release another super attack like I did before to knock them out. All I could do was stall for time so the Mutant didn't go after the others while they were dealing with Seath. As it chased me, it set off explosions left and right of me as I ran for my life. The explosions around me were bright and powerful and blew up parts of buildings and paths, so I decided to fly up to the sky to avoid causing as much damage as I could to the kingdom. So I flew up as fast as I could to try and escape them, but while flying up, they grabbed onto my right leg and set off a small explosion on my plate, which caused it to crumble away into specks of nothing. After the explosion, I kicked their face, then escaped its grasp just barely. They continued to follow right behind me. They kept on blasting at me nonstop, damaging and breaking apart my armor plates all over, with every explosion hitting me causing a bit of my time trance to develop. Half of my plates were either damaged or completely withered away into dust. The only thing that was barely protecting me anymore was my scales, which were also heavily damaged. Some parts of my leg and side were completely damaged, with it not even regenerating back at all. I realized the Mutant had disappeared. So I stopped and looked around aimlessly, terrified of where it could have gone. Suddenly a horrible feeling overwhelmed me inside. I turned around behind me and looked up to see the Mutant about to set off a huge explosion. With no time to react, I was blasted with everything they had. The explosion they hit me with was one of the biggest explosions that Dragonborns could possibly make. It was the size of a castle, with magenta flares flying all over the sky and around me. The pain was absolutely agonizing from the attack.

I plunged downward from the sky like a fireball, covered in flames. My eyes were closed throughout most of the explosion. When I opened them, the sky above was filled with endless dark magenta smoke. The only reason I could breathe fine was because my scales that masked my face filtered out the smoke and particles around. But through the smoke, I saw the eyes of the Mutant glowing. They beamed down on me for a minute until they charged at me and tackled me with their claws covered in their lava slush. The Mutant dragged me down even faster and started to scratch away what was left of my plates and burned me right through my scales, with the entire thing in slow motion in my eyes. Before I knew it, the little armor I had left was covered in scratches and was crumbling away bit by bit. When I tried to push them off me, they got angry and stabbed their claws into my right side, which made both of my sides messed up. In horrible pain I tried to draw out my sword to fight, but when I did, the Mutant grabbed it from me and threw it to who knows before I got a chance to swing it. After they did that, they crashed me to the ground hard with my front first, still holding on to me. I tried to escape their clutches, but they held me down with all their might, then suddenly they grabbed my left horn and pulled hard on it.

I struggled and tried to escape from them as much as I could, but I had no strength at all left. After a minute of them pulling on my horn as hard as they could, I heard a loud, clean crunch sound and felt the worst pain I've ever had in my life from the top of my head. The pain felt like getting a limb torn off with someone twisting a knife in the wound. Pulsing with pain, I screamed out in bloody murder helplessly as the Mutant got off me and walked away. As I shook on the ground from pain, I reached for my head. I noticed that my left horn had been ripped off. Only a tiny chunk of it remained still attached. I deactivated my armor form, and a rush of blood came down the left of my face instantly. I looked up from the ground and saw that the Mutant was clenching my horn in their hand, just staring intensely at it. Before I could gain any strength to mutter out a word to them, the Mutant summoned their wings and flew off into the sky, leaving only the trace of bright magenta specks of flames from its wings.

My entire body was in horrible pain from everything that had happened to me. As I lay there on the ground, I was so weak that my jacket stopped glowing with power. I put my hands down and noticed my gloves were covered in blood and were also practically destroyed from everything that had happened. I took them off and also saw my bandages practically burned up, so I took those off as well and threw everything aside. I didn't even care at the moment about the birthmark on my hand; everyone around already knew about me and my powers, so why bother. My vision started to darken as I lay in a small puddle of my own blood from my wounds. I thought I was done for until I felt someone's aura nearby. They stopped in front of me and said in a familiar voice in Dragonborn, "Get up."

I looked up to see who it was, and I saw the Teal Dragonborn from the other day.

"W-what?" I asked back in Dragonborn, in a daze.

"You need to get up—this fight isn't over yet. Will you just lie here and let your friends die?" they asked, then dropped my sword in front of me and said, "I've been watching you fight from a distance, and I know you're not done yet. You also gave me quite a laugh at the beginning—it was quite a surprise to see you alive after all this time. It was also quite nice to see that you had been doing well since everything that happened back then. It's been quite an awfully long time, Aika."

"Who are you?" I asked, confused.

"Oh, don't worry about that right now! Instead just think of this: Why hasn't Seath attacked you yet? All he's done was poison you with his sludge at the very beginning, and that was all," they told me.

I was silent for a moment, thinking. Then I said quietly, "Oh… yeah, you're right."

"Interesting, isn't it! You think he would like his revenge after what happened to him after he supposedly 'killed your entire bloodline.'" Then they crouched down to me and said, "Hey… you want to know why he hasn't tried to battle you yet?"

I picked myself up a little from my blood puddle onto my knees and forearms, then asked, "What do you know?"

They laughed a little to themselves and said back, "It's because they're injured, my little friend!"

"He's injured!" I said back, surprised.

"Yep, that's right! How he got injured was quite funny to watch, might I add! You see, right before he started chasing down that lunatic Electric

Dragonborn, he got in a nasty fight with the 'Mutant,' which you people call her, and put a control device around her neck, which turned them into a weapon for Seath. Before when she attacked you, she was just losing their mind, like the others that attacked. They've been a real mess back in our land… that's for sure."

I asked them, "Are you a Defender?" pointing at their scabbard.

They laughed a bit and said, "Hey, I told you not to worry about who I am right now. But anyways, after he got control of them, Seath and his main backup soldiers got stupidly injured from them. Why else do you think his goons there were so easy to beat compared to other Dragonborns. They were last-minute backups; he had to wait till evening for all of them to arrive. So, do you know what time it is?" they asked me as they put out their hand.

I smiled back at them and grabbed my sword, then their hand.

As they helped me back up, I told them, "It's ass kicking time!" then activated my armor form. It was all busted up still from the battle, but my jacket glowed a bit once again.

They told me, "Give me a good opening, and I'll take care of your Mutant for you, and I'll leave kicking Seath's ass to you!"

"Do you know where they are?" I asked.

"They flew over near your friends. If I were you, I would hurry, though. It didn't look good over there the last time I saw them," they told me.

I asked them, "Why are you helping me out so much?"

They snarkily replied, "Oh, please, I already told you the other day. I need your help with something important." Then they flew up high into the sky.

So, filled with determination to fight, I summoned my wings and flew up into the sky to spot the others. But while I was fighting the Mutant and talking to the Teal Dragonborn, Bolt and the others had a fight of their own going on.

When the others arrived with the other Slayers, Bolt had immediately asked, "Hey, are you guys doing all right? Have you seen Seath anywhere around?"

A random Slayer asked, "What do you mean? No one has been around here."

Jack told them, "We saw Seath fly over here to you all—were you all not paying attention or something?" he asked, a bit annoyed.

"Oh, don't worry yourself too much to find me," a voice said from above them.

Everyone turned to where they had heard it, and behind Bolt, Seath flew down from the top of a roof, watching them without his armor form.

Bolt stepped forward to him and asked, "What are you here for? I thought you would be watching the fight over there waiting for a chance to attack Aika!"

Seath laughed a little at Bolt's question, then replied, "Oh, but I am watching them fight! Look at all those marvelous explosions in the sky over there! I'm just watching from a safe distance… that's all. That monster is my greatest and most powerful 'War Dragonborn' that I've ever made. After they are done blowing the Blue Ultimate to bits, they will fly over here and burn you all to ashes."

Jack shouted out to Seath confidently, "Ha, like Aika would lose to the Mutant. Last time they fought, she kicked their ass using limited power."

Suddenly the huge final explosion lit up the sky above everyone, and magenta flares flew above them in the sky.

"You sure about that?" Seath asked as he smirked back at him.

"Tis but a scratch for Aika!" Jack said, sounding very confident in himself.

Bolt tapped his shoulder and told him, "Uh, Jack I don't know about this one. I'm worried, that looked real bad just now."

Jack told him, "Bolton! This is Aika we're talking about! Since when has she ever completely lost a fight?" he asked him.

Then they all heard me yell out bloody murder from a near distance. Everyone froze with fear.

"Oh geez!" Bolt said to himself, frightened.

"Hey Jack, I don't think she's okay," Niki said to him.

"Hehe… I bet that that was a victory yell?" Jack said, unsure.

Then they saw the Mutant fly over and land on the roof next to Seath, holding my horn in their hand covered in my blood and blue splatters.

"Ah, very good! Now stay put," he demanded as he snatched my horn from their hand. He jumped down and started walking toward Bolt and the others, examining my horn. "My my my, they put up quite the struggle, didn't they? Hmm, it really was worth my time and strength to capture this monster of godly powers. But at last I have the final component," Seath said to himself.

Bolt asked, "Why do you want her horn?"

Seath looked over to Bolt and said in a smug attitude, "Like you would understand why I would."

Bolt told him, "No, I understand more than you think! Dragonborn horns are useless to other Dragonborns—they are just hollow armor plates that don't even protect you well. The only use they have is that they are filled with liquified aura that only the Dragonborn themselves can use for an emergency power boost, but it's almost completely useless because it hurts too much to break off. That stuff is useless to you!" he explained.

Seath asked back, "So it's useless to me, why do you care?"

Bolt shouted back, "Exactly, it's useless! So why do you have it? What are you planning to use it for?" Bolt demanded.

Seath laughed to himself and replied to Bolt, "Heh, I like you, kid, so I'm going to give you and your other two friends there one last chance since you three got some guts! You get out of my way, and I'll spare you for now. If I were you, I would take it and run over to my friend over there bleeding to death."

Bolt angrily yelled out, "Heck no! We're Dragon Slayers—we protect people from Dragonborns like yourself, never will we walk away!"

Jack shouted after him, joining on to his little speech, "Yeah! Also Aika would kick our asses if we ran away after all she's done!"

Niki also joined in and said, "Oh please, you're bluffing about Aika. You need her alive, don't you, to use her powers. We all know that if she died, all traces of her powers would disappear."

Seath stared at the three for a moment, laughed a little, and said, "Oh, look at you three trying to be so brave and such standing up to me. What are you going to do, Blondie? All your arrows are and dumb tricks are all used up. What could you possibly—"

Bolt then suddenly snatched my horn out of his hand and ran back quickly to the others.

"Hey, what the?" Seath questioned.

"Never underestimate us Infinitans with our combined determination and stupidity!" Bolt shouted as he ran back to the two, while Jack was laughing his ass off at Seath and Niki was smirking at Seath with an evil grin.

"Come back here with that horn!" Seath hollered out to him as he drew out his sword and chased after him.

But before Seath got close to Bolt, Niki slid in from the side and swung out at Seath's sword. "Are you the real Seath from Aika's story? Because you're a hell of a lot slower than Aika!" Niki teased him.

"Shut up!" he shouted back at her.

Then Seath went to knock away her sword with a slash, but before he swung, an arrow whizzed by him close and threw him off guard.

"Hey, asshole, I'm not completely out of arrows!" Jack shouted to him as he lowered his crossbow, still giggly.

As Seath was distracted by Jack, Bolt swung against his sword with his and said, "Do you really think we made Aika be involved in all of our plans? Well, guess again, we may not have powers, but that doesn't leave us defenseless! Niki, analyze!" Bolt commanded her as he took a step back away from Seath.

Niki said out loud to everyone, "Seath here is wielding his sword with his right hand, keeping his left far away as if it's weak or injured. Then his back is a bit slumped, so he is also injured there, or his old age is getting to him. They will keep a high guard on us after that last attack you just did, Bolton, so he'll most likely defend instead of bluntly attacking."

Seath looked at her in shock and asked, "What? How… how did you figure that out?"

Bolt ordered, "Jack, list our options!"

Jack said out loud, "Well, Bolton, we can do multiple different attacks, but the best one for us right now is to make him feel pain and keep on charging at him till he runs away like a coward or the possibility of Aika appearing, if she can still fight. We should probably try to hit him on his left and from behind because of what Niki pointed out before."

Seath took another step back and gripped his sword and yelled, "Oh, you three really think you can defeat me! You are all just the support to that short idiot!"

Bolt ran forward at him and slashed back against his sword hard and replied, "We're not always the support in battle! We went through five years of training to fight you people, and let me tell you…!" Bolt said as he kicked Seath on the side of his leg, causing him to almost flinch, "I know all of your hidden weak spots!" Bolt said a bit ominously to him.

"Shut up!" Seath hollered as he shoved Bolt out of the way. "You're weak! Pathetic! I am a god compared to you in power!"

"A god? Ha, now that's hilarious!" Jack laughed at him. "I've heard too many people from my past yell about how godly you are!" Jack told him as he swung his sword at him, and Seath deflected it.

"You don't think I'm a god, huh? Well, how about this!" Seath yelled as he summoned his armor form and sprouted out toxic sludge from his hands above them like thick rain.

Niki questioned Seath, "Do you really think that stuff will affect us? You said it yourself that your powers were made to kill other Dragonborns, not Infinitans."

Seath shouted, "All right, but can you Nons resist this!" Then he blasted a path of fire toward Niki, but she stood in place and smiled back at him and pulled out a flask that was blue inside and threw it on the ground. The flask broke, and a wall of blue fire was created before her.

"What, how did you—" Seath questioned.

Bolt interrupted, "We can't resist your fire or create any for ourselves, but we can use someone else's fire to block your attack."

Niki ran over and swung her sword at his again and said, "I can't believe this is all you got! Aika talked about you like you were the final boss, but you can't even defeat three Infinitans!"

Seath pushed her back, but Jack swung at him and said, "I bet he's not even a general anymore! If he was, I bet he would have had much stronger goons."

Seath swerved his sword and shouted back at him, "Oh please, what do you know about me and my position?"

Niki replied, "Oh nothing much… just that all information about you came to a halt right after the war ended. What, did you royally screw up after you supposedly killed all the Blue Ultimates?" Niki teased him with an even more evil grin.

Seath ran over and tried hacking at her with his sword, but Niki threw a flask at his sword and it shattered, causing fire to cover Seath.

"Ahhh, you pest!" Seath yelled as he patted the fire out on him, but as he was doing so, Bolt slashed at him.

Seath stepped aside to dodge him as he patted out all the fire, then swung his sword out at him.

Bolt dodged and jabbed his sword into Seath's sword.

Seath asked him, "Don't you think it's pathetic you need dumb little tricks to defeat me? You people are useless without powers like us!"

Bolt replied, "Oh, we don't need powers to take you down! All we need is our 'dumb little tricks,' which you call them!"

Bolt diverted his sword, and Seath took a step back and Jack ran close and said, "You call them dumb, yet they are very effective against you!"

Jack tried knocked his sword away and when Seath stepped back from him Niki slashed her sword against his and teased, "What's wrong? Getting aggravated that you, the person who single-handedly destroyed the strongest Dragonborn clan, is losing to three 'weaklings,' as you call us?"

Jack said, "Person? Why be so nice to call him that, why don't we call him a monster like Aika?"

Seath, losing his composure, then screamed loudly, "Shut up! I'll show you how pathetic your race really is!" He averted back her sword and stepped far back away from them and ordered, "Kill them my monster!"

The Mutant jumped down in the middle of Seath and the others, then released a path of fire toward them all.

"Get behind me!" Bolt called out to everyone. Then he threw a flask on the ground and a shield of fire was created, protecting everyone from the Mutant's flames, but it started to fade fast. "Jack, how many more flasks do you have?" Bolt asked him in a panic.

Jack threw a flask into the same spot he did, and the fire got a bit stronger.

"That was my last one. Damn, how did Aika fight back against their fire before that day?" Jack questioned.

Niki replied, "She passed out in a coma afterward. I bet she was pushing herself beyond her limits by a long shot."

"Niki, do you have any more flasks?" Bolt asked her.

"Only one, but I doubt it'll do much to hold it back for long," Niki replied.

Bolt said, "Oh, goodness… I… I don't know what else to do against the Mutant. They're just too powerful for us at the moment. And I know the Slayers aren't going to risk their lives for us right now after all that's happened."

Seath laughed at them from afar, at their hope fading, but suddenly he looked pissed off. As the fire from the flask burned out and the blaze of the Mutant came toward them, I suddenly slid in front of them from the sky and shielded everyone from the Mutant's flames with my own.

"Aika, you're okay?!" Bolt called out with a combination of relief, happiness, and confusion.

Seath shouted, "How… how are you moving? You got exploded repeatedly from my monster! Half of your armor form is broken!" he yelled out in confusion and frustration.

My armor form was almost completely destroyed. The only thing left were some patches of scratched-up plates on my forearms, left shin, and chest. All the armor on the bottom of my right shin was gone, with just scales left behind, like my left side. In some other spots, my scales wouldn't even regenerate because I had exhausted all my power and started to wither away. My pants and shirt flowed behind me with my jacket in the breeze I made when I flew down.

Seath's reaction to me still fighting made me laugh a bit, and I answered his question. "Oh how am I still moving? Well, it's really quite a simple answer," I told him, then deactivated my armor form and revealed how messed up I looked to everyone. My sides and face were covered in blood from my wounds, with my arms and legs bruised up under my blood-drenched clothes and my right leg burned a bit from the massive explosions. My shirt wasn't even tucked in my pants, which were not tucked into my boots either, like usual. Finally everyone could see my element birthmark on my hand, which was the electric symbol that matched the symbol on the back of my jacket.

I shouted out loud, "I was smart for once to wear my spare outfit and equipment today. Those explosions really did do a number on me… but do you really think it would knock me out? Well, think again, because I won't stop until every last drop of blood I have is gone!"

"Also don't forget about hitting your head real hard on something," Niki butted in at the end.

"Also, hitting my head badly on something hard will knock me out!" I added.

Bolt yelled to me, "Aika, catch!" and threw my horn.

I caught it and threw my horn down to the ground and crushed it with my boot. My horn disappeared into aura particles and combined with the aura swirling around me. The tips of the fire that I was using to shield against the Mutant turned multicolored, to every color in the rainbow. Everyone behind me watched in disbelief at my power, and Seath watched in rage what he was seeing.

"Ultimus dammit, you activated that power!" he shouted.

My eyes and aura had never glowed that bright before while using my powers. My aura around me swirled greatly, and I was filled with power I had never experienced before. This was the very first I ever used my power like this, and it felt awesome! With my newfound powers, I pushed back the Mutant's fire and overwhelmed them with my fire instead.

I shouted out to Seath and everyone, "Oh yeah, I also forgot to mention! While I was bleeding out over there in that field, some asshole walked up to me and told me that you were injured, Seath," in a carefree tone to him.

"Uh, Aika, we already know that," Jack told me.

"What?" I turned to Jack in confusion.

"Yeah, Niki already discovered it for us," Jack explained.

"You're… you're kidding? Right?!" I asked, astonished.

Niki replied, "Oh please, it was simple. He's avoiding you while fighting, making his goons fight you for him, and he only bothered to fight us because we don't have powers. Did you really not consider it?" Niki asked me.

"Uh… no?" I replied, confused.

Bolt face palmed, and Jack said, "To be honest I would have been surprised if you'd found out sooner than just now that he was injured."

"Oh, screw you guys, I'm not that dumb!" I yelled at them.

"Aika, what day is it today?" Niki asked me.

"Uh… Wednesday?" I replied, unsure.

The three of them looked at me stupidly for a moment.

Niki told me, "Today's Friday, idiot."

"Really, but I thought you said yesterday was Tuesday?!" I replied to her.

Everyone looked at me like I was a complete, utter idiot. Even the Mutant stopped their attack and stared at me disappointed, as if they knew me all too well.

"Oh my Ultimus… you're still an idiot after all these years?!" the Teal Dragonborn said from above, watching me in a combination of shock and stupidity.

"Oh, come on, really! Does everyone think I'm an idiot?" I asked everyone, and they stared at me silently.

"Yeah," some random person from the Slayers shouted out.

"Really? Bolton, do you think I'm that stupid?" I asked him.

Bolt got nervous and said, "Uh well… sometimes you can be."

"Oh my Ultimus, this is the saddest thing I've ever seen for a distraction!" The Teal Dragonborn said, as they watched at me.

"Oh screw you… person… who I don't even know the name of!" I yelled back at them.

"This is the saddest thing I've ever seen in my life, and I've been in war," Seath muttered to himself.

"Hey, shut up there!" I shouted at Seath.

"You know what… screw it, I'm losing precious brain cells listening to this," the Teal Dragonborn said as they dropped from the sky and tackled the Mutant down and ripped off the control device from around their neck and threw it toward Jack, who picked it up in an excited hurry. They held back the Mutant trying to grab at them with claws and said playfully, looking back over to me, "Well, I've done my part. I'll be seeing you again real soon… Lil' Aika!" They summoned their wings and grabbed the Mutant's hands and dragged them off into the darkness of the sky, disappearing from sight.

I looked over back at Seath, who was in disbelief at what just happened before him.

So I asked him, "So what's the plan now, Seath? Your little goons over there can barely move a muscle after what I did to them, your little mind control device on the Mutant is destroyed and they got dragged someplace else, and now I'm here ready to kick your ass after everything that happened."

All Seath replied was "Shut up! I don't need that monster to kill you! I'll do it myself!" he screamed angrily as he clenched his fists.

I laughed at him and said, "Oh please, neither of us are in any condition to fight! So let's make this easy," I said as I pulled out the Sound Radiator.

"Aika, no wait, don't do it, please!" Bolt called out to me.

I turned to him and said, "I'm sorry, Bolt, I'm out of options," then turned back to Seath. "You can either run away now or find out what this lovely little device does," I told him ominously.

"Were you the one who took that from me?" he asked, surprised.

"Oh, that doesn't matter right now. Tell me what you're going to do," I said.

Seath scoffed at me and said, "You think after all this time I'm just going to run away because you got that device? Pathetic I would be!" he said.

I sighed and said back to him, "Well, I warned you," then I powered on the SR at high volume. Immediately all our ears were filled with the horrible clangor from it, which burned right into our eardrums, causing our ears to ring and our auras to weaken.

"Wha-what is this?" Seath asked, shaking a bit.

I told him, "Don't you love it! It's a lovely little device that the Slayers dubbed the Sound Radiator, or for short, the SR. It emits sound frequencies that deafen our powers and creates noise that only we hear that paralyzes us! It still hurts a lot for normal people's ears too, but for us it's worse!" I explained cheerfully.

Seath shouted back, "This… this is nothing, come on!" Then he started running after me and sprouted sludge at me.

"Oh geez!" I said as I dodged his attack and ran.

"Get… back here!" he hollered out of breath already from trying to use his powers once more.

"Uh… no," I answered as I ran in a mini circle with him chasing right behind me.

As I ran, he continued to attempt to blast me with sludge all right in front of everyone, who watched us in a combination of horror and stupidity.

"Yeah, you go, Aika!" Jack cheered out to me.

"Don't any of you have any arrows?" I asked them.

"Oh, we fully ran out of arrows, sorry!" Jack shouted back to me.

"Of course you all are!" I shouted back to him.

After I hollered at him, Seath finally got me and hit my back good. "Ahh dammit, that hurt!" I yelled to Seath, pissed.

"Why don't you use your powers?" he asked.

"Oh, why, I never thought of doing that!" I yelled sarcastically as I ran near the Slayers again and finished another loop.

A Slayer approached Bolt and asked, "Uh, is that really the same Dragonborn who beat all of the other Dragonborns near the castle?"

Bolt sighed and replied "Yep," as he watched me flip off Seath while running back to them again.

Jack said, "I'm honestly surprised they haven't tripped by now."

Niki said, "Just give them like… five minutes max and they will probably trip or almost trip."

"You think I'll be that clumsy at a moment like this!" I yelled back to them as I proceeded to almost trip on a pebble.

"See, exactly like I said," Niki said as she smirked, watching me.

Bolt said, "All right, I'm going to help her out—do you guys want to join?"

"I'll back you up just in case but watch from afar for now," Jack replied.

"I'm just going stand by and watch. I want to see if I can get any more data from Seath," Niki replied after him.

"All right, I'm off then," Bolt told them as he gripped his sword and ran to Seath.

"Oh great! Now I get to deal with you again," Seath said, annoyed, now just noticing Bolt run over.

"What kind of battle did you have with Bolt?" I asked as I stopped running and drew out my sword and swung at him.

Seath slashed his sword at mine, but Bolt ran over and jabbed his back.

"Ugh, pest," Seath said, kicking me back and turning to Bolt and swung his sword against his.

"I can't just stand there and watch Aika run, while injured," Bolt said to him.

"Oh, thanks for being the only one to helping me out, Bolton," I said to him as I slashed my sword at Seath, but he stepped aside, dodging me, and tripped Bolt.

"So now you're just playing dirty because you're losing, huh?" I asked Seath as I caught Bolt's hand.

"Quit your mockery, I'm no Defender who fights honorably. I'm a Conqueror, I fight for the thrill of battle!" Seath screamed back.

I stared back at Seath and said, "I'm going to enjoy what I'm about to do to you," then ran at him and swung at his sword hard and yelled, "Now it's even more personal, Seath! Because how dare you mention my clan after what you did to it!"

Seath laughed and said, "What's wrong? Wasn't it supposed to be the strongest Dragonborn clan out of the five? To me it either makes the

Defenders look weak, or I'm just the strongest out there."

I replied, "Oh just keep buttering yourself up! Because now that you know I'm alive, there's no point in hiding from you and the rest of the world!"

I pushed back Seath, and he said to me, "Good luck with that, the entire world thinks all the Blue Ultimates are dead. You can thank me for that, by the way. You and your former father are both quite a handful."

I scowled at him pissed and was about to slash at him again, but Bolt ran before me and swung into his sword hard and said, a bit pissed off, "Don't you bring up her dad after what you did to him!" and glared right at him with his eyes glued to his.

Seath smiled and replied, "Wow, and here's something you don't see every day! You, boy, got the eyes like us! That glare you give me shows it all too well that you got a bit of our blood mixed in you a little."

"What?" Bolt asked, confused, taking his sword away and stepping back.

"Eh, don't think about it for too long, you'll find out soon enough," Seath replied to him.

I asked Seath, "Hey, aren't you getting tired yet? We've been running around for a bit now with the SR blasting."

Seath replied, "Ha, no never! This is nothing, I told you!"

I stepped back in front of Bolt and everyone else and said, "Oh, you're right… this is nothing!" a bit ominous to him.

"What..? I mean, come on, bring me the worst you got!" Seath replied as he glared at me a bit.

So I told him, "Yeah this thing, the SR, it's only a little above half!"

"Wait, this ain't max!" Seath asked, sounding a bit shocked.

"You sure this ain't messing with you at all? I saw your face just now, and your voice shrieked a little. Do you want me to put it on max to show you how great it is?" I asked as I turned up the volume a bit, making the noise even more unbearable than it was before.

Seath didn't answer and just watched at me from a distance.

I shouted out to him, "I heard this thing at max once, but only for about a minute. During that time I fell to my knees and lost my hearing for about five minutes." As I explained, Seath scowled at me, looking more and more frustrated, clenching his fists harder. "You see, Seath… neither of us can keep this up. But there's a big difference in our situations. I have someone to catch me when I collapse… but who do you have? All your goons are down, you have no strength, and I have an entire army of Dragonborn killers behind me. This is your last chance to run away now," I told him.

Seath was silent for a moment, then he shouted out "Fine!" So I lowered the volume a bit, and he summoned his wings then flew up and said, "I'll come back and get my revenge for this one day, and when I do, I'll make you suffer like you never have before! Until then, don't you die so I can be the one to kill you for sure."

He flew over to where his henchmen were at. A minute later he flew back up into the air carrying his henchmen, and glared at me one last time, then flew off into the distance. When he was far enough away to know he wasn't coming back, I turned off the SR, then turned around back at everyone. Everyone was either frozen with fear, disbelief, slightly or definitely freaking out, or just plain confused on everything that had happened.

"Aika?" Bolt called to me, worried, as he took a step to me.

So I gave Bolt a wave and turned to everyone else and gave them a smile and asked, "So is everyone else okay?" Then my legs went completely numb and I fell back slightly, and my vision went dark.

I heard a voice call out repeatedly "Aika… Aika… Aika, you okay?"

When I opened my eyes, I found myself in Bolt's arms. His face was full of concern, on the verge of tears.

So I casually replied, "Oh hey, Bolt, what's up?"

Bolt sighed, then said back "You know… sometimes I forget how reckless you can be," while brushing my bangs out of my eyes.

I noticed Jack and Niki standing behind Bolt, with Jack looking a bit worried and Niki writing a whole bunch of information down in her notebook.

So I asked them, "Hey, guys, on a scale of one to ten, how badass was I out there?"

Jack immediately broke out into laughter and said, "Oh man, that's the first thing you ask us? That's great!"

I told him, "Hey, if I looked cool enough out there, do you think they will overlook the entire 'I'm actually a devil' part?"

Niki, standing beside Jack, who was hysterically laughing to himself, replied to me, "I'll give you a seven out of ten score because you're an idiot but you did save us multiple times."

Bolt just looked over to them and back to me, dumbfounded by us, then said, "You three are so unbelievable right now. Everyone over there is watching us terrified of what just happened, and you're all making jokes?"

I told him, "Oh please, Bolt, what are they gonna say? I'm a devil for making a joke at a time like this? Anybody who's ever met me knows I'm like this."

Niki told me while walking around Bolt, then crouching beside me, "Oh Aika, it's going to be so much fun rubbing it in everyone's faces that I was right all along and how no one believed me!"

"Like what you did to me for an hour straight?" Jack asked as he walked to the other side of Bolt, smiling from my question still.

"Even worse!" Niki replied to him.

Jack asked me, "So Aika, what exactly happened to you? All your clothes are drenched in blood."

"Oh, I was just lying in a puddle of my own blood from getting blown up multiple times and stabbed," I replied casually.

"Oh geez, that's why you look so pale!" Bolt said worried as he carefully carried me up in his arms.

"Hey, next time I'm going to be the one who carries you all romantically like this," I told him.

"I… let's just get on moving inside so we can help your injuries," Bolt told me, then said to the others, "All right, guys, let's get on moving," then he started walking toward the Slayers.

Niki walked to the right of Bolt near my head and asked, "So anyways, Aika, how do you feel right now?"

I told her, "Kinda dizzy and completely numb. I can't move my body except my head, but besides all that I'm doing fine. Got some good revenge for myself by ruining Seath's pride," I explained.

Bolt stopped in front of Zane and asked, "Commander, sir, may I get Aika some medical treatment before we start explaining this whole mess?"

Zane glared down at me for a moment, then back to Bolt and said, "You can bring them into one of our rooms. There should at least be one open for them. There you can help them—don't expect us to make anyone help you, though." Then he moved aside for us to get by.

"Thank you sir," Bolt said, then continued forward to inside the emergency chambers.

As we passed by a bunch of Slayers and citizens, they all stared at me, either scared or threatened.

I told the others, "Guys, I think everyone's scared of me."

Bolt told me, "They're scared of all of us. Us three were the only ones who knew about you. That stood out a lot to people after they saw Charles's reaction to you. But don't worry, I'll handle it. this was my big task to do after you got revealed, remember?"

Then we walked by a big room of people to Bolt's left. They all looked over to us gossiping about what happened, but what caught my attention was Charles in the very back staring at us in distrust. He must've noticed that I was looking back at him, because he suddenly turned around and walked away.

"Just ignore them, Aika, those morons don't know a thing," Niki told me.

Jack joined in and said to me, "Yeah, we'll handle everything, no sweat!" as he walked in front of Bolt, near my legs, so he would block my view.

I told them, "I think I just saw Charles looking back at us rejected."

They went silent, unsure of what to respond back with.

Jack told me quietly, "Don't worry about Charles right now. I'll talk to him later about you. I'm the closest to him, maybe he'll hear me out."

Niki butted in and said, "Hey, if Charles doesn't understand and forgive you guys, I'll just replace him."

Jack and Niki started arguing back and forth with each other about dumb stuff. As they did, I started to feel my senses shut down and their voices get fuzzy, and my vision blurred a bit.

I looked up at Bolt, and he looked down back at me and noticed I wasn't doing well, so he told me softly, "Hey, just rest up. I got it from here, I told you. I'll explain everything I can to them, and if they still insist on calling you a devil or try to hurt you… then hit them with your story about who you are. Don't worry about anything, I'll be by your side throughout everything that happens."

I told Bolt, "You know… it's kinda funny that some people think we're gods and others think the complete opposite and say we're devils. Do you think that once they all learn the truth about our different cultures, people will stop calling us devils?" I asked.

"Maybe, but we won't know for sure until we try," he replied.

"Well, it is just a distant dream. I just hope they won't lock me up in a dungeon for all of eternity. Eh, maybe they will do that to Niki instead after she makes fun of everyone for being an idiot," I said.

"Well, let's just hope that they don't lock any of us up for now, okay. And if they do, then we'll break them out," Bolt told me.

"Oh, hell yeah, for sure!" I told him.

"But hey, I mean it this time: rest now. Today's fight is over for you," he replied.

"Heh… all right, Bolty," I replied as I closed my eyes.

But as I finally rested, something was still bothering me a bit. How did that Teal Dragonborn know me? Who were they, and why did they call an "old friend?" The strangest part to me was how familiar they seemed to me when they called me "Lil' Aika." But all of this was just the beginning for me. Little did I know that this was only the first act of my adventure. The moment after I woke up, a whole new story started for me and my friends.

For what would be *Act 2*.

Thank you all to whoever got this far, I hope you all enjoyed my novel and if you want to get the latest news sneak peaks of further books visit my Instagram j.bernier1835, where I make dumb art and post silly things, which contains the link to join my Discord server, The Book Slayers.

And most importantly leave an honest review of my book on Amazon!!!

Acknowledgments

I would like to thank my close family for supporting me thought my writing journey. It took me a long time getting to this point in publishing my book. To my mom, dad, brother, grandmothers, uncles, aunts, and everyone else, thank you all for helping me grow into the person I am today.

I also want to give a special thanks to my good friends who helped me write my book, give me advice, and who were there in my worst days. To Dare, Jacob, Shay, Nax, AJ, Minister, Paige, Aiden, Inez, Adam, and all the others, thank you all for the motivation that kept me going and being the first group of people who I could talk about my book with.

Authors Bio

J. Bernier writes in the genres of Fantasy, Comedy, and Adventure/Action. When she's not writing, she watches Anime that fuels her inspiration and plays dorky Nintendo games. More books in the series Dragon Slayers will come out eventually in the further with a lot more jokes and action. It took a little more than four years to write, but that was because she would mostly write in school at every second of her free time.

To contact J. Bernier
Instagram: j.bernier1835
Discord server: The Book Slayers (Link in Instagram)